European Experience

Experiences: Book 5

Subspace and Love on a Visit to Europe

Simone Freier

OTK Publications
www.OTKPublications.com

European Experience

EXPERIENCES: BOOK 5

By Simone Freier

Published by OTK Publications
http://otkpublications.com

Copyright © 2015-2018 OTK Publications
All rights reserved

ISBN: 978-1-942054-12-2
v1.5

Manufactured in the United States of America

COVER DESIGN BY OTK PUBLICATIONS

This is a work of fiction. All names, characters, and incidents in this work are fictitious. Any resemblance to actual events or to real persons is purely coincidental. No humans or animals were harmed during the creation of this work.

Caution: This work contains mature content, including graphic sexual descriptions and scenes, and is provided for adults only. Neither the author nor the publisher intends to encourage or promote any of the activities depicted in this work. Many of the specific activities and scenarios described in this work can potentially be dangerous, and should not be attempted without special knowledge or training and, as appropriate, use of sterile single-use supplies. No information contained herein is intended to constitute advice or serve as instructional material, and this work should not be relied upon to ensure safe practices in real life.

Table of Contents

CHAPTER 1: MARGARITAS & BUBBLE BATH

It was another hot August day, and the cool air from the shopping center felt refreshing, as I pushed open the glass door, and entered the first floor of the large complex. I looked forward to having lunch with Julie, Linda, and Kathy – the first time we would be meeting since my birthday party.

School would be starting again in a couple of weeks, the doctoral program requiring that I attend a couple of 'seminar' classes, in addition to working on my dissertation. I walked past the Victoria's Secret store, glancing through the window at the current stock of lingerie on display, but thinking about the beautiful satin négligée that Sam had bought me for my birthday.

As I entered the Mexican restaurant and took a table in the bar section, thoughts of the birthday party filled my mind: All of us sitting nude on the king size sheet on the lawn; the group massage in the jacuzzi; Sam creating a needle art corset on my back, as my friends watched; the pirate scene! That had been incredible.

Then there was the barbeque dinner Sam had prepared; my birthday spanking ... along with the participation of my friends; and the slumber party – during which Julie and I got it on for the first time. And, Sam's stupid 'spank poker' game, where he put us on the turntable he had called a 'Lazy Sam'. Julie, Kathy and Linda had really been good sports, taking in stride whatever crazy experiences Sam threw at them.

But it had been more than 'in stride'; my friends had been enthusiastic and receptive, even sexually. That was far beyond Sam's expectations. Or mine. We all had planned on a nice summer day, lounging around nude, and skinny-dipping in the pool. Sam had planned to take me from behind at the 'climax' of the pirate scene – with my friends watching, but from afar, and with Sam and I mostly hidden behind a boulder.

My mind's eye flashed an image of Sam's beautiful backyard: The black-bottom pool and jacuzzi, with a rock waterfall, and surrounded by boulders; and the perfect, green lawn with some magnificent trees, extending to a winding path, lined with Tiki torches, on the other side of which were flower beds, still mostly in bloom although summer was nearly over. And the forest beyond.

I focused, and looked at my watch: My friends had not yet arrived, but they were only a few minutes late, so far. My friends who I now viewed – as I'm sure we all viewed each other – in a different light, having shared and discussed some intimate things together; some experiences, that we never would have tried, if not for Sam's prompting.

We all knew that Julie loved to act wild; I had only realized in the past few weeks that she was always 'acting', almost never herself – whatever that was. But we had seen a 'real' part of her when she and Linda had visited, and Sam gave Linda a birthday spanking; Julie then letting Sam spank her ... and ending-up masturbating in front of us!

My muscles clenched, and I looked around, nearly tempted to put my hand down my pants. I adjusted my sitting position, and continued to think about the friends who thought they had known each other well ... until coming to Sam's house a couple of times.

And Linda! She had surprised us all, with her openness and sexual responsiveness. It was something we had never seen, and could barely imagine. I guess that wasn't fair to Linda; but I think we all now had a different view, and a higher level of respect for Linda's capabilities, and her sensuality.

She had been receptive to Sam's interest in spanking, evidently stemming from her own schoolgirl paddling experiences. But she had also been surprisingly receptive to some of the things Sam had done during the 'spank poker' game. *And*, Sam had informed me that she had requested that he masturbate her, in the pitch-black playroom during our slumber party. We had all surprised each other. I wondered how this might affect our friendship.

Kathy, usually the most relaxed of us, had also taken everything at the birthday party in stride, but she hadn't seemed very enthusiastic. She had been somewhat distant. Still, she had let Julie go down on her in the jacuzzi, and actually *came* in front of all of us.

Incredibly, each of my friends had masturbated in front of Sam ... or allowed him to masturbate them. And, the next morning, they had treated Sam to a multi-girl oral experience, preparing him for me.

Sam had relaxed, and enjoyed it, although I knew he was still hung-up about sexual contact, mostly related to his concerns regarding sexually transmitted diseases. And it appeared that my friends had enjoyed it, too. I thought again about having a ménage with Julie and Sam.

"Hi, Kelly!" Linda bent down and hugged me lightly. Julie and Kathy were walking into the restaurant. Linda asked, "Where *were* you?" I gave her a questioning look, and she clarified, "You were staring out into space, and didn't even notice me, when I walked up right in front of you."

I shrugged, "Just thinking back to the birthday party."

Linda nodded, as she pulled out a chair and sat down. Before she could make a comment, Julie and Kathy said 'hello', and Julie bent down and kissed me on the cheek. I looked up at her, and she smiled seductively. Everyone sat down, and the waitress took our drink order; this time, we decided to get a *pitcher* of margaritas.

Linda looked across the table at Julie, and glanced at Kathy, "Kelly was catatonic when I got here, thinking about her birthday party." Then, Linda looked at me seriously, and said, "I have to admit, that was quite a party." Kathy and Julie were nodding. Linda continued, "We've really learned a lot about each other in the past few weeks."

There was a loud cough, and we looked at Julie, who had choked on a tortilla chip. Kathy patted her back, and Julie seemed OK, after she'd had a drink of water. Julie tried to speak, but her voice was hoarse.

Kathy kept patting Julie's back, and said, "We never really talked about sex that much before, except relating to our boyfriends. I couldn't have imagined us masturbating in front of each other. And, in front of a strange man."

I laughed, "Well, he *is* pretty strange!" Everyone laughed. Now was my chance, "So what did you guys think about Sam, now that you've spent some time with him?" It was certainly a loaded question. We were briefly interrupted when the Margaritas arrived, were poured into salt-rimmed glasses, and passed around the table.

Linda volunteered, "Like you told us, he *is* very creative." We were all laughing again.

Julie was nodding, "That pirate scene was quite a production. It took all of us to get the mast up, while Sam tied-off the ropes. Then we had to help him get into his pirate costume."

Linda blurted, "And that was a beautiful Victorian dress you wore! I guess he knew your size ..."

I nodded, "Sam knows *everything* about me. He has probed me, and prodded me, and taken all my measurements." I pictured the exam room, that Linda and Kathy had not seen, yet. "But he did make a nice choice – and even got me all the accessories. He's very thoughtful."

Linda nodded, "Yeah, thoughtful about your dress, just before he rips it off, and flogs your breasts!" Now, we were all in an uproar, and people from a few other tables were looking across the room at us.

I said, with mock indignance, "He didn't rip it off! He carefully unbuttoned it. I'm sure he thought about that when he bought the dress. That was part of the fantasy I had described to him."

Kathy laughed, "So how close was it, to your fantasy?"

It took a few moments to think about what I had told Sam, and picture a few fragments of the fantasy I'd had more than a few times. "Sam incorporated most of what I had told him – pulling my hair, tying me to the mast, flogging my breasts, and then dragging me down to the cabin and making love to me. Of course, I pictured being on a rolling ship, with the wind gusting and the salt spray hitting us in the face ... but it was pretty close. We hadn't discussed it since our second lunch, so I guess he was listening to me."

Then I felt my face warm. I smiled at my friends, "It was a little challenging to let Sam make love to me while you guys were watching, even if we were behind the boulder. I think the blindfold helped." I licked some salt off the rim of the glass, and took a big swallow of margarita, as my friends laughed.

Julie said, "Kelly, if anything, we're jealous of you. Somehow Sam has gotten us all more comfortable with doing intimate things in front of each other." Julie took a quick sip of margarita and continued, "I like Sam. He's a nice guy ... and also pretty wild. And I'm not even saying 'for his age'; he likes 'shock value', as I do, and he's probably more 'open' than any of the guys we've known."

Kathy nodded, and commented, "As energetic and compulsive as he is, Sam was very relaxed around us – even when we were undressing, or while we were sitting around nude, talking. It's obvious that he's gone to nude beaches a lot: He hardly noticed when I pulled my top off, and wasn't wearing a bra. And he seemed perfectly comfortable taking his own clothes off."

I agreed, "Yes, Sam is very open in a lot of ways. But, like everyone, he still has his hang-ups." I wasn't going to offer any further explanation, unless my friends pried, which they didn't.

Linda chuckled, "Well, if he'd had a boner while we were undressing, I don't think I would have been very comfortable walking around naked in front of him all day." We were laughing again, but Linda persisted, "But Sam acted like 'one of the girls'."

We were still laughing; but it was true: Sam could be 'one of the girls' when he wanted to be. I wondered how Sam would feel, if I dressed him up as a woman, and took him out to some clubs.

The waitress came, and we ordered the food; this was going to be a long lunch. Linda went to the rest room, and I took the opportunity to comment on the 'new' Linda. I whispered to Julie and Kathy, "Linda seemed to be pretty enthusiastic at the party." I arched my eyebrows.

Julie and Kathy were nodding. Kathy said, "We've never seen her in a sexual situation. And she's usually too reserved to talk much about sex with any of her hook-ups." Kathy looked around the table, "But it's pretty fun doing 'things' together – like at your party – now that we've gotten more open with each other."

Linda returned, as Julie added, smiling, "I thought almost everything was fun at the party, probably Sam's turntable being my least favorite."

Linda agreed, "Ugggh! How does Sam come up with those things?"

We all stared at Linda, and Julie piped up, "Linda! You certainly seemed to like 'spank poker' during the game. You let Sam masturbate you until you had an orgasm! Don't 'Ugggh' us!"

Linda looked down, "I guess, now that I think about it, I didn't mind the game too much." We were all laughing again. Then, she looked up at us sheepishly, and added, "And I liked sticking Sam with needles. That was a turn on for me."

Now, Kathy said, "Ugggh!" We all looked at her. Kathy shrugged, and looked directly at me, "Kelly, I think we all had fun ... most of the time. I didn't mind Sam giving me a few spanks ... or even putting his finger in my rear ..." None of us said anything; we were all thinking about when that had happened to us.

Kathy continued, "But I was uncomfortable being tied down on that turntable – it was a feeling of helplessness, which I didn't like; I'm glad Sam was only doing that to get a point across, and untied us for the rest of the game."

She continued, "And the main thing that bothered me was the needles. I get a little sick to my stomach just thinking about them. The so-called 'needle art' on your back was bad enough; and, I guess I didn't mind sticking Sam with a couple of needles. But I didn't like having them stuck in my butt."

I would agree that Sam tended to overdo his needle fetish. Now, I would test my friends' interest in doing something with us again. "I'm going to tell Sam that if we do anything else with you guys, he'll have to lay off the needles." There was general nodding around the table, but nothing indicating that my friends would not try another 'experience' with Sam and I. That was promising.

I thought again about Julie, who was sitting next to me, glowing. Maybe we should surprise Sam with the ménage? I had no doubt that he would be thrilled. And he had already 'shared body fluids' with Julie. So, by his own definition, he's already had sex with her.

Now, for the next topic ... "So what did you guys think about getting spanked? None of you have complained about that, yet." I chuckled, and poured myself another glass of margarita.

My friends were silent for several moments, just shrugging. Finally, Kathy spoke up. "They hurt more than I thought they would – especially that belt thingy. But it wasn't a big deal."

Julie concurred, "It was completely different, just playing around, rather than actually being punished. Sam wasn't spanking us hard, and there weren't very many strokes. Like Kathy said, it wasn't a big deal. Sam did give me a punishment spanking, when I spilled the beans about Kelly's adoption ... but even that wasn't too bad. I'm actually more curious now, what a 'real' spanking feels like – of the type Kelly says she can withstand."

Linda said, "I thought the spanking part was hot. But like Julie said, it was just playing around – not really hard spanks. I have no doubt I could get turned on by taking a long spanking from Sam." Linda smiled and looked at me, "And I enjoyed spanking *you*, Kelly." I remembered that it had been Linda's spanks that had finally gotten me wet.

I looked at Kathy and said, "Well, it seems Linda and Julie got excited by some of the things Sam did. But Kathy, of all of us, I would have thought you would enjoy the day the most, since you're the most open of us. But you didn't seem very enthusiastic."

Kathy was shaking her head, "I don't think I'm that open ... especially compared with Julie. And I *did* enjoy most of the day. I would go skinny-dipping with Sam anytime. But I think I was in a funk because of my period."

Kathy stopped speaking suddenly, and swallowed hard. She took a sip of margarita, and looked around the table at us. "And, I might have a new boyfriend." That was a surprise! We all smiled and clapped.

Kathy took another swallow of margarita, set it down, and explained, "A guy I met in Mexico. He's an American, but working down there on some land deal. We had dinner together and went to the beach a couple of times. It didn't get that serious ... but I was thinking about him throughout the party. I've called him since, and I'll probably go down there during Christmas break to see him again."

We chatted a while about 'boyfriends'. I asked Linda about her latest hook-up, a guy who had taken her to a Disney animation movie. "Oh, he's a shlub. A nice guy, but not the type who will get me 'excited', if you know what I mean."

Julie laughed, "We do, now!" Again, we were all laughing and, when the waitress came, we ordered another pitcher of margaritas. It *was* going to be a long lunch!

Julie reminded us of a couple of guys she occasionally 'dated', but informed us that she was still looking for someone who would excite her. Julie always had guys lined-up to take her out.

Then, Julie looked at me, and said, "Kelly, I can really understand why you're happy with Sam. He's a sweet guy;

'dominating', you might say, but not macho. As we said earlier, he can be 'one of the girls', but he's still definitely a man. He really knows how to take care of a woman ... in many ways." I was nodding, as were Kathy and Linda.

Linda said, "It's interesting ... I can understand now why you told us that he was 'sweet' and a 'nice guy', even though he spanked you. And he *is* thoughtful, as you said: For example, giving us the pareos, and the birthday t-shirts, and the picture of all of us in pink."

Julie laughed, "And the 'triple threat' rabbit vibrators!" All our eyes were on Julie now, and the table erupted again. Fortunately, we were the only ones left in the bar at this hour, and the wait-staff were nowhere to be seen.

Kathy said, "So have you tried it?" Although we were still all looking at Julie, in my peripheral vision I saw Linda flinch.

Julie replied, "Of course. Haven't you?" As Kathy shook her head slowly, Julie said, "It actually works pretty well. If you don't mind part of it up your butt." We chuckled.

I wasn't going to push Linda, but gave her a knowing glance. Her eyes went down, and back up to Julie and I. Then she said, simply, "It was the best birthday party favor I've ever gotten!" We were hysterical.

I hoped the bartender wouldn't call taxis for us, thinking we were too drunk to drive. Or, maybe he should. The margaritas were pretty weak, but the conversation was getting stronger, as the afternoon progressed.

It seemed that nobody was going to ask Linda to give details, so I exclaimed, "Well, the Europe trip that Sam gave me is the best birthday present I've ever gotten."

Amidst nods around the table, Kathy asked, "So have you guys figured out the itinerary, yet?"

I shook my head, "No. Sam is working on a proposed itinerary that we're going to review together later this week. But everything sounds great. Since I haven't been anywhere, it's all going to be new. And Sam has friends he wants us to visit, and some special places he wants us to go". Sam had already explained this to my friends.

"I still have to meet with my advisor at the university, before we can pick exact dates for the trip. Sam is conflicted, because he wants to show me some things that are only around during the summer, and others that are only during winter: Everything from kayaking to skiing. But we can't do it all in one trip, so he's having to make some compromises."

Linda said, "It sounds pretty exciting to me. Even if you don't get to kayak or ski."

She was right. It was going to be an incredible trip. Not just seeing some great cities of the world; or the geography – including some famous mountains and famous rivers; or the incredible art and museums. As Sam had explained to me, and I was now fully realizing, we would be visiting some 'special' places, and doing some things that furthered our journey of openness and sexual exploration. As well as experiencing a few different segments of European culture.

After we had chatted a while longer about Europe and travels – including Kathy's return trip to Mexico – I had to ask just one more thing, related to the birthday party. "I told you guys that Sam arranged for the lights to be off so that Julie and I could 'play around' a little." I looked directly at Kathy and explained, unnecessarily, "Since Linda and Julie came over to Sam's house and Julie masturbated in front of us, I have been turned on by the thought of playing with Julie; even though – until recently – I had never been with another woman before."

I glanced at Julie and back to Kathy, "And I think we found that it was a turn on for both of us." Julie was nodding. Neither Linda nor Kathy made a remark.

I continued, "And when I asked Sam what he had been doing with you guys, he said, 'satisfying your needs'. I don't mind whatever he did, but I'm curious as to what actually happened. If you don't mind sharing."

Kathy and Linda looked at each other. Linda said, softly, "Kelly, Sam was a perfect gentleman. I asked him to satisfy my needs, and he did … with his hands."

Linda looked into her lap; I could see that her face was reddening. "And he was very good." Of course, I knew that, already. Linda concluded, "After I came, he kissed me goodnight, and crawled away. Like a spirit in the darkness."

Then, Linda looked into my eyes, and said, "What's so amazing to me is that he never got turned on. I mean he never had an erection. He was doing it all for me. At least, that's what it felt like." Linda looked down again.

I said, "Linda, that's great. I'm glad you enjoyed your time with Sam. He's a very considerate person, and really does care about your needs. And he has very good control over himself: I'm not surprised that he didn't get turned on. But I'm a little surprised that he didn't use his tongue, as he knew that Julie and I would be going down on each other. Although he's still hung up about STDs."

Then I looked at Kathy. She shrugged, "Sam was 'visiting' each of us, as he had asked to do; lying next to us, and asking how we were. He asked if he could help get me off, and I told him yes." Linda, Julie and I looked at Kathy, who looked back at us and continued, "I took him up on his offer to be my 'bed', while I masturbated on top of him. I let him lie face-up, but he wasn't allowed to touch me in a sexual way. As Linda said, he was a perfect gentleman. It was fun, feeling his body under me, relaxed, as I fantasized about Carlos – he's the guy I met in Mexico."

We all laughed, but Kathy continued, "When I was done, I thanked Sam, and he said 'But, I didn't do anything'. I told him 'that was the point' – it was an intimate experience, shared with him, but without any obligations – it was just for me. But I'm pretty sure Sam enjoyed it."

I chuckled, "I'm sure he did!"

Kathy continued, "I really expected Sam to ask for a hand job, or something, in return. But he didn't. Like Linda said, he never even got hard. And I'm sure he knew that I would do it, if he asked. Not a big deal. But he never did. I don't know what he would have done, had I offered."

I didn't know, either. "Probably accept your offer. But maybe he was 'saving' himself for me. That would be too bad, because I was too tired to make love to him." There were a few chuckles.

Julie said, "After he finished with you guys, he waited in my bed – I'm sure so that he wouldn't miss sleeping with Kelly. I had to shake him awake. I thanked him for giving Kelly and I the time to be together, and offered to get him ready for Kelly. But he suspected that Kelly would be too tired, and said he would take a rain check."

Julie shook her head, "I have to agree with you guys: Sam was a perfect gentleman."

I suddenly cracked up, shocking my friends by my outburst. "Sam is a 'perfect gentleman'. Who throws skinny-dipping parties with young women, ties them to a turntable and spanks them, and visits each one at night to make sure they're sexually satisfied." I looked around the table, and we were hysterical again.

Linda poured the rest of the margaritas into our glasses, and we toasted to Sam: A creative, kind, and thoughtful person, if not more than a little perverted. But he was *my* perverted gentleman. I was proud of Sam, and very glad that my friends approved of him. I guess that would be an understatement.

It had been nearly a week since Kelly's birthday party, and we sat out by the pool enjoying the late summer breeze, and slightly cooler temperature. Puffy cumulus clouds dotted the deep blue sky, and loud chirps came from birds that were no longer spring hatchlings.

Kelly looked beautiful, even wearing her pink 'birthday' tee, and without makeup. The youthful skin of her freshly scrubbed face glowed. Her hazel eyes looked iridescent, and her amber hair fell, straight, to her waist in back.

"Sam, thank you for being so nice to my friends."

"I try to be nice to everyone, Kelly. *Especially* your friends." I chuckled.

"I'm serious, Sam. You pushed them, as I knew you would, but they all thought you were a 'perfect gentleman' – their words. They were especially impressed that you were able to satisfy them during the slumber party without putting any pressure on them to reciprocate."

"Well, they rewarded me well, the next morning." I was already getting hard thinking about three beautiful women going down on me as I woke up wearing a pink t-shirt.

Kelly laughed, "Yes, I didn't expect that. It was Julie's idea for you to wake up surrounded by a bunch of nude women, and make a 'Sam Sandwich'." Then, Kelly looked at me and added, "And it was nice that you accepted their reward, without being hung-up about the definition of sex."

"I was ambushed. I didn't have a choice." I pleaded, although Kelly knew otherwise.

"Of course, you had a choice. And you made it – I think it was the right one." I had to be thankful that Kelly was accepting of the relationships that were developing with her friends.

"Well, at least you said they didn't have any boyfriends, currently."

Kelly was perturbed, "I didn't say that. I just said they have hook-ups who they do different things with. I'm sure that includes sex, at least with some of the guys. And Kathy just informed us that she now has a Mexican lover, from her trip before my party."

"God! I've now had sex with some Mexican guy!"

Kelly laughed, saying, "He's Mexican-American," but I didn't think it was so funny.

I was curious to hear what Kelly's friends had said about the birthday party. "Your friends seemed pretty relaxed about all of us going nude, having a group massage, and seeing our demonstrations – the needle art corset and the pirate scene. They even played the 'spank poker' game for a while; I guess that got to be too much for them."

"Sam, you have to admit that my friends were amazing. They didn't turn down any experience. But they didn't like being tied down at the beginning of that 'spank poker' game. And, the needles were too much for them – especially Kathy. She gets faint at the sight of a needle. If we're going to play with them again, you're going to have to keep that in mind."

Then, Kelly batted her eyelashes at me, and added, "But I'll play with you – even if it includes needles and shots. Actually, I don't think Julie or Linda were too bothered by the needles, either, but don't push it."

"Yes, Ma'am. I'm sure you noticed that Linda didn't seem to mind the rectal insertions much, either. She was actually turned on by them. And, allowed me to masturbate her."

Kelly nodded, "Yes, that was surprising. There were a lot of surprises, and decade-long best friends learned some interesting new things about each other. This may fundamentally change our relationship; I just don't know how, yet"

"So what's the verdict on Julie? Was she as hot with you as she was with herself?"

Kelly laughed, "Yes, we had a good time together. But you have nothing to fear about losing me to a woman: Julie and I are both interested in men ... as well as some women." Kelly gave me an inscrutable look, and smiled, informing me, "So, instead of losing a lover, you may gain a ménage."

Now, I arched my brows at her. "Yes, Sam, I think Julie and I would both love to get it on with you – together." Now *that* was interesting news! I guess we'd all had 'sex' of some kind with each other, already. And Julie had turned out to be really hot for both Kelly and I. The perfect ménage was brewing on the horizon.

Kelly and I spent the rest of the afternoon talking about the Europe trip. I showed her a proposed itinerary, and we made some edits and a few additions. We discussed the hotel selection, and routing for our flights. Then, we went downstairs to the playroom, and I looked at flight schedules and hotel availability.

Finally, we'd had enough travel planning for one day. We were going to have an early dinner, so headed up to the master bedroom to get dressed. However, my body had other plans and, as I climbed the stairs from the basement 'playroom', something else rose as well. By the time we got to the kitchen, I had a full-on erection, and decided to suggest another 'experience'.

Kelly turned and saw my bobbing hard-on, then took me in her hands. "Do you need some help, mister?"

I was tempted to let Kelly 'help' me right there, using her mouth, but suggested, "Why don't we try some of the furniture, on the way up to the bedroom?"

Kelly looked confused, "'Try' the furniture?"

I nodded, "An extension of our Kama Sutra positions." Then I thought, "Or spanking positions. Let's see what we can do with the furniture. I slipped off my running shorts."

Kelly laughed, and looked around the kitchen, as she removed her underwear. "You've already used the spoon on my bottom, with me bent over the kitchen table."

I pulled out a chair, and sat down, then pulled Kelly down, straddling me. She lowered herself the rest of the way, my member sliding deeply into her. We rocked on the chair a minute or two, and then decided to move on.

I had Kelly get into the 'chair' position in one of the dining room chairs. But the arms were a bit close together, not allowing Kelly's legs to separate widely. I gave her a couple of playful spanks, and then we went into the living room. Kelly bent over the arm of the couch, and I gave her a couple more spanks, and she giggled. Unfortunately, she was too low for me to enter her comfortably.

She got on her knees on the couch, and I positioned myself behind her. Perfect height! I entered her again, and made long, slow strokes into her warm wetness. At that moment, I knew that we weren't going to make it to the bedroom.

Reaching under Kelly with my right hand, I moved my fingers in a circular pattern over her clit, as I tried in vain to lengthen and slow my strokes. After two more strokes, I came violently, pounding against Kelly's rear, emptying myself gratefully into her. I kept up the motion of my hand over Kelly's clit, but she reached under and moved it. "I'm sorry, Kelly. I guess I was a little too fast, today."

Kelly got off the couch, and took my hand. "That's OK, sir. Your satisfaction comes first." As we climbed the stairs, she looked over at me, and added, "But now, it's my turn." We turned into the guest bedroom. Kelly took the 'standing position', and asked, "Will you please spank me, Sir?"

That wasn't an offer I would refuse, but I gave Kelly an inquisitive look. She pointed to the bed, and instructed me to sit in front of the pillow with my legs out, feet towards the foot of the bed. She then climbed onto the bed, facing the foot, and maneuvered herself backwards, straddling my legs, then gradually lowered herself, as I pulled her legs around each side of me.

Her bottom was now in my 'lap', but turned 90-degrees from the normal spanking position. Kelly relaxed into the bed, between my legs, and put both her hands under her. She turned her head to the side, and said, "Please spank me slow and hard. Well, you can start at medium, and increase the force as you go. I'm going to take care of myself as you spank me."

That was something new. I massaged her bottom, alternately pulling her globes apart, exposing her pink rosebud, and squishing them together, making a double-mound of flesh. I then lightly rubbed her buttocks, my hands grazing over them in circular motions. Kelly closed her eyes, and began satisfying herself. She quietly said, "You may begin spanking me now, Sir."

I smiled, and did as she bid – giving her about one spank every two seconds, as she worked on herself. I hoped that she was already turned on, or this could become a painful sex experience, and painful for my hand, if it took 500 spanks before she came.

As I felt Kelly quicken her pace, I quickened mine – with harder spanks now spaced about a second apart. One thousand. Two thousand. Three thousand. The slaps on Kelly's bottom resounded in the small room, but the only sounds from Kelly were heavy breathing and a few grunts.

I watched Kelly's bottom bounce up and down with the spanks, and her own rhythmic motions. I could see her arms working, her fingers buried under her. Looking down, I could see Kelly's relaxed anus and, below that, the glistening pink tissues of her vulva.

Quickening the pace again, I spanked Kelly harder, and she breathed harder – now panting into the bedspread, her hips bucking, and her bottom thrusting up to meet the spanks I was delivering. Beginning as a guttural roar, Kelly let out a savage cry that increased in pitch and in intensity, to a final series of shrieks synchronized with the bucking of her hips.

I gave her two final spanks, before Kelly's body collapsed onto the bed, all of her muscles simultaneously relaxing, a rag doll with her legs draped over my hips. Kelly gave one final sigh, and then purred, as I softly massaged her bottom, thighs, hips, and lower back.

Eventually, Kelly crawled forward on her stomach, her legs coming free from around me, and continued off the foot of the bed. We stood up and hugged each other. As my hands reached around to rub her bottom, Kelly said, "Thank you, Sam. That was nice."

I shrugged, "You did it yourself. But it's always nice to hear someone thank me, after I've spanked them."

Kelly chuckled, and gave me a quick peck on the lips. "Shall we dress for dinner, now?"

We both laughed, as we walked into the master bedroom, and through the master bath to the large closet. Kelly took off her tee, and donned a pair of black lace panties and matching bra. Then, she slipped on a silk blouse.

It wasn't until she was pulling up her jeans that I grabbed my own belt from the rack, and thought back to the time I surprised Kelly by having her bend over for the belt, the hem of her dress pulled up and laid over her back. I had given her only one stroke, but she had submitted without question. I knew that I could have done the same tonight, but I'd just spanked Kelly, and knew that she'd had enough for a while.

When we got back to Sam's house after dinner, I told Sam that I had our evening planned. At first he gave me a wary look, then shrugged, and said, "I'm all yours, Miss."

I led Sam upstairs, and we undressed each other in the closet. Then, I turned the hot-water faucet of the giant jacuzzi tub and, after the water was hot to the touch, I closed the drain and let the tub begin to fill.

"Sam, do you have any more of those large candles, like you used in the playroom when we first made love?" Sam got the idea immediately, and nodded once curtly, before running downstairs. The tub was filling slowly, and I looked through a few drawers, until I found some bubble bath powder, which I set on the side of the tub.

Sam came back with an armload of candles, and began setting them, in their holders, around the tub, on the windowsills, and on the tiled counter next to the sinks. I told him to hold-off lighting the candles, so he sat down on the edge of the tub, and waved his hand through the hot water, as I sat down to pee. Sam let out an 'Ow!' as he put his hand under the faucet. The tub was ¾ filled, and I told Sam to turn off the water.

Then, I led Sam back downstairs. We'd had iced tea at dinner, so I asked Sam to open a nice bottle of wine. He had me taste the wine, and then set the opened bottle and two crystal glasses on the bar in the playroom. The wine was a Bordeaux, dark and luscious. I would have to suggest another Europe trip – focusing on France, so Sam could teach me more about wine.

We went into the downstairs bath, grabbed a couple of towels, and opened the smoked glass door of the sauna. Sam complained that I should have let him know earlier, so he could heat it to the proper temperature, but I was glad there would only be moderate heat. We entered the dim, red-lit space, and I inhaled the cedar aroma.

We spread our towels on the benches, and lay down – Sam on the upper bench and me on the lower one. Sam turned the sand dial over, and I looked up at the ceiling, thinking again of my birthday party, our upcoming Europe trip ... and Sam.

I closed my eyes, and relaxed into the warmth of the sauna. Some time later, Sam came down and sat on the lower bench, and I put my legs across his lap. I was becoming so relaxed I thought I might fall asleep.

Sam quietly suggested we get under a cool shower. That sounded good, but I could have stayed in the sauna much longer. Sam had overheated quickly on the upper bench, while I was still comfortable lying on the lower bench.

But we had much more of the evening left, so I got up, and we stepped back into the brighter lights of the shower room. Sam adjusted the temperature of the rain shower to lukewarm, and the leg jets to cool. We hugged, closed our eyes, and let the water flow over and between our bodies.

When we had cooled down, I took a Loufah, and squirted some body wash onto it, then started scrubbing Sam. Beginning at his neck, and working down with a circular motion, I exfoliated him thoroughly, all the way to his feet. Sam complained a few times that I was scrubbing too hard, but I told him not to be a baby. I carefully washed Sam's genitals, and inserted a finger deeply into his rectum, in order to massage his prostate. Sam moaned, appreciatively.

Then, Sam washed me, trying to duplicate my technique. I had to keep telling him to scrub harder, but he finally got the idea, and bathed me well. Sam also washed my genitals, and put his finger in my front and rear, but did this in a perfunctory way, not trying to turn our shower into a sexual event.

When we turned off the water, Sam and I were both pink and glowing. We took new towels and dried ourselves, then put on terrycloth robes from the narrow closet. Sam smiled at me, and said, "That was fun."

We retrieved the wine and glasses from the bar, and took them upstairs. I sat on the edge of the tub, and put my hand into the water: It was still hot, but not scalding. I turned on the hot water again, and poured the bath powder under the stream. Bubbles filled the tub, as the water level rose, and the water became nearly too hot to touch. Sam lit all of the candles, and set the wine and glasses on the wide, tiled back edge of the tub; then he turned off the lights.

I slowly slipped into the hot water, wondering if we would need to add some cold water; but I finally made it all the way in, and lowered myself until the water was up to my neck. Then I sat up, and Sam lowered himself into the water, whining the whole time that it was too hot. Finally, we were both in the tub, facing each other, Sam's legs outside each of my hips.

Sam poured the wine, and we toasted to another nice day together. A few minutes later, Sam caused a tsunami by moving around me, until I was sitting between his legs, lying back on his chest. Sam put his arms around me, under my breasts, and we lay that way for some time, enjoying the flickering flames of the countless candles, and the soothing soak in the scented spa.

By the time we decided to get out of the tub, the candles had burned halfway down, and we had finished more than half of the wine. Sam held and kissed me, then helped dry me with a huge, fluffy towel.

As I took all of the decorative pillows off the bed, and pulled down the covers, Sam moved the candles into the bedroom, carefully placing them in the centers of the dressers and side tables. Then he turned on some soft music, turned off the light, and climbed into bed next to me.

It was like our first time again: Candlelight, music and the aroma of burning wax, if not roses. I climbed on top of Sam, and let my hair fall over his chest, moving my head so that my hair was swinging across him, brushing his nipples, swirling over his taut stomach.

I crawled down his body, and stroked his growing manhood, finally taking him in my mouth. I swirled my tongue around him, sucking and lapping until he was fully ready. Then, I straddled his hips, and guided him into me. I lowered myself onto him, my breasts pressing against his firm chest, and we kissed lovingly. We moved our hips in counterpoise, and I adjusted my position so that Sam was pressing against my most sensitive tissues.

Sam softly said, "Legs straight, please." As soon as I had straightened them, Sam held me around the back, and flipped us over, with him now on top. Taking long, slow strokes, Sam filled me, bringing me nearly to the point of no return ... but then he pulled back, coming nearly out of me, stopping momentarily, while I felt his cock throb.

Sam was an expert in self-control, and I wondered whether he actually practiced Tantra – an ancient Eastern technique for prolonging sex. As in Tantric sex, Sam controlled his breathing and his movements with precision. He brought us to the edge and back several times, until I was ready to scream at him to let me come.

Sam sensed my readiness – urgency – and thrust into me, his aim precise, and my response predictable. We both experienced explosive orgasms, nearly simultaneous, but Sam had waited to be sure I would come first. He was very considerate. I loved this man.

We continued to move until we were both spent, the sauna, bubble bath and wine taking their tolls on our energy level. The candles had nearly burned down to their bases, and the music still played softly, as we snuggled. I lay next to Sam thinking of Europe. All the places Sam had shown me now flew through my head, their images coalescing, as I drifted off to sleep.

CHAPTER 2: ALEX VISITS

Kelly had stayed with me the last two weekends, and I had worked with her, strategizing and planning her dissertation. The research would be done at the university, but she needed to 'package' it in the context of a background, and conclusions summarizing the meaning of the results and potential future applications of the technology.

We researched the literature together, and compared notes. We outlined the thesis, and drafted executive summaries. Of course, there was only so much we could do, as her lab work had not yet started. But it got Kelly back into the educational spirit and, hopefully, accelerated her progress, so that she could take time in October to travel through a little of Europe with me.

Kelly was upstairs, unpacking some clothes for the Labor Day weekend. She was still planning to stay at home during the week, focusing on school, and stay with me over the weekends. She would have to see how her schedule worked out, after her seminars began.

Kelly came bouncing down the stairs, into my arms, "I missed you." We kissed each other tenderly.

"I missed you, too. At least we have one more long weekend before school begins." Kelly nodded, looking distant. We grabbed a couple of Diet Cokes, and walked out onto the patio.

As Kelly popped the top of the can, she looked around and said, "This place always looks beautiful. It's a place I want to come back to."

I chuckled, "Well, it's not quite as nice in the winter. But I agree that I'm always happy to come back home to this backyard." We sat at the glass table, and sipped our Cokes.

Finally, I asked, "What would you like to do, this weekend, Kelly? I could do hamburgers or steaks on the barbeque on Labor Day, if that sounds good to you."

Kelly put her Coke down, and looked at me, "Actually, Sam, I have bad news and good news. Actually double bad, and double good."

I waited silently, and Kelly continued, "The bad news is that my parents always put on a Labor Day bash – mainly for all my Dad's sports friends. They watch college football and drink a lot of beer. They're more likely to cook hot dogs than steaks."

Kelly smiled, then frowned, "They really want me to be there, so I can say hello to their old friends." She looked at me and said, "I'm sure they would be happy to have you to the party ... but I'm not sure it's such a good idea."

I sat back in the chair and thought about it. "I agree with you – it's not worth it, unless you're ready to introduce me as your current boyfriend. Man friend."

Kelly laughed, but shook her head, "I don't think so." Then, she smiled sweetly at me, and announced, "And I'll probably get my period before the end of this weekend." Well, that couldn't really be considered bad news; most unmarried couples would be thrilled that Kelly's period was on-time. And it wouldn't really affect our weekend; at least the first part of it.

I asked, "So what's the *good* news?"

Kelly looked down, and then back at me, "My parents' Labor Day party always degenerates into a television-watching get-together in the early afternoon. So I can plan to leave around that time. I can probably be here between three and four o'clock. And either hamburgers or steaks would be fine." I nodded. We can still have dinner together.

Kelly looked at me brightly and said, "And, I would like to suggest that we invite another guest." I shifted my position, my groin suddenly spasming, as I thought of a possible ménage with Julie.

Then, Kelly clarified, "I spoke with Fiona last night. She told her boyfriend about needle art, and now he's getting enamored with it. Fortunately, he likes the art on *his* body." We laughed, but Fiona had shown her mettle when she visited us, and I knew that she would submit to needle art, if her boyfriend asked her.

Kelly continued, "He hasn't proposed, yet, but Fiona thinks it might be soon. Anyway, Fiona told me that Alex just got back yesterday from Europe. I mentioned that it was great that Alex would have the long weekend to get over jet lag, and explained that we would be here, probably barbequing. We both thought it would be a good time to invite Alex over; so you could get to know your neighbor."

I was surprised at this turn of events, but agreed that it might be nice to get to know Alex a little better. Kelly had said something about Alex and I being in the same age range, but I was at least five years older than Alex, although her conservative nature made her seem older than her years. I wasn't sure that we had similar values, however, with my liberality and stress on openness, and her focus on high-society and art; money and things. We would have to see.

I said to Kelly, "I guess we could have her join us for dinner. We can have her come around 5PM, to give you a chance to get here and settled."

Kelly shook her head, "No, Sam. You should invite her to spend the afternoon here, maybe come around one or two o'clock.

Now, I was shaking my head. "I don't want to be stuck with her that long, having to make idle chit-chat, with you not here."

Kelly sighed, "Sam, she may not be that bad; she went skinny-dipping with us in the pond. Fiona thinks there's hope that she'll open up a little. It sounds like all her other relationships are formal; she really has no friends with whom she can relax, and let her hair down."

I grumbled, "I'm not sure she ever lets her hair down."

Kelly laughed, "Look, I'll try to get here by around 3PM. Why don't you invite her for 2PM. That's only an hour. Maybe, she'll go in the pool or spa with you?"

"I really doubt it. I will certainly make the offer, but I don't think she'll be very comfortable, if you're not here."

Kelly argued, "Nonsense! Fiona thinks she'll go out of her way to show some openness with us. Give her a chance."

I reluctantly agreed, and Kelly gave me Alex's number; I suggested that we both get on the call. Alex sounded tired, but was glad to hear from us. Kelly told her that she would be tied-up for a while on Labor Day afternoon, but that Alex should plan to come over between one and two o'clock. I waved at Kelly, but she just shook her head and smiled, as she said, "Great! We look forward to seeing you on Monday."

Then, she hung up the phone, and gave me a 'look'. "Don't worry. You guys will do fine together." At least Kelly hadn't tried to play the 'age' card.

The weekend flew by: Kelly and I planned further details of our Europe trip, and we had a nice relaxing time together. The only notable 'event' was the second installment of our Kama Sutra adventure ... that didn't get much farther than the first one. We stopped before Kelly got too sore. It was interesting, but not really a turn on.

Kelly had left this morning to attend her parents' party, kissing me as she walked out the door, then turning and saying 'Good luck!' with respect to Alex.

I really wasn't sure what to expect: Alex seemed to be a nice, well-to-do woman, who was a little too hung up and conservative for my taste, but who seemed to want to try to loosen up, make friends, and enjoy life more. At least, that was my take on the situation.

For our Labor Day dinner, I decided to make steaks with stuffed baked potatoes, and asparagus, along with a big salad. In a slight nod to being realistic, I chose a quick brown butter for the asparagus, rather than the classic Hollandaise sauce. Ah, Holland. The Netherlands: Land of tolerance. And one of the world centers of the fetish scene.

The morning disappeared: By the time I had returned from the market and prepped the food, it was already 1PM. Alex could show up at any time. I put on a pair of cargo shorts, and a muted Hawaiian 'Aloha' shirt, and was walking down the stairs to the living room when the doorbell rang.

I opened the front door and greeted Alex. She wore flowing white linen slacks, pleated at the waist, and a leopard patterned silk blouse, with sleeves rolled up to just below her elbows. The sheer blouse was unbuttoned to expose the top of her black bra, and the cleavage of her full breasts.

A thin brown belt accentuated her narrow waist, and a couple of simple gold bracelets graced her left wrist. Her thick dark brown hair, parted on the left side, fell straight, to the middle of her back. Her lips had a very light peach gloss, and she wore just enough makeup to look elegant, but not overdone. A pair of white strappy sandals completed the outfit.

I was a little surprised that Alex hadn't worn shorts, as this was a Labor Day party, but I suspected that most of the parties that she attended were held at museums, art galleries, and other swankier venues. She sported a pair of fashion sunglasses, and my first impression was that she looked like a film star, walking along the boulevard in San Tropez, or maybe Rodeo Drive in Beverly Hills.

We hugged, and I invited her into the house. She handed me a bottle of French red wine, a small bow tied around the neck of the bottle. "Thank you for inviting me over, Sam. I had kept this weekend open, knowing that I'd be tired after the return flights from Europe. But it's nice to get together; Fiona has been suggesting that I call you, but my schedule usually doesn't give me much time for social visits."

Alex looked around the living room, as I led her into the kitchen, where I put the wine on the counter.

"Thank you for the wine, Alex. It wasn't necessary, but it's appreciated. I'm glad you have a little time for relaxing after your trip; and Kelly has also been suggesting that I call you." Almost as an afterthought, I added, "Kelly and Fiona seemed to really hit it off together."

I had no idea whether Fiona would have mentioned her experience with Kelly to Alex, but I doubted it. Alex just nodded, as she glanced around the kitchen.

"Why don't I give you the nickel tour?" Alex agreed, and I began by taking her out to the patio.

As Alex surveyed the backyard, she said softly, "This is very nice. Your lot is much bigger than mine, and you have a lot more large trees. And we never put in a pool." I walked her along the path around the pool, next to the flowerbeds, and the expansive lawn. It was another beautiful day, the placid water of the black bottom pool reflecting the blue sky above.

I told her, "We used to use the backyard a lot more, when our kids were at home. But it hasn't been used much for the past decade ... until recently. Kelly liked the atmosphere back here enough that she picked my backyard for her birthday party."

Alex gave me a look, and explained, "Yes. Fiona mentioned that Kelly was going to have a 'skinny-dipping' birthday party with her friends. She would have liked to come, but had to fly back to Toronto."

I nodded, wondering what Alex thought about a bunch of young women frolicking nude around the pool with an older guy. "It was a fun party. Kelly's friends seemed to be very comfortable being nude, but I gave them a couple of things to wear as party favors."

When Alex looked at me questioningly, we walked into the pool room, and I found a couple of the photos I had taken, left on the massage table. I handed Alex a photo, which showed the five of us in our pink 'happy 25th birthday' t-shirts, and another shot of the four girls from behind, the pirate logo displayed on the back of each tee.

She smiled, "That's cute."

I told her that I had also provided pareos, as a cover-up during lunch; but I didn't mention that most of Kelly's friends had wrapped it around their waists, covering only their lower bodies. I explained that the pool room was used for various things, although it was mostly empty now.

I hoped that Alex wouldn't ask about the large round wooden turntable strapped to the wall.

Alex looked at the professional massage table – still positioned at the edge of the sliding glass door to the patio – and asked, "Are you a masseur?" She ran her hand along the faux-leather surface of the table.

Chuckling, I said, "I'm not licensed, but I've had some training from a friend who's a great masseuse. I'm pretty good, but don't have the opportunity to practice much, these days."

Alex looked at me, and then stared out to the backyard for a few moments. "I love getting massages. It's one of life's little pleasures. I make sure to get a massage after I've flown internationally, and checked into my hotel; it really helps me get over the jet lag."

That was a great opening. "Well, if you haven't had a massage since you returned, I'd be happy to indulge you. It's something I enjoy doing. And it's a great way to give someone a nice experience, using only your hands."

Alex nodded, but didn't reply. We continued the tour, walking downstairs to the playroom. I had lowered the giant screen, and closed the electric curtain behind it. "I call this the 'playroom' – a combination family room, office, and entertainment center." I didn't mention the additional 'entertainment' that the king size bed would provide, nor how most of the furniture was also used for our spanking sessions.

I flipped on the video, which happened to be cued to 'Winged Migration', an incredible film with close-up videography of birds flying on their thousand-plus mile migratory journey. Alex gasped when the video came on; it really was as good as any theater.

Then, I walked to the bar, and offered Alex something to drink. "We have wines, beers, mixed drinks, bottled water, Diet Coke, and various juices, if you're interested."

Alex nodded absently, and said, "A Diet Coke would be great." I opened a can, and poured the Coke into two crystal glasses with tiny cubes from the icemaker under the bar. We carried our drinks as we backtracked through the playroom.

Alex was briefly surprised, when I turned into the bathroom, but she understood when we entered the shower room, and I pointed out the multiple temperature-controlled jets, and the lounging area.

"And this is the sauna." I opened the smoked glass door so that she could see the cedar-lined room. It was already warm, but I turned the temperature up, just in case Alex got adventurous and agreed to take a sauna with us later. I offered, "Perhaps you'll try the sauna with Kelly and I, later?"

Alex said, "Perhaps." Then we walked back upstairs, and out to the patio, where we sat at the table.

"I haven't made any appetizers, yet, but I can put out some nice cheeses and crackers, if you like. Or macadamia nuts?"

Alex shook her head, "I'm fine." Then, she smiled, and said, "But I wouldn't turn down the macadamias."

I hopped up and ran to the kitchen, where I filled a small bowl with whole macadamias, which I brought out to the patio table, along with another can of Diet Coke.

Alex smiled, as she popped a macadamia into her mouth. "I guess I should have brought a bathing suit. I wasn't sure what you had planned for the afternoon."

I shook my head, "No worries. There is really no plan – just relaxing and getting to know each other. Kelly should be here in an hour or so. I'm planning to barbeque steaks for dinner, if that's OK." I hoped that Alex wasn't on a vegan diet.

"That sounds great. The jet lag is hitting me today, so I would be happy to just relax."

I ventured, "And you never need a bathing suit here – we don't use them." Alex scrunched her face, and I added, "You seemed to enjoy the pond without a suit."

Alex gave me another 'look'. "Fiona was pushing me, and I decided it would be the most sociable thing to do, as you guys were naked. As you can probably guess, I don't normally take off my clothes in front of people who I don't know." Then, she smiled, and added, "Even people I *do* know."

I laughed, "It certainly was 'sociable'. And we don't normally discuss our spanking and submission fetish with people we don't know." Touché.

Alex put down her Coke. "Sam, I'm not embarrassed about my body, or even letting someone see me nude. It wasn't a big deal to go skinny-dipping at the pond. It just isn't the social environment that I'm used to. Fiona thinks I'm hung-up, and not adventurous enough. She also thinks I'm an 'old maid', and she can't stop trying to find me a date. But I'm not looking for anything like that; my life is full of social contact without having to meet the expectations of a man."

That was interesting. "Expectations?"

Alex looked out at the backyard, and back to me, "Yes. Like sex. Or cooking for him. Or washing his clothes."

I chuckled, "Is that what you think men want?"

Alex shrugged. "I had a life tending to my husband's needs, and now I'm enjoying my life without responsibilities or commitment to anyone else." Alex looked at me, and I could see that she was deciding whether to tell me something.

"I do like men. And I like sex. Just not all the strings that are usually attached." I was nearly compelled to ask Alex whether she masturbated, which would then open the subject of fantasies and sexual preferences. But I held my tongue. Perhaps I could pursue that later, when Kelly was here.

We were quiet for several minutes, munching macadamias and looking out into the backyard. Then I asked Alex where she had been, on her recent trip to Europe. I found out that she had spent almost all the time in London and Paris, with a brief side-trip to Milano. All her activities were related to foundations and the arts.

I told her about the evolving plans for Kelly's first trip to Europe – at least the basic itinerary, but not mentioning the clubs and saunas. We still had to confirm the schedule with Kelly's doctoral advisor, and I was still trying to expose her to some of the summer activities as well as the winter activities – not an easy feat, during a two- or three-week trip.

Alex and her husband had traveled to most of the places on our itinerary – such as driving along the Rhine river, and into the Neckar valley, staying at 'schloss' (castle) hotels. We talked about the great food of each region, as well as the wines.

Alex looked down and shook her head. Then, she looked at me and asked, "Would you really want to give me a massage?"

I was dumbfounded. That was probably the last thing I had expected Alex to ask. "Of course! I love giving massages, and I love seeing people relax and enjoy it. As I said, I'm not a licensed professional, but I always try to give the most 'professional' massage that I can."

I looked at my watch. "Actually, it would work out just about right – your massage will be finished about the time that Kelly is supposed to return from her parents' house." I looked at Alex, who had a distant gaze, and asked, "So?"

Alex refocused her eyes and nodded, "OK, Sam. I would like that. It really might help me get over the jet lag." Then she smiled at me, and said, "But I might fall asleep. I've done that during massages before, when I'm already tired, and then get very relaxed."

I nodded, "Yes, that can happen. But that would be fine. I have no 'expectations'."

Alex laughed, "OK. But could we possibly have a little wine, first? That might loosen me up a little more." Then she smiled, "But it might also put me to sleep." We laughed.

"If you fall asleep, I'll just cover you with the draping, and we'll wake you for dinner." More laughing. "Would you like me to open the bottle you brought, or pull something out of my cellar?"

Alex shrugged, "Either. I brought a merlot, but I'm open to anything." It was nice hearing that Alex would be 'open to anything'. Maybe Kelly and I would have a chance to find out how true that was.

I brought the empty can of Diet Coke, and the glasses into the kitchen, and found some large-bowl glasses with a tapered lip that would allow faster oxidation of the wine that Alex had brought, as I wasn't going to decant it, and we didn't have time to allow it to breathe.

I carried the glasses and bottle of wine to the patio table, and Alex and I toasted – to good neighbors, openness and adventure. We sipped the wine. It wasn't bad: A soft, medium-body, fruity wine, with hints of black cherry and plum, and very little tannin. It was lighter than my usual preference, but nice for drinking in the afternoon. I tilted the glass, and confirmed the orange-red brick-color of the rim – characteristic of merlots.

Alex took several long swallows of the smooth, red liquid, and I re-filled her glass. "If you fall asleep too quickly, you won't enjoy your massage!"

Alex laughed, took a couple more swallows of her wine, and said, "OK. I guess I'm ready."

I led Alex back downstairs, and pulled a terrycloth robe from the narrow closet in the shower room, hanging it on a hook on the tiled wall. "Please undress, and put on this robe. You can wear some flip-flops from the bin. When you're ready, I'll meet you in the pool room." Alex nodded, and I exited the bathroom, pulling the door shut behind me.

I went upstairs, and put on a pair of running shorts and a tank, grabbed a clean sheet from the upstairs linen closet, then prepped everything in the pool room for Alex's massage. I put a towel over the massage table, and then selected some oils that I placed on the rolling metal table that I positioned next to the massage table.

I opened the sliding doors, bringing the outside in; there was a slight breeze, but it was warm enough that Alex wouldn't get chilled when I uncovered parts of her for the massage. I sat at the patio table, and finished my glass of wine. But I didn't pour any more, as I had to stay awake too! I hoped I had the stamina to give a full-body massage.

A few minutes later, Alex came out to the patio, wearing the robe and a pair of too-large flip-flops. She looked more relaxed, already. As did I. She looked strangely at my casual outfit, and I explained, "It takes a lot of energy to give a good massage; I might even get sweated-up. So I decided to put on my 'working' clothes." Alex nodded blankly.

We walked to the massage table, and I unfolded the sheet, and held it up, between myself and Alex, to act as a privacy screen. Alex took off the robe, and slipped out of the slippers, then climbed onto the table, lying face-down, with her head in the face cradle. As she lay down, I covered her from neck to toes with the sheet, letting the extra fall off each side of the table. Alex settled into position, and I took each of her arms, laying them alongside her body, palms up. I gathered her hair, and let it fall to one side over her shoulder. Then I leaned down and whispered, "Are you comfortable, Ma'am?"

I'm not sure why the 'ma'am' came out, but Alex chuckled, and said, "Yes, Sam, I feel fine."

Then, I asked, "I usually use a coconut-based oil, but I have several others if you have a preference ... or an allergy."

Alex said, through the hole of the face cradle, "Coconut oil is fine."

I folded the top of the sheet to halfway down Alex's back, and then folded it again, exposing her back down to her waist. Then, I squirted some oil into my palms, and rubbed them together vigorously, to warm it.

Standing at the head of the table, I placed my hands on either side of Alex's spine, near the base of her neck, and leaned forward, putting increasing pressure on her muscles, and then slowly glided my hands down to the small of her back. Maintaining contact with her skin, I lightly pulled my hands back up, and repeated the stroke, this time using my thumbs to follow the contours of her spine, pressing into the spaces between each vertebra.

My strokes continued, as I gradually moved my hands away from her spine, and towards her sides. For the final strokes, my hands were at the edge of Alex's back, my fingers curled around the sides of her body. I could not help but notice Alex's breasts squishing out from each side of her, as they pressed into the massage table.

I then folded the sheet again, exposing a few inches of Alex's upper buttocks. My strokes started lower on Alex's back, and continued down to the sheet and, eventually, under it, both hands kneading Alex's buttocks before coming up from under the sheet. I would have liked to fold the sheet down to her gluteal cleft, but decided on a more modesty-protecting draping.

I unfolded the sheet back up to Alex's neck, and then stood at the side of the table, and folded the sheet over Alex, so that her right side was exposed, from her waist down to her toes. I tucked some of the excess sheet between her legs – perhaps not the most comfortable for her, but hopefully communicating that her 'privates' were not exposed.

Alex was being very open to allow me to give her a massage, and I was not going to push her; I would be seeing most of her body, but wanted to make her as psychologically comfortable as possible by ensuring that she knew I was protecting her modesty – at least as much as feasible while still giving her a full-body massage.

Massaging her right buttock, I pressed down hard, and glided my hand from her waist down, over her hips to her thighs. Alex had a firm body – for her age (I winced as I thought that) – but she had a relatively large butt and wide hips. Her flesh rippled under the pressure of my palms, as I stroked farther down, along her right leg, and down to her ankle.

I pulled the sheet over to cover her right buttock, leaving only her right leg exposed. Then, I circled her leg with my hands, and slid my hands down, from her thigh to her knee, continuing down to her ankle. After considerable focus on her leg, I flopped the sheet back over her, leaving only her right foot exposed.

I squeezed more oil into my hands and massaged Alex's foot, my thumbs stretching her Achilles tendon, then moving over her heel, and down the sides of her foot.

I then covered her right foot, and exposed her left, performing the same movements on that side. In a reverse of the massage on her right side, I folded the sheet over to expose Alex's left leg, up to her gluteal crease (where her lower butt meets her upper thigh). I circled my hands around Alex's right ankle, and stroked upward, along her leg, to her thigh. I worked my way up, always keeping at least one hand in contact with Alex's body.

As I stroked upward around Alex's right thigh, I was careful to end the stroke before my hand reached her sensitive areas. It was very important to me to build Alex's trust, and not overextend my 'welcome'.

When I was done with her leg, I massaged Alex's left buttock, again squeezing and kneading, and slipping my hand up her lower back, and along her side, under the sheet. Finally, I re-draped Alex with the sheet, and let my hand glide over the sheet along her body, as I walked toward her head.

Alex hadn't made a sound and was breathing regularly, and I wondered whether she had actually fallen asleep. I leaned down next to her head, and whispered, "How are you doing, Alex?"

She wasn't asleep. "I'm doing fine, Sam. And you're doing a great job – this is a really nice massage. I think I'm finally starting to relax from the trip."

My right hand was casually making circles, rubbing Alex's back lightly through the sheet, as I talked with her. "I hate to disturb your serenity, but are you ready to turn over, now?"

Alex chuckled, and started to turn herself over. I stood at the side of the table, and held the sheet up, casually looking toward the foot of the table, to give Alex more privacy, as she turned over onto her back.

I adjusted the sheet, which still covered Alex from her neck to her toes. I decided to work my way up from her feet, so moved to the foot of the table. I uncovered both of Alex's feet, and squeezed more oil into my hands.

Starting on her right foot, I massaged each of Alex's toes, and pressed my thumbs into the sole of her foot, stroking upward from heel to the base of her toes. I spent at least five minutes giving Alex a foot massage on the right side, and then on the left. I heard Alex softly purring, as she relaxed even more.

Then, I folded each side of the sheet up to her leg, and folded again, and again, until the sheet was mostly between her legs, uncovering both her left and right legs from her toes up to her thighs. I made long strokes down her legs, from thighs to toes, first on one side and then the other; and then, I ran my hands down both her legs simultaneously, pressing her into the table.

Alex now looked a bit like she was wearing a white dress with slits at each side, her legs completely exposed through the slits, while her upper body was completely covered.

I asked Alex if she was cold, but she replied that she felt perfect, so I left both her legs uncovered, a mess of sheet filling the space between her legs, and covering her groin. My next step was to fold the sheet down from her neck, uncovering her on top. Alex was obviously expecting this, and seemed very relaxed; and, she knew I had already seen her breasts at the pond. But I decided to err on the modest side. I leaned down to her, and whispered, "I'll be back in just a minute." Her eyes still closed, Alex nodded slightly. I ran over to the bathroom, and took a couple of washcloths from the shelf, returning to Alex's left side.

Even before I lowered the sheet, there was a sexy scene before me: Alex was almost completely covered by the sheet – at least, from her neck to her waist – but the sheet had contoured around her breasts, showing their shape three-dimensionally, while her nipples pushed up dimples on the sheet.

I looked at Alex's face, which was very relaxed. She wore little makeup and, of course, I could see her age (she had evidently not had a facelift, thankfully); but she was still a beautiful woman, with a strong jaw, high cheekbones, and large eyes, framed by perfect brows. At that moment, I decided to work on her head, before venturing lower.

I squirted oil into my hands, and rubbed them together, then placed them on each side of her neck, my thumbs pressing into the nape of her neck. I slowly massaged her neck, feeling muscles tense, and then relax. Then, I put the tips of my thumbs together in the center of Alex's forehead, and slowly pulled them to each side, stretching her skin.

Working this way for several minutes, I moved down to her ears, and gently massaged her lobes, using circular motions of the thumb and forefingers of each of my hands. I put my thumbs on her cheeks, and pulled them down slowly, stretching more skin.

Finally, I moved to the side of the table, and prepared the next step, placing each of the folded washcloths on Alex's chest, and slowly moving them down over her breasts, as I lowered the sheet. In one smooth motion, Alex was now uncovered, and I folded the sheet, and folded it again, until it was just above Alex's pubic hair.

I ran my finger along her skin, from one side to the other of the sheet, subtly letting Alex know how far it had been turned down.

Alex was now uncovered down to below her waist ... except for a folded washcloth sitting on each breast; covering much of them, but as she was a good C-cup, the washcloths actually sat on top of each breast, with a lot still exposed.

As I prepared to begin her upper-body massage, Alex raised her head slightly and opened her eyes, looking down her body, and seeing the washcloths sitting on her breasts. She laughed, and put her head back down. "That wasn't necessary, Sam. I know that to give me a massage, you're going to have to see my body." She was still laughing.

"I'll move the washcloths, when I get to that area." Then, I explained, "I'm just trying to be professional, Alex. I want to make you as relaxed as possible. That's what I think a good massage should do." Then, I added, "And give you a tingling feeling, when we're done."

With her head down and eyes closed, Alex replied, "You're being very 'professional', Sam. I'm very impressed with your skills. And your sensitivity and thoughtfulness."

That was nice. Then I thought – as I had when Kelly's friends thanked me after a day of spanking them – here was a beautiful, elegant, woman, thanking me for touching – and seeing – her body. I wasn't about to become a professional masseur ... but it was a profession I could enjoy!

I oiled my hands, and began on Alex's chest, massaging both sides, my hands going upward over her shoulders, around her neck, lifting her head, and then gently lowering it, and repeating the stoke.

Then facing down the table, I ran my hands from Alex's shoulders, across her chest, and down between her breasts – between the folded washcloths. I continued the stroke down across Alex's taut stomach, and below her navel, turning at the folded sheet, and moving out to each side, over Alex's hips, and under her – lifting her bottom – before coming back up her sides to her chest. I repeated this many times, diving down between her breasts, and making a circle around Alex's upper body.

At this point, the sheet was folded in a thin line across Alex, covering her private parts, and then vertically down, between Alex's legs.

I carefully folded the sheet from her hips down between her legs, leaving Alex completely uncovered from head to toes, except for the washcloths over her breasts, and the small area of sheet still covering her pubic area. Essentially, Alex was showing about as much skin as she would when wearing a bikini bathing suit.

Now I drizzled some of the fragrant oil over her stomach, which reacted by moving up and down a little. Then, I massaged across her abdomen, my hands going in opposite directions, across her body, and over her sides. Finally, I did a few strokes starting on her stomach, and moving down her hips and upper thighs.

Leaning down again with my head near Alex's, I whispered, "We can finish, now. Or, if you don't mind being a little more uncovered, I can continue."

Alex, her eyes closed, smiled, and said, "You may continue, Sam."

As I said, "Yes, ma'am," I heard footsteps, and Kelly appeared at the door of the playroom. She stopped and surveyed the scene, smiling broadly, and hitting her forehead with her hand. I smiled at her, and she gave me the diver's 'OK' signal, then she disappeared back into the kitchen.

I oiled my hands again, and slid them from Alex's chest down between her breasts, and then around them and back up to her chest. Each time around, my hands moved outward, more over Alex's breasts, until the washcloths were pushed down on each side. I put them on the table below Alex's hands, and continued her breast massage. My hands went directly over the center of Alex's breasts, from her chest down to her stomach, and then followed the contours of each breast, back up to her chest.

Then, my hands went down from her chest, over her breasts, my fingers splayed, so that her nipples were caught in the 'V' of my fingers on each hand. I went back up her breasts, and then back down, catching her nipples again. The third time, I continued down, Alex's firm nipples grazing along each of my palms, as my hands slid across her stomach, down around her waist, and under her bottom, then pulling back along her sides.

One last oiling of my hands, and I stepped down the table, next to Alex's hips. I decided to push Alex, just a little bit. My hands started on her hips, and dived along the fold of her inner thigh, down, and under her. I didn't bother moving the sheet, but my hands moved it aside, as they massaged Alex's upper thigh.

I didn't touch her private parts. Well, my hands might have grazed her labia ... but the main pressure was toward her leg. I moved around the table, and did the same on the other side. By now, the sheet was pushed out of the way, and Alex was completely exposed. I massaged her pubic area lightly, circumventing the rectangular patch of dark hair, and dived between her legs, under her bottom, and back out. Alex seemed completely relaxed, although by her slightly heavier breathing, I could tell she wasn't asleep.

Then, I replaced all of the sheets, reversing the order of folding, until Alex was again covered from neck to toes. I moved to the head of the table, and leaned down until my face was nearly touching Alex's. I kissed her lightly on the cheek, and she opened her eyes and smiled. "The main part of your massage is over, ma'am." Then, I smiled at

her, "Would you permit me to give you a 'happy ending'?"
I held my breath.

Alex was still smiling, and she didn't respond
immediately. She appeared conflicted, and then said,
"Sam, you've been wonderful. This has been a great
massage: I *am* tingling. But I just don't think I can let you
do that; at least today. I'm not saying it can't happen in the
future, but I just wouldn't be comfortable with it, right
now."

I bent down and kissed Alex on the tip of her nose.
"That's fine, Alex. Sometimes, I can push too hard, but I
really want you to be comfortable. The massage was for
your enjoyment and relaxation. I just wanted to make the
offer, in case ..."

Alex lifted her head, and gave me a peck on my closed
lips. "Thank you, Sam, for being so understanding."

I retrieved Alex's robe, and held it up for her, as she
sat, and swiveled on the massage table, holding the sheet to
her chest. Then, she smiled, and dropped the sheet,
pushing the rest off of her, as she slid off the table, and
stood before me, nude. She put her arms into the sleeves
of the robe, and I closed it around her front.

After she had tied the sash, she turned to me, and we
hugged. It was a nice hug, not passionate, but close, and
sincere.

We separated, and I said, "Kelly's back." Alex gave me
a shocked look, and I elaborated, "She just got back a few
minutes ago, and peeked into the room. I think she was
very impressed that you allowed me to give you a
massage."

Alex laughed, as we headed for the kitchen. "I think
Fiona has everyone believing that I'm totally hung-up and
close-minded."

I said, "Alex, you are obviously not hung-up or close-minded. It took a lot of trust to come over to a strange guy's house, take off your clothes, get on a table, and be comfortable with him touching you."

I smiled at Alex, "Although I would argue that I'm not really that 'strange' a guy."

We laughed, but Kelly had heard the end of the sentence, and informed Alex, "He's actually a *very* strange guy!" Alex laughed harder, as Kelly continued, looking into my eyes, "But he's *my* strange guy. And I love him." Kelly pulled me toward her and gave me an exceedingly passionate kiss; more passionate than I had ever experienced while someone watched.

Alex nodded, "I can see that." Alex hugged Kelly, "You've got a catch, there, Kelly. If you decide you don't want him, maybe I'll take him." We all laughed. But it made me wonder if there was any meaning to that, and what Kelly thought about Alex's casual statement.

I put the potatoes in the oven, then turned to Kelly and asked, "How was the party?"

Kelly crinkled her nose, and said, "As I expected. It was all my Dad's 'jock' friends – although they're all armchair quarterbacks now. They're almost all fat and bald."

I winced, but Kelly quickly clarified, "I don't mean just their age – they're all in terrible shape. I bet some of them are younger than you," I winced again, and Kelly continued, "but they look at least ten years older. And the wives! That's what I think of, when someone asks if I want to be a 'housewife'." Alex and I laughed. "Anyway, I made them happy by putting in an appearance, and I'm sorry I couldn't get out of there sooner."

I poured Alex some water from a pitcher in the fridge with a lime, and said, "You need to keep hydrated." A half bottle of wine was still sitting on the patio table. Alex nodded, and drank the water appreciatively.

Kelly gave me a funny look, like she knew some inside joke, and then turned to Alex seriously, "You're going to have to get that oil off you before dinner ... although you're welcome to come to dinner in the robe, if you want. But I don't think that coconut aroma will go well with the steaks."

We all laughed, but Kelly quickly interjected, "You know, Sam's really good at bathing women. Why don't you let him get you ready for dinner?" I choked, and Alex's mouth dropped open ... but Kelly was serious; I think the poker games with her friends when she was young developed her skill for bluffing, as I knew she was about to crack up, seeing Alex's face right now.

Alex turned toward me, and said, "I guess I could do that. You've already seen and touched my whole body. And, if you're half as good at bathing as you are at massaging, I should be squeaky clean for dinner." We all laughed louder. Kelly was nodding, and I think we were both visualizing what 'squeaky-clean' would mean to us; probably not exactly what Alex was thinking.

I held out my arm, made a small bow, and said, "Ma'am?" Alex took my arm, turned her head to Kelly and shrugged, and I escorted Alex downstairs.

When we entered the shower room, I saw that Alex's clothes were on one of the chaises, a set of black lace underwear and bra on top. I took off my tank and running shorts, and put them on the other chaise, then helped Alex out of her robe. I adjusted the rain shower for hot, and foot jets for warm, and we stepped under the shower together.

We rinsed off, and I asked, "Would you like me to wash your hair ... or let you do it? Pointing to the tiled shelf I said, "We have these and other shampoos and conditioners, if you want?"

Alex declined the shampoo, and as she washed her own face, I began washing her back, up and over her shoulders, and reaching around to her breasts. I didn't linger, but continued soaping Alex with my hands, working down to her bottom, molding and squeezing her generous spheres, and moving my finger quickly down her butt crack, and over her anus. I moved it up and down, and then around a few times, but never entering her. I continued soaping, moving down her legs.

Then, I took the Loufah and scrubbed her, lightly, covering her entire backside from head to toe. I took Alex by the shoulders and turned her around to face me.

She was being very passive, but smiled at me as I began soaping her front with my hands, starting at her neck, working over her chest, around her breasts, and then spending a full minute on her breasts, holding them, squeezing them, and moving my hands over every part of them, finally taking her nipples in my fingers ... but for only a moment. I continued soaping downward, across her stomach, and down to the small patch of hair.

I moved my hand down over her genitals, a finger or two sliding between her labia, up and down, but again not entering her. My hand slipped under her, and I put a finger over her anus, and moved it in a circular motion. Then, I pulled my hand back, and continued soaping, down her legs, and to her feet. I would describe Alex as passive, docile; she was uncomplaining, and evidently enjoying being washed by a man.

I took the Loufah again, and scrubbed her front, including her breasts, and her private parts, gently; nothing sexual, but washing every part of Alex in detail, and with care.

I took the shower attachment off its hook on the wall, and rinsed Alex, the water of the attachment joining with the large drops from the rain shower above. I ran my hand over her body again, rinsing, including across her genitals, and down her butt crack. Then, I hung up the shower attachment, and turned Alex to face me. I scanned her body, from head to foot; she certainly was a beautiful woman.

"May I hug you," I asked. Alex didn't say a word, but nodded, and closed her eyes. We held each other, our bodies in intimate contact, and I put my cheek against hers. The water from the rain shower flowed over us, down our cracks and crevices, and fell onto our feet, as the leg jets massaged our hips, thighs, and legs. Still holding her, I pulled back, and said, "I hope you enjoyed being bathed."

Alex nodded, leaned forward, and gave me a quick kiss on the cheek. "Thank you, Sam. That was really nice." We stepped apart, and Alex looked at me – down at me. I was completely flaccid, as there was nothing sexual involved in bathing Alex, and I had specifically tried to avoid anything too intimate.

Again, my mind spun, as I realized that 'not too intimate' was everything, except putting a finger into her. Amazing. And this was the woman that Fiona had complained was too 'hung-up'.

Alex asked, "May I bathe you, now, Sam?" She smiled at me seductively, although I knew she wasn't trying to be seductive, at all.

"It would be very nice, Alex. But I don't want you to think you have to ... If you want to get dressed and visit with Kelly, I can bathe myself. Of course, if you're comfortable bathing me, I wouldn't turn it down."

Alex laughed, "I'm happy to do it, Sam." Then Alex looked down at me again, and added, "I'm especially pleased that you're not turned on. That would make it a little more challenging for me." We laughed. She said, "Of course, I was married for years, so it's no big deal. I guess it's not about the nudity at all, just the potential for it to turn into sex. Which is not something I'm looking for."

I nodded, "Me too. I'm not looking for sex – other than with Kelly. And you've hit one of my 'buttons'."

Alex cocked her head, and, under her breath said, "Oh no."

I laughed, "No, not that kind of button. It's disturbing to me that so much of the population equates nudity with sex. But they have nothing to do with each other."

Alex was nodding, so I continued, "We had fun at the pond, you had a nice massage, and we're here now enjoying each other's company, taking an innocent shower: Just 'good clean fun'. And none of it has anything to do with sex. But we had to be open enough with each other, and trust each other enough, to be with each other without clothes."

I took a deep breath. "It doesn't seem like it would be a big deal. But religion and our social mores have made it a big deal for many people." Alex had been washing my back, and was now down to my butt. I wondered whether she would insert a finger into me ... like Liz did, years ago.

But, in light of our conversation, I doubted that Alex would risk getting me turned on. She slipped her fingers down my butt crack, and pressed on my anus, as I had done with her. She soaped me there, and then quickly inserted a finger, and pulled back out. It was a thorough washing, but no prostate stimulation.

Alex squatted down and washed my legs; I turned around, so she could do the other side, and I helped her up, when she had reached my groin. Alex looked into my eyes, as she washed my penis, which was still flaccid – although

I could have gotten hard very quickly, if I had allowed myself.

She continued washing me, over my stomach, and up my chest. She tweaked my nipples between her fingers, and then gave me another peck on the lips. We both rinsed off, and I finally turned off the jets, and grabbed a couple of fresh towels from the shelf in the closet.

We dried off, and I brushed her hair. Alex put on her bra, and then stepped out of the shower room, and sat on the toilet. I sat on the chaise and put on my shirt.

When Alex returned, we both finished dressing. Before we left the shower room, we hugged one more time. It had been a close experience for two older people, at least one of whom would normally never have dared to risk social ridicule – or worse – to enjoy the afternoon we'd had together.

Perhaps Fiona had pushed her. Maybe I had pushed her. But however it had happened, I hoped that Alex had gained an appreciation for a different value system, a different lifestyle. It was still fully ethical, fully 'moral' – whatever that means – but free, open, and trusting. Enabling the enjoyment of being with another person, with or without clothes, with no sexual pressure.

When we got up to the kitchen, Kelly had made the salad – awaiting the dressing that I had made, and the potatoes were ready. I suggested that Alex and Kelly visit out on the patio – and maybe finish the wine – while I got dinner ready. It wasn't difficult to convince them.

I scooped out the potatoes, added all the ingredients, and stuffed them again, sprinkling Parmesan cheese over them, and putting them on a tray to go into the oven. I cleaned the asparagus, and set up the steamer. Finally, I took out the steaks, trimmed and seasoned them, and put them on a tray to take out to the barbeque.

I grabbed a beer from the fridge, and went out to the patio; the women were deep in conversation. I started the fire, cleaned the grill, and soaked a little hickory. I started steaming the asparagus, and put the stuffed potatoes in the oven.

Then I gathered the pink tablecloth and napkins, the candles, and silverware, and joined Alex and Kelly at the patio table. We quickly set the table, and I carried in the spent wine bottle. I brought a bottle from the cellar – a fourth-growth Bordeaux – and the appropriate glasses out to the table, and opened the wine to let it breathe.

Kelly served the salad, and I lit the candles. Then, I remembered that both the Tiki torches and tree lights were still set up from Kelly's birthday party. I lit everything, and the backyard turned, once again, into a wonderland. The sun hadn't set, yet, but we could already feel the air getting cooler. Summer was over.

When we finished the salad, I put on the steaks, and checked how Alex liked hers cooked. The asparagus was ready, and I prepared the brown butter, which I poured over the asparagus, adding salt and pepper, and putting it into a bowl. The potatoes were nicely browned, so I took them out, and put them on a large plate.

Then, I went out to the barbeque, turned the steaks, and tossed some hickory over the charcoal. I closed the barbeque, and glanced at the clock next to the kitchen door. Five minutes later, I was taking the steaks off the fire, and bringing them in on a platter.

I explained, "I wasn't sure what kind of steaks you guys like, so I made a couple of filets and a couple of New York strip steaks. Take whatever you like – or some of each. We filled our plates, and went out to the patio for our Labor Day dinner. Not exactly the usual barbeque, but a nice meal on the occasion of Alex's visit.

Alex had really surprised me with the openness that she had shown today. I believed that there was hope for almost everyone – if they were just open to new experiences, and willing to be trusting. Of course, you had to know who you could trust ... which I guess was one of the main challenges to the theory.

The wine was luscious, as were the women. We all enjoyed the meal, and each other's company. It wasn't long before Kelly couldn't resist, and asked Alex, "So, did Sam bathe you properly?"

Alex laughed, "Yes, he did a great job." She glanced at me, "And he's a very good masseur."

Kelly nodded, "He's only given me one massage, and it was my first one ... but I loved it."

Alex put her wine down, and looked at Kelly, "Are you bothered at all by Sam 'playing' with other women? Like massaging and bathing me?"

Kelly shook her head, "Not at all. Sam and I don't 'own' each other – we allow each other to have friends, regardless of gender. But that doesn't mean that we have sex with other people." Kelly looked at me, and I thought back to her birthday party. Four women had gone down on me and, with multiple transfers of body fluids, we had definitely had 'sex' with other people.

Kelly continued, "And it doesn't take anything away from me, if Sam sees a beautiful woman nude – or even massages her or bathes her." Kelly glanced at me again. "In fact, by Sam's curious definition of 'sex' as transfer of body fluids, it's not sex to help someone masturbate, but it *is* sex to eat or drink after each other, or kiss each other. So we've had to modify his original definition, to make it practical." I wondered exactly how far we would 'modify' the definition ... to fit our desires.

While Alex had a busy social life, attending art openings and other events, she'd had little real interaction with people on a personal level, since her divorce. I could see that she was craving this newfound interaction, with people who were open and could be trusted to be honest with her.

We cleared the patio table, and put away the leftovers. Then, we retired down to the playroom with the last of the wine, and continued our conversation on the couch. I thought that Alex might be ready to leave, when Kelly asked, "Would you like to try out the sauna, Alex? Then, we can cool off in the pool; it's great at night."

Alex looked at Kelly, and then at me. I shrugged and nodded. Alex glanced at her watch, and shrugged, "Sure, I'll try it." She looked at me again, "I am actually very comfortable being with you guys, even without clothes. Maybe Fiona will stop bugging me about being more open, now." We all laughed.

Kelly suggested that we get undressed in the playroom, and I offered to provide Alex a clean robe to wear. She laughed, "Don't bother, Sam. There's no point." Alex slipped off her sandals, stood up, and unfastened her belt. Then, she unzipped her pants, and slid them down her long legs. She smiled at us, as she slowly unbuttoned her blouse. Kelly pulled her t-shirt over her head, and stood up, unbuttoning her own shorts and pushing them down.

We were now all in our underwear, and a couple of minutes later, we were walking, nude, through the playroom. Kelly sat on the toilet, as Alex and I continued into the shower room. By the time I had adjusted the jets Kelly had joined us. We rinsed off quickly, I handed Alex and Kelly towels, and we entered the sauna. As with the pool, it had never seen so much use, until the last few weeks.

Alex looked elegant, even without her high-fashion clothes: Her C-cup breasts were perfectly formed, firmer than I would have expected for a woman of her age, and her body evidenced Alex's care in keeping herself in good condition. Her body was well proportioned – perfect as far as I was concerned – although I guessed that other women might criticize her wide hips and relatively large bottom. Perfect for spanking ... although I doubted that would ever be part of our relationship with Alex.

The sauna was now at 185 degrees Fahrenheit, ready for a multiple-sauna course, but it would limit how long we could stay in before having to get cooled down. Sweat was already beading on our skin.

"Alex, if you like, Kelly and I can move to the lower bench, so you can lie down."

Alex laughed, "That sounds nice, but I'm afraid that if I lie down, I'll be asleep soon. Your massage already had me very relaxed before dinner, and with the wine ... and the jet lag ... I'm sure I'll sleep well tonight."

We sat in silence together, enjoying the cozy warmth and stillness of the sauna. Glistening drops coated our skin, refracting light from the red bulb that illuminated our bodies against the backdrop of cedar paneling. We were all wiping sweat from our faces. I watched as drips fell from both Kelly's and Alex's breasts, and streamed down their naked bodies.

I looked at the sand dial: We had only been in the sauna eight minutes, but I wasn't sure how much more we could take. Less than a minute later, Kelly looked at me, and I nodded. We stood on the lower bench and stepped down to the tile floor, and I held the glass door open for the women. Kelly got the shower going, and we all huddled under the cool rain shower, as jets sprayed water on our legs, making them feel cold, after the heat of the sauna.

Wrapping our towels around us, we walked upstairs and out to the patio; it was much cooler now, and our bodies were steaming. The backyard looked beautiful, with the Tiki torches, path lights, and tiny lights strung among the branches of the trees. I turned off the patio light, and we dropped our towels on the table, before climbing down the ladder into the deep end of the pool, enjoying the refreshingly cool water.

Although the pool had a black bottom – looking almost like a pond during the day – the pool lights, filtering through the water, now turned the clear liquid a sparkling blue, with shimmers and speckles of light dappling the trees and eaves of the house. The three of us glided through the intimate coolness, our bodies now tingling.

Alex and Kelly were talking at the other end of the pool, and I swam over to them. Alex smiled, "This *is* nice! I'm glad you guys talked me into it." I didn't recall it taking much effort, but I was glad that Alex was spending more time with us. She still wasn't my 'type', but I was starting to like her.

"The stars are great, when the sky is clear, and it's dark. Put your feet up on the side like this." I showed them how I lay back, floating on the surface of the water, my usually-sinking feet propped up on the edge of the deck. "Just lay back and float – your legs will keep you up – and let your eyes adapt after I turn off the lights."

I climbed out of the pool, and switched off the lights in the trees. Then, I walked down the path, extinguishing all of the Tiki torches. The backyard was now quite dark, as the quarter moon had already set, the only the light coming from the pool, and now silhouetting Kelly and Alex.

I made my way back to the pool, and slipped into the water, taking a couple of strokes to reach Kelly and Alex, who were laying back, their eyes skyward. I did the same – with the three of us now next to each other, jutting out from the side of the pool into the water.

I closed my eyes for a few moments, and then opened them, looking directly up. The stars were magnificent – the great square of Pegasus now high in the sky, the Cygnus cross, Ophiuchus. I didn't see any satellites, but as we lay quietly in the water gazing up, a meteor streaked across the sky. Kelly and Alex both went 'Oooooh'!

Alex turned her head to me, and said, "This is a wonderful experience, Sam."

I agreed, "Sometimes you just have to take the time – and effort – to 'smell the roses'," I pointed up, "or watch the meteors. I'm glad we could share this with you." I first thought it was Kelly with whom I'd seen satellites and a meteor ... but I now remembered that it had been with Julie, when we took a break from the slumber party.

I looked over at Alex, floating calmly, her hair spread in a corona around her head, the blue light of the pool twinkling through the strands. Alex's breasts bobbed below and above the surface, waving like seaweed with the ebbs and flows of a current.

As our eyes became 'dark adapted', we saw more stars, including the great fuzzy arc of the Milky Way, our home galaxy. There had been very little conversation, but we were sharing an intimate connection with the universe ... and each other.

Kelly said, "I'm getting chilled. Let's go in the jacuzzi." Without waiting for a response from Alex or I, Kelly swam to the ladder and climbed out, a cascade of water falling from her body, illuminated by splatters of sparkling blue light from the pool. Alex and I followed Kelly to the spa, and we gradually lowered ourselves into the hot water. I realized that we probably wouldn't be going back into the sauna, after we were warmed up.

Alex was sitting on the bench, her back to one of the jets, and her head tilted back, eyes closed. Kelly snuggled with me, and leaned over to kiss me playfully.

Alex had been incredibly open with us today, and I wasn't going to push it ... but I couldn't help visualizing a group massage, Kelly and I 'taking care' of Alex. I had already given her a real massage, so it wouldn't be a big deal. But the mood was too good to be spoiled. As I regarded her, Alex opened her eyes, and smiled at me.

I said, quietly, "Alex, I was very proud of you today: I thought you were very relaxed and open. And, I think you know, I wasn't trying to push you. But it was a nice way to 'get to know' a neighbor!"

We all chuckled, and I elaborated, "I think you've had a taste of our 'open' lifestyle – such as it is, as it evolves with our relationship. And it certainly isn't about *sex*." Then, under my breath, but loud enough for Alex to hear, I said, "Although you *could* have allowed me to give you a 'happy ending' to your massage." We all laughed, but I had been serious.

We got out of the jacuzzi, and I turned on the patio lights and lights in the trees. We dried off, and wrapped ourselves in the large towels. "If you would like to sit out here for a while, I could bring some after-dinner drinks." Then I remembered, "Oh no! I forgot the strawberry shortcake!" Alex was shaking her head, but Kelly just shrugged, and pulled out a chair for Alex.

I went into the kitchen, and assembled the dessert, decorated it with fresh mint, and brought the plates out to the patio table, which was still covered by the pink tablecloth. I then asked, "Should I put on a pot of coffee?

Or, could I offer you an espresso, or cappuccino to go with your dessert?"

Kelly shook her head, and Alex thought a moment and replied, "It sounds nice. But I'm hoping to get some sleep tonight, so I won't take the chance." I was sorry I couldn't offer decaf, but seldom had it in the house.

After we finished dessert, we brought the dishes into the kitchen, and walked downstairs. Kelly suggested, "Let's get rinsed off in the shower."

We all went back into the shower room, but did more than a rinse. We quickly soaped each other's backs – and fronts – and rinsed with the hand shower attachment. We did not dwell on each other's bodies, but took an efficient 3-way shower together. I pulled out fresh towels for everyone, and we dried off.

Alex carried her towel casually, as she walked, nude, back into the playroom. I admired her ample bottom, which brought my mind back to spankings ... but I couldn't picture Alex participating in a spanking scene. Nor a medical scene.

Kelly was wearing a robe, and I slipped on my clothes as I watched Alex dress. She looked sexy in her lacy black bra and underwear. She was even cuter wearing the silk leopard-print blouse, which intermittently hid her underwear. When Alex was fully dressed, she was again the elegant society-woman.

We walked upstairs to the front door, and I said, "Thank you for coming to our party, Alex. I hope you enjoyed it as much as we did." Kelly was nodding.

Alex looked into my eyes, and there was a moment of suspended animation. Then, she stepped up to me and hugged me tightly. "Thank *you*, Sam. For inviting me, massaging me, feeding me ... and being a nice person. I didn't feel that you were pressuring me, at all. And I enjoyed everything we did."

She laughed, and glanced at Kelly, "And I probably would have enjoyed the 'happy ending', also ... but I just wasn't comfortable going that far. Maybe, sometime in the future, I'll be relaxed enough, open enough, to do something like that. I think it's great that you guys can be open."

Alex hugged Kelly, "And, thank *you*, Kelly; for making the dinner and being the hostess ... and for allowing Sam to massage and bathe me. You're lucky to have such a gentleman who loves you, as I know Sam does."

We said our goodbyes at the door, since neither Kelly nor I were wearing shoes. As Alex drove off, Kelly remarked, "Well, I guess I can report to Fiona that her aunt is turning over a new leaf ... maybe a fig leaf." I chuckled, and Kelly continued, "She's a nice woman, and I think she enjoyed herself, in spite of the nudity."

I nodded, "Alex is a mature woman. Nudity is not a big deal, per sé, but today she was in a different kind of social situation than she's normally used to. I think she was enjoying actually being able to relax with other people; I don't think she gets the chance to do that, much."

I chuckled, "But I *was* surprised that she requested a massage – that's pretty intimate contact, and you weren't even here to chaperone us." Kelly laughed, as we walked back into the house.

It was mind-boggling how in the past couple of months my close relationship with Kelly had developed; we had done a lot of intimate things together.

And, we had done intimate things with Kelly's closest friends – Julie, Linda, and Kathy. Then, there was Fiona, who showed us her piercings, allowed us to give her a needle experience, and played with Kelly on the bed, as I photographed them.

Now there was Fiona's aunt, Alex, who we had met at the pond, but with whom I now had become a much 'closer' neighbor, with all the experiences we'd had today.

Suddenly my formerly empty and unfulfilled life had blossomed.

CHAPTER 3: MÉNAGE À JULIE

Kelly had begun the school season, figured out her seminar schedule, and gained approval from her advisor to miss a couple of weeks during October, for our Europe trip. Actually, Kelly had said that she could take the most of October and early November, provided she did some work on her dissertation during the trip.

That expanded the possibilities, and I was still revising the itinerary; however, I would need to purchase airline tickets soon. I crossed-off huge swaths of Europe, that could only be covered in future trips.

There were the Dolomites in spring, flowered hillsides with steep craggy peaks, still covered in snow, beautiful lakes below. Ah, Sirmione – a small walled town on a peninsula jutting into long, thin Lake Garda, the wonderful palace hotel at its tip. And the wine regions of northern Italy, tiny port towns, such as Portofino, and visiting my friends in Torino.

My mouth watered, thinking about the white truffle spaghetti I'd eaten as just one course of an incredible meal in a small hillside restaurant, covered in vines.

There was Monaco, St. Tropez, and small towns, such as Le Lavandou – the jumping off point for the Îles d'Hyeres, where Sarah and I had first experienced a nude beach, on the Île du Levant, so many years ago. On that trip Kelly and I could visit the Pont du Gard – an ancient Roman aqueduct, and perhaps even detour through the

Pyrenees to Andorra, before we headed down to the Costa Brava, Costa del Sol, and Barcelona. Well, that trip would take about a month!

As Kelly had mentioned learning more about wines, a trip through France would be nice – the Rhone and Loire valleys and, of course, Bordeaux. It would be fun to show Kelly Paris, and take a few side-trips, such as to Reims in the East, and Le Mont Saint-Michel, the tiny castle hill on a tidal island in Northwest France. And there was Mt. Blanc towering over Chamonix in the Southeast. OK, another month.

Scandinavia would be fun, too. I loved København, with its Tivoli gardens – where Sarah and I had once attended an international jazz festival. The sand dunes on the northern beaches of Denmark were perfect for naturist activities, although with rather cold water. And we could visit Stockholm, where I had seen the *Vasa* not that long after it had been recovered from the harbor.

And Oslo was a beautiful city, where we could visit the Kon Tiki museum, and Frogner Park, with its 200 Vigeland sculptures; and, see the disturbing expressionist images in the Edvard Munch museum. We could travel to Stavanger, and up to Bergen; I wondered if the old mail ship was still running – there were probably dozens of tourist ships, now. Another month.

And then there was the former Yugoslavia – now Croatia, Serbia, and Slovenia. The mostly clothes-free Island of Hvar – which advertises money-back, if there is rain during your stay.

Ah, Greece – the culmination of ancient culture! I envisioned Kelly and I watching the sound and light show at the Parthenon – where Sarah and I used to walk freely, without fences, years ago. And I would love to take Kelly to the Greek islands; even the unassuming Crete had its

Minoan art and palaces, excavations continuing to the present.

I was looking forward to visiting many of the Greek islands for the first time, including Rhodos in the Dodecanese, Mykonos and Santorini in the Cyclades, and Lesbos in the northern Aegean. Well, that might be appropriate, considering Kelly's current predilections. Again, it would be at least a month-long trip.

There were many other trips that we could consider in the future – England and Scotland, countries along the Danube, and various islands, such as the Balearic Islands of Spain – including Mallorca, Minorca, and Ibiza.

Even Switzerland could be a stand-alone month-long trip: Sailing in Interlaken, taking Kelly up to the Jungfrau, and shopping in up-scale Geneva or visiting the more 'small town' feeling Zurich, and perhaps historic Basel and Lucerne.

I would love to take Kelly on any of these trips. And these were only the ones I could immediately think of in Europe; the rest of the world awaited us. But the trip I had planned had a dual purpose: To give Kelly a taste of European culture, and to show her a side of the culture that many people missed – and others probably *didn't* miss. I had to be realistic about how much we could cover, but the trip promised to be an epic event for Kelly. And I.

I e-mailed Henk, and we planned a Skype call, when our travel plans were a bit firmer. I was glad to hear he was still with Zoë; she might provide further insights to Kelly, in her exploration of bisexual adventures.

I also e-mailed a friend in Zurich, but found that he would be traveling most of October in the Far East. Although I had several other friends in Europe, they were in cities that we probably would not be visiting on this trip.

Kelly was finished with her last seminar around noon on Friday, and came directly to my house to spend the weekend. She seemed quite excited, and I asked for the latest update from school – how she liked her seminar classes, what she thought of her instructors and advisor, and her progress in setting up the lab for her research project. She filled me in on all these things ... but that turned out not to be why she was excited.

"I had lunch with Julie this week." She arched her brows, but I wasn't sure what she was trying to communicate. She smiled, "How would you like to have a ménage this weekend?"

I was surprised, but not shocked or stunned; we had already talked about the possibility generally, and we both had gotten the vibe that Julie would be game for playing with us. Perhaps more than 'playing'. I knew that the original meaning of *ménage à trois* went beyond a love triangle, and referred to a 'household of three' – a threesome romantically or sexually involved, and living together. I assumed that Kelly was referring to group sex, not adding another person to our living arrangement.

I responded, "You know that's always been a fantasy of mine. And I think Julie's hot." Then, I looked at Kelly seriously, "But how far do you think we should go, in terms of sex with your friends? I'm still nervous about STDs. Of course, all three of your friends went down on me the morning after your birthday party, so we've had oral-genital contact already. I guess I could use a condom with Julie?"

I really was conflicted. I assumed that Julie had an active sex life, and the chance of STDs increases with multiple partners.

Kelly shook her head, "Sam, I mentioned your fears to Julie when I spoke with her. She said she just had her annual gynecology exam a week ago; she also told me that she doesn't have a current sex partner, and hasn't had sex with anyone all summer." Well, that was *something*.

I laughed, "Is that the longest Julie's gone without sex?"

Kelly slapped me playfully, "Sam! She's not the 'hussy' that you think she is." Then, Kelly smiled at me, and said, "Anyway, Julie and I had 'sex' during the slumber party. And, you saw how proficient she is at taking care of herself!" We laughed, but I still had lingering doubts about whether this was the 'right' thing to do.

It wasn't a moral, ethical, or religious issue: It came down to basic health safety. I thought back – it was only three months ago when I had told Kelly how much intimacy there could be between people without transferring body fluids. Now, I realized that my concept of non-sexual 'play' may have been theoretically valid, but difficult to put into practice.

Of course, it wasn't about birth control, as my vasectomy would address that issue. But HPV was at an epidemic level in the U.S., with nearly 30% of women being infected overall, and nearly half of women Julie's age. And there were many other STDs – such as herpes virus – that could be transmitted via unprotected sex, and were incurable.

"Kelly, I've studied this area, as our pharmaceutical company developed some of the early drugs for STD prevention and treatment. There is a vaccine available, but it only protects against four types of HPV, out of the dozens of types that exist – including at least 20 types that are considered 'high risk'." Kelly's expression was blank.

I continued, "And that vaccine includes three shots spread over 6 months – not exactly practical for doing something this weekend. Also, the shots are usually given only up to age 26; so you would be eligible for them, but I'm not. Ideally, you would also get hepatitis vaccines; there is now a combined vaccine for Hep A and B ... but it doesn't protect against hepatitis C, D, or E. And, that vaccine is also given in 3 shots over 6 months. I've already gotten that vaccine, but it's something you might want to do." This was an information overload for Kelly.

Sam was really hung-up on the issue of STDs. My friends and I were healthy; we had annual checkups and our doctors would have told us, if we were infected. Of course, there might be *some* risk − but there's risk in everything: Our plane to Europe could go down, and my brilliant future career would be snubbed before it got going; and here (as the chances of one of us having HIV was virtually nil), Sam was talking about the risk of getting some genital warts!

Later, as we were playing around in the huge bed in the playroom, casually watching television, Sam suddenly asked me, "Sarah and I played with another couple when we were first married, but I've never been part of a ménage before; I wonder how it will work?" He smiled, "I guess there can be lots of combinations ..." I could see Sam's eyes glaze over as his brain worked to imagine the possibilities.

Then, he smiled again, and voiced a surprised, "Oh!" Sam jumped up and ran to the credenza behind his desk, rummaged around a little, and walked back, carrying a strange contraption. When he got back to the bed, he separated the straps and held two devices up, one in each hand. "In my BDSM buying sprees, I picked up these: 'strap-ons'.

I laughed, and took one of the ungainly things with the penis-like dildo and nylon straps. Was this a vaginal or anal toy? At least the dildo wasn't that large in diameter, perhaps an inch. A little dilating and a lot of lube would make anal insertion no more difficult than with the butt plugs we'd played with. Now, I could fuck Sam in the ass!"

I envisioned fucking Julie with one of these. My mind whirled, as I thought about taking Julie vaginally from the rear, over the corner of the bed, as Sam often did with me. My muscles clenched, as I thought about Julie, Sam and I playing tomorrow. Sam was right: There were a *lot* of possibilities!

Sam suggested that we all take enemas, before playing together. I knew this was from some combination of Sam's hang-ups, his health-focus, and his desire to keep the sex as 'clean' as possible. It wasn't a very 'romantic' way to start our threesome ...

But we hadn't discussed romance at all: I think we all looked at this as just a fun experience between the three of us; a way to continue the closeness we had developed, and our fondness for each other.

"OK, Sam, as long as Julie agrees, we can give each other enemas. But *I'll* decide how we do it." Then, I thought of something else that would undoubtedly come up during our play together. "And, I don't want you to start sticking us with needles. I know that turns you on, but I don't think it's what either Julie or I would consider appropriate for our sexual adventure."

Sam frowned. He had probably been fantasizing about sticking needles in Julie and I as we bent over in various positions to satisfy each other. I sighed, "OK, Sam. We can make up one shot for each of us ... but only if Julie agrees to take one. And, again, *I'll* decide when and how those are given. Those are my ground rules."

Sam nodded, "OK, Kelly, I guess I can live with that. Are those *all* of your ground rules?"

Now, I had to think: What else would Sam suggest tomorrow? I knew Sam pretty well, by now, and didn't have too many other concerns. "I guess so. But let's try to make this a fun experience for all of us – not one of your 'submission challenges'."

Sam looked at me and smiled, sheepishly, "Yes, Ma'am."

Now, there was only tonight to think about. I looked at Sam, and said forcefully, "OK, young man. Help me get strapped into this thing, and let's give it a try!"

Sam stared at me, having evidently not considered that I might want to try the strap-on tonight, with him on the receiving end. He closed his eyes, and shook his head. As he took the strap-on from my hand, I heard him mutter, under his breath, "Monster!"

I ignored him, and got off the bed. Sam figured out how the contraption worked, and helped strap me in. I hopped once, and looked down, watching the dildo bounce up and down. Suddenly, I felt a surge of power!

Sam disappeared, and a minute later returned with the tube of KY and an exam glove. Handing them to me, he asked, "How do you want me?"

How did I want Sam? Let me count the ways ... I laughed, "How about over the corner of the bed?" Sam pulled down the pillow, and straddled the corner of the bed, lowering himself onto the bed, and letting his ass cheeks separate and anus relax.

Looking at Sam in position, and realizing that I would be stimulating his prostate, I ran to the bathroom, and brought back a bath towel. I asked Sam to get up for a moment, and placed the towel under him, and hanging off the corner of the bed. Then, I pulled on the glove, and squeezed a dollop of KY onto the tip of my middle finger. As I placed the pad of my finger on Sam's anus, and moved it in small circles, Sam relaxed and sunk further into the bed. His head was buried in the pillow.

I slowly advanced my finger, twisting it around clockwise and counterclockwise, lubing Sam completely. I turned my palm down, and bent my finger, stroking and pushing against his prostate. I heard Sam purr, and his body slowly rocked fore-and-aft, as he moved himself against the towel. I left my finger in Sam, as I bent over him, and kissed his back.

Rather than spending time dilating Sam with progressively larger butt plugs, I decided he was ready for the strap-on; I would take my time inserting it. My muscles clenched again, unexpectedly, distractingly. I pulled my finger out of Sam and took off the glove, leaving it, inside out, on the towel next to Sam. I squeezed a little more KY on my fingers, and lubed the dildo of the strap-on. It was now glistening black; I did a few Kegels, contracting my PC muscle every few seconds.

Then, I stepped up behind Sam, holding his hip with my left hand, and guiding the strap-on with my right. I placed the tip of the dildo against Sam, and leaned forward, putting gentle pressure on it. The tip disappeared inside him and, as I thrust my pelvis forward, Sam's anus expanded, and took in the thicker part of the phallus.

I heard an 'Mmmm' from Sam, and increased the pressure on the dildo; it gradually slid into him. I now held Sam's hips in both my hands, and slowly pulled and pushed, pulling the dildo partially out of him when I pushed, and thrusting it back into him as I pulled his hips toward me.

The harness was actually giving me some physical stimulation, but my main stimulation was mental: The image of me taking Sam from behind, giving me total control. As I looked down at Sam's bottom, bouncing against me, I envisioned giving Sam an injection; I could understand his turn on, even though it seemed antithetical to the idea of making love.

I came out of my daydream, and realized that – although I still had Sam's hips in my hands – Sam was doing most of the moving, now thrusting his hips against the towel, and back against me, the dildo undoubtedly pressing against his prostate as it moved deeply into him.

I thrust against Sam, as he thrust against the towel, and very soon Sam was coming, muffled cries coming from the pillow. I pulled Sam's hips against me, and held the dildo as far as it would penetrate into Sam's butt. Then, I swayed my hips left and right, up and down, to move the tip of the dildo against Sam's sensitive gland, as he continued thrusting into the towel.

Finally, Sam was spent, and I slowly leaned back, the dildo sliding easily out of him.

Sam turned his head on the pillow, and said, "Thank you, ma'am." We both laughed. He stood up, and wiped his sticky-wet cock with the towel. Turning around and looking down at the strap-on, Sam commented, "Well, I guess it works pretty well." We laughed again.

I collected the used glove, and Sam carried the towel, as we walked to the bathroom. Sam rinsed the cum off the towel, and left to drop it into the washing machine, as I struggled with the harness of the strap-on. When Sam came back, he extricated me from the device, and washed the dildo, as I sat down to pee.

I told Sam, "My only suggestion would be to put something into the harness to allow me to get stimulated, too. The harness and straps don't allow me to 'do' myself."

Sam nodded, "Well, the other strap-on has a removable dildo – it's held in by a large metal ring. So, maybe next time, we can use that one – and hook it up with your triple-delight vibrator?" I laughed, but it was a really good idea. Too bad we hadn't thought about that this time. But I was sure Sam would take care of me properly.

And he did.

Kelly and I slept in Saturday morning, and I made a late breakfast of waffles with fresh fruit (to be healthy) and a side of bacon (to be unhealthy), which we ate at the patio table, enjoying the start of another sunny day. I had fresh-squeezed some oranges, and we'd finished half the pitcher of juice already.

I wondered how our ménage with Julie would go. I had visualized many different combinations of the three of us getting each other off, but my mind was now a swirl of images, and I had no real ideas for how to organize our activities. I finally decided that they should not be 'organized', but organic – evolving from each other spontaneously. I knew Kelly would appreciate that approach, so we did not discuss the ménage any further.

After breakfast, I went down to the playroom to take the duvet and decorative pillows off the bed; I left the top sheet on, but tucked it in, so that the bed was now merely a platform – the 'stage' for our upcoming performance.

That got me thinking (again), and I thought about recording the event, which only required pressing a few buttons on the panel behind my desk. I had no plans for using – or even watching – the recording, but there seemed little downside to it; although these kinds of recordings always seemed to get people in trouble. I finally decided to leave the ménage to our memories.

I checked the preset on the playroom remote that set the lighting to focus on the bed, and dim the rest of the room. I queued up some music, and even a few videos, should we decide that appropriate. And I pulled out a bottle of my favorite chardonnay from the cellar fridge, and opened it, leaving the bottle and three crystal glasses on the playroom coffee table.

While I was doing all this, Kelly was in the exam room, making her own preparations. I wasn't sure what she had in mind, but would let her 'have her way' – whatever that was. It felt good to leave someone else in control, and I tried to relax, finally deciding that I should 'taste' the wine. It was barely noon, but admittedly, I was a bit nervous about actually having sex with Julie.

As much as I theoretically wanted to have sex with multiple women, and as open as my relationships had been – even while I was with Sarah, it still seemed against some 'principle' to share myself with someone other than Kelly, who was the woman I loved. I guess it was about proving to Kelly how much I loved her. But Kelly already knew that, and wanted this experience; I hoped for herself, as much as to please me.

I took another swallow of wine, and put the glass down, shaking my head at my good fortune at even having to worry about these kinds of things.

Soon enough, the doorbell was ringing, and Kelly and I went upstairs to greet Julie. We all hugged, and brought Julie downstairs. She carried a beach tote, and wore tiny cut-off shorts and a white blouse. I was surprised that Julie had brought a whole bag of stuff. I looked at Kelly, who laughed and said, "I suggested she bring a few things."

Julie reached into the tote, and pulled out the new toy I had given her as a 'favor' at Kelly's birthday party, "Like my favorite vibrator!" We all laughed.

Kelly whispered to me, "But I didn't tell her exactly *why* she should bring the vibrator." This was getting fun, already! I poured the wine, and we toasted to what should be an interesting afternoon.

Julie surprised us by asking, "Can we start by taking a dip in the pool?"

I looked at Kelly, and she responded, "Sure! That would be fun. We haven't really planned out the day." As we each took our glass of wine, and headed toward the stairs, Kelly said, under her breath, "Just a couple of shots and a couple of enemas." I smiled. Kelly had evidently planned at least *part* of the day.

I felt a stirring below, but quickly thought of something else, so I wouldn't get turned on. That was funny! I would probably be turned on in front of Julie most of the day; so I guess it wasn't a big deal, even if 'it' *was* 'big'. I grabbed some towels from the bathroom, and ran up the stairs to catch up to the girls. I chuckled, as I held the door from the kitchen to the patio open for Kelly and Julie. We sat at the table, and sipped our wine.

Enjoying the effect of shocking people as much as I do, Julie opened with a stunner. "So, Kelly tells me that you're a little hung up about having sex with me." My mouth dropped open.

I looked at Kelly and back to Julie, "It's not that I'm 'hung up', exactly ... but I've been very careful over the past three decades to not put myself in a position where I had to worry about sexually transmitted diseases. I think you know that my wife and I were very open sexually, until the AIDS epidemic in the early 1980s. Since that time, I haven't had sex with anyone else," I looked at Kelly, "until Kelly. At least, sex as I defined it to mean 'transfer of body fluids'."

I looked Julie in the eyes, "And until you guys went down on me the morning after Kelly's birthday party."

Julie looked back at me, "I understand, Sam. And I will understand if you don't want to have sex with me, or if you want to wear a condom. But I really don't think I'm putting you at risk: I just visited my ob/gyn, and she did not find any evidence of me having an STD. I don't have a current boyfriend or sex partner. I've never used IV drugs. I'm not sure what else I can say."

I wasn't sure what I could say, either. "Julie, I would love to make love to you," I glanced at Kelly, "or 'have sex' with you. I think you know by now that you've been a turn on to both Kelly and I." I laughed, "And you can see that my principles broke down – or at least weren't *that* absolute – as I've been making love to Kelly."

I knew I probably shouldn't start down this path, but decided there would be no better time. "Julie, have you had the HPV or hepatitis vaccines? Kelly and I were talking about that last night." Julie shook her head.

Repeating the information I'd given Kelly, I told her, "The HPV vaccine must be given before you're more than 26 years old. And neither of these vaccines is perfect – they only protect against some forms of the diseases. But they're the best we have, at the moment. If we all have sex together today, would you consider getting those vaccines? Actually, I'd love to see all of you guys get them – Kathy and Linda, too. Maybe, I could organize it, and take you all in together?"

Kelly laughed, "Then Sam gets to watch us all get shots." Kelly glanced at me, and back to Julie, "And each of those vaccines is actually a series of three shots – the first, then a second one after a month, and then a third one at six months. I am going to get them; after Sam told me about them, I did some research ... and they are a good idea."

Julie turned to me, "I would want to check with my own doctor first, but I would be OK getting those vaccines." Julie looked at Kelly, "Especially, if we all get them together." Then, Julie looked into my eyes, "So, Sam, are we going to have a 'romp' together today?"

Before I could reply, Kelly jumped in, "And, Sam, you know that I'm OK with doing this today; actually, more than OK with it. I think you should loosen-up about 'sex'; especially if we're just talking about my friends. And today, we're only talking about Julie. And all three of us have had 'sex' together already, if you count oral sex."

I sighed. Kelly had a point. And I didn't want to live a life of fear: I wanted to open-up, and be more casual about sex. I had wanted that all my life. At my age, I wasn't too concerned about genital warts, and I highly doubted that any of Kelly's friends had HIV. Maybe I *was* making too big of a deal about STDs.

Of course, I *could* wear a condom if I was going to have genital contact with Julie; that was probably the most responsible thing to do. But I wasn't going to infect Julie with anything, so the decision only related to a slight increased risk to *me*.

"OK. I'll try to loosen-up; starting with our ménage with Julie today." My mind flew ahead to the various combinations of sexual activities we might do today. "But I will insist on wearing a condom, if I have anal sex ... with *either* of you."

Julie nodded, "That sounds like a good idea." She glanced at Kelly, "But with all your openness, and focus on the butt, I'm surprised you guys haven't done that, yet."

I just shrugged, "It was on my sexual 'to do' list." The girls laughed.

Now, Kelly turned to Julie, and said seriously, "Sam does want us all to take a couple of enemas, to clean us out.

And I knew he was going to suggest we play with needles. But I gave him an ultimatum: I told him we might agree to the enemas, and even a shot or two, but that *I* would decide when and how they would be given." Kelly didn't volunteer any information to Julie about our having strap-ons.

Julie shrugged, "I guess I'm OK with that." Julie looked back and forth at Kelly and I, and continued, "Are there any more 'conditions' for today? If not, can we take a dip in the pool, now?" We all laughed.

Then we stood up, and started undressing, placing our clothes on the patio table. Julie was wearing a black thong under her ragged (fashionably tattered?) cut-off shorts. She wasn't wearing a bra, her B-cup breasts not really requiring one. Kelly had been wearing her pink 'birthday' tee, also braless, over a pair of cotton flesh-colored bikini underwear.

I pulled off my tank and running shorts, and we all walked to the ladder at the deep end of the pool, and lowered ourselves into the sparkling water. We floated or swam around the pool separately, thinking – I'm sure – about our ménage.

After only a few minutes, Kelly got out of the pool, and into the jacuzzi. Julie and I followed her, and I pressed the air switch in the deck to turn on the jets.

Kelly and Julie sat on either side of me – a 'Sam sandwich', as they had called it the morning after Kelly's birthday party, when they had surrounded me in bed. Kelly took my head in her hands, and turned me to her, then gave me a mouth-watering, tongue-twisting kiss.

Then, Julie took my head in *her* hands, turned me to her, and gave me her own wet and lingering kiss. Julie broke away and stood, then, knelt on the bench of the jacuzzi, her legs straddling me, and my head once again pulled to her, her mouth insistent. We held each other, and kissed – more passionately than I had intended.

When we came up for air, I glanced at Kelly, who sat next to me, smiling at us. She nodded. I put my hands under Julie's bottom, and pulled her closer to me, my budding erection vertical between us, rubbing on her hairless pubes.

Julie slipped her hand down and took hold of me, stroking slowly, as she leaned forward to kiss me again. I squeezed and molded Julie's buttocks as she pressed her breasts against my chest, our mouths joining urgently.

Eventually, Julie leaned back and smiled at me. She moved toward the edge of the bench, and lifted a bit, taking my now-hardened shaft, and rubbing it against her labia. I whispered, "We may need to get some lube."

Julie just smiled, and pressed the head of my penis between her labia. I jerkily slipped into her, and we rocked as we held each other, my manhood throbbing, as her vaginal muscles clenched and pulled me farther into her. It felt great, and she had plenty of internal lubrication to allow me to move within her.

I was startled when Kelly's voice broke the constancy of the bubbly noise. "If you guys are ready, maybe we should go downstairs, and get started?" Julie and I looked at each other and laughed, both of us having been in our own world with each other. I came out of her, as she wiggled off of me, and we stepped up onto the deck, my member at full mast.

Julie curled her fingers around my shaft, and pulled, saying, "Come along, boy!" Her thumb stroked my frenum as she followed Kelly, and led me downstairs, briefly swinging by the patio table to collect our clothes and towels, which Julie piled in my arms, keeping my hands busy, as she led me by my manhood; I felt like a pull-toy.

When we got to the playroom, we dried off and, upon instructions from Kelly, spread our towels on the bed. I lay down on my back on one of the towels, and Julie straddled me, lowering herself until she could take my flagging penis in her mouth. I wasn't 'flagging' very long, as Julie was quite talented in using her oral resources.

I heard some jangling sounds, and lifted my head to see Kelly walking toward the bed carrying both of the IV poles, from which hung enema bags. I let my head drop back onto the bed, and tried to focus on Julie.

When I had both of the enemas set up, I leaned over to Julie, and whispered, "I'll start your enema, now."

Julie took Sam out of her mouth long enough to say, "Whatever."

I hadn't told Sam that I'd spoken with Julie on the phone, and informed her of what I had planned for our ménage 'preparation'. Sam wanted us cleaned out, before we started using the butt plugs or engaged in anal sex.

Julie had agreed to take two enemas ... *and* a couple of small shots. I would let them 'get it over with', while they had sex for the first time. My own muscles were clenching, as I watched Julie expertly go down on Sam ... and saw Sam's reactions.

I put on an exam glove, placed some KY on the tip of my middle finger, and then swirled my finger over Julie's butthole. Julie didn't react, just kept up her ministrations of Sam. My finger slipped into Julie's rear and, once she was lubed, I removed it and picked up the enema nozzle – one of the bullet-shaped stainless steel plugs that I had selected for both Julie and Sam. I pressed the cold steel against Julie and the nozzle slowly advanced into her. She still didn't show any reaction to the attention I was showing her butt.

I said, "OK, Julie, that's enough." My mind could hear Sam replying, 'that's easy for you to say!' "Let Sam work on you for a while."

Julie and Sam switched positions, Julie laying back on the towel, with Sam between her legs, bending down to caress her. A few moments later, as Sam went down on Julie in earnest, I slipped on another glove, and repeated the procedure with Sam.

With my finger deep in him, I pressed down, against his prostate, in a pulsing motion. With my other hand, I held his balls, and the base of his cock. Sam's breathing was heavier, and I realized I was getting him too turned on. It would be embarrassing – for me – if Sam came within two minutes of the time he entered Julie.

I took my finger out of his rear, and replaced it with the shiny nozzle, which slid into him, as I applied only a slight constant pressure. Once it was in place, there was only a shiny disc showing between Sam's cheeks, the thin tube dropping down to the bed, and over to the IV stand, where it was hooked up to the enema bag. A small roller valve was positioned a few inches from the nozzle, and now hung in mid-air, halfway down to the bed.

Sam turned his head back, and said, "I'm not sure who's permission to ask before entering Julie." Sam coughed, and added, "Do you want to get me a condom, Kelly?"

I wasn't sure how to respond. I thought that Sam should relax, but if he insisted, neither Julie nor I would fault him for wearing a condom. I replied to Sam, "Not really. Unless you insist."

Sam shook his head, and sighed. Then, he took his position, and lowered himself, as Julie reached under and guided his cock into her. Sam continued to lower himself onto Julie, and they began their rhythmic motions. I reached over, and opened the valve slightly, so that a slow flow of warm saltwater was now flowing into Sam's ass.

Their motions continued, and I was fascinated seeing the view from behind Sam, his cock plunging deeply into Julie, his balls slapping lightly against her. Now, we were ready for the next phase of Julie and Sam's first lovemaking experience.

"Whoever wants to get their shots first should be on top."

Sam groaned, but Julie said brightly, "I'll go first, Sam." Sam and Julie rolled over, so that Julie was again on top. I opened the valve in Julie's enema tube to begin the slow flow into her.

I chuckled, "I'll give the shots whenever Sam tells me." Julie and Sam continued their motions, slowly.

Sam said quietly, "While I'm kissing Julie." Julie didn't need any prodding, as she began kissing Sam, with evident passion.

I swabbed Julie's right hip, and quickly inserted the needle. As Julie continued to move on top of Sam, I slowly injected 3cc into her bottom and pulled out the needle. Sam and Julie were still kissing.

Sam turned his head to the right, looking at me over Julie's left hip. I pointed to an injection site that Sam could see, and he nodded subtly. He whispered to Julie, "Are you ready for your second shot, now?" Julie emitted an 'Umm hmm'. I positioned the needle above Julie's bum.

A moment later, Sam said 'Now', and I darted the needle through Julie's skin, and pushed it in, up to the black hub. I let go of the needle, and Sam and I watched as it wiggled slightly with Julie's sensual motions. Then, I slowly injected the sterile saline. Julie had not made a sound.

After letting them continue for another minute or two, I said, "Time for you guys to turn over, again." Sam let out an involuntary sigh, and he and Julie rolled over so that Sam was on top, while I made sure the enema tubes didn't tangle. Sam lowered himself onto Julie, and now lay nearly flat.

Julie volunteered, "You can give Sam the shot while I'm kissing him, like he did with me." Julie began kissing Sam, and I swabbed him and inserted the needle. It was a turn on, seeing him in simultaneous pleasure and pain. I injected 3cc, and left the needle in a while longer. I saw a spasm ripple across Sam's flesh, and pulled out the needle.

Julie and Sam continued moving, and I thought they were both just about ready to come. I waved, and Julie looked up at me, and smiled. I smiled back, and pointed to Sam's hip. Julie nodded, and I gave Sam the shot, as Julie watched.

Julie held Sam, and they continued their motions, as I opened the valves fully and allowed the last of the enemas to drain into them. I sat on the bed and watched, as the intensity of Julie's and Sam's lust heightened. Julie's nails were clawing at Sam's back, leaving long streaks of white against his tanned skin.

The sounds of sex filled the room: Bodies colliding, heavy breathing, and moans emanating from both partners. Julie suddenly arched her back, unseeing eyes staring at the ceiling, her body jerking, and taking breaths in gulps. As she began to relax, Sam reached his release, thrusting into Julie, his head turned away, a guttural sound coming from his depths.

Watching porn videos does not usually turn me on, but this was the first time that I'd ever watched another couple getting it on, close-up and in-person. It was hot! My own muscles tightened, in time with Sam's movements, and my breath caught, as he came.

It dawned on me that I was actually enjoying being a spectator, and that I was not at all bothered by Sam making it with Julie. We were sharing an intimate experience with each other, but that did not mean that I was losing something. I was happy for Sam. And I was happy that our relationship had progressed to the point where we could do this with Julie.

The sounds subsided, as Sam relaxed his body on top of Julie, as she relaxed hers into the mattress. Sam gave Julie a peck on the lips and, running his hand through her hair, said, "Thank you, Julie. That was really nice."

Julie took Sam's head in her hands, pulling it toward her, and kissed him, languorously. Then, she smiled and said, "It was nice for me, too."

Sam thrust one more time, trying to keep his waning hard-on inside of Julie. I asked, "Would you like me to take this nozzle out, now, Sam?"

Sam didn't chuckle, but said, seriously, "Yes, please. Miss." Now I was chuckling, as I extracted the shiny bullet-shaped nozzle from Sam's rear. I wrapped it in tissue, and placed it on the end of the towel.

"Now, it's Julie's turn," I said cheerfully. Julie had not complained, and apparently neither Julie nor Sam had experienced any cramps. Or, maybe they just hadn't noticed them?

Sam backed out of Julie, and slid off the bed. I handed him a couple of tissues, as Julie rolled over and got into a knee-chest position. I asked her to give a little push, and pulled the nozzle by the shiny disc; it slipped out easily, but I decided to move it in and out of her a few more times. Sam was watching, curiously.

MÉNAGE À JULIE

I handed Julie a couple of tissues, and she wiped herself, still in the knee chest position. Then, she climbed off the bed, and stood next to Sam. I looked at them and smiled, "It looks like you enjoyed each other, even with me rudely interrupting your lovemaking with enemas and shots." We all laughed. I was impressed that Julie had done so well, but perhaps it shouldn't have been surprising.

"Well, I guess it's my turn. I'll need to wash the nozzles and tubing, and make-up another batch. Unless you guys want to let me off the hook, this time." Sam was shaking his head. I considered offering to take my enema on the exam room table, but decided to see if either Julie or Sam would stick around long enough to get me off, now that I was turned on by watching them.

"OK, I'll get everything ready – if you guys think you can hold your enemas." Sam and Julie looked at each other and nodded.

Five minutes later, I carried out a filled enema bag, which I hung on the IV pole, and a cleaned and already-lubed nozzle connected to a long tube, which I handed to Sam. Then, I climbed onto the bed, and got in a knee chest position on one of the towels, folding a pillow under my middle. I heard Sam behind me, asking Julie, "Would you like to do the honors?"

I felt the cold rounded tip of the nozzle pressing against me, wiggling, and then invading me. It felt big. I felt the narrow neck, and then the nozzle was being pulled out again. Julie was obviously returning the 'favor' of extra attention with the nozzle.

Finally, it was pushed in all the way, and Sam whispered, "I'll start the flow, now." A moment later, I felt the warm water flowing into my ass. It wasn't horrible, but I still wasn't used to the feeling. Actually, it wasn't too bad.

I asked, "Would one or both of you like to help me, now? I seem to have gotten a little wet, watching you guys make out."

I heard a moan, and Julie announced, "Well, I don't think I'm going to be able to hold it any longer. I really have to go!"

Sam said, "Why don't you take the bathroom off the pool room? I'll take care of Kelly." I heard feet pattering across the carpet and out of the playroom.

I lowered myself, and relaxed, my hips being raised a little by the pillow; I let my legs separate, and felt Sam climb onto the bed next to me. Then, his hand was under me, stroking, alternately diving into my wetness and moving his fingers over my clit. It wasn't going to take long. Sam used two fingers putting swirling pressure over my hood.

My mind was flooded with images – of Julie scratching Sam's back, Julie straddling Sam in the jacuzzi, and Julie masturbating in front of Sam, Linda and I. As my body spasmed, Sam's fingers stilled; and as I cried out, Sam inserted two fingers into me, pressing on my G-spot. I orgasmed again, and Sam again spiraled his fingers over my hood, slowly, circling the area, then finally honing in and lightly squeezing my clit between two fingers. I screamed, and reached down to remove Sam's hand. It was too much stimulation.

Sam got the idea, and took his hand out from under me. Then, he held my hips, moving me slightly forward and back, as warm water flowed into me. Sam groaned, and said, "Sorry, Kelly, but I'm going to have to go, now." I understood. He had done very well.

He climbed off the bed, and informed me, "There's another quart left. Just relax. I'll come down as soon as I can." Sam groaned again, and ran to the stairs. I was now alone in the playroom, feeling the water flow into me, and thinking about our experience today so far. We were still in the preparation phase, with the 'main course' still ahead. I closed my eyes, and gave in to the images that were again forming in my mind.

When I opened my eyes, my belly felt full, and I felt the nozzle in me, but it wasn't objectionable; I realized that I might have even fallen asleep for a few minutes. Looking back, I saw that the enema bag was empty. I reached back and pulled the enema tube until I could feel the roller valve. I shut the valve, and then removed the nozzle. I brought the IV poles back into the exam room, and cleaned up everything on the playroom bed, but left the towels. Then, it was my turn to use the bathroom.

As I released one of my last floods, Julie appeared in the doorway; she turned to go into the playroom, but I called to her, "Julie, it's OK. You can visit with me if you want; while all the water comes out."

Julie stepped into the bathroom, "Yeah, it's not that pleasant. But it does feel good afterward."

A few moments later, Sam stepped into the bathroom. At that instant, another flood of water gushed out of me. When I was ready to wipe, I looked at Sam and Julie, and said, "It's getting a little crowded in here." Sam and Julie went into the playroom, as I finished on the toilet.

When I walked into the playroom, Sam was pouring wine into three glasses. Julie sat on a towel that had been laid across the couch. We were all nude. I walked up to the bar, and took two glasses of wine, handing one to Julie, as I sat next to her on the couch. Sam sat on the other side of Julie. I raised my glass in a toast, "Here's to a close friendship between us all. And to your first ... coupling." Sam and Julie laughed.

Sam said, "Yeah, Julie's great in bed." Then he looked down at himself, and added, "And I don't *feel* any warts, or stuff, yet."

Julie yelled, 'Sam!" And I threw a decorative pillow at him, nearly knocking the glass out of his hand.

Then, Sam raised his glass, "And here's to Julie. Our friend. Our very open, and now very close friend! Thank you for playing with us. And for putting up with Kelly's fixation with enemas and shots."

Now, I threw another pillow at him, but it sailed over his head. My aim might have been better had I spent more time playing ball, as my dad had wanted. My ammunition was running low. "*My* fixation? You wanted it, but the deal was that I would decide when and how."

Sam smiled at Julie, answering me glibly, "Uh huh."

Julie looked at me, and said, "Come on, Kelly, admit it: You're as turned on as Sam by this stuff. I could tell when you called me that you were getting excited."

Well, maybe. But it was an overstatement to claim that this was my thing. Although, I would have to admit – to myself – that I *was* turned on by the shots. I don't know why. Maybe, I had caught something from Sam?

Well, it was time for me to prepare the next enema experience. I hoped that after all this, we actually would have fun with the strap-ons and maybe this would be the first time for Sam and I to have anal sex. "I'm going to get our next enemas ready. You guys can play by yourselves for a while."

Sam whined, "Kelly, maybe we don't need another enema. I feel pretty cleaned out, already." Julie and I laughed.

"Sorry, Sam. Plans are plans. And Julie and I need to be ready for you ... and the strap-ons."

Julie hooted, "Strap-ons? That should be fun. I've always wanted to try one of those!"

Sam interjected, "I've been trying to figure out all the combinations. I could do anal with you, while you do Kelly in the rear."

Julie laughed, and then translated, "You mean you'd like to fuck me in the ass, while I fuck Kelly in the ass?" Now, we were all laughing. I went to the exam room, and started preparing our next enemas.

I put my wine down, and looked at Julie sitting on the couch next to me. "Well, Kelly told us to 'play by ourselves for a while'..."

Julie took a sip of her wine and put her glass down. Leaning toward me, she kissed me on the lips. Then, grabbing my hair, and pulling my head toward her, she opened her mouth, and we kissed fervently. Julie reached down with her other hand, and held my re-hardening shaft, curling her fingers around me, and stroking the underside with her thumb.

She smiled at me, and lifted her butt off the couch, moving herself toward me, as she guided me into her. She wrapped her legs around my waist, and we rocked, holding each other tightly, and feeling the glorious sensation of our bodies joined with me inside her. I ran my hands down Julie's back, and held her bottom, molding her buttocks, and pulling her to me – although I was already in, as they say, 'up to the hilt'. We continued rocking, holding each other

I couldn't resist asking Julie a stupid question, "So what do you think about our 'open' lifestyle, having sex with your friend's lover, being ravished by an older man?"

Julie shook her head slowly, her eyes quickly going to the ceiling before looking into mine, "I'm not thinking much about it. Just enjoying the feelings and sensations. Why do you have to be so analytical? Or, is it 'anal'?" We chuckled.

Then, Julie said, seriously, "Sam, I think we're all having fun. It's an interesting experience, and I think you guys are great to be able to share it with me." Then, I saw a twinkle in her eye, and she added, "And your age has nothing to do with it. At least, you don't have to take Viagra!"

I laughed, "Yeah, that's all I need! I already get turned on pretty instantly, and it's actually a bother to get an erection various times throughout the day, as I happen to think of things that turn me on."

Julie shrugged her shoulders and, with a straight face, said, "I guess you can't keep a good man down." We were hysterical, still rocking, as Kelly came back into the playroom, carrying a bunch of supplies.

Kelly watched us for a moment, before saying, "It looks like you guys are having fun together. Hitting it off, pretty well."

I shook my head, and said, "No, the spanking part hasn't started, yet." At that, both girls turned their heads to me, but it only took a moment to realize that I was joking: No spankings were planned for our threesome today.

Julie laughed, "Well, before Sam got in me, you could say I was 'spanking his monkey'." Then, she added, "Or 'whipping his willy', or 'bopping his baloney', or 'flogging his log'." We were hysterical again.

Julie and I stopped rocking, and Kelly said, "I was planning on having us get into the 'chair position' on the couch, each one of us squirting one syringe into the next person, down the line, until we were all filled. But I think it will be more practical if we use the bed, and get in a knee chest position. Then each of us can take turns squirting the warm saltwater into each other."

Although I wasn't looking forward to having water squirted up my rear, I guess my throbbing organ still inside Julie was already anticipating my emptying syringes of water into the two girls, their bottoms in the air, anuses relaxed and open, awaiting the not-so-rude intrusion of warm liquid.

I leaned back, and Julie extricated herself from me. Then, despite the stickiness on me, Julie took my erection in her hand, and led me to the bed. We laid the towel along the side of the bed, and Julie and I climbed up and each got into a knee chest position. Our heads were turned toward each other, and Julie reached out and held my hand, as I felt the tip of the syringe against my anus.

"Just relax, Sam," Kelly said, as she squirted six ounces of water into me. It only took ten seconds, and wasn't a bad feeling."

I heard Kelly preparing a second syringe, and then saw her put it against Julie in my peripheral vision. Kelly held the syringe against Julie's anus, and said, "Julie, I would like to echo Sam's thoughts. *Thank you* for playing with us. And even putting up with the needles and nozzles that Sam has to poke and prod us with." Then, Julie squeezed my hand lightly, as Kelly emptied the syringe of water into her.

I turned back to Kelly, and asked, "Who's doing the poking and prodding?" Kelly chuckled, and we switched positions, Kelly taking the knee chest position on the bed, as I stood on the carpet surveying the situation. Kelly had made three one-gallon Tupperwares of enema solution, which sat on a towel on the floor, a separate 200cc syringe sitting next to each of the jugs. The jugs and syringes were labeled with tape, 'K', 'S', and 'J' – our initials; and each of the jugs sat on the floor below the person who would be getting that solution.

I drew in six ounces of water from the 'K' jug, and stood up, taking in the sight that I had fantasized about a few minutes before: Both girls in a knee chest position, bottoms high in the air, awaiting their enemas. I pressed the tip of the syringe into Kelly's anus, and used both hands to squeeze the plunger of the syringe, spraying water into Kelly's rectum. Kelly was silent, her head turned toward Julie, who was giving Kelly a knowing smile.

Then I loaded Julie's syringe, and stepped behind her. Once again I was amazed at the openness and enthusiasm of Kelly's friend. When I had met Julie – only a couple of months ago – at the restaurant, I would never have imagined in my wildest dreams that I would be standing behind her with a syringe in my hand, as she waited patiently for me to squirt water into her rear. And I'd had some pretty wild dreams.

I noticed the glistening pink tissues below and, as I pushed the syringe against Julie's anus with my left hand, I slipped my right hand below her and did a few light strokes, finishing with a circular motion of my fingers over her clit hood. I heard Julie gasp and, after a few more strokes, began injecting the warm water from the syringe into her.

Kelly was smiling as she watched Julie take her enema. When the syringe had been emptied into her, I kept holding it against Julie, as my hand slipped down once more under her. I advanced two fingers deeply into her wetness, and Julie rocked her body back towards me, and emitted a quiet 'Hmmmmm'.

Then, I climbed onto the bed and got into a knee chest position next to Kelly, and said, "It's your turn, Julie." She smiled at me, as she slithered off the bed. I turned my head to Kelly, who was smiling at me, and took her hand in mine. I whispered, "I bet you never pictured this scene: Julie shooting enemas into our rears as we hold hands."

Kelly chuckled, "Never." Then she closed her eyes, as Julie injected the second syringe of water into her. Soon enough, Julie was standing behind me, and I felt the tip of the syringe against me. Suddenly, Julie's hand was holding my balls – lightly, sensuously, finally reaching further, and giving me one nice stroke from head to base, before she began injecting the water.

It still didn't feel bad, and it was exciting to visualize Julie, standing behind me, in full control of what was going to happen in the next minute or two. When the syringe was empty, Julie again stroked me several times, stopping when my penis began bobbing on its own; I was close to having an orgasm, but the combined expertise of Julie and I kept it on the edge.

Julie took her position to my right again, and Kelly got off the bed to begin our third round of enema injections. We continued in this way, speeding up the process, with each of us taking only a minute or so to inject the other two. Ten minutes later, we each had taken ten syringes of water – about two quarts.

When it was Kelly's turn again, she said brightly, "We're halfway done! Just another ten syringes, each." Julie and I groaned. We were starting to feel the water expanding our bellies, although none of us had yet complained of cramps. Kelly laughed, and said, "I was going to have a contest to see who can take the most, but I guess we can stop after this round, if you guys are too weak to play the game."

She was taunting us, and both Julie and I shouted "Weak?" Kelly laughed, and said, "OK. But let's make this more efficient. Julie, can you please get off the bed and help me?" Uh oh ... what now? My question was answered when Kelly explained that she would load the syringe and Julie could inject the water into me. Within two minutes, I had taken another six syringes of water.

I asked, "Do you think that's enough, yet? I think I'm going to be pretty cleaned out. Any more, and I might explode!" The girls laughed, and Julie and I switched positions.

Now, Kelly was filling the syringe and I was emptying it into Julie, one after another. After another four syringes of water, Julie started cramping, and we decided to end her enema at that point. Finally, Julie and Kelly switched positions, and Julie filled the syringe repeatedly, as I injected the water into Kelly; who wasn't complaining.

So, we kept filling and injecting the syringes of water into Kelly, using nearly the entire gallon of solution before Kelly began whining. "OK, guys, I think I've had enough. I'm filled to the top." She chuckled, "I mean the bottom. Whatever." We helped Kelly up, and I carried everything back to the exam room.

Kelly looked at me, "It's your turn to take this bathroom." I shrugged, and walked into the bathroom, but before I sat down, Kelly said, "And I think Julie should sit with you for a few minutes." That shocked both Julie and I. Julie's hands were rubbing her stomach, as Kelly explained. Julie smiled at me, and straddled me, as I sat on the toilet – as I had done with Kelly during her first experience here.

I was still embarrassed, but not as much as I would have been a few months ago. Julie held me, and we kissed, as a flood of water came out of me. I looked at Kelly, and she smiled and nodded, "Come on, Julie. I'm going to sit on your lap while you expel your enema." There was an instant of shock on Julie's face, but then she shrugged and smiled at me, getting off my lap, and leaving me in peace, as she and Kelly went upstairs to do their business.

Our enema experience finished, the three of us stood under a hot shower, bathing each other. As Kelly washed my backside and Julie washed my front, I realized that I'd grown to like taking showers with multiple people. Kelly took her turn washing my front, and Julie asked her to pull my buttocks apart; she gladly complied.

Julie held my 'package' as she stuck out her tongue at me, then bent down, and tended to my private parts. I realized that she was 'rimming' me – running her tongue around my anus, and probing my depths, flicking her tongue and teasing my sensitive tissues.

I moaned, and said, "Julie, that feels wonderful ... but I'm not sure it's such a good idea."

Julie looked at Kelly questioningly, and she said, simply, "Germs."

Julie was astounded, "What? I just bathed you. Scrubbed your privates with soap and water." Kelly just shrugged. I had to admit that what Julie was doing was probably safe, but I still didn't like the idea of it ... although I couldn't complain about the feeling that Julie's tongue was giving me.

We finished our shower and dried off, putting the towels around our waists, as we walked into the playroom. I went behind the bar, and poured some Diet Cokes for us. As we sipped the bubbly black liquid, Julie asked, "What now?"

I smiled, "Now, it's a 'free for all'. Let's just play it by ear." Then I glanced at each girl, and said, "Or 'play it by *rear*'."

Julie laughed, "Well, my ear won't fit you, but I have a couple of other places that will." I collected some things from the credenza behind my desk, and we walked over to the bed. But not before I had flipped a couple of switches on the electronic wall panel.

Julie asked to try the strap-on, and I gave her the one with the more flexible phallus, which was realistic to the point of having veins on the sides. As Julie figured out the harness and put it on, I suggested to Kelly that we might want to start her with a large butt plug, to get her ready for our first anal sex experience.

I lubed the bumpy glass butt plug, but Julie grabbed it, and said, "I'll take that!" She took Kelly's hand, and led her to the end of the bed, then had Kelly lay back, her butt at the edge of the bed. "Hold your feet up, and I'll insert this thing into you." Kelly did as Julie had asked, and Julie seemed delighted to be in control, as she took her time inserting the glass device.

Then, Julie stepped between Kelly's legs, and pulled Kelly closer to the edge of the bed, as she guided the dildo of the strap-on between Kelly's folds, and deep into her vagina. Julie held Kelly's hips, and thrust into her, Kelly's legs now vertical, against Julie's shoulders. It was quite a scene. Julie had a palm over Kelly's clit, the dildo sliding next to it, as she rocked her palm slowly.

Kelly glanced at me, standing on the sidelines, and signaled me to come over. I climbed onto the bed, and got on all fours, between Kelly's head and the headboard of the bed, then slowly crawled forward, until my now-hard member was over Kelly's face. She reached up and pulled me into her mouth, and I spread my knees to lower myself slightly, as Kelly used a deep-throat technique she had never demonstrated on me.

I looked up, and into Julie's eyes. She smiled, and leaned forward, continuing to thrust into Kelly, her palm still in place over Kelly's clit. Julie and I kissed, our mouths joining hungrily, but both our hands relegated to other tasks.

Closing my eyes, I tried to visualize the scene that the three of us were making: Kelly lying on the bed, her legs up against Julie, a butt plug in her rear, and Julie's strap-on dildo moving in and out of her, as Kelly went down on me – actually, 'up' on me. I realized that Julie was the only one not being 'stimulated', except mentally by using the strap-on.

I didn't want to come prematurely, so decided to leave the party for a few minutes. Kelly was surprised when I lifted off her, leaving an empty mouth behind, but – based on the gleam in her eyes, I knew that she had figured out that I was 'up' to something.

I went back to the desk, and pulled out a small device that looked like a small mouse with a long tail, and grabbed a keychain with three buttons on it. I also lubed two medium-size butt plugs before I walked back to the bed. As Julie continued to thrust slowly, I showed her the small mouse-like device, and pointed to her groin.

She gave me a 'look', but took the device, and was able to slip it under the strap-on harness, and into her. Then, I showed her one of the butt plugs, and she shrugged and bent forward. I walked behind her, and inserted the plug into Julie's rear. Then, I bent over the bed, next to Kelly, and handed the other butt plug to Julie, who duly inserted it into me.

Climbing onto the bed, I again positioned myself over Kelly, who re-started her oral ministrations. With the keychain hidden in one of the hands that was holding me above Kelly, I leaned forward, and Julie and I kissed again.

As her tongue swirled around mine, I pushed the first button on the keychain remote. Instantaneously, Julie yelped, first into my mouth, and then she pulled her head back, laughing, as the small remote-controlled vibrator inside her hummed.

I told her, "That's what Kelly was dealing with, when you guys saw her in the restaurant. Except, she was at level 2 or 3." Julie looked at me curiously, then, with dread, she realized what was about to happen. I tapped the second button, and Julie stood up straight, still laughing, and still thrusting into Kelly. I was still in Kelly's mouth, but she was now laughing, too. I smiled at Julie, and said, "Now, it's time for some orgasms!" I pressed the third button on the remote, and Julie squealed.

We worked together to get each other off: Julie, with the butt plug and vibrator in her, using the strap-on to 'do' Kelly, who also had a butt plug in her, and was deep-throating me. I also had a butt plug in me, and Julie and I were kissing again. All of our orifices were filled, some more delightfully than others, but all making their presence known as the three of us continued our grind.

Kelly came first, arching her back, taking me even more aggressively into her mouth, little hums coming from somewhere deep in her throat. Julie took her palm off Kelly and slowed her thrusting.

I came next, filling Kelly's mouth, the thick, sticky, white liquid overflowing onto Kelly's chin and cheeks, as she struggled to swallow. My rapid movements and panting breath did not allow me to continue kissing Julie, but when I opened my eyes, Julie was smiling at Kelly and I, obviously amused to watch the ebb and flow of our dual orgasms.

Well, that was interesting! While Sam was cleaning himself in the bathroom, I walked to the bar, and poured more Diet Coke to wash down the cum that remained in my mouth. Julie called to me from the bed, and asked, "Can I take this damn vibrator thingy out of me, now? And the butt plug?"

I laughed, and gave her permission. I had no idea what Sam had in mind, but neither Julie nor I had found his remote-controlled vibrator to be much of a turn on. Looking at Julie, I said, "You're the needy one, now. How about if I go down on you?"

Sam was walking back into the playroom, and added, "Yeah, Kelly can go down on you, while I take her in the ass." Julie was reaching under the strap-on harness, and trying to extract the vaginal vibrator. Sam offered, "May I help you with that, Miss?"

Julie laughed, but already had the vibrator out. She walked up to Sam, still wearing the strap-on, and dropped the vibrator in his hand, turned around, and bent over. Sam did the honors of removing Julie's butt plug, and headed back to the bathroom to wash the toys, as Julie walked up to me and hugged me. "Yes, I would like you to go down on me, Kelly. But, first, don't we have to finish something?" I had no idea what she was talking about, and looked at her questioningly.

As Sam entered the playroom, Julie gave me an enigmatic hint of a smile, then reached out and pinched both my nipples, then twisted them roughly. "You're *my* bitch, now!" Julie's face was contorted, vehement, evil. I was stunned.

Julie grabbed a handful of my hair, and pulled me toward the bed. That hurt! Julie turned to me and said, "I'm going to fuck you in the ass, now. And stick you with needles. Bitch!" We were at the bed, and Julie was still pulling my hair. Sam was walking up to us, looking bemused, when Julie turned to him, reached out, and twisted one of *his* nipples!

"Ow! That hurts!" I suddenly flashed on the fact that Sam and I would certainly be talking about this experience well into the future. Sam looked startled.

Julie, now looking like a wicked witch, cackled, and exclaimed, "*You're* my bitch, too. And, I'm going to fuck *you* in the ass, bitch!" I suddenly couldn't help but laugh – on the inside; but I didn't dare laugh at Julie. Was she *acting*? I had recently realized that Julie was always acting ... but I had never seen her in a role like this.

Julie was now taking off the strap-on, which surprised both Sam and I. We had no idea where she was going with all this. Then, Julie put on the other strap-on, the one with the slightly thinner, but much harder cock. It dawned: Julie *was* going to fuck Sam and I in the ass. Julie was spreading a thick layer of KY over the dildo. Then she climbed onto the bed, and lay on her back, her head on a pillow, the cock pointing to the ceiling. Julie turned her head to me, and said, "On the bed, bitch!"

I got on the bed, and crawled to Julie. She instructed, "Get in a knee chest position and let my other bitch take that butt plug out of you. I'll need that space." I got into position, and Sam pulled out the butt plug.

Julie commanded, "Get your ass over here, and get in the reverse cowgirl position, bitch!" It took me a few seconds to realize what Julie wanted. I straddled her hips, looking down her long legs that were together, her ankles crossed.

Julie was maneuvering the dildo, as I carefully lowered myself onto it. After the large butt plug, the well-lubed strap-on dildo wasn't a big deal. I slid myself down onto it, moving up and down to get it comfortably situated in my butt, 'comfortable' being a relative term.

Then, Julie surprised me, and I realized what was coming. She told Sam, "Bring me the bitch's shot!" I looked over my shoulder, and saw Sam collecting everything from the dresser, then crawling to Julie on the bed. I settled myself on the dildo of Julie's strap-on, and looked across the playroom, as I awaited the needle.

Sam asked if he should give me the shots, but Julie insisted on doing it herself. Sam quietly explained to her the procedure, including pulling the plunger of the syringe back to check for blood, before injecting the sterile saline. Then, Sam was maneuvering himself over Julie's legs, in front of me; he was trying to figure out if he could get in me, while Julie fucked me in the ass, but he finally gave up, and straddled Julie's legs, as I was, and we leaned toward each other and kissed.

I felt Julie swabbing the left side of my bum, and the needle going in. I was getting used to the feeling of cold stainless steel plunging through my skin, but it still didn't feel good. Sam held my head, and we kissed, as Julie fumbled with the syringe. I felt the saline being injected for a few seconds, and then it became a dull, but uncomfortable, pain – like someone pinching me.

I tried to ignore what was happening behind me, but I felt Julie thrusting the dildo into me, as much as she could with me on top of her. I began moving up and down, slowly, letting the dildo slide in and out of my ass. The feeling wasn't much of a turn on, but the thought of what was happening did excite me.

Sam reached down, and fingered me – first sliding his hand over my vulva, then moving his fingers over my hood, and finally inserting two fingers and putting light pressure on my G-spot. He moved his fingers slightly one way, and another, until my 'Hmmmm' let him know that he was in the most effective position. Sam held his fingers in position, as I slowly moved my hips up and down. I leaned forward, and Sam and I kissed again, as I visualized what Julie was seeing at this moment. I put my arms around Sam's neck, and closed my eyes. I realized that I was actually enjoying the sensual feelings of my body, although I wasn't really turned on, sexually.

Julie had finished the first shot, and was now swabbing my right hip. Sam leaned forward, and watched over my shoulder, his fingers still in me. I settled onto Julie, the dildo now fully inside me. I heard Sam whispering '3 ... 2 ... 1 ..." and felt the needle stick. I took a deep breath, and tried to relax. Julie injected me, as Sam watched.

My eyes looked across the playroom, but I was seeing the quaint streets of Amsterdam, as I had seen on the 'net, the stepped gable of a narrow house, on one of the canals. The shot was now hurting, and I was ready for us to move on to something else. Finally, I felt the needle being pulled slowly out of me.

Sam crawled around me, and took the syringe from Julie, then got off the bed, and headed to the desk area. Julie pushed upwards on my bum, and I got the message, lifting myself until the dildo came out of my rear. Julie and I got off the bed and I watched, as Julie removed the strap-on.

When Sam returned, Julie commanded, "Over the corner of the bed, bitch!" Sam complied, and Julie took her time inserting an interesting butt plug that Sam had set on the dresser: It's tip was angled, in order to better stimulate the prostate. With the plug halfway into Sam, Julie twisted it, so that the angled tip was facing 'down'. Then, she continued to insert it, moving it roughly side-to-side and in-and-out inside Sam. When it was finally in all the way, Julie gave me a mischievous smile, and ordered, "Come with me, bitches!"

Julie lay back on the other corner of the bed, her legs down, straddling the bed. She gave me the 'come here' signal with her pointer finger, and said, "Eat me out, bitch!"

I straddled the bed and lowered myself to Julie, having to push back slightly so that my tongue was positioned over her clit. But Julie had turned her feet in, pinning my legs against hers and the bed, so my pushing back positioned me well for Sam. Sam had gone around the bed for something, and was now walking back behind me.

He said quietly, "You're going to need to be dilated in a few minutes, when we do anal, so it's best that I insert this butt plug." I groaned; there had been something up my butt for most of the afternoon, already. But I wanted my first anal experience with Sam to go well, and knew that he was right: Being expanded by large plug would help me take in Sam easier.

Sam stepped up against me, and I reached under with my right hand to guide him into my pussy, the feeling wondrous. I left my hand under me, doing myself, as I ate Julie. I wondered whether all three of us could have a simultaneous orgasm.

After a few strokes of his cock in me, Sam pressed the plug against my butt hole, and the large thing slowly invaded me. Julie was now reaching out with both hands, and pushing my head down onto her, so I began licking and kissing her, trying to ignore the feeling in my ass. Finally, Sam pushed the plug all the way in, where the narrow waist allowed my poor, sore anus to relax a bit.

As Sam began long, slow thrusts into me, I flicked my tongue under Julie's hood. I retracted her hood with my left hand and sucked her clit hard. I had learned some of Julie's preferences when we had 'made out' the night of my birthday party; she liked rough play. I lightly slapped Julie's hood with my hand, and moved my tongue under it, seeking her hardened knob. My right hand unconsciously pressed on my own hood, as a random thought entered my brain: I wondered how this would feel, if I were wearing a VCH piercing, like Fiona's.

I was now, suddenly, very turned on. The room was quiet, except for the heavy breathing, and the sounds of my slurping Julie's clit, and Sam's front slapping against my bottom. I saw the three of us, as if from above, each in our own bubble, approaching orgasm, all of us helping each other. This was hot!

Julie cried out, as I lightly bit her clit, and she arched her back, and thrust her hips, and I kissed her clit over and over. I realized that Sam's motions were increasingly urgent, and I pinched my own clit, the pain and pleasure exquisite, as my own excitement crescendoed and peaked.

I was surprised, as Sam slowed his movements; he hadn't yet come, his control amazing, considering the two women orgasming as he watched. He leaned over me and whispered, "Is it time for anal, yet?" I realized that had Sam come, it might have taken another 30 minutes before he was ready again ... and I was glad I didn't have to have that damn butt plug in me that long.

I answered, hesitantly, "I guess I'm as ready as I'll ever be." I'd only taken it in the ass once before, with a boyfriend who hadn't been that gentle, nor considerate. It was amazing that Sam had waited this long for anal sex, but I realized that he was a little squeamish; I would need to continue working on him. Perhaps someday he would be as 'open' as he claimed to be.

Julie interrupted, "Just wait a minute, bitches!" I guess she was still in her 'role'. I meekly replied, "Yes, Mistress."

Sam followed my lead, and also said, "Yes, Mistress," although he was laughing as he said it.

Julie got out from under me, and I watched as she strapped on the strap-on again, and walked behind Sam. "Reach back and spread your cheeks for me, bitch!" Sam complied, and Julie removed the butt plug from Sam's rear.

I saw Julie standing next to the bed, holding out her hand, and Sam leaned over me, and whispered, "Give a little push, Kelly." I pushed, and Sam pulled out the butt plug, finally giving my bum a break. But it was a short break. Sam fumbled a bit, then guided himself into my ass.

His cock felt larger than the butt plug, but I focused on relaxing my anal muscles, and he was fully inside me in less than a minute. He moved back-and-forth a little, then suddenly pushed into me, his body tensing.

Julie said, calmly, "Just relax, Sam. My dick isn't that big; you can take it." Julie chortled, as she inserted the dildo into Sam's rear. Now, the three of us were coupled, Julie in Sam, and Sam in me, as we began to move in unison.

The feeling was amazing: Julie's strap-on penetrating me, and pushing against my prostate, as my entire length slid into Kelly's rear. Her clenching anal muscles brought me to a higher level of excitement each time I pulled nearly out, and then thrust back into her. I closed my eyes, and wondered how long I could keep this feeling going ... but grateful that these two incredible women were willing – and enthusiastic – to give me such a beautiful experience.

I seemed to be in a trance, images of our ménage with Julie flying through my head. My motions continued, moving forward into Kelly, and back into Julie – her strap-on plunging into me. Julie had been massaging my bottom, but now gave me a quick spank on each side. Then, she continued massaging for a while. Suddenly, she gave me a flurry of spanks, as she thrust the dildo into me and held it there.

The spanks didn't hurt, but must have 'hit a nerve': I looked down at Kelly's bottom, my hard shaft sliding in, as I held it there, and gave Kelly a few spanks on each side. Then, both Julie and I were moving again. It took only one more round – Julie spanking me and me spanking Kelly – before my orgasm detonated.

My quickened motions made Kelly yelp, and I nearly yelped from Julie's strap-on roughly moving around, as I impaled myself on it. It took nearly a dozen thrusts before my energy was spent. I leaned over and put my head on Kelly's back, my hands pulling her hips toward me, so that I could stay inside her as long as possible. Then, Julie pulled my hips towards her, as she held the dildo deep inside me, and put her head on my back.

We stayed that way for several minutes, until my breathing had slowed, and I was ready to come out of Kelly. I couldn't resist thinking how much I liked having a 'Sam sandwich' with the girls.

When we were all standing at the corner of the bed, I turned to Julie, and gave her a small kiss. As I turned to give Kelly a kiss, she exclaimed "What!??! You wore a condom? Even after those enemas – and pumping a gallon of water into me?"

She stood there shaking her head, but I took her head in my hands, and gave her a deeply passionate kiss: A meaningful statement of my love for her. Despite – or in spite of - our intimacy with, our lovemaking to, Julie. This was the ultimate fulfillment of many of my fantasies – of openness, trust, and intimacy. But, actually, it went far beyond my fantasies, which had generally stopped short of having sex with my female partner.

As the three of us walked to the bathroom, I tried to recall what other combinations of positions I'd envisioned for our ménage ... but at the moment, I couldn't think of anything specific that we hadn't already done. At that moment, I felt quite satisfied and happy: Contented.

Julie sat down to pee, as Kelly helped me take off and dispose of the condom. Then, Kelly sat down on the toilet. I informed her, "But I have to pee, also." She just stared, as I straddled her, and pushed her legs apart. I pointed my penis down between her legs, and we both peed together.

I got off, so that Kelly could wipe, and stood next to Julie, who said, "I can see that you guys are *really* close." We all laughed, but it was true: Kelly and I were very close, in many different ways.

We took another nice shower together, bathing each other thoroughly – along with a lot of hugging and kissing. I realized that this was the first time I'd had sex – actual intercourse – with anyone other than Kelly, since my wife passed. Suddenly, I became very emotional, tears flowing from my eyes – fortunately they were hidden in the streams of water cascading over my body from the shower.

I was crying from sadness – thinking about Sarah; and from joy – thinking about Kelly: A most unique woman – intelligent and strong, but also enthusiastic and humorous. Someone I could love fully, share experiences ... and make a life with.

Julie, Kelly and I didn't talk much after our ménage, but enjoyed the closeness that we had developed. I brushed the hair of both women, and opened a split of champagne for one last toast. We dressed together in silence, each of our emotions responding to the experience we'd had together. Kelly and I saw Julie off, and then we held each other for a long time, standing on the front porch.

I couldn't imagine a more perfect threesome experience, and could even less imagine what experiences we might have in the future.

CHAPTER 4: READY, STEADY, ...

Our travel plans firmed up, as I made the airline and hotel reservations, and confirmed with Henk the timing of our visit to Amsterdam. Through a deal offered by one of the major credit card companies, I was able to purchase two business class tickets for the price of one and, due to my status on the airline, put in a request for a further upgrade to first class. My years – decades – of business travel had to count for something. We were on standby for the upgrade in both directions, and I would just have to keep my fingers crossed.

Kelly was now well into her school year, with her research planned, and she was spending a lot of time in the lab preparing the experiments that would be the basis for her dissertation. She stayed with me over the weekends, and we finally finalized the itinerary of our upcoming European adventure.

Last weekend, I had taken her shopping, and we bought some jackets and other clothing items for the trip. Kelly was taking off today, Friday, and would be coming over this morning. Then, Julie, Linda and Kathy would be dropping by, and we would have a medical experience.

This time, the experience wasn't going to be in my exam room (which only Julie had seen); it was going to be a *real* medical experience. Kelly and I had convinced her friends that they should get HPV and hepatitis immunizations; they were all near the maximum age for the HPV shots, but it still seemed a reasonable precaution for them to take.

My own doctor had agreed to provide the prophylactic treatment, and each of the girls had checked with her own doctor. Their main comments had been that the HPV vaccination would be of limited usefulness, but that it would be a good idea to get the hepatitis injections. There would be a course of three shots in each of the series, the first being today, and then returning in one month and in six months for the rest. The girls were neutral: They neither felt a great need to get the shots, nor did they think it was a big deal; except for Kathy.

We would be departing in less than a week, and I was trying to determine which of our toys and supplies I should bring, considering that we would probably be buying additional toys in Europe. I cleaned the camera that I planned to take, along with a single zoom lens that would have to suffice. I have traveled long enough to know that lighter is better: I didn't want us to get bogged down with our luggage. We would each be taking a rolling case, and a small backpack.

Hoping that we would be able to ski at least once, I stuffed my backpack with the small items that I wanted with me when I skied; I also packed a shell jacket, sweater, and ski pants, but we would need to rent skis, boots, and poles. It wouldn't be practical for me to bring my helmet, with its built-in camera and Bluetooth audio, but I didn't plan on taking Kelly off-piste, anyway.

When Kelly arrived, we went upstairs to hang her clothes for the weekend. We were also going to sneak in a quick lovemaking session, as it had been nearly a week, and her friends wouldn't be arriving for another hour. As we stood together in the large, walk-in closet, I eyed the belts hanging on hooks, remembering the first time Kelly had come over, and bent over for one stroke of the belt here in the closet, as I dressed for dinner.

Kelly looked at me, and smiled. "I'll bet you're thinking about that belt that got me so horny that I masturbated on top of you." Ah, the joy of shared experiences; we had been 'together' for less than six months, but already had a huge number of shared erotic and exotic things that we could talk about.

Kelly said, "If we're going to make love, I wouldn't mind getting a little turned on, first." She continued to eye the wide leather belt hanging on the last hook. My manhood stirred, and I reached down my pants to adjust myself. After Kelly and I got undressed, we stood in the middle of the closet and hugged each other. My hands went down to cup her bottom, and rub it a little, envisioning how red it would be in a few minutes.

I took the belt off the hook, and asked Kelly, "Where would you like to do it?"

Kelly shrugged, "I guess over the foot of the bed." I nodded, and we walked into the bedroom. Kelly took a large decorative pillow from the head of the bed, and placed it in the center of the foot of the bed. I held the strap and waited. Kelly crossed her arms, and stamped her foot, as she stood in front of me, also waiting.

Finally, Kelly squawked, "You're *my* bitch, now! Get over that pillow!" I realized my mouth had dropped open, and I closed it again; now *I* was the fish. Of course I had assumed that Kelly had wanted *me* to strap *her*. My bottom was already starting to hurt.

"Kelly ... Am I being punished for something?" I didn't know if I'd done something wrong to deserve this.

Kelly laughed, "No, silly." She batted her eyes at me. "You've been wonderful. But, it's all your fault!"

I was confused. "What is?" I asked Kelly, as I stared at the belt in my hand.

Kelly laughed again, "You taught me what a turn on it can be for someone to submit – to some pain or embarrassment – just because you ask them to. Because they love and respect you enough to accept some pain, if you request it. For any reason."

Well, I had to admit that Kelly understood what turned me on ... and now, evidently, also turned her on. And I *did* love her, and was willing to do anything for her. Well, almost anything. I calmed myself, realizing my near-term fate, and being fully willing – as Kelly had said – to submit; just because she asked me to.

I looked at her, my eyes diverted downward, and said, glumly, "Yes, miss." Then, I handed her the belt, and climbed onto the bed, positioning my hips over the pillow. It was a hard pillow, and didn't squish, so held my hips well above the bed; my legs were hanging off the foot of the bed, my feet not touching the ground.

I realized that it would take some self-control, so I asked Kelly, "May I have a pillow for my head, please, miss?" Kelly smiled, and pulled one of the 'real' pillows from under the cover, and put it under my head. I reached around the pillow with my arms, and held my hands together, wanting to be sure I behaved during my strapping, and not reach back to rub or shield my bottom, as my instinct was sure to command.

I looked back over my shoulder, and said, "I'm ready for the belt, now, miss." I pushed my face into the pillow and locked my hands together tightly. Then, I heard the SWOOSH of the belt flying through the air. 'WHAP!'

The first stroke was stunning. I was, literally, stunned! It was as if a hot poker had been laid across my bottom. I cried out into the pillow, then realized that my feet were kicking, and pushed them down against the bed. The second stroke seemed even worse, if that was possible. It seared a line across my bottom, and I screamed into the pillow. Thankfully, Kelly rubbed my bottom; it must already have had huge welts across it.

I waited, tears in my eyes, thinking how much I loved this woman ... and how much of a 'monster' I had turned her into. I smiled inwardly: Kelly wasn't a monster, but she had been a good student, and somehow had been turned on by many of my own turn-ons. I heard the SWOOSH of the belt again, and closed my eyes. 'CRACK!'

That was too much. My body convulsed, my upper and lower bodies jackknifing, my feet kicking, and tears now wetting the pillow. I knew not to complain or try to reduce the 'punishment'. And I now realized that *I* didn't have a safe word that Kelly would recognize to stop the ordeal. I knew Kelly would call me a 'baby', but those had to be the hardest strokes I'd ever taken ... or given. I whimpered into the pillow.

Just as I realized that Kelly hadn't told me how many strokes to expect, Kelly rubbed my bottom, and declared, "You're getting 24 strokes, so you have 21 to go." Again I was stunned. I didn't know whether to just get off the bed, or verbally refuse to take such a serious punishment. Maybe Kelly was testing me? But I already had a very sore bottom. I wiped my eyes with the pillowcase, and waited.

It was at this point that I wondered whether I could ever be a sex slave. *Or* a master. I kept waiting, stifling the huge urge to reach back and rub my bottom. I jolted as something was placed on my back; I realized it was the coiled-up belt. Then, I heard Kelly peeing, and the toilet flushing, as she walked back behind me, and took the belt from my back. I involuntarily whimpered into the pillow.

In a stern voice, Kelly announced, "You've done very well, so-far, young man. Stand up and face me, immediately!"

I pushed myself back and slid off the bed onto my feet, turned around, and assumed the 'standing' position, my feet widely apart, and my hands on my head. "Yes, miss?" I stammered.

Kelly had the coiled belt in her hand, and was walking back and forth in front of me, looking menacing, despite the fact that she was nude, her soft body looking inviting, at the same time. Then, she set the belt on the bed, and took my head in her hands, giving me the biggest kiss I'd had in a while.

When we came up for air, my hands still on my head, Kelly stepped back, and asked, "Did that punishment make an impression on you, young man?" Then, she looked at me and asked, "Do you need the other 21 strokes? My arm is getting tired." Then, despite trying not to, Kelly was laughing.

I stayed in the role until I was sure the coast was clear. "Yes, miss. That punishment certainly made an impression ... on my bottom." We laughed, and I continued, "And, NO, miss! I can save your arm the trouble: I don't think I need another 21 strokes."

Kelly nodded, and said, "Thank you, Sam. You may relax, now." I was very relieved, and so was my bottom. Kelly explained, "As hard as the spankings have been that you've given me, I don't think they're as hard as they can be. That belt looked mean, and it didn't take much effort to swing it; I knew that it would be a challenge for you. I expected you to complain and maybe rebel ... but you submitted very well. That was a big turn on for me."

Then, looking down at my rising 'flag of truce', now at half-mast, Kelly added, "I guess it was a turn on for you, too. Even though I made you cry."

I hugged Kelly tightly. "It's only a turn on after it's over. That really hurt – probably more than I've ever felt with any of the implements we've used. I didn't – *don't* – think that I could have kept myself under control for 21 more strokes ... but I was going to try. Because I do love you, and am willing to submit to you."

I chuckled, adding, "And I trust you to not hurt me that bad very often!" Kelly laughed, but I was quite serious. Then, I remembered about the safe word, and suggested to Kelly that I use the same one as hers: Horseradish. Hopefully, she would never make me use it.

Walking through the bathroom to hang the belt in the closet, I turned my back to the mirror and looked over my shoulder to survey the damage. There were three two-inch wide, parallel, red stripes crossing my bottom. I wondered whether I would be able to sit down, without my butt smarting.

When I returned to the bedroom, Kelly had pulled down the spread and blanket, and was lying on her back, casually fingering herself. She smiled at me, and said, "You've earned my permission to make love to me, any way you want." That was a great offer! There was anal, and oral ...

But I told her, "Kelly, I'd just like to make love the usual way." Then my bottom reminded me, "But I'd like to be on top, if you don't mind; so my bottom gets some air." Kelly laughed, nodded, and gave me the customary beckoning sign with her pointer finger.

I mounted her, and we made love, simply, and lovingly. I only had to remind Kelly once to not put her hand on my bottom. Then, Kelly reminded me that she was due to get her period soon. We both had hoped that she would have gotten it by now, so that it would be over before we left on the trip.

We got dressed and were walking down the stairs just as the doorbell rang. Julie, Linda and Kathy came in and we all hugged each other. Julie kissed me on the mouth, and said, "Hello, Sam." Her eyes sparkled, her hair shone, and her skin looked fresh.

Linda and Kathy also looked great. Linda wore a simple shift, and Kathy was in a pair of 'designer-thrashed' jeans, holes in the knees, and one strategically placed on her hip. Julie was in a pair of black slacks and a red blouse. Kelly was wearing a loose black dress with nude-color bikini underwear, and I was in one of my standard pairs of black slacks and a dress shirt.

I offered the girls something to drink, but they refused, and Julie said, "We'll need to leave soon, to get to our 11AM appointment." So we all exited the house and piled into my car. The girls chatted as we drove to the clinic, mainly about the new fashions and what was happening in a few popular television programs. As far as I knew, Linda and Kathy weren't aware of the ménage that Julie, Kelly and I had experienced a couple of weeks ago.

I parked, and we went into the lobby of the clinic, and checked in at the desk. It was not busy, and we were called within a few minutes. It seemed surreal, as I followed the four girls - women - to an exam room.

As this wasn't their usual doctor, the girls had to fill-out a several-page form, listing their diseases, medications, and allergies, as well as listing contact information for themselves and an emergency contact. Linda and Kathy sat in the two chairs, Julie took the rolling stool used by the doctor, and Kelly hopped up on the exam table. I was happy to remain standing, my bottom still feeling the effect of the three strokes of the belt Kelly had given me.

It seemed like at least twenty minutes had elapsed before the nurse returned, scanned all of the forms, and stapled them into separate manila folders. Then, she informed the girls, "I'll be back with your shots in a few minutes." They continued chatting, apparently not at all nervous that they were about to get a couple of shots. Of course, I wasn't nervous, as I was too old for the HPV vaccine, and had already taken the hepatitis immunizations.

Ten minutes later, the nurse returned to the exam room with a tray on which there were several paper cups, each with a couple of syringes sticking out the top. She placed the tray on the counter, and washed her hands. Taking one of the cups from the tray, and placing it on the counter, she asked, "So who wants to go first?"

Linda stood, looked around at us, and said, "I guess I can go first." I think everyone was surprised; but then I remembered that Linda had volunteered a few times at Kelly's birthday party. Linda looked at the nurse, and asked, "Should I lie down on the table?" Kelly hopped down, and stood next to me against the wall.

The nurse responded, "Well, you can, if you want to. But these are small shots, so it might just be easier bending over the table for them." I had suggested to my doctor that all the shots be given at a gluteal site, although at only 0.5 and 1.0 cc, they could have been given just as well in the arm.

Linda nodded, and stepped up to the table, pulling her shift up to her waist, and lowering her pale blue bikini underwear to mid-thigh. She bent over the exam table, her generous bottom on display and ready for the shots. The nurse walked to Linda's left side, swabbed her, and quickly inserted the needle. The shot was over in less than three seconds. Linda looked back and said, "That was quick!"

The nurse dropped the used syringe and needle in the sharps container, and took the second shot from the cup. She stood to Linda's right, swabbed her upper hip, and darted the needle in. This shot took a little longer – perhaps five or six seconds – and then it was over.

The nurse put a small round bandaid on each of the injection sites, and moved the next cup to the counter, as Linda pulled up her underwear and pushed down her shift. She smiled at Kathy and said, "That wasn't bad."

Linda sat down and Kathy stood. "I hate shots. Why haven't they invented a way to give shots without needles?"

I knew the answer, but the nurse was the one to reply, "They have – using high pressure air to shoot the drug directly through your skin. But it was too expensive, and wasn't accepted well." As the nurse told her this, Kathy undid her belt and unzipped her jeans; then, she lowered her jeans and underwear together, nearly down to her knees. She looked back at Julie, giving her a sour look; Julie smiled back.

I thought Kathy might decide to lie down on the exam table for her shots, but she bent over the table and put her forehead against the crinkly paper. As with Linda, the nurse was very efficient, giving the smaller shot on the left side, and the larger one on the right.

Kathy gave a little groan as each of the needles were inserted, but otherwise did fine. After the nurse had put on the bandaids, Kathy turned around, and said, "Horrible!" as she pulled up her underwear, and then her pants. She walked back to the chair and plopped down, not looking too happy.

Julie stepped up to the exam table and dropped her slacks. She was wearing a pair of high-cut black bikinis that she pulled down to just below her bottom. I could see the white of a pad inside them, and realized that Julie must be having her period. Julie bent over the table, and took her shots without making a sound. As she zipped her pants, she turned, and smiled at Kelly, then took Kelly's place, next to me, as Kelly took a few steps to the exam table. Kelly reached under her dress and lowered her underwear, then gathered the dress around her waist, and bent over the table.

This was going very efficiently, almost like an assembly line; the girls were taking their shots, one after the other, and we would be done in just another couple of minutes. The nurse gave Kelly the first shot, which couldn't have taken more than three seconds. After disposing of the used syringe and picking up another from the cup, the nurse again positioned herself to Kelly's left.

The nurse said, "Let's give you this one on the left side also, and then you'll get the big one on the right side."

As she started swabbing Kelly's hip, Kelly and I said in unison, "What!?!?" Kelly asked, "I have to get *another* shot?"

The nurse explained, "Yes. You will be traveling, and the doctor thought that if you were concerned about hepatitis, it would be a good idea to give you some protection during your trip, with an injection of gamma globulin. It won't be that bad – not much worse than getting a penicillin shot." Kelly shook her head, and glanced back at me with a strange look; I was dumbfounded, and just shrugged.

She turned back to the exam table, and bent over, and I heard her exhale a deep breath. The nurse gave her the second small shot on her left side, and then took a third shot from the paper cup: This one looked like the practice shots that we had given each other, with the large 10cc syringe half filled, and the yellow hub indicating a relatively large 20 gauge needle. All of the smaller shots had been given with a 22-gauge needle, as I could determine from the black hubs.

Linda gasped, "That's a big shot!"

The nurse swabbed Kelly, and inserted the needle. Then, she slowly injected the clear liquid, as we all stared at Kelly's bottom; except Kathy, who was studiously ignoring the shots by reading a magazine.

I glanced at my watch a couple of times, and realized that the shot had taken more than 45 seconds, already. Finally, the nurse pulled the needle out, and put a bandaid over the injection site. Kelly pulled up her underwear, and let her dress drop.

Now that we were done, I decided to offer the girls a small reward, "How about if I take you all for ice cream, now? As Linda started to nod, the nurse said, loudly, "We're not done, Mr. Johnson. You haven't gotten *your* shots, yet."

What? I calmly retorted, "I've already had the Hep series, and I'm too old for the HPV vaccine."

The nurse was nodding, "Yes. But the doctor checked your record, and you're due for a tetanus shot. *And*, as you'll be traveling too, she prescribed a gamma globulin shot."

Oh, my God! I wasn't planning on *receiving* any shots today, just watching the girls take theirs. The nurse picked up a small syringe, and looked at me, "I was instructed that all of the shots were to be given glutcally. The doctor said you would understand."

Yes, I understood very well. My doctor was giving me my comeuppance, since I had insisted that the girls take their shots in the rear, and now she was going to make me take some shots in my butt, also. I sighed, and stepped up to the exam table, as the nurse waited. I glanced over my shoulder, and Kelly smiled sweetly at me. Linda's hand was covering a smile on her face.

I turned back to the table, undid my pants, and let them drop. There was no giggling about my European-style underwear; the girls had already seen me in them, and the nurse was probably too professional to say anything. Or, she had seen it all. As I reached down and lowered my underwear, it hit me: Oh, my God, again! I realized that I still had three red large welts, in parallel stripes, across my bottom!

I had to think quickly: How could those have gotten there? Maybe I fell on a grate that was shaped like that? Then, I realized that if this were an accident, the nurse might ask the doctor to come in and examine me. That would really be embarrassing; not the exam, but admitting to her that I was into S&M.

I decided on the nearly-honest approach. "I was a bad boy this morning, and my significant other took the belt to me." Kelly, Linda and Julie were sniggering, while Kathy continued to read her magazine.

The nurse stepped to my left side, and 'harrumphed', as she swabbed my hip. Almost immediately, the needle was in me, and she was injecting the medicine. She squeezed my bottom around the needle, and roughly shook it; this seemed awfully long for a simple tetanus shot. The medicine burned a little, hurting worse than the saline we used for practice shots; and I realized that the real 'pain in the ass' would come later, as my body reacted to the drug.

The nurse placed a bandaid on me, and massaged the area with her thumb. Then, I heard her walking behind me, getting the 'big' shot. As she stepped to my right side, I looked back, and was surprised to see that the syringe was filled more than halfway. "I'm getting more than 5cc?"

The nurse swabbed me, and said, "Yes. It's calculated for your weight." Then she jabbed me with the needle. I could definitely tell that this needle was larger than the ones we usually played with.

As she began the injection, the pinching feeling started, the pain growing, until I was really ready for it to end. I think the nurse drew the procedure out, making me suffer, as the needle must have been in me for well over a minute. I sighed again, and finally the needle was pulled out, the nurse taking her time putting a bandaid on me. I pulled up my underwear, and the nurse left the room.

I lifted my pants and turned around, tucking my shirt in, zipping up, and re-buckling the belt. "Well, that was certainly unexpected." The girls laughed.

Kathy slapped her magazine down on the counter, and said, sourly, "There's no reason you shouldn't suffer with us." Julie, Linda and Kelly laughed louder, but were nodding.

Kelly gave me a peck on the lips. Then Julie stepped up to me, put her arms around me, and hugged me, dropping her hands down to cup my bottom, right where I had gotten the shots. "You were a good boy. Would you like me to take you for some ice cream, now?" We were all hysterical, as we walked out of the clinic.

Well, we had all taken our shots; at least the first ones in the series. We now had an appointment for the week after Sam and I returned from Europe, to get our second doses. The small HPV and hepatitis shots weren't a big deal. And, it had been worth taking the large gamma globulin shot, to see the look on Sam's face, and give him a 'dose of his own medicine', in a manner of speaking.

It had been difficult to keep a straight face, and to pretend that I didn't know I was getting a third shot; and not laugh, when Sam found out that he would be getting shots, too.

It had been lucky that I'd been at Sam's house when he had spoken with his doctor; I'd listened surreptitiously and, after the call, when Sam was in the garage, I had hit the redial button, and spoken directly with the doctor. I had explained to her that we were all OK with the shots, even getting them in the rear, but that this was a turn on for Sam.

I had suggested that Sam get a couple of shots, and the doctor had said she could prescribe a big gamma globulin shot for Sam, but that it would only make sense if I got one too, as we would both be traveling. I agreed, and the stage was set for today's 'fun and games'.

Sam did take us for ice cream. He felt he deserved a double cup, while Linda had a double cone, Julie and I had a single cone, and Kathy got a frozen yogurt. When we sat down, Linda – in-between licks of her cone – asked, excitedly, "So what did you do to misbehave, this time, Sam?"

I laughed, and informed everyone, "Sam didn't misbehave at all." I leaned over and gave him a sticky kiss, both our mouths already full of ice cream. "He's been wonderful. I just wanted to test him; see if he would submit to me."

Sam took offense, "Kelly, I always submit to you, when you ask me to." Sam had a point. Although he sometimes whined and complained, he never refused to submit to me, when I asked ... or when he thought it appropriate.

I explained, as I stroked Sam's cheek, "Yes, you do. But you like shocking me, and I thought I would shock you with what that belt can do ... in the hands of a strong woman." Sam smiled, but he wasn't laughing. My friends were listening intently.

I said to Sam, "I think you were right, when you said that you'd never given me strokes that severe. I'm sure the other implements can also be used harder than we've done so far." I realized that this discussion might have an 'impact' on our future spanking experiences, but I was just being honest with Sam.

While I had been somewhat shocked by the range of things we had done, and the seriousness of Sam's spankings, during my first experience with him, Sam had never really been rough or hard on me. He truly didn't want to hurt me. But I was now really psyched about Sam's submission this morning, and I briefly drifted into a fantasy of Sam being the sex slave, and me the Mistress. I had no doubt that I could 'shock' him, plenty.

Sam was awaiting my further explanation. First, I looked at Julie, "Julie, you were right: I do get excited by some of this stuff."

Then, I turned to Sam, "You were surprised when you realized I wanted to use the belt on you, but you got into position, as I asked. I gave you some very hard strokes that I know must have hurt, but you didn't complain, try to reach behind you, or rebel against me. The first stroke might have just been too shocking for you to react, but after the second, and then the third, I knew that you really were submitting; that you would at least attempt to cooperate during your spanking."

I chuckled, "I thought you would ask, when I didn't tell you how many strokes you would be getting, and when I finally told you it would be 24 strokes, you whimpered, but didn't complain. I'm proud of how well you did, young man!" My friends giggled and snickered a little, but I knew – after seeing Sam's butt – that they were impressed, also.

When we got back to Sam's house, my friends came in for a while, and we shared our Europe itinerary with them. We would be hitting a wide range of places and climates, cultures and activities – during a relatively short trip, Sam finally insisting that we take three weeks, and not rush it like typical tourists.

We wouldn't be going very many places, but I knew Sam had some interesting experiences planned. I couldn't wait; and wouldn't have to, for long.

CHAPTER 5: MILE HIGH CLUB

We drove to the airport early Tuesday morning, and first had to take a two-hour flight to our 'gateway' city for the long flight to Europe. On this flight, we would be in first class, Sam having somehow wrangled the upgrade, although we were still waitlisted for a first class upgrade on the European flight. We would be flying through Heathrow airport in London, then taking another short flight to Amsterdam, where our European experience would begin.

We boarded first, and I sat at the window, as Sam always sat in the bulkhead aisle seat. I listened to some Miley Cyrus and Rihanna, as Sam unloaded his 'supplies' for the plane – first class socks, his iPad, Bluetooth noise-cancelling headphones, and even a small bottle of Tabasco sauce for the Bloody Mary he would be ordering on the flight.

I looked out the window, watching all the activity on the tarmac, almost not believing that I was on my way to Europe for the first time, with a man I loved. Yes, an 'older' man, in some respects; but able to keep up with a bunch of women my age. He was handsome, the flecks of silver hair around his temples being the only real indication of his biological age. Although I had found a few white chest hairs on him, as well; I hadn't mentioned those to him ... yet.

It was now late September, and Sam hoped that we would be able to do some summer-like and some winter-like activities during the trip. It was a bit ambitious, but typical of Sam's style: He always tried for more, a higher level of whatever he was doing. But I had never seen him complain of what he did have; I think he appreciated life, perhaps more after he had seen how tenuous it was, when his wife died in that tragic traffic accident in England. I shivered, although the temperature in the plane was pleasant.

Sam held my hand as we took off, and our drinks came within minutes after we were off the ground. We toasted, me with my screwdriver (light on the vodka), and Sam with his Bloody Mary. We were served warm nuts, and put our feet up on the bulkhead. What a way to travel! I hadn't been on that many flights, anyway, and had always sat in the back, usually squashed between people in the center seat. It was quieter up here, not only because we were well away from the engines, but because there were no crying babies around us.

The flight attendant took our orders – an omelet for Sam, and cereal for me. I was impressed that our places were set with tablecloths and silverware, and our breakfasts included a nice bowl of fresh fruit, and choice of steaming breads, bagels, croissants, and muffins. We weren't even on our Europe flight yet, but this was pretty nice!

When we landed, Sam took me directly to the airline's first class lounge. I had been in an airline club lounge once before, but it had been nothing like this. We were in a hushed space with subdued light, beautiful decorations, and only a handful of people. I walked around, and found an open bar, with an incredible array of appetizers and desserts. I poured a Diet Coke, and took a miniature éclair.

Sam declined the alcohol and the food, saying that he would wait until we were on the flight.

The éclair was delicious, and I decided to go back to sample a few more of the sweets, which were all very good. Now, I would just need to drink another ten Diet Cokes, to compensate for this many calories! I decided to take advantage of a bathroom on the ground, rather than wait until I was on the plane. I was glad I did, as these were really deluxe facilities.

When I returned to the sitting area, Sam informed me that we should walk to the gate for our flight, soon. Then he smiled, and said, "I do have a few things in my backpack that might help to 'set the mood' for our flight. And we have time for you to go back to the restroom and put them in place."

I just shook my head. I knew that one of Sam's fantasies was to have sex on the flight – join the 'mile high club' – but I wanted to enjoy the first part of the flight, without discomfort or annoyances. I grabbed the handle of my roll-on, and said, "Let's go to the gate." Sam dutifully followed me out of the lounge, and down the long corridor to our flight.

I had never been on a 'triple-seven' before; it was a huge plane. As we stepped from the jetway onto the plane, Sam whispered, "Here's where I would like to turn left, instead of right." He chuckled, as we turned right, down the aisle a short distance, then right again into our spacious bulkhead business-class seats.

I explored the seat controls, the lights, and the entertainment system, as Sam took out all his supplies and stowed them; he knew all the nooks and crannies, how he liked his seat adjusted, and how to access the power port for his electronics. We put our shoes in the little receptacles, and donned socks provided in the small fake-leather amenity bags that were on our seats. We had large pillows for headrests, and Sam took a blanket from the overhead, which he stowed on the window-side of my seat.

The flight was smooth, and the meal service seemed to never end. Sam said he hoped we would be able to come back in first class, as that offered even more elaborate food. First class and business class had the same wines, and they were good. We began with champagne, drank a white and two red wines during dinner, and liqueurs with our hot fudge sundaes.

Sam said he usually chose the fruit and cheese plate, but I didn't believe him for a minute. I now knew why he hadn't taken advantage of the free bar in the lounge – or the array of tidbits. I was stuffed, and fairly inebriated, and put my seat back as the cabin lights dimmed.

Sam leaned over and kissed me, then whispered, "We can take a nap now, and have some 7-mile-high fun later in the flight." That was OK with me. It was only mid-afternoon by my body clock, but already bedtime in Europe. I yawned, and continued pressing the 'bed' button on the seat control, until it was nearly flat. I put the pillow under my head, and the blanket over me, drifting off, as I dreamed about Sam and I traveling through Europe.

When I woke, the cabin was dark, except for the reading lights that a few passengers were using. Sam was watching a movie on his iPad, and listening with the large headphones. I pushed the button, and my seat slowly rose, but he didn't notice me, so I tapped him on the shoulder.

Sam paused the video and took off the headphones, leaning over and kissing me. "Good morning, starshine!" It wasn't morning here, but must have been, somewhere ahead of us. Sam suggested that I look out the window, cupping my hands to avoid reflections of light from inside the plane. It was incredible: I could see the Milky Way galaxy, cutting across the sky, the stars shining brightly, the sky beyond, black.

I turned to kiss Sam again, but he had stood, and was now trying to position himself over me on my seat. It might have been possible, but Sam eventually gave up, and signaled me to come with him. We stepped into the aisle, and just a few steps toward the front of the plane, and entered the lav. It was a good thing, because I had to go.

I sat on the toilet, and peed, as Sam looked in the mirror. He said, "I think my beard grows twice as fast in the air." He felt the new growth on his cheek with his hand. I thought it was perfect: Miami Vice style. Fortunately, I had gotten my period last Friday evening, right on schedule. I was still spotting, but removed the tampon, as I knew what Sam had planned.

Then, Sam took his turn, artfully peeing into the toilet, as the plane flew through some light turbulence. Sam closed the toilet seat and sat down, and I straddled him, the two of us grasping each other, hugging, and kissing. Sam nibbled on my ear lobe, and I kissed his neck. Then, we kissed passionately, my eyes closed, the hum of the plane hypnotic, as I drifted into another world.

At some point, Sam whispered, "Take off your underwear." He had convinced me to wear a dress on the plane, but I had also brought leggings, which I planned to put on before we landed. I got off Sam's lap and removed my panties, which Sam wadded and put into his pocket.

Then, He lowered his pants and underwear, and I began working on him, until he was ready, his cock sticking up between his legs, and ready for the taking. I straddled him again, and slowly lowered myself, as Sam guided his throbbing organ inside me. I had to thrust my hips forward to allow Sam to enter me fully, but finally we settled into a rhythm, rocking back and forth, our eyes closed, feeling the vibrations of the plane transit through our conjoined bodies.

Sam reached down, and kindly diddled my clit, and I held his head, as we kissed deeply. We suddenly hit some turbulence, and I bounced nearly off Sam, and then back down, impaling myself on his cock. That got me excited.

I bounced myself on Sam, his eyes closing, and face contorting, until he finally released his load into me. I continued to bounce, and Sam did his part, pressing his thumb over my clit, and biting my nipples through my dress and bra. I pulled his head to my bosom, and squelched a scream, as I came. *Became* ... a member of the 'mile high club'.

We landed at Heathrow and, after a bus tour of the entire airport, Sam took me to the British Air first class lounge. We'd already had a small breakfast before landing, so skipped the beautiful buffet. Sam escorted me to the bathing facilities, and offered to pay for a massage, but we really didn't have time, and I was too excited to relax. I was standing on European soil, for the first time. Well, at least British soil.

Then, Sam suggested that we take a shower; together. I guess first class service and discretion trumped the Victorian attitude of the British, as the attendant for the showers didn't bat an eye when we both entered the assigned room. We got undressed, and I dug through my rolling case for a fresh pair of underwear and bra, as well as a tampon – hopefully, the last one I would need to wear on this trip. Sam shaved, while I got the shower started and washed my hair.

After our 'mile high experience', I had started watching one of the movies on the plane's entertainment system, but decided to rest a while. I had slept another three hours, waking as the breakfast was being served. So the trip had been easy, so far. I felt reasonably rested, and was invigorated by the hot and forceful shower. I guess they didn't have a water shortage here.

Sam got in the small shower with me, and we struggled to bathe each other. When I got to his genitals, I knelt in the corner of the shower, as Sam straddled me – his butt against the glass shower door, and I washed him, and then took him in my mouth.

Sam was always 'ready', and it didn't take long before I tasted his pre-cum. I took him out of my mouth, and stroked him with my full hand, fingers curled around him. It only took a few strokes before he came violently, his cum spouting across the narrow shower, and dripping down the wall. I finished cleaning him and the shower, and he got out, allowing me to finish bathing myself.

I felt much fresher after the shower, and put on clean underclothes. I wore the dress and leggings, expecting there to be a chill in Amsterdam, when we landed mid-afternoon. We hung around the lounge a while longer, Sam tasting a few of the interesting selections at the wine bar, and then we did some window shopping along the main 'mall' of the terminal.

Finally, we made our way – it seemed a very long way – to our flight to Amsterdam. I found that there was no 'first class', only business class ... and we were in coach, but Sam had gotten seats in the front row, the drapes of the nearly empty business class section just in front of us. Although we felt squeezed, Sam mentioned that the seats behind us were even worse, especially if the seat ahead was reclined.

I visited the rest room before we took off; it was tiny. We obviously wouldn't be having a 'mile high' experience on this flight!

CHAPTER 6: AMSTERDAM

An hour later, we landed at Schiphol airport, just outside of Amsterdam. We took a taxi to our hotel, a quick ride. I was amazed at the ease with which Sam made small talk with the taxi driver, in Dutch. The hotel was a 3-star establishment, not the luxury level, but relatively small, and located in a mostly residential area of the 'Old South' part of Amsterdam, on one of the offshoots of the Amstel canal.

The staff greeted Sam, as if they knew him – actually, they did recognize him, and welcomed him by name, in flawless English. Sam responded with a couple of sentences in Dutch. We took the elevator to our room on the top floor (except for the restaurant above us), with panoramic glass windows that look across Amsterdam, and down on the canal. It was very picturesque, and it suddenly hit me that the trip was *real*; Sam was real. My life had fundamentally changed – regardless of whether I stayed with Sam long-term, or not.

We unpacked, changed into jeans and a thin jacket, and left the hotel on foot. Although it was already early evening, the sky was bright, and there was no lack of traffic – the trams, cars, and, especially, bicycles. Nobody wore helmets! Infants and small children rode on the back of bikes nonchalantly, the cars speeding by.

Sam bought a *Chipkaart* for each of us, a multi-day tram and bus pass, and we boarded a tram only three blocks from the hotel. I was mesmerized by the sights: The canals, the people, the bicycles. It was a beautiful city. Actually, from what I could see, Amsterdam was more of a small town; with the restaurants, entertainment, and sights of a big city. Sam startled me when he said we needed to get off the tram.

We walked around the area, Sam pointing out the historic bell tower, and the Hotel de l'Europe, where he had stayed once. We walked through a square with tables set up, people selling books. I could have spent an hour or two looking through them, although after I saw a few titles, I realized that most were in Dutch or German.

We turned down an alley, and Sam held me. "I am not asking you to submit, we can do whatever you want. But, if you would like to sample a typical Dutch *tourist* experience, we could try this place." Sam pointed to a nondescript building, people sitting at high-top tables in the window, and a sign that said 'Coffee Shop', with a green palm frond, which I realized was actually a marijuana leaf.

I shrugged, and nodded. I didn't get stoned often (although, I realized, we had all smoked at my recent birthday party), but if Sam wanted to, it might be fun. I felt high already, after the long flights and time change.

We stepped into a surprisingly small den, with subdued light, and quite a few people; in fact, there were very few seats available. A large bar crossed the room, and there was a smaller room in the back with a counter, where several people were lined up.

Sam asked, "Would you like to try the beer?" I nodded and Sam pointed to a table in the corner.

As Sam went to the bar to get the beers, I surveyed the place. There were people of all ages, and several ethnic backgrounds, talking many different languages, most of them smoking. The place reeked of marijuana smoke, and

I realized the entire place was in a cloud of smoke, but it smelled a little sweeter than I had remembered.

Sam returned, disappointed that the Amsterdam 'coffee shops' were no longer allowed to sell both alcohol and marijuana. He handed me a Diet Coke and a menu. I doubted that we would be eating here – the smoke alone would make it awful – but I took the menu from Sam, to see what they offered. It was a leather bound book, done very nicely. On the first page, it listed the drinks – from tea and coffee, soda and juices, to Kombucha and other more exotic offerings.

Then I turned the page. There were at least half a dozen plastic pages, each page with twelve pockets. In each pocket there was a picture, description and price, not of marijuana (which I found on the last page), but of hashish. The names sounded romantic, from far away places; I wondered how 'far away' I would be if I tried any of these delicacies.

Sam and I toasted with our Diet Cokes, and we both drank half before putting them down. I guess we were a little dehydrated. I looked around the room again, marveling at the diversity of life displayed here, when I saw Sam fumbling with something.

When I looked closer, I saw that he had opened a small square plastic zip lock bag, taken a piece of soft, black stuff, and put it in a small wooden pipe. "I didn't know you were going to smoke. Where did you get that pipe?" There were things about Sam that I still didn't know ... but I was learning.

Sam smiled at me, and said, "I bought it. At a shop here in Amsterdam. I'll take you there in a while, just for window-shopping. As you know, I don't smoke very often ... but when I'm in Amsterdam, I sometimes partake, as it brings back memories." He lit up, and took a long toke, then passed the pipe to me. I took a puff, and handed it back to him. The smoke was sweet, but after I exhaled, I realized how powerful it was. I coughed, and took a large gulp of my Diet Coke.

The tiny amount of hash in the pipe allowed us to take only three or four hits each, but it was enough: I was higher than I'd been in a long time; it brought back memories for me, too. We finished our drinks, exited the 'coffee shop' and turned the corner, walking by a small market and several shops.

Sam turned to me and asked, "Do you have the munchies?" I realized that I *was* hungry. We hadn't eaten since the small breakfast on the plane, so I nodded to Sam, as I took in the scene before me: The street opened up to a wide cross-street that was set up as a flower market. Sam took my hand, and we stopped at a small corner shop, advertising *Vlaamse Frites*. Sam explained that this meant 'Flemish' fries which, of course, we call 'French' fries.

Several cooks filled steaming bags with the potatoes, and squirted on one of a dozen different sauces, from mayonnaise, to curry. Sam bought a small order, which came in a cone-shaped paper container, and he squeezed more of the mayonnaise on top. Then, he cautioned, "I'm hoping we have a nice dinner tonight, so let's not overstuff on these. But I wanted you to try them."

I took a couple of fries that stuck out of the sauce, and tasted them: Definitely not low calorie, but possibly the best French fries I'd ever eaten.

We walked through the flower market, several blocks of a street that paralleled a boulevard and tram, eating our fries. Before half the fries were eaten, Sam pointed to a trashcan, I nodded, and he dumped the rest. Sam told me that we were walking toward *Centraal Station*, the main train station of Amsterdam, which was the center of the rings of canals.

We came out of the narrow streets to an area with water, and docks filled with boats. Walking down one of the planks, we boarded a glass-topped tour boat that was about to depart. We took a seat, and Sam kissed me gently. "We'll be doing a lot of walking here, but this might give us a nice break, and you'll get a good overview of Amsterdam, this way."

The boat pulled away from the dock, and Sam put his arm around me, as we passed many of the sights of Amsterdam, which were explained over the boat's PA system. We passed the Anne Frank house; the *Kleine Trippenhuis* – the narrowest house in Amsterdam, only eight feet wide; and many other attractions. It was now dusk, and the lights of the city were on.

Our boat passed under lit bridges, strings of lights in the trees hanging over the canals, bright lights near the harbor, and even red lights in the windows of Amsterdam's famous 'red light' district. Sam sat back, relaxed, as he had seen all these things many times. He whispered "We'll be seeing more of these sights ourselves, over the next day or two." Then, we would be traveling south of Amsterdam, to stay with his friends, Henk and Zöe.

After the boat tour, we walked past the Marijuana Museum, and up a street that was obviously meant mostly for tourists – with many coffee shops (a green leaf on their signs), 'accessory' shops – with hundreds of glass pipes and water pipes in the windows, clothing shops, and sex shops. It was touristy, but pretty interesting. I had never seen such a line-up of stores catering to hedonistic pleasures.

We ducked into one of the many sex shops, walking down the aisles and perusing the extensive array of sex toys they offered. Sam took a few different butt plugs and vibrators off the rack, and looked at me questioningly. I helped him make a selection, and picked some beautiful glass dildos from the cabinet. I saw many of the things that Sam already had in his collection, including butt plug horse tails for pony play, strap-ons, and a lot of BDSM equipment – leather collars, fur-lined cuffs, spreader bars, and ball-gags, plus a lot of stuff I didn't recognize, and couldn't imagine how it would be used.

We paid for our purchase, now carrying a rather large plastic bag down a street that was crowded with pedestrians, but still had cars trying to maneuver through all the people. We continued walking and eventually turned into a 'smokes accessories' store, called 'The Old Man'. Again, we saw hundreds of pipes – glass, metal, wood, and polished stone. Sam and I walked quickly past the glass cabinets, and up a narrow stairway. The second floor had several rooms, including one with clothing, and another with knives and other weapons.

We didn't buy anything, but it was an interesting experience – not only seeing the stores, but all the people that were actually buying the stuff. And the tattoos, body jewelry, hairstyles and colors, and fashions these people were sporting. Hearing a multitude of languages around me, I realized there probably wasn't a Dutch person in the store, except for the employees … and even that was questionable.

Walking a short distance further down the street, we came upon a large plaza – 'Dam Square'. There were hotels and restaurants on our side, and the Royal Palace across the square. Crowds of young tourists sat on the steps and edge of the pool of the National Monument, a phallic-looking statue in the center of the square.

We passed Madame Tussaud's wax museum, and continued past the square into some smaller streets. Sam turned left, obviously knowing where he wanted to go; after another block, we walked up the steps into a tiny shop on the corner ... that specialized in sexy underwear for both men and women. We were greeted by a very old, very short, woman.

There were many racks for each gender, and I had to giggle, when I saw some of the men's versions that must be intended for performers at a male strip club. Sam held a couple up for me, and I shook my head; now, I realized that Sam actually wore some of the most conservative European underwear, at least judging by what was offered at this shop.

Sam bought a couple of pairs of the nicer underwear, and bought me several pair that he wanted to see me wear. A couple of them were cute, but a couple of others were totally impractical for normal wear.

The bag that Sam was carrying was more filled, and we were getting hungry again. Sam asked me whether I preferred another snack, or dinner. It was already after eight, and I wasn't sure whether it was jet leg hitting me, or the hash we'd smoked ... so I suggested that we go to dinner.

It was a big decision for Sam, but as we walked, he reasoned, "We'll try some typical old-Dutch food tomorrow for lunch. And maybe we'll invite Henk and Zöe to dinner in a couple of nights to a great Indonesian restaurant here in Amsterdam, then they can bring us back to their village.

Tomorrow night, we can plan one of the more 'fancy' restaurants – not really that fancy, but one of the traditional good restaurants; he had several in mind, including the famous 'Five Flies'. Finally, he suggested that we eat at one of the good Indian restaurants only a short walking distance away.

Our dinner was great; I really hadn't eaten very much Indian food before, and the dishes here were each distinctive and incredible – not tasting like the 'curry' powder we got at home. Sam had his favorite dishes, and we ordered way too much, especially as I was beginning to fade. I knew that Sam also cooked Indian food, but he hadn't yet made me the 'feast' that he'd described to me a few times; no matter, we were having a feast tonight.

After dinner, we got on a tram, and I thought we would be returning to the hotel, but Sam wanted to get off at *Leidseplein*, an interesting square, with street performers surrounded by crowds of tourists, several restaurants with outdoor tables and umbrellas, and a major American ice cream store.

We got a couple of cones, the ice cream great; Sam promised me that we would find an authentic Italian gelato shop during the trip so that I could compare the flavors and styles.

We finally made it back to the hotel. Sam had pointed out the Rijksmuseum, the Van Gogh museum, and the Concertgebouw, the famous concert house, but I was too tired to notice or care. When we got to the room, I had undone my pants and had pushed them down before the door finished closing. I took them off along with my underwear, and went into the bathroom.

Sam was somewhere in the room, unpacking the goodies we had purchased during our afternoon tour of the city. I finished undressing, and put on one of the robes that the hotel had provided. When I walked into the bedroom, Sam gave me a surprised look. "You're not going to *bed*, already? I thought we would dress up, and visit one of the clubs."

I knew that Sam was joking; he had to be as tired as I was. He stood, and put his arms around me. "Are you tired? Really?" I nodded. Yes, Sam, I am *really* tired. He said, "OK, I guess we don't have to go out." He smiled. "Or, try out some of these toys we bought." I was very glad to hear that, being almost asleep already.

He took my hand, and said, "I'll put you to bed in a few minutes, but would like you to experience the atmosphere ... outside." Outside? I was already in a robe. Sam opened the sliding glass door, and we stepped out onto a very small balcony. Sam said, "They usually don't have chairs, but the hotel knows what I like."

We sat down on the chairs, and I closed my eyes, my body spinning. When I opened them and looked around, I realized that we had an incredible view: The canal below us, small boats moored next to the back of the hotel, a quiet residential area across the canal, and the lights of Amsterdam above the nearest houses.

Sam put me to bed, and tucked me in, asking, "Would you like me to 'service' you, Miss, before you go to sleep?" I chortled, and shook my head. It was a nice offer, but I was exhausted. Sam leaned over the bed and kissed me. I saw him walk towards the sliding door to the balcony with his pipe, lighter and small plastic pouch in his hand. He smiled at me, and switched off the lights, then walked out onto the balcony, closing the door behind him.

Sam continued to surprise me. My Sam, the person I loved. I couldn't believe that I was falling asleep in Europe. I had dreamed about such a trip many times, and now I would be dreaming within the trip. The last thing I remembered was turning onto my side, and whispering into the darkness, "I love you, Sam."

CHAPTER 7: GOING DUTCH

When I woke, Sam was snoring next to me. It took a few moments, in the dim light, to realize where I was, and when it was: Amsterdam, Thursday morning. I quietly got out of bed, and peaked through the blackout drapes at the view of Amsterdam. There were low clouds, occasionally punctuated colorfully with blue sky. The canal below us was quiet, only a single person rowing along the far bank, the water dark below him.

I took my time in the bathroom, and put on a pair of running shorts, a sports bra and a tank. When I came out, Sam was sitting on the bed, looking around, apparently having just awakened. His hands were in his lap, and I could see that he was stroking himself.

"Good morning, Sam!" My voice was more chipper than usual, and I realized that I was feeling good: Refreshed, no jet lag, energetic, and enthusiastic to see more of Amsterdam.

He looked at me and blinked, "Are you going for a run?" I had been thinking that I might use the hotel gym, while Sam slept.

"That sounds good. Are you interested? I might not find my way back, if I go alone."

Sam laughed, "Of course, you would." He got out of bed, and walked to the coffee table. "Here's a small map of Amsterdam. It's an easy layout, and you have a pass to take any bus or tram. While we're here in Europe, I would like you to be responsible to keep those kinds of things, and a little money, on you whenever we go out."

He smiled at me sweetly, "I don't expect to let you stray very far from me. I will take care of you … but you also have to be ready to take care of yourself." He kissed me, and we hugged – after he lifted the obstruction between us, and nestled it between our stomachs. Sam said, quietly, "I was hoping to make love to you this morning."

Of course, I wouldn't deny him, but I was now ready to go for a run. I had even put one last tampon in, to make sure my period was over. I kissed his nose, and offered, "Let's make love *after* our run." He gave me a sour look, and I added, "But if you'd like a blowjob or a hand job, I would be happy to oblige."

Sam smiled, and hugged me again. I walked into the bathroom, and moistened the corner of a hand towel, and when I re-entered the room, Sam was already lying cross-wise on the bed, still stroking himself. He really couldn't get enough sex; I guess that was a good thing.

He was surprised when I got on the bed behind his head, and then crawled, straddling him, until I was in position, my head above his triangle of dark pubic hair. I briefly flashed on having him submit to me by shaving himself … or maybe I could give him a wax job.

Then, I briefly considered stripping, and making love to Sam right now. But Sam was ready, and I lowered myself onto him, taking him in my mouth, while I slowly lowered my hips, until much of my weight was on Sam. I was not smothering him, but I was low enough to pin him to the bed. As I thrust my hips, I felt his nose, not too far from where it might have done some good.

I enjoyed oral sex and, obviously, Sam did, as well. The thick gooeyness and saltiness of Sam's cum didn't bother me, although it wouldn't be my choice for my first European breakfast. Sam had explained to me that it wasn't a big deal to him if I didn't swallow – no big deal in spitting it out – but that letting him come in my mouth and continuing to suck and lick his dick was the best part of oral sex for him.

I settled in, sucking Sam's length, and taking his frenum between my lips, and pressing them tightly, then moving them, like a cow chewing her cud. I lowered my hips until my shorts were over his face, and I wiggled my butt, as I attended to Sam's other end. Sam's hands were now on my bum, pulling me even closer to him, until I was concerned that he really would suffocate.

It didn't take long, and Sam exploded into my mouth, the jet of cum hitting the back of my throat. I continued to suck vigorously, as Sam writhed under me, thrusting over and over, and moaning softly.

I spit most of the cum into the towel, folded it, and used the previously-moistened corner to clean Sam. Finally, I pushed off with my right hand, and flipped backwards, off Sam. As Sam went into the bathroom, I opened the drapes, entranced by the view; we really were in Europe!

Sam was quick, and we put on our shoes and took the things we needed for the run. It would only be a few miles, so I grabbed the complimentary bottle of water provided by the hotel, and stuffed the map, my *Chipkaart*, and a ten Euro bill that Sam had given me into the pockets of my running shorts. Sam took a bunch of unnecessary stuff (like his phone, GPS, and camera), putting it all into a small fanny pack.

We exited the hotel, walked to the end of the block, and then ran across the bridge over the canal, continuing through a mixed residential and small mom-and-pop store area, arriving a few minutes later, at a beautiful park.

As we turned onto a dirt pathway, and settled into our run, Sam said, "This is *Vondelpark*, one of the biggest parks in Amsterdam, more than one hundred acres, and it's probably the most popular park."

We saw quite a few other runners, a few people on bicycles, and one or two mothers, pushing a stroller. It was only 7:30 in the morning, and the sun was just rising behind us, as we ran down the length of the park. We passed cafes and teahouses, sculptures and fountains, and a large rose garden, before swinging around the far end of the park, and running back – now into the sun that sat just above the trees – on the other side of the park.

When we left the park, and waited at a signal, Sam looked at his GPS and said, "We've only run about 3.5 miles, so far. Maybe it will be four miles, by the time we're back to the hotel. We could run around the park again, but I would like to get to the Van Gogh Museum well before 10AM, so that we won't have to wait in a long line."

I told Sam, "I'm fine. That was a good morning workout, it got my juices going."

As I realized what I had said, Sam smiled at me, and said, "I'll take care of you when we get back ... but let's stop for a small breakfast, first."

The morning was getting brighter, and we sat at a small table on the sidewalk, outside a corner café. We ordered cappuccinos, and Sam insisted that I try the *stroopwafels*, which looked like miniature waffles, or thin, bendable cookies. Utilizing the traditional Dutch method (according to Sam), we rested the stroopwafels on the demi tasse coffee cups and, within a few moments, we took them off, and bit into a delicious combination of baked dough and a thin caramel filling, with just a hint of cinnamon.

It was delightful, sitting here, drinking perhaps the best coffee I'd ever tasted, eating the sweets, and watching the people on the street.

When we got back to the room, we quickly stripped off our clothes. As I was peeing, Sam came in, holding up two of the butt plugs we had bought yesterday. "Which one do you want to try?"

I laughed, "I'll take the thinner glass one; you can take the one that's tilted to stimulate your prostate." When I came out, Sam had already lubed the two butt plugs. He got into the chair position, and I inserted 'his' butt plug, twisting it until Sam confirmed that he was receiving the intended stimulation. I reached under and stroked him, until he was ready.

Then, I bent over the front of the chair, and Sam entered me from behind, sliding in easily, as I had lubed myself with a dab of KY, having taken out the tampon and being too dried out for comfort. I was definitely over my period, the next one not due until after we returned home.

Sam moved against me, with long, slow strokes, pushing deeply into me, and then pulling back, nearly coming out of me. I was just getting into the rhythm, when Sam stopped, and I felt the glass butt plug against my anus. Sam was gentle, as he moved the colorful, ribbed phallus into me and back out slightly, now thrusting his own phallus into me in synchrony.

My holes were filled, and my muscles clenched involuntarily, as I gazed out the windows over the city. When the butt plug was fully inside me, Sam reached around, and slid his hand down to my clit. Sam's hand moved over me with each thrust of his hips, and soon my eyes were closed, my body tingling, and my own hips thrusting back to meet his. I squeezed my hand under us, next to Sam's, and grabbed his balls lightly. I held on while we thrust together, Sam 'holding on' to my clit, both of us moaning, and quickly reaching our dual consummation.

Kelly and I took a short tram ride to the Van Gogh museum, arriving in time to join the other tourists waiting near the front door. When the museum opened, we took our time, moving in an upward spiral, following Van Gogh's artistic career. We also toured the special exhibit in the East Wing of the museum. Stepping out into bright sunlight, the sky mostly blue, with picturesque cumulous clouds floating by, we walked along the park, buying soft drinks and perusing the exhibits of post cards and tee shirts; we bought a couple of them as souvenirs.

Then, I took Kelly to my favorite modern art museum in the world, the *Stedelijk Museum*, on the corner, next-door to the Van Gogh museum. I told Kelly, "This used to be an old-fashioned building, but was in disrepair and closed down by the fire department. The entire collection was moved to a temporary location near *Centraal Station* and the harbor, but it's finally back here, in this ultra-modern building."

We enjoyed walking through the modern art exhibits, and had snippets of discussions about art, history, and philosophy. Then, we sat in the museum restaurant, where I suggested we sample a couple more Dutch delicacies. We got a plate of *krokets*, along with a beer for me, and a Diet Coke for Kelly.

The croquettes were deep fried, with a meat ragout in the center. They were filling, and I decided that we would be having a late lunch. Kelly bit into one of them, and burnt her tongue on the filling inside; steam was pouring from the opening she had made with her teeth. I had forgotten to warn her. I dipped one into some mustard, and bit carefully through the breadcrumb outer layer, savoring the meaty sauce inside.

As we would be having a late lunch, I took Kelly across the street and down a couple of blocks to the *Concertgebouw,* the famous concert house, where we were able to purchase tickets for the lunchtime 'practice session'.

The concert was nice, mostly Mozart, which was refreshingly light, compared to some of the other music I'd heard here, including Mahler. At the end, there was an organ piece by Jan Sweelinck, one of the few famous Dutch composers.

This was a nice way to begin our tour of Europe; in fact, what a nice first morning! We had taken a run, tasted some Dutch treats, made love, seen some incredible art, and were now seated in a fancy concert hall hearing beautiful music. I reached over and held Kelly's hand, as the organ piece concluded.

We took a tram to *Leidseplein*, where we sat at one of the outdoor tables, under a dark green umbrella with the name of some beer or other in white letters. I'd had a beer with the *krokets* – a great combination. But I decided to quench our thirst further, and try another delicacy - *bitterballen* (which was very similar to the *krokets*), before taking a walking tour of the area.

Kelly joined me, and we clunked our mugs together, and sat back in our chairs, watching the trams go by, people walking in every direction, and small throngs of tourists watching the street performers in the square.

Now feeling a bit mellower, we walked a few blocks around the area, and I showed Kelly streets with restaurants of all nationalities lined up, block-after-block. Most of these were tourist joints, and I probably could have been happy with a plate of spaghetti for lunch; but I wanted to share more traditional Dutch specialties with

Kelly. I felt pressured, as our time here was limited. It would really take a week or more to see the city properly.

We continued walking, alongside a canal, and I asked Kelly if she knew about Anne Frank, the Jewish girl who had hidden out in an attic to avoid being found by the Germans during World War II. Kelly had heard the name, but wasn't sure about her story.

"Anne had been given a diary on her 13th birthday, in which she documented her experience hiding from the Germans. Although Anne and her family lived more than two years in hiding, they were eventually discovered, and deported to concentration camps, where only her father, Otto, survived.

"When he returned to Amsterdam, friends gave him the diary that Anne had written, which he eventually published, Anne's story being told around the world." By the time we bought our tickets and began touring the house, I was in tears; it happened every time I came to this emotional place.

After the Anne Frank house, we continued a short distance further, and walked around the *Jordaan* district, a renovated warehouse area, now very upscale neighborhood of art galleries, shops and restaurants. I was tempted to stop for a typical Indonesian lunch of *nasi goreng* or *bami goreng*, basically fried rice or fried noodles, respectively, with shrimp, chicken or other toppings. There were also some very nice bistros from which we could choose.

But I kept my plan to introduce Kelly to some *real* old-Dutch food, not available very many places in Amsterdam, any more. We took a short tram ride, and walked down a street with expensive clothing shops, interior design stores, hairdressers, and assorted other businesses. Then, we entered a nondescript restaurant that I knew still served some of the traditional dishes.

Kelly tried the *stamppot* (mash pot), a combination of mashed potatoes, peas, sauerkraut and endive, topped with a *rookworst*, a traditional smoked sausage. I had the similar *hutspot* (shaken pot), a tasty but filling combination of mashed potatoes, carrots, onions, and bacon.

I told Kelly, eruditely, "The '*hutspot*' was originally made from whatever was leftover. When it was brought to England, it became 'hotchpot', which was a jumble of available ingredients, mashed together. That is the origin of the word 'hodge-podge'." Kelly nodded, as she dug in to her dish.

She looked up at me, "This is delicious, but I'm already getting full." She took a sip of her Diet Coke, and I toasted with my beer mug.

"You don't have to eat it all – I just wanted you to try it. These dishes aren't available many places any more." Then, I chuckled, "And there are several more dishes I would like you to try." I glanced at my watch – it was already mid-afternoon.

"But we might not make it to that good restaurant tonight; maybe we can put it off until tomorrow." Kelly was nodding vigorously, and put down her fork, clearly filled to capacity from the meal; and all the snacks we'd already eaten this morning.

We walked out of the restaurant, and I wasn't sure which direction to turn: There were great sights all around us, and we had to set some priorities for the day. "Kelly, there are so many things to see here, that we can't possibly cover them all on this trip; and, tomorrow, maybe we can take the train to a few other places, outside Amsterdam. I'm happy with anything you want to do."

Kelly looked at me blankly, "I'm happy now, and would be fine with anything *you* select. You know the place, and I'm happy 'submitting' to your whims." She batted her eyes at me.

I chuckled, "OK, if you want some 'whims', how about this ..." We walked to the center of a bridge, stood next to a mass of bicycles, and looked at the beautiful canal scene in front of us.

"The most famous museum here is the *Rijksmusem*, which is huge, and has the 'Night Watch', and other important Rembrandt paintings. It also has rooms of Dutch culture – textiles, and other stuff. But it's back towards our hotel, at the beginning of the *museumplein*, where we were this morning. And, I'm getting museumed-out." Kelly nodded. We actually had only seen two museums, plus the Anne Frank house ... and the concert house.

I continued, "But if we skip that for now, we should at least visit the Rembrandt House, which isn't too far from here. I love his etchings." We started walking in the direction I had suggested.

Kelly looked sideways at me, and asked, "Etchings? Is that like when you asked me to 'come with you to your boudoir'?"

I laughed, "No, in this case, the etchings are real. But after visiting Rembrandt, we can skip the other museums ... although I really wanted to show you the Maritime museum, also ... and maybe go to a typical Dutch sauna." Now, Kelly smiled. We turned onto another small street.

"That sounds like fun," Kelly said, adding, "And I think I might be starting to feel a little jet lag."

I laughed again, "Just wait another 48 hours – Saturday afternoon. That's when it will hit you the worst. But we'll get some chances to relax. I've got our timing 'wired'." Kelly just shrugged, and we kept walking.

Kelly did enjoy Rembrandt's House. We covered it thoroughly, but didn't linger. Then, we walked toward *Centraal Station*, passing through the *Nieuwmarkt* area, where locals had rioted to prevent the construction of a highway through the neighborhood, settling for a metro stop, instead.

We made a slight detour, and visited the Erotic Museum, which was small but interesting. They displayed an incredible variety of erotic drawings, prints, paintings, and sculptures. Kelly and I studied a few of them, wondering whether we could get into those sex positions, and whether they were shown in the *Kama Sutra*.

Then, we entered a room with erotic photographs, many from the early 1900s, featuring women masturbating, spanking each other, and wearing leather or latex suits. It was perfect fare for Kelly and I, and we spent considerably longer here than we had at the Rembrandt House museum.

A little more 'pumped up', we continued our walk, crossing a canal to the *Oudezijds Voorburgwal*, the original old wall of Amsterdam – the 'dam' on the Amstel River. Kelly looked up at the arched windows and towering spires of 'the old church', a landmark of Amsterdam.

I explained to Kelly, "This has been the main church of Amsterdam for 800 years. All the famous people came here, like Sweelinck, the guy who wrote the organ music we heard earlier today – he played here all his life, and is even buried here."

As we walked into the church, I whispered, "And, Rembrandt came here often – it's the same now as it was when he saw it 400 years ago." We walked around the impressive space, looking up at the arched wooden ceiling, and around at the intricate and colorful stained glass windows.

We squinted, as we exited the church into a bright sunny day, the clouds having burned off, somewhat rare for Amsterdam, this time of year.

Walking just a few more blocks, we came out on the main drag across from the train station, and were lucky to catch the bus to a district north of Amsterdam in less than five minutes. This would not only expose Kelly to a very 'local' and quaint area, but also to her first Dutch 'sauna' experience. She would learn that I wasn't the only one enjoying hedonistic pleasures with disregard for clothes.

I gazed out the window of the bus, as it wound north, into industrial areas, picking up people off an early shift, then driving through residential areas and several villages, past empty fields, and finally bearing left into a small village, where Sam and I got off, and started walking – north, again.

The village thinned, and we were walking down the main drag – in fact, the only, very narrow road – along an extension of the village. Between the charming and all different, houses, I could see that to our right lay empty fields, and to our left was a narrow body of water – a lake, or canal, maybe.

We continued to walk, Sam leading the way, as my mind wandered – perhaps feeling the beer I'd had this morning, the jet lag, or whatever. At lunch, I'd only had a Diet Coke, but I was still spinning. I let my mind drift, as we kept walking up the road, passing cute houses on either side, each with a manicured yard.

As usual with Sam, it had been a whirlwind: Two museums, a special exhibition, and a concert in the morning – this was after our run and breakfast stop! I was stuffed, from lunch and also from all the snacks we'd eaten.

I would have to start watching my weight, if I kept up this lifestyle. Sam had been an incredible tour guide: He not only knew the layout, without looking at a map, but could also give me the history and meaning of most of the things we saw and sights we visited.

I took Sam's hand, and closed my eyes, as we walked together down a sidewalk through the picturesque village. I visualized some of the phallic pieces we'd seen at the Erotic Museum. I saw the vaulted wood ceiling of the old church. And then, unbidden, for reasons unknown, an image of my parents formed in my mind's eye; looking at me lovingly, sweetly, kindly: My birth parents. A shiver ran down my spine.

Sam's hand pulled me to the side, and I stopped, and opened my eyes. Sam looked at me, neutral, awaiting my comments, respecting my thoughts, and caring about my feelings. I hugged him, long and hard, closing my eyes, and spinning, again. Why had I thought of my birth parents? I suddenly became emotional, but I wasn't sure why. Sam held me, as I took control of myself.

We continued walking in silence; north, always north, the wind-swept water to our left, a magnificent blue sky with puffy clouds dominating this old-world village.

Sam pointed, and we finally approached an industrial-looking building – not exactly what I had pictured as the sauna that we would be visiting on our first day in Europe. We walked up the steps, and entered the lobby. We were the only ones in the reception area, and the road had been empty of cars and pedestrians, but the parking lot outside the concrete building was nearly full.

Sam paid, and took two thick towels, two robes, and two pairs of flip-flops. He smiled and thanked the receptionist behind the desk in Dutch, which she seemed to accept; then she thanked us for coming – in perfect, nearly accent-free English.

I followed Sam through the double doors, into a small locker room. There was a woman, sitting at a narrow counter in front of the mirrored wall, drying and combing out her hair; she was wearing a nude-color bra, and had a towel around her waist. She looked up at us briefly, and smiled.

Sam looked at something in his hand, and searched for our lockers. We went down a couple of rows, passing a handful of men and women in various states of dress – or undress. Finally, Sam pointed, and handed me a plastic bracelet with a small key, with which I opened a locker.

We undressed, hanging our jeans and tops on the wiry coat hangers, and leaving everything else on top of our shoes at the bottom of the locker. Sam put a one-Euro coin in each of the locker doors, and closed them, saying we would get the coins back, when we re-opened the locker. We sat on a bench, on our towels, and I mimicked Sam, as he put the plastic bracelet with the key around his ankle and buckled it, turning the key horizontally, along the bracelet.

Then we stood, put the towels around our waist, and exited the locker room, carrying our robes, which we hung on a row of hooks on the wall just outside. Sam pointed, and I nodded, as we each entered a tiny toilet room, coming back out together a minute later. We had barely walked into the main area, when Sam headed to the left, hung his towel on a hook, and entered the shower area. We each took one of the tiled shower positions, Sam standing next to an older woman – probably older than him – and me next to a girl about my own age; she was beautiful, with perfect breasts and long blond hair.

I was suddenly a tiny bit jealous ... but I didn't know why. I probably should have put my hair up, but had left it long. As I soaped myself, I glanced at the 'girl next door' again: I had more defined muscles than her, but her slight extra bit of fat made her look more rounded, somehow more sensuous. I had once seen a gigantic Rubens painting, which had shown even more-rounded Dutch beauties: Rubenesque. The girl next door was trim, but still had curves in all the right places. Her skin was nearly white – obviously, she didn't get out in the sun, much.

I turned, and watched Sam, his eyes closed, as he turned around and around under the water gushing from a rectangular showerhead. His eyes popped open, and he gave me an inquisitive look; I shook my head and shrugged.

As we walked out of the shower area, we grabbed our towels, and again put them around our waist. The next stop was a footbath, half a dozen people sitting on the ledge, their feet in a shallow, tiled pool of lukewarm water. One couple was chatting quietly, but everyone else sat in silence. I leaned over to kiss Sam, and he gave me a quick peck on the nose, but shook his head. I guess showing feelings was inappropriate here.

We rose, and walked a few feet, leaving our towels on another hook, and each entered a tiled vertical silo, in which there were various shower heads at different levels – very similar to the leg jets in Sam's downstairs bathroom. I turned one of the knobs, and was shocked when cold water poured on me from above. I quickly turned that off, and cautiously tried some of the leg jets. I was starting to get chilled.

Sam exited his shower stall, and we took our towels and turned the corner; this place was quite large, and there were dozens of people in the open area. Sam pointed to the nearest sauna room, and I nodded. There was a red digital readout above the door that indicated '85°', obviously Centigrade; at 100°, we would boil, literally. Sam held the door open for me, as we both quickly entered the darkness, and then he pulled the door shut. It took a few moments for our eyes to adjust, and I realized that we were in a huge sauna, perhaps twenty feet across, with three tiers of curved benches formed of wooden slats similar to the ones in Sam's sauna.

There were probably a dozen people in here, a few sitting as couples, or partners, others lying on the top bench, their head on a wooden triangle. As Sam had instructed me, everyone had a towel under every part of their body – the people sitting letting their towel fall to the lower bench, with at least enough horizontally so they could put their feet down without contacting the wood of the lower bench.

Sam and I walked across the sauna to the other side, and climbed up to the top bench. Sam positioned his towel and sat on the bench, while I spread my towel, and sat cross-legged, facing into the sauna. It was much darker in here, than in Sam's sauna, but my eyes were finally getting used to the dim yellow light. Sam pointed, and I leaned over and inverted one of the sand dials on the wall.

Closing my eyes, I again saw my birth parents, in black-and-white, formally dressed, and staring at me, as if from a picture. I let my head loll forward, as images flew through my brain: Of my adoptive parents, my brothers, my girlfriends ... and Sam. The warmth felt good, and beads of sweat began forming all over my body.

As drips of sweat rolled from my forehead, I wiped my face with the corner of my towel. The sauna was silent, save for a few crackles of the rocks in the sauna heater. Sam's eyes were closed, his face relaxed and his mouth forming a contented smile. I looked at the hourglass of the sand dial, and saw that we had been in here nine minutes. I moved down to the bench on the second tier, again arranging my towel and sitting cross-legged.

I took my time to survey my surroundings and, especially, our sauna 'companions'. There were several old men, and a couple of old women – much older than Sam, perhaps in their 70s, or maybe 80s. There was a couple, probably in their 30s. And, there were several women, most likely in their late 30s to late 40s. There were many different body types, but everyone seemed comfortable in their skin.

Sam tapped me, and I nodded; we stood, walked down the benches to the tiled floor, and exited the sauna. There were showers next to the saunas, which we used to rinse off the sweat and cool down. We carried our towels – letting them hang in front of us, for a minimal show of modesty – and walked outside to the deck. There were more showers, a small cold pool, and a huge swimming pool. We left our towels on a deck chair, and entered the pool; it was cool, but not uncomfortably so, and felt very refreshing after the sauna.

The sky was still blue, with puffy clouds, and the air temperature was nice – just slightly cool. Looking away from the building, we saw open fields, with dozens of sheep. Sam explained that these long narrow strips of land, demarcated by narrow waterways, were 'polders', or reclaimed land, kept from flooding by the dikes, as they were below sea level. It was a very pastoral and calming scene; almost like a painting.

We swam a few laps, and floated around the pool. There were only a few other people in the pool with us, most somewhat older – perhaps from their late 30s to their late 50s. But there were also a couple of cute girls, around my age, sitting on the steps, talking quietly. As I side-stroked toward the steps, one of the girls looked up and smiled at me. "*Goede middag*," she said, with a guttural voice.

I smiled, and said, "Hi!"

The girl shook her head and said, in perfect English – with perhaps a very slight British accent – "Oh, I'm sorry. Hello! I thought you might be Dutch. Are you visiting Holland?"

I swam over and sat on the steps, giving me time to look at them a moment longer. They were both cute, and both had medium-length hair, one nearly blond, and the other a sandy brown. As they moved to a higher step, I could see that their full, but firm breasts were nearly identical. In fact, I had noticed that nearly all the women had similar breasts – at least the younger ones. My breasts weren't much different than those of the Dutch girls.

"I'm visiting – in Europe for the first time. My partner," pointing at Sam, who was still in the deep end of the pool, floating on his back, "is giving me a tour; we have three weeks, but will only be seeing a few places. Actually, this is our first full day here – we flew from the U.S. yesterday." Or had it been two days? Or three? It sure seemed like we'd been here more than a day!

One of the girls smiled and nodded, "That's great. I hope you have a good time here. We have some unique things to see and do in Holland."

Smiling, I said, "You mean, like the saunas?" I let my arm swing around, pointing at the beautiful surroundings, totally different than the old streets and buildings, and *tourists*, in Amsterdam.

Now, the women were shaking their head. "No, going to a sauna is normal, throughout most of Europe. I mean like the great art, the historical architecture, the fantastic local food," She stopped for a moment, and looked at me strangely, then continued. "And the sex clubs." Now, *that* was a surprise. Not that every big city didn't have sex clubs, but it seemed strange that she would mention them.

I pretended to be naïve, which I was. "Sex clubs?" I noticed that Sam was slowly swimming our way.

The other woman explained, "Amsterdam can get pretty wild ... if you know where to go." Then, she laughed, "There are places that specialize in just about every sexual persuasion – from gay and lesbian, to transgender, and a variety of fetishes."

Now, I had to smile; I couldn't play dumb much longer, as I wanted to elicit more detail. "Fetishes?"

Both women smiled and nodded. "Yes, like dungeons for BDSM play." She glanced at her friend, "It's really very interesting. But you have to be into it, or you probably wouldn't understand." My hand went down between my legs, disappearing under the water made choppy by a few swimmers.

Should I share with these women? Why not? I would probably never see them again, and they wouldn't have brought up such a subject, unless they had *some* interest in it. I think. I glanced at Sam, now floating in the middle of the pool. "Actually," I couldn't help but smile broadly, "my partner and I are into BDSM, a little."

The girls smiled, and put on mock shocked expressions, and I explained, "Sam is into spanking and submission." I gulped, wondering whether to go on ... but the women just looked at me with interest, and nodded slightly. "And medical fetish." Sam had said the Dutch were tolerant, but I wasn't sure what to expect, after my revelation.

Now, the other woman piped up, "Nice. We're into the scene, too ... although it's just the two of us, as our husbands won't 'play' with us." They both laughed, in a pained way.

"But they're OK with you guys going to the clubs? And having sex with other people?"

Both women shook their heads brusquely, "*Yes*, they're OK with us going to the clubs, but *No*, we don't have sex with other people. Greetje likes to tie men up, and I like to whip them. Not usually at the same time." The women laughed.

I looked at the other woman, "Your name is Greetje?" I pronounced it like 'Great ya'.

She nodded, "Yes, like 'Greta'. And this," pointing to her friend, "is Sofie." I nodded, and Greetje explained, "I'm into 'Kinbaku', the Japanese art of binding people – sometimes, now called 'Shibari'. I'm a wizardess with rope; it's really an art form."

Sofie snidely remarked, 'Yeah, and it sure beats macramé!"

We all laughed as Sam swam up to us, and we introduced each other. "Sam, this is Greetje and Sofie. They're into BDSM." I knew that would have an impact. Sam gave me a questioning look, and I nodded, adding, "They go to sex clubs, and tie-up and spank men."

I gasped, and hoped I hadn't made a mistake: Not by letting the women know about Sam or him about them ... but, I wondered whether just bringing up this subject would give Sam a hard-on ... *not* something that would be well-accepted at the sauna.

Sam smiled at Sofie, and calmly said, "Well, I wouldn't mind letting you spank me, sometime."

The women chuckled, "If you're in town long enough, I'm sure that can be arranged." They gave Sam the 'once over' with their eyes. I felt no jealousy, just pride.

We all got out of the pool, and headed inside, the women going into one of the saunas, Sam and I getting into the jacuzzi. The warm water felt great after the relatively cooler pool. I smiled at Sam, "Well, that was a coincidence! As wild as Amsterdam may be, there can't be *that* many people going in for BDSM. Can there?"

Sam shook his head slowly, "I don't think so. The Netherlands is really a very conservative country." I could see thoughts flitting through Sam's head, and knew he was trying to devise a plan where we could meet-up with those women in a setting more suitable for playing around. But we only had today and tomorrow in Amsterdam, and then would be visiting Sam's friends somewhere to the south, near Utrecht. I also wondered whether Sam would really allow Greetje to tie him up.

We got out of the jacuzzi, and went into another sauna, this one up a flight of stairs, and having a panoramic view of the polders that stretched to the horizon. The jet lag was hitting me again, and I lay on the top bench of the sauna and closed my eyes.

A few minutes later, I was startled by a group of four people entering the elevated sauna, evidently two young couples. I sat up, and rubbed my eyes, then wiped the sweat from my face. We all smiled at each other, and the two couples chatted quietly. The *other* thing I had noticed about the people here at the sauna, in addition to the consistent-looking breasts of the women, was the uncircumcised penises of the men; I think Sam may have been the only circumcised man here.

Sam decided to wake me up, so after boiling in the sauna for a while, we walked downstairs, and outside, where Sam jumped into the cold pool. He came up bellowing, but finally found his voice, "This is very refreshing. Come on in!" I felt the water with my big toe, and it was freezing – almost literally. Sam wanted me to try it, and I wanted to submit to him ... voluntarily; before he decided to ask me to submit formally, and jump into the pool.

I slowly lowered myself down the ladder into the cold water. As I got to my waist, I let myself fall, submerging entirely, before I popped back up next to Sam, and screamed. Then, I promptly climbed up the ladder, and onto the deck, looking around for my towel.

I'm not a screamer ... but the water had been shocking. I didn't wait for Sam, when I realized that my towel was inside the door, at the bottom of the stairs to the glassed-in sauna. I went through the door, grabbed my towel, and climbed the stairs up to the sauna. Greetje and Sofie were the only people in the sauna; they sat on the middle bench against opposite walls, their backs against the wall, and their knees up. I'm sure Sam would like the view – and I wasn't thinking about the panorama of the polders.

Sam followed me into the sauna, and we climbed up to the top bench. We chatted with the women a while longer, answering their questions about what we'd seen in Amsterdam, and where we would be traveling on the trip. Then, we all went downstairs and got into the showers. I noticed that Greetje, with the blond hair, was bare down below, while Sofie, with the brown hair, had a neatly trimmed landing strip of dark pubic hair. My 'do' fit in perfectly, and I was glad that I had done the waxing.

The women headed toward the jacuzzi, while Sam led me back to near the lockers, where we swapped the towels for our robes. We then walked back into the main area, and up a few stairs, into a bar and restaurant area, where we took a table next to a wall of glass that overlooked the sauna facility and, through it's glass wall, to the pools outside, and polders beyond.

Sam ordered an eclectic mix of snacks, and I doubted that we would make it to dinner, tonight. It was a Thursday night after work, and the sauna was getting more crowded; looking through the glass to the floor below, there had to be more than a hundred people here now. All were nude, and all were comfortable with their bodies ... although some of them were far from perfect (I thought this, as I noticed a couple of *very* heavy women walking toward the jacuzzi, below).

Our first course came – the *erwtensoep*, also called '*snert*' – traditional Dutch split pea soup. It was steaming and delicious. Before we were half done with the soup, a plate of *loempia* was served – Southeast Asian spring rolls. They were very good, also.

Then, as a large plate was set on the table, Sam said, "I thought about getting the 'satay' – the Indonesian skewers with peanut butter sauce – we'll get those when we have a *rijstaffel*. But I wanted to check out the farmer's plate – a selection of sausages, cheeses, olives and cornichons."

I picked up one of the sausage sticks that Sam said were called *frikandellen*, and tasted it; it was very good ... until Sam said, "Please don't ask me what goes into it." I put my *frikandel* down, and tried one of the cheeses, which was also good. I ate another loempia, and was stuffed.

We walked out to the deck, still wearing our robes, and looked out at the polders, the sun now very low on the horizon. Sam asked me whether I would like to take another 'course' of sauna, and I shrugged, "It's been fun, but I wouldn't mind getting back to Amsterdam. Especially, if we have to walk five miles back to the bus."

As we went back inside, Sam laughed, "It's not nearly five miles." He gave me an evil smile, "Probably not much more than three miles. We can walk off the snack, so we'll be ready for dinner, when we get back into Amsterdam."

I gave him a 'look', "I'm not sure I'm going to be hungry for dinner at all, tonight." I hoped Sam wouldn't be too disappointed, as I knew that he savored every opportunity to try new foods during his travels.

We walked into the locker room and, across from us were the two women we had met. One was wearing a thong, and the other was in bikini underwear; both were putting on their bras. Sam turned to them, and asked, "You ladies wouldn't be headed into Amsterdam, would you?"

It turned out they were; saving us a long walk to the bus. Sam and I piled into the back of a Mercedes 450SL and, as the sun set over the polders, we rode back to Amsterdam in style.

Sam offered to take the women to dinner and, I'm sure, hoped to go to a club with them, but the women had to get back home to their families, and dropped us off on the north side of town, where we took a tram back toward the city center. They did, however, hand Sam a business card for one of the sex clubs, with their home phone numbers on the back, and suggested we contact them if we were here on the weekend; they also gave us a few names of the club's managers, and said they would see that we got in and were treated well.

We got off the tram at Dam Square, and turned onto a large canal. It was nearly dark, the sky now deep purple, reflecting in the canal, long fingers of yellow and red lights from the shops and houses above also reflected in the shimmering water.

Then, we turned onto a smaller canal, cars parked along one edge, and bicycles amassed on the other side. Trees lined the canal, and lent a haunting feeling to the place, in the semi-darkness. We walked past restaurants and coffee shops, strip joints and sex shops. The street became more crowded, and I heard an incredible number of different languages being spoken by the people around us on the narrow, cobblestone road.

We now entered Amsterdam's famous red light district, along with about a million other tourists. Slowly making our way down the street, we looked up at window after window, fringed in red and lit in red, a half-naked woman inside – sometimes sitting and talking on a cellphone, sometimes dancing in the window, and occasionally bending over to give the sailors – and tourists – a thrill. Some of the girls could have been cute, had they not overdone the makeup, and had they been wearing real clothing.

It seemed strange: The nude women at the sauna seemed perfectly natural, while these sluts seemed under-dressed, even though they were covering most of their assets. I guess it wasn't fair to call them 'sluts' – prostitution is legal in Amsterdam, and some of these girls were probably students, trying to pay their way through school. But most of them *looked* pretty 'slutty'.

We ducked into one of the many sex shops, and Sam decided that we should each pick out a few items. I selected a combined cock ring and anal plug, along with a prostate stimulator, for Sam, and a set of gold Ben Wa balls and 'double delight' strap-on for me.

Sam picked out a cute riding crop, with a heart-shaped paddle, and a flogger with a clear plastic handle; both of these looked cheesy, compared to the stuff Sam had at home. He did find a nice set of nipple clamps, with chain, and I found myself clenching my muscles. We selected a couple of new butt plugs together, and then we got to the clothing section.

The outfits were cheap, both in price and in quality, but Sam insisted on selecting a few outfits that I could try later, including a black fishnet chemise with matching G-string; a halter black lace dress, also with G-string; and finally a schoolgirl skirt and a nurse outfit. I had no idea how we would get all this into our suitcases. We were again walking with a large shopping bag. At least, it was filled with interesting things; sexy things.

We stopped at one of the famous 'brown cafes', a small, dark space with heavy wood fixtures, and a bar running its length. We sat at one of the few tables, and Sam brought back several things from the bar; then, he went back to the bar, and brought several more things to the table.

Sam pushed a beer, and small, tulip-shaped glass of clear liquid to me. Holding up his glass, he said, "This is *genever*, a juniper berry-flavored traditional Dutch liquor, from which the English developed gin. First, let's take a sip." We did, and it burned my throat; but it did have an interesting aftertaste.

Then Sam smiled, and said, "Now, for the more traditional way." Sam upended the tulip glass, draining it in one big swallow. He set the glass on the table, his eyes wild, and then picked up his beer, and took a couple of big swigs. Then, he let out a satisfied, "Aaaah!"

I looked at my glass, still nearly filled to the rim. Once again, I would 'submit'; well, it wasn't really submission, but trusting Sam, and agreeing to do something that I knew would be uncomfortable, if only for a short time. And there might actually be some pleasure afterward. Like most of the things Sam and I did together.

Picking up the glass, I smiled at Sam, and drank the fiery liquid, my mouth and throat instantly burning, and my stomach suddenly feeling warm. Sam handed me the mug of beer, and I drank it appreciatively. OK, I did that; but I probably won't do it again, anytime soon.

I was fading rapidly, the alcohol not helping. I tried to focus on the plate of food on the table, but couldn't actually make-out what was on it.

Sam pointed, "This is smoked eel, one of the local delicacies." Then, he added, "Although not as local as in Volendam, where you can eat the eels as they come off the boats in the tiny harbor. That's on the *Ijsselmeer*, the huge body of water in the north of Holland." I forked a piece of eel, and put it on my plate. Finally tasting it, I realized that it was quite good – a smoked flavor, like a very delicate version of beef jerky. I drank a swallow of beer; I was tired.

"Here's to your first day in Amsterdam!" Sam held his beer up, and I 'clinked' his glass, finishing the rest of the beer in mine. Had we really been here only one day? It felt like a week ... at least considering the number of things we had done; and all the things we'd eaten. The sauna had been a nice relaxing interlude. I just hoped that Sam wouldn't suddenly get the idea to go to a club tonight.

We walked to the tram, Sam insisting that we 'clean our mouths out' with some gelato. It did taste good, after the genever and eel. And perhaps it would give me enough energy to get back to the hotel, before crashing. Sam was right: The flavors of the gelato were strong, vibrant, compared to those in most of the American ice cream.

The rocking of the tram lulled me to sleep, Sam having to shake me awake at our stop. He offered to carry me the remaining three blocks to the hotel, but I found enough reserve to get there under my own power. But as soon as we entered our room, my clothes came off, left where I dropped them on the floor. I walked into the bathroom and peed, watching Sam get undressed and hang his clothes in the small closet just outside the bathroom. I brushed my teeth, and took a look in the mirror; I wished I hadn't.

I walked into the room to find Sam sitting on the couch, taking out our cache of sex toys and clothing from the bag. As I continued past him toward the bed, Sam held up one of the pretty glass butt plugs. "May I see how this fits you, tonight?"

I mumbled "Umm hmm. Unless you wake me up." I smiled inwardly.

Sam came over and stroked my hair, "Are you really that tired? We rested most of the day at the sauna!" I smiled and kissed him. Then, I decided to give Sam five minutes of my beauty rest, and turned over into a knee chest position. I felt the dildo slide into my rear, my anal muscles relaxed, as did the rest of my body. When the butt plug was in, Sam moved it slowly, and I let my knees slip until I was lying on my stomach, my head on the pillow.

The bed was really comfortable, and I didn't mind the feeling of the thin glass shaft inside me. Visions of the day flitted through my head: The incredible collections of Van Gogh and modern art, the Anne Frank house and art galleries of *Jordaan*, and the view from the sauna: Sheep in the polders, as the sun set.

Sam's hand slid under me, and he tried to stimulate me, but I was out. All I could muster was "Sorry, Sam." And I was asleep.

Kelly was gone; probably a combination of jet lag and the alcohol we'd consumed. And it *had* been a long day. We'd covered many of the essentials of Amsterdam, but I felt guilty that we wouldn't have time for so much more that the city offered. I didn't want to rush the trip, but we had a limited amount of time. Perhaps I was pushing Kelly too hard?

I turned off the room lights, and sat on the balcony, wearing a hotel robe. I had closed the door to the bedroom, and hoped it would open again, or I would be in trouble. I lit the pipe, and took a long toke of the sweet, but pungent, smoke from the hash. Ah, Amsterdam!

I looked down at the canal, now reflecting a distorted image of the nearly full moon. It *was* a beautiful city, that offered an incredible range of experiences: Not a bad introduction to Europe for Kelly. I took another puff and smiled – *I* was enjoying it too. I went inside, and tried out some of the toys on myself, in the dark, before climbing into bed next to Kelly.

Visions of the day filled my head: Running in *Vondelpark* with Kelly, visiting the erotic museum, walking through the red light district and shopping in the sex stores; and meeting two women who enjoyed BDSM and spanking. My hand slipped under the sheet, as I drifted off, thinking about what *might* have happened, had the women wanted to 'play' tonight.

CHAPTER 8: DRESSED FOR SUCCESS

We woke together, and lay for some time, looking into each other's faces. Without averting her gaze, Kelly reached over, and held me, and I realized that we hadn't properly made love since the night before we left on the trip – three nights ago.

Kelly rolled me onto my back, and straddled my hips, taking me in her mouth and finishing the preparation. Then, she inserted my length into her, as she sat on me, adjusting her position slightly one way and then the other, and moving up and down on my rigid member. She fell forward onto me, and I held her tightly, as we moved our lower bodies in counterpoint, savoring the feeling of being joined with each other.

As we finished our morning rituals, Kelly asked, "Are we going to go for a run, today?" She held up her running shorts.

There were so many possibilities, but I made a snap decision. "How would you like to go for a run on the beach?" Kelly's eyes widened, and she nodded enthusiastically. We packed our backpacks with our supplies, including towels from the hotel, underwear, jeans, and a t-shirt, and walked to the tram stop. We took the tram to *Centraal Station*, and a train to the nearby town of Haarlem.

Walking across the square to the bus station, we found that we had twenty minutes until the next bus to the beach.

My mouth watered when I saw a *poffertjes* stand. I explained to Kelly that *poffertjes* were small, but thick pancakes – more like small muffins – served with a lump of butter and covered with powdered sugar.

We ate the delicious sweets off a paper plate, stabbing them with a wooden fork. And, we drank traditional Dutch coffee, although probably not the best example, coming from a streetside stand. We also bought a couple of bottles of water that we stashed in our packs.

The bus took us to Zandvoort, the south end of a national park – mainly consisting of sand dunes – that borders the beach. We stood on the bluff, surveying the 180-degree expanse of North Sea, which looked cold, with mist or fog limiting the visibility out to sea, and low clouds overhead.

As we walked one of the many trails through the dunes down to the beach, passing only a few hikers and runners, I informed Kelly, "On a nice weekend day in the summer, this beach can get crowded; all the nice beach restaurants and bars are packed."

We finally stepped onto the beach and, looking south, I said, "Zandvoort beach stretches five miles to the south. There are many outdoor restaurants, and a *naturiste* – nude – beach a couple of miles south of the town. But we're going to run to the north, along the national park. Then, we can explore the dunes, and maybe have some lunch, before heading back to Amsterdam."

Walking along the beach, hand-in-hand, we passed several empty restaurants. Hundreds of chairs were set out for the weekend, but it was still a bit nippy for a beach day. We continued north, beyond all of the 'civilization', and sat down by the bluff.

"We can run from here. If we're really energetic, we can run to the North Sea canal, where all the ships pass on their way to or from Amsterdam; it's probably only about six miles from here. Then, we could walk through the park trails. But it may be close to ten miles by the time we get back to the bus stop."

Kelly shook her head, "I don't know if I'm that energetic today, but we can try."

We took our water bottles out of the packs, and sipped a little. Then, we began our run, slowly at first – getting warmed up, and then settling into a pace that could get us to the canal in under an hour. After 20 minutes, we took a short water and pee break. As we started running again, a young couple passed us, running the other direction, nude.

I glanced at Kelly, and she shrugged; the morning was getting warmer, and there was virtually nobody on the beach. We took off our running clothes, stuffed them in our backpacks, and continued north. I let Kelly run slightly ahead of me, and admired her beautiful body; I never tired of the sight. Kelly's muscular legs carried her gracefully over the ground, her bottom moving rhythmically, her long auburn hair swinging across her back, its tips reaching to below her waist.

We saw more beach cafes ahead, and walked to the bluff to put on our clothes. Kelly said, "I'm really too big on top to run without a bra; it's not very comfortable." We sat down, and drank from our water bottles.

Then, Kelly stood, and exclaimed, "I haven't come all this way to the beach to not go in the water. She ran across the wide beach, down to the water. It was quite calm, small waves breaking farther out, and foamy white water flowing onto the beach, and ebbing back into the sea. She turned and waved, and then waded into the water, getting much farther than I had expected, considering the water temperature.

So as not to be an old fuddy-duddy, I walked slowly to the water, letting it cover my feet. Kelly bent down, and splashed water onto me, but instead of splashing back, I rushed her, and kissed her long and hard.

As we walked back to our packs, I said, "I considered tackling you, so that we would end-up lying in the water, rolling around and kissing, like those scenes in some of the old movies. But I didn't think you'd appreciate getting your hair wet and salty."

Kelly laughed, "You're just a baby – afraid of a little cold water. I saw showers next to some of those restaurants, so I'm sure we could get salt off, if we really wanted to lie in the water." Then, she stopped laughing, and said, seriously, "But it *was* a little cold. And it's getting a little windy." She smiled sweetly at me, "So I guess we can continue our run."

We got dressed again, and ran to the end of the beach – the south dike that formed the entrance of the North Sea canal. We ran partway back to the national park, then walked, cooling down. The breeze dried our sweaty clothes, as we climbed one of the trails into the park. We followed meandering trails, heading mostly south, and finally came back out onto the beach, where there were several restaurants.

Kelly turned suddenly, and I saw that there were some open showers. She put her backpack down, and took out her clothes. Then, she stepped onto the concrete pad, pulled off her running shirt, and started to take off her sports bra. "Would you like to be a gentleman, and hold up a towel for me?" I always liked being a gentleman.

I held the towel horizontally, but it didn't hide much of Kelly's body; fortunately, there were very few people around, and nobody was coming down this particular trail to the beach. Kelly took off her sports bra and running shorts, tossing them toward her pack. Then, she took a quick shower.

I wrapped her in the towel, and she dried off. She pulled up her underwear under the towel, and put her arms into a fresh bra, letting go of the towel, and completing the maneuver, now standing in bra and bikini panties without having exposed herself.

She pulled on a t-shirt, and stepped into her jeans, then bent down, and handed me a brush, as she finished buttoning the jeans and buckling her belt. I looked at the brush, and back at Kelly. Smiling at me, she chided, "No, silly, it's not for *that*."

I hit the flat back of the brush against my palm; it smarted. I sighed, thinking again what could have been, and brushed her hair, from the bottom up, being careful to not pull the knots. It took several minutes, but looked beautiful when I was done, the brush sliding easily down from roots to tips. Then, Kelly held a towel for me, while I rinsed off under the shower, and got dressed.

We walked over to the first restaurant, and sat at a small table just in front of the building. Kelly and I checked out the menu, and I ordered – an *uitsmijter* and Diet Coke for Kelly, and an order of *rollmops* and a beer for me.

The *uitsmijter* was basically a fried egg, ham and cheese open face sandwich, now usually eaten for breakfast or lunch, but originally made for late-night bar-goers, before the proprietor threw out his patrons and closed down for the night.

The *rollmops* were pickled herring filets, rolled around pieces of onion and pickle, and held together with small toothpicks – delicious, but perhaps not the most breath-freshening food. It had been a pleasant morning, even invigorating, with the exercise of the run. We finished our snacks and walked to the bus, finally getting back into Amsterdam around noon.

As we had come back via *Centraal Station*, we walked the short distance to the National Maritime Museum, and the three-masted sailing ship from the Dutch India Company. The building dated from the 17th century, and I was shocked to see that, inside, it was an ultra-modern complex; it had been completely renovated since I'd last been here. We enjoyed the special exhibits, and learned a lot about the history of Holland's romance with the sea.

I knew I would feel guilty if I didn't take Kelly to the *Rijksmuseum*, so we took the tram, and got off at *Museumplein*. Kelly followed me, as my nose sniffed out a *pannekoeken* stand, where we each ordered one of the plate-sized pancakes, nearly as thin as a crepe, and wrapped around one of a multitude of fillings. Kelly selected a traditional apple pannekoek, and I ordered, a bit more adventurously, a pannekoek with Camembert cheese and chicory. Now, I *really* needed to find some breath mints!

We went into the museum and saw the Rembrandts, and many other examples of Dutch art, as well as some of the arts and crafts, textiles, and other exhibits highlighting Dutch culture. I didn't think it was as interesting as the Erotic Museum had been.

We walked out of the museum and up a path through the huge triangular grass area behind the string of museums. The afternoon was warm (at least, for Amsterdam), and we decided to spread our towels, and relax, like dozens of other people scattered around.

As I sat down, my cellphone rang: It was Henk! We spoke for a few minutes, and then I gave Kelly the rundown. "Henk is coming into Amsterdam tonight – going to a special club. He isn't sure that we'll want to go to the club, but he wants to meet us there, and then we can decide. He didn't tell me exactly what kind of club it was, but he said that I would be shocked."

I laughed, "Now, you *know* that there's not much that will shock me. So I have no idea what he's talking about, but it should be interesting. Zöe won't be coming tonight; Henk said they would pick us up tomorrow morning, and bring us back to their place. We'll stay there over the weekend, and then leave Monday morning to start the driving portion of our trip." Kelly nodded, her eyes closed, as she lay on her towel on the grass, the sun now bright.

I offered to take Kelly to more museums, walk around the parks and gardens, or even go to one of the local saunas here in the city. Even our hotel had a sauna ... but I wasn't sure if it was 'mixed' – men and women together, without clothes.

Kelly suggested that we head back to the hotel, and I realized that this might be the first time that we could try some of our new toys. It seemed like I had been a little 'sex starved' lately, although I couldn't blame Kelly for that. Perhaps I was becoming – or had already become – a 'sex addict'?

Back in our room, we unpacked our packs and Kelly started pulling things out of the shopping bag – where I had put them, after a little 'playing' of my own last night. I sat out on the balcony, taking a few puffs of the hash; it didn't take much, since I wasn't used to it, having not smoked for many years ... except at Kelly's birthday party, when Julie had pulled out the little plastic pipe and lit up.

I heard the door open, and turned to see Kelly, standing in the doorway, in a sexy pose, and even sexier outfit: The black fishnet dress we had bought at the sex shop last night. It was incredible, almost entirely see-through, except where a pattern of solid black – perhaps dragons or animals – covered a small amount of her.

Kelly's full, but firm, breasts made the dress look even more incredible: She had exactly the type of body that filled the dress as sensuously as it could get. The black G-string was clearly visible through the dress, and the hem of the dress barely came down to the bottom of the tiny triangle of black material.

Kelly turned around, and I found myself drawing in a huge breath: Two thin straps came down from her shoulders, and held up the fishnet, which was entirely see-through in the back. As she was wearing a G-string, her bottom was brazenly on display, only a single, thin horizontal line of the string interrupting the view of Kelly's backside. It was a little shocking, even though I'd seen Kelly nude for the past six months. Kelly ducked back into the room, and I took another couple of puffs on the pipe.

Again, I heard the door open, and again I looked back to see Kelly – now, in the second dress we had bought her. Well, it looked more like lingerie; nobody would actually go *out* wearing something like that. Again, it was black, and mostly see-through, although there were black 'flowers' of material that hid more than the fishnet had.

The top was a deep scoop, and Kelly's breasts now sat in more of a fitted, bra-like part of the dress, her contours – especially her hips – beautifully outlined by the dress. There was a thick black band of ruffled material, cut very high on her left hip, and running diagonally down her thighs; it looked Spanish. I could see the G-string underneath, but it was not as apparent, the black ruffled hem covering much of it.

Then, Kelly turned around. Shocking, again: With thin, diagonal straps high on her back, and a low-cut scoop at her lower back, the dress was almost totally see-through, the flower pattern thinner, and not hiding much. Again, I could see the horizontal line of the G-string around her waist. I got up and stood in the doorway, taking Kelly in my arms, my mouth on hers.

We walked back into the room, and I whistled, "Boy, that's sexy!"

Kelly rubbed her body on mine, like a cat rubbing against someone's leg; she batted her eyes at me, and said, "Do you like what you see, mister?" I couldn't get undressed quickly enough. Kelly took off the dress, and pointed to the nurse outfit, questioningly. I shook my head, and pointed to the heart-shaped riding crop, the flogger, and the Ben Wa balls.

Kelly shrugged, smiled, and assumed the 'standing position', her legs apart, hands on her head, looking straight ahead, seriously. And then, she started cracking up. Her hand came down to cover her mouth, and she bent over, coughing, but I could tell she was nearly apoplectic about something. She stood up, put her hands back on her head, and said, "Sorry, Sir!" only laughing a little as she tried to get the words out.

I pointed to the bed, "On your back, young lady, knees to your chest!" I was surprised when Kelly made a detour, but understood, when she brought the towel from the bathroom and laid it on the bed. Then, she hopped up on the bed, lay back, and pulled her knees to her chest, as I had instructed; all the while trying to stifle a laugh.

I picked up the toys from the coffee table, and walked to the bed. "Would you like to explain what's so funny, young lady?"

Kelly sputtered, "Well, the 'heart-shaped' crop, for one." She continued to laugh, her body rolling a bit on the bed. I put the other toys down, and raised the crop so that Kelly could see it. Then, I brought it down on her bottom, close to the towel. Kelly let out a little shriek; but continued laughing.

I held her legs against her chest, as I gave her another two dozen snaps of the crop against her now-reddening bottom, making them much stronger at the end. "Ow! Ow! Ow! That really hurts!" Kelly cried; but she wasn't crying; she was still laughing – although she was now rubbing her moist eyes. Moist from laughing, or crying; or both. I admired my handiwork: There were now red hearts all over her bottom.

I lubed the Ben Wa balls, and showed them to Kelly. She nodded, and I carefully inserted them into her vagina; they were quite large and heavy, solid metal, with a gold finish. Kelly squealed, "Those are cold!" I would have to remember in the future to warm them, first. I picked up the flogger by its heavy plastic handle, some two dozen thin strips of leather – probably faux-leather – hung down, and I dragged it over Kelly's genitals, up her stomach, and over her breasts.

Kelly cooperatively held her legs further apart, as I let the flogger do its work – swinging it lightly across her breasts, and then vertically down her body, covering the insides of her thighs. These strokes were light enough to make Kelly's body tingle, and not hurt too much.

I climbed onto the bed, and swung the crop carefully, so that the ends of the leather strips landed on her anus and perineum. Kelly again squealed. She wasn't laughing any more, but was very quiet, holding her legs, and controlling her breathing, her eyes closed.

Increasing the strength and speed of the flogging, I slowly moved the flogger so that it was falling on Kelly's exposed bottom. I got off the bed again, and flogged her from high to low, the leather strips landing lightly on her vulva. Kelly was moaning softly; by now, I could tell the difference between a 'moan' and a 'groan'.

I separated her labia, which glistened with secretions. I let the flogger fly a few flings further, onto her fecund feminine flesh, Kelly first flinching, then feeling her flaps flutter and her fears fade, as she fell freely through her consciousness.

Then, I put the flogger down, and lowered myself between her legs, kissing her ravenously. I showered small kisses down her body, over her breasts, on her navel, and down to where it really counted. Then I went down on Kelly in earnest, licking and lapping, sucking and biting.

Lifting my head, I put my hand under her, and pushed up repeatedly against her perineum; then, placing my hand over her vulva, I pushed rhythmically, morphing the motion into a gentle slap. We clearly heard the clicking of the Ben Wa balls inside her. I went down on Kelly again, swirling my tongue around her clit.

Then, I put two fingers inside Kelly, my knuckles against the Ben Wa balls, and the pads of my fingers against her G-spot. I had wondered whether I would need to take out the Ben Wa balls, but everything fit inside Kelly, tightly. Kelly's body contorted, and I adjusted the position of my fingers until I heard a purr; perhaps Kelly *was* more feline than I had realized.

I held my fingers against her sensitive tissues inside, while my other hand covered her outside, the heel of my hand putting light pressure on her hood, and moving it in tiny circles. When we had begun, I assumed that I would be making love to Kelly, just using a bit of oral to get her going. But I decided to focus on Kelly's needs, and perhaps give her a new experience.

I very slightly increased and decreased the pressure of my fingers pushing on her G-spot, and Kelly moaned. Her body started moving, rhythmically, in waves, her hips rising to force my hand harder against her hood. I slightly lessened the pressure of my fingers, and Kelly relaxed her body. Repeating these steps, I was able to keep Kelly 'on the edge' for several minutes.

Finally, she began squirming, and I knew that she was ready. I increased the pressure of my fingers inside her, alternating the pressure between them rapidly, as if playing a trill on the piano. I quickened the motion of my other hand over Kelly's clit, without increasing the pressure.

Kelly moaned loudly, then thrust her pelvis up, a low howling sound coming from her lips, as I pushed both fingers deeply into her G-spot. That did it: Kelly thrust her body repeatedly, squirting clear liquid several inches, onto the towel. I followed her cues, as she continued to thrust, her vaginal muscles squeezing my fingers against the metallic spheres. I took my hand off her hood, and put it under her, pushing her perineum rapidly, until it was vibrating, the balls making a continuous clicking sound. Kelly screeched, panted, and said, "OK, Sam. That's enough! I can't take any more!"

I took my fingers out of her, then climbed up her body, until my mouth could reach hers. We kissed briefly, but Kelly was out of breath, her eyes closed, arms straight out to each side on the bed. I kissed Kelly on the nose, and said, "Was that your first 'squirting orgasm'?"

Kelly's eyes opened, and she looked at me curiously. "Is that what happened? Was it pee?"

I shook my head, "I don't think so; it was a clear liquid. I'll have to read up on it more, but I always wondered whether there was really such a thing as a squirting orgasm."

Kelly smiled, "Well, I don't know what it's called, but it felt incredible." She lifted her arms and reached around my neck. "Thank you, Sam." We lay together, Kelly's breathing slowing gradually. A few minutes later, Kelly giggled, and said, "And now it's your turn. We can do anything you want."

Wow! It was another irresistible offer. "Actually, Kelly, I would just like to make love to you. Maybe you could get me ready using that new 'prostate stimulator'."

Kelly laughed, "Is *that* all? You can't imagine how much strength and submission it took to make that offer." We both laughed. But I understood Kelly: She was *trusting* me to not be too hard on her ... and was willing to show her *submission*, if I did want to do something challenging. There certainly was no issue about openness, any longer, and there hadn't been for at least four months.

I offered, gallantly, "Would you like me to take those metal balls out of you?" She didn't answer immediately, and I added, "Or would you like to do a few jumping jacks?"

There was a loud laughing cough, and she said, "You may do it if you like, Sir." I inserted my fingers, Kelly pushed a little, and I retrieved the first ball. Then, my fingers eased in farther, and Kelly pushed again, so that I could grab the second ball. Kelly got up, taking the Ben Wa balls with her into the bathroom.

I went to the coffee table, and opened the prostate stimulator, a strangely-shaped plastic device, then lubed it, and carried it to the bed, setting it on the towel. I got up on the bed, and into a knee-chest position over the towel, and waited.

Kelly returned a couple of minutes later and, without saying a word, put the prostate stimulator against my anus. I relaxed, and it slid in easily. Kelly twisted the device, moving it around, and pushing it in still further until, at one point, I gave a loud, involuntary moan. I closed my eyes, as Kelly kept the device in position, rocking it around as it pressed repeatedly into my prostate. It was a great feeling, augmented a moment later by Kelly's hand reaching under and taking hold of me, stroking expertly.

I really hated for this to end, but also really wanted to make love to Kelly. "I think I'm ready, Kelly." It wasn't a subtle hint, but it would have taken only a few more strokes before I came. I turned over onto my back, and Kelly mounted me, inserted my throbbing shaft into her, and leaned forward, moving herself on me as I slowly plunged myself, upward, into her.

I hadn't been inside her for more than two minutes, when I had a massive orgasm – my tensions leaving me instantaneously, as I relaxed back into the bed.

We got dressed – me in my typical 'business casual' attire, with a lightweight jacket; and Kelly wearing a cute black dress ... although the leggings she put on didn't enhance the outfit's sexiness. But it was going to be cool tonight, and I wanted her to be comfortable. I didn't feel as though I needed to impress Henk with Kelly's beauty: He would recognize it without my help, and regardless of what Kelly chose to wear.

There was plenty of time, so I brought Kelly out to the balcony, and pulled out the pipe again. I wasn't going to force her, but after I lit up, took a couple of tokes and handed it to her, she followed suit, drawing in the aromatic smoke and holding it for several seconds before exhaling. I distracted her, so that she wouldn't think about how much smoke she was getting. "Kelly, what did you think about our tour of the Red Light district, last night?"

Kelly coughed out a lungful of smoke, and gasped, her eyes wide, "That's what I wanted to ask *you*." I wasn't sure I understood, so waited for Kelly to elaborate. She explained, "With your concepts of openness and sex, I was wondering what you thought about prostitution." Kelly looked down at the pipe in her hand and said, "I felt sorry for those girls. Although, I realize that they're just trying to make a living." Kelly took another puff, and passed the pipe back to me.

I'm not sure I had fully-formed thoughts about prostitution, but tried to work through my feelings as I explained, "I think a woman has the right to do what she wants with her own body; as long as other people aren't being hurt." I looked at her, "Like bringing home an STD to your family." I took a puff, finishing the last tiny piece of hash that I'd bought.

"I think a woman has the right to have sex with whomever she chooses, and also has the right to charge for it." I chuckled, "I actually feel sorry for the 'Johns' – I have never paid for sex, and never plan to; I think guys who have to get sex from a prostitute must be pretty pathetic."

Kelly argued, "That's not really fair. I can think of a number of reasons why a guy can't get sex from a normal partner, and feels the need to use a prostitute."

I nodded, "OK, maybe. I think guys also should have the right to pay for sex ... but I just can't understand why most of them would do that."

Kelly laughed, "Sam, I think it's been easier for you to get sex than a lot of other guys." That wasn't really true: I'd been married for twenty-five years, so hadn't *tried* to get sex from anyone for most of my adult life. Until recently; and I had been very *lucky* to find Kelly.

I continued, "And I don't think that most prostitutes are suffering 'degradation' by their clients. Of course, I'm not talking about unwilling prostitutes – the young women who are kidnapped and turned into prostitutes. But the girls you see in the windows here in Amsterdam aren't being degraded, unless they're doing it to themselves. And

I doubt that any of them would say that they feel degraded by their customers, or their profession."

I chuckled, "As you can probably guess, I would be all for 'free sex', if there were no STDs – or pregnancies, or emotional problems – as a consequence."

Kelly shivered, "I don't know. I'm very open about sex. Your friend, Henk, for example: If he was cute, and asked me, and you were OK with it, I would probably make it with him ... and he's a stranger. But the thought of having sex with *anyone* who paid me for it is disgusting." She pronounced my friend's name as 'heenk', when it was just like the American 'hank'.

I was surprised at this turn of the conversation, "You're saying you would have sex with Henk and you haven't even met him?" I accented 'hank', subtly letting Kelly know the correct pronunciation.

Kelly shook her head, "No, I'm saying that my emotional perspective changes dramatically, depending on whether I view sex as something fun, versus something that you have to do, to make money. And, whether you can pick someone that turns you on, or have to make it with any guy that comes along." Neither of us made a joke of the 'comes' in her statement.

We left the discussion there, and left the hotel, taking the tram, and getting off at *Leidseplein*. After watching the street performers for a while, we walked several blocks, past dozens of restaurants.

I offered Kelly, "I know a good Italian restaurant nearby – not one of the touristy ones. But, if you'd rather, there are Argentinean steak houses, Japanese restaurants, and almost everything in-between. We could eat barbeque, Mexican, Chinese, or Middle Eastern food. Henk said that we would be going to an Indonesian *rijstaffel* restaurant on Sunday."

Kelly licked her lips, "Italian sounds great." Then, she added, snidely, "I think I must have had just about every Dutch snack food, and I'm ready for a good meal." She was wrong about having tried nearly everything, but we were both ready for a nice dinner. I had considered picking one of the classic Dutch fine-dining establishments, but agreed that we should take a break from Dutch food.

Our dinner was very nice, typical Italian fare. We both selected a salad and pasta, leaving the heavier dishes – sausages, chicken, or veal – for another time. We drank an *Amarone*, and Kelly was surprised at how good the wine was. I told her a little about some of my favorite Italian wines – some of which were on a par with the Bordeaux.

I explained Henk's background – as marketing executive for the pharmaceutical company that I worked for. I related to Kelly the visit that Henk and Zöe had made to see Sarah and I shortly before Sarah's accident. Although we had gone in the jacuzzi and sauna together, I'd thought that Zöe had been a little stand-offish with me.

I told Kelly that, based on her comments, Zöe was bisexual, and may also be into some fetishes, although I had no idea what they might be. I wasn't sure about Henk's relationship with Zöe, but knew that they slept together, and they'd been together for more than five years.

My summary of Henk was that he was a consummate professional, respected within the company and the industry. I admitted that I might have been rash to share my lifestyle and fetish interests with Henk, but he hadn't reacted badly. As I had explained to Kelly, the Dutch were very tolerant, and Henk was no exception.

We walked towards the club that Henk had suggested for our get-together, the lights of the city lit and reflecting in each of the canals, as we crossed the bridges over them. The streets were more crowded, now that it was Friday night, although it wasn't even eight o'clock, still early for most of the restaurants and clubs. As we walked, Kelly whispered, "Sam, I'm still really high."

I laughed, "Don't sweat it. You don't *look* stoned." Kelly just shook her head.

We found the bar, '*de Nieuwe Vrouw*', which I translated, 'the new woman'. It was just one more bar, café, or restaurant of thousands that looked almost the same. I wondered how someone living here selected a bar; or someone living out of the city, and needing to pick a place for a meeting, selected one.

I held the door open for Kelly, and she walked in, me following close behind. It wasn't that dark inside, but the walls had strange artwork, and musical instruments hung from the ceiling. There were a few tables by the window, some long communal tables, and a high banquet along the right side of the long, narrow space. At the far end of the room, to the left, was a small stage, complete with a curtain and microphone on a stand. There seemed to be a lot more women in here than men. Evidently, Henk had not arrived, yet.

As I put my hand gently on Kelly's back, pushing her forward toward the bar, looking for a good table, I heard a loud, and high-pitched, "Sam!" I looked around, unable to detect where the voice had originated. We took another step into the restaurant and, from our left, by the front windows, I heard, "Sam! Over here!"

I looked at the woman sitting at the corner table; she was now getting up, and started walking toward us. She was somewhat cute, in a horsey sort of way – long face, thick hair, tumbling over her shoulders, and, from her cleavage, big on top. She wore a red dress that came down below her knees, and her makeup seemed a bit overdone; I wondered briefly, whether she might be one of the local prostitutes.

Then, a jolt of electricity passed down my spine, and my whole body convulsed. "Henk?" The woman was not a woman at all: She was Henk! My knees were weak, and I hoped we could sit down soon. I still wasn't sure what I was seeing; *who* I was seeing. Maybe, it was Henk's sister? A hand stretched out to me, and I shook it, unbelieving. My mouth was open, but that was the least of it – I felt faint, disturbed, in shock.

The woman turned to Kelly, and said, "Hi, I'm Helga. I'm Henk's alter ego; actually, Henk is *my* alter ego." Kelly shook his – her – hand.

Kelly said, "Pleased to meet you. Sam's told me a lot about you." She looked at me and smiled; I thought she might crack up again, as she had in the bedroom a few hours ago. Then, she turned back to Henk – Helga – and qualified her remark, "But, I guess he didn't tell me *that* much about you." We were all laughing, now.

Henk – Helga – replied, "Well, I've only recently 'come out'. And, until Sam retired, we both worked for the same company; a conservative – so-called 'ethical' – company, that wouldn't be happy about having a cross-dressing male executive. I did give Sam some hints, when I visited him, but I guess he didn't pick up on them."

He – she – turned to me, and said, "Come on, Sam, let's sit down and have a drink, and I'll try to introduce you to *my* 'fetish'." Then, to Kelly, "Come sit next to me, Kelly." They slipped into the booth in the corner, and I followed, and sat next to Kelly, still dumbfounded.

We ordered drinks, and I calmed myself. I wasn't critical of, or bothered by, cross-dressers ... but I just hadn't pictured Henk in this way. It took some re-training of my brain. I looked around the bar, and back to Kelly and Henk. Usually, I would be delighted to sit between two beautiful women ... but in this case, I was glad to have Kelly as a 'buffer'.

That caught me: I didn't need a buffer; I was a mature, open-minded, and liberal man. I certainly would accept my friends, no matter their sexual preferences. We all had our stories ... and, it appeared, fetishes. I finally found my voice, "I'm sorry, Henk. Helga. It was just such a surprise. My brain couldn't reconcile the information from my eyes with it's memory bank." I looked at Kelly, and back to Henk, "So, tell us."

Henk chuckled, "When Zöe and I visited you and Sarah, you told us all about your fantasies and fetishes, and where they came from. Mine is pretty obvious: I was eight years old, playing in my parents' room, and went into my mother's closet, where I put on some of her clothes.

"As I tried on different things, I became turned on – possibly for the first time; I can't remember ever getting turned on before that. I sat on the floor in her closet, imagining different things ... and that has stuck with me, and molded my perceptions of what turns me on, ever since then."

Kelly ventured, "Helga, may I please ask you a few questions? I'm really interested in learning more."

Henk – Helga – responded, "Of course, Kelly. Ask me anything." Henk glanced at me and smiled, "And, like Sam, I will be open and honest with you."

Kelly smiled, and looked down, obviously trying to organize her thoughts. I was still trying to organize my own. Kelly asked, "Are you gay? Do you get turned on by men or women?" My shock seemed to have been renewed, as I listened to the exchange.

Helga – Henk – said, "No, I'm not gay. I'm interested in women. Zöe and I have a bit of a strange relationship, as we're both heavily into our own things, but we still consider ourselves a 'couple', and we certainly have sex together."

Now, Henk – Helga, looked down and smiled, "Although when we're making love, I'm sometimes fantasizing about wearing women's clothes." He quickly added, "Of course, Zöe is aware of that. We know each other quite well – probably as well as most married couples. And we've thought about getting married ... but neither of us is ready, yet." He looked at Kelly, "So, I'm definitely heterosexual."

Kelly asked, "Do you feel like woman ... or that you should have been a woman? Is there a 'sex change' in your future?"

My friend laughed, "No, no, and definitely not! I'm not transgender." He looked around the bar, "Some of these girls *are* transgender – in various stages of their transsexual transformation."

Then he looked back at Kelly, "But I'm comfortable being a man. I just get turned-on by wearing women's clothes. Actually, by 'being' a woman, for a while. Sometimes, I dress up and just watch television at home. It's just a 'feeling' that it gives me. A turned-on feeling, that I first felt when I was eight years old, in my mother's closet."

Kelly stared at Henk, I mean Helga, and I could see that she was ready to answer more questions. Kelly obliged her, "So how do you do it? Make yourself into a woman, I mean?" A waitress brought another round of beers for Kelly and I, and another Margarita for Henk.

Helga (I finally got it right!) chuckled, and said, "We all have different techniques. And, of course, there are forums where we can share information. But, like Sam, I'm in the medical industry, and have access to things most people don't have." Kelly cocked her head, obviously enthralled by Henk's detailed explanations.

Helga (!) continued, "For example, I use surgical tape, and squeeze my chest together to make this cleavage." He bent forward, and I could have sworn that I was looking at a big-breasted woman's chest. Helga continued, "I've gotten laser hair removal on my face, waxing of my legs, and shaved off most of my body hair. Zöe uses a hair-removal cream on my back."

Then Henk said, "But I've left my pubic hair." He glanced at me, "It's more comfortable for me to go to the sauna, that way, although I don't think anyone would pay any attention." She turned to Kelly and said, "I go to second-hand stores and street sales for most of my clothes, and I've studied makeup styles. And I have a nice collection of wigs and falls."

Kelly asked, "Helga, where are the bathrooms? I should go, before I start on the next round of drinks."

Helga nodded, and took Kelly's hands in hers, "Yes, dearie, I have to tinkle, also. I'll take you." The two of them squeezed out of the booth, and disappeared into the restaurant. I pulled out my cellphone and searched Henk in my Contacts, then added 'Helga' in parentheses. I looked at my phone and had an urge to photograph Henk – Helga. I would have to ask ... her.

I realized I was spinning, and it took a moment to appreciate that my thought about photographing Henk was so that I could show Sarah. That hit me hard, and I sat back in the hard wooden booth, and closed my eyes. As I opened them, and rubbed away a couple of spurious tears, Henk and Kelly were getting back into the booth.

Henk asked, "Sam, are you crying because you've lost a male friend? Don't fret – you've gained a female friend!"

I shook my head, "No, Henk, it's not that. I was thinking about Sarah."

Henk immediately leaned over and put his hand on my arm, "I'm so sorry, Sam. As you know from our e-mails, we were devastated to learn about Sarah's accident. Zöe and I really liked her."

I nodded, and muttered, "Yeah. I really loved her." I looked at Kelly, and she leaned over and kissed my cheek.

Our drinks came, and we toasted to all our varied fantasies and fetishes.

Henk said, "I saw a television program recently, where scientists put a little 'jacket' on young male virginal rats. Then, they were put in a cage with a female rat in heat. The rats copulated, and this was repeated for some weeks. Then, the jackets were taken off half the rats: While the ones still wearing jackets copulated as usual, the ones without the jackets couldn't get it up – they were impotent."

Henk looked at me and smiled, "So that's basically the same as in my case: I feel more 'sexy' when I'm wearing certain clothes." Then he looked at Kelly, and confirmed, "But I can still have sex without wearing women's clothes ... just thinking about them."

Henk looked at his watch, and said, "The music's going to start soon, so let's move up to those seats," he pointed to the banquet, "I think you might find the show interesting." We took our drinks, walked up the few steps to the upper area in the back of the bar, and squeezed into the wooden seat running along the side wall.

The music started – mainly Karaoke or lip-synching, all the performers in drag. It was a pretty good show, singing being the main event, everyone accepting the cross-dressing. I now realized that most of the 'females' in this club were born males.

Henk swallowed the rest of his beer, slid out of the seat, and approached the microphone. He was announced in Dutch, but I couldn't understand what they had said. The lights dimmed, and colored spotlights illuminated Helga; now, she was definitely Helga, as she made sensual movements with her body, and began singing.

As Helga sang a love ballad, with tremendous feeling, Kelly leaned over and whispered, "She's really good!" Yes, he was.

By the time the show was over, it was after eleven o'clock. We left *de Nieuwe Vrouw,* and walked along one of the canals, Helga apparently comfortable walking down the street dressed as a woman; in high heels. I wondered how often she was hit-on.

We turned down a small alleyway, and entered a tiny bar: There was only room for half a dozen patrons at the bar, and there were four tables that sat about ten people in total. The bar was nearly filled but, luckily, one of the tables was vacated as we walked in, and we grabbed it, pulling an extra chair over. Helga told us, "This is one of the great Belgian beer bars of Amsterdam. They have more than 40 of the best Belgian beers."

I loved Belgian beers – sometimes. At home, I usually drank IPA, a very hoppy beer; Belgian beers were on the opposite end of the scale, being very malty. Both types of beer typically came in a high alcohol percentage: 8-12%. I ordered a Kwak, and Helga ordered a Duvel, while Kelly decided to try the Framboise, a raspberry-flavored Lambic beer, the style made before hops were used to flavor beers. Lambic was one of the lowest alcohol content beers, weighing in at less than 3%.

Our beers came, each in its specific glass. Kelly's was a tall, fluted glass with the distiller's name and logo on it, and a gold rim around the top; the head was a pink foam, the beer itself looking like a dark red ale. Helga's glass was the traditional short and stout, tulip-shaped glass, with 'Duvel' stenciled across it in gold.

Kelly's eyes widened, when she saw my Kwak arrive: As usual, it was served in a tall glass, bulbous at the bottom, and widely flared at the top, with a long center section, and held in place by a wooden stand. I lifted the glass out of the stand, and we toasted.

I knew to be careful tipping the glass, as I have gotten a face full of beer when I didn't control the bottom of the glass, and the whole thing suddenly tilting up as I drank. It was similar to the 'half yard of beer' and 'yard of beer' glasses that are sometimes seen in the U.S. Some people use the wooden stand as a handle for the glass, but I've found it challenging enough just holding the glass itself. I savored the malty liquid, as it slid easily down my throat.

We finished our beers, and I realized that Kelly and I were finished; we were fading rapidly. Helga asked, "So are you guys ready to party, now? It's a big Friday night in Amsterdam." Kelly and I just chuckled.

Fortunately, Helga had been joking. "Well, I have a long train ride home – actually two trains and a car," he laughed, "but no busses or boats. We'll drive back and pick you guys up tomorrow morning. How about 10AM?"

Kelly and I looked at each other and shrugged. "Sure, Helga, we'll be ready." My friend smiled, apparently pleased that I was finally calling *her* by name. We left the beer bar, and walked to the nearest tram station, but we were headed in opposite directions. Helga had to go to *Centraal Station* first, then transfer to a train to Utrecht, and then retrieve her car and drive back to her small town. Kelly and I had only to transfer trams once to get back to our hotel.

We climbed into bed, very tired, but at least able to make love. We lay on our sides, Kelly's leg over my legs, and her arm across my chest, as we made love slowly, both of us thrusting toward each other. Kelly got a brief second wind, doing most of the work, and getting herself off, as well as me.

Then, she sunk on top of me, and we pulled the covers over us. Kelly kissed me once more, but her eyes were closed, and she missed. I kissed her gently on the lips, and she whispered, "Good night, Sam."

I drifted off, as my flaccid organ slipped out of Kelly. Although I knew that she was asleep already, I whispered, "Good night, Kelly."

CHAPTER 9: SEX CLUB

Sam and I woke up around 7AM, my body not feeling any jet lag. Sam was used to international travel, but the overnight plane flight and change of time had really affected me. I had awakened during the night, and actually spent several hours doing some research for my project.

We took turns showering, while the other packed for the move to Henk's place. As I bathed, I thought back to our unexpected experience with Henk ... and Helga ... last night. Evidently, Sam had never suspected, and was totally shocked seeing Helga for the first time. I would have laughed at Sam, but was afraid Helga might have taken it the wrong way.

It had been interesting, hearing about Henk's fetish, which I assume is what cross-dressing would be called. I would have to do some Internet research to understand better the differences between a 'cross-dresser', a 'transvestite', a 'drag queen', and a 'female impersonator'. Or, I could just ask Henk ... or Helga. I wondered whether Henk was turned on just by being 'Helga', or whether the showiness, the exhibitionism, also played a role.

We ate a buffet breakfast in the rooftop restaurant of our hotel, taking our time. It was only offered on the weekends, and only for executive members, like Sam. He seemed to have an 'in' with all the hotels, as well as the airlines. The buffet was small in size, but very nice, with various meats and cheeses, pickles and olives, many types of breads and croissants, with a selection of jams, boiled eggs, short fat sausages, bacon, a few types of fish, and several platters of fresh fruit.

After eating our fill, we went back to the room to make sure we hadn't forgotten to pack anything. We sat on the balcony, looking down at the canal, a few boats puttering along; there was smoke rising from chimneys across Amsterdam, as we looked over the rooftops of the nearby houses. It had been a very pleasant stay here in Amsterdam, in spite of my jet lag.

Henk and Zöe picked us up in a gray Peugeot 308 that looked nearly new – probably leased by the company he worked for. Within a few minutes, we were out of Amsterdam, and heading south on the freeway, passing modern-looking industrial parks – one with an IKEA, then a long stretch of polders with sheep. A canal ran alongside the road, and I pointed at a ship.

Henk looked at me in the rear-view window, and said, "Yes, this canal to our left connects the Ijselmeer – the water north of Amsterdam – with the North Sea canal.

I smiled, and proudly informed Henk and Zöe, "We saw the North Sea canal yesterday morning." Henk gave a surprised look, and I explained, "Sam and I ran from Zaandvoort past the national park to the North Sea canal."

Now, Zöe turned to look at me, "That's a long run!" It wasn't that bad, but Zöe's perceptions were different than mine. While Henk was very tall and trim, Zöe was around Sam's height, and solidly built. She had shoulder-length brown hair, and a nice face – almost porcelain white, like some of the women we had seen at the sauna.

We passed the city of Utrecht, and then headed left on another freeway, then a two-lane highway, and finally entered Henk's village, called Driebergen. It was a tiny place, but very nice, with parks, and neat rows of houses.

Sam asked, "Can you take a train here?"

Henk laughed, "No, we're pretty out-of-the-way. I leave my car at a train stop south of Utrecht, where I can get on the highway, and zip home in ten minutes." We drove through an area of condominiums, and pulled into a driveway. Henk's house was a townhouse, nearly – but not entirely – separate from the next-door neighbor. The area was beautifully neat and clean.

We put on our backpacks, and dragged our roll-on suitcases inside. Henk grabbed mine, and bounded up a very narrow staircase, calling "Your room is up here."

I held onto the rail, but nearly got vertigo when we turned the corner after the second floor, and continued up to the third. It was a small attic – a mattress on the floor, made-up with nice linens and big pillows. There was a skylight above, tilted open, to bring fresh air into the room.

Two small windows faced another townhouse, and the street in front. Henk put down my suitcase, and said, "Sorry the room's not bigger. You can use the bathroom on the first floor, or the half-bath on the ground floor."

We went downstairs, and Henk offered us drinks. We all drank small glasses of soda, and sat down on the couch that faced through a wall of glass doors out to a small patio and garden.

Henk glanced at his watch. "Sam, I'm very sorry ... but you know the company. They want me to come in for a few hours for some meetings. I thought I had evaded it, but I was roped back in." He continued, "But Zöe suggested that she take you to a sauna to relax. Then you guys can help Zöe do some marketing, and we'll make a simple dinner at home. We'll need to leave around eight tonight."

Sam and I looked at Henk. He glanced at Zöe briefly, and said, coyly, "We thought you might be interested in visiting a sex club, tonight." *That* was a stunner! I looked at Sam, as his mouth dropped open – again. Before either of us could comment, Henk stood, and said, "I'll be back around four. Zöe will tell you about the club, and you can decide if it's something you'd like to do."

As Henk picked up his keys and headed for the door, he turned and said, "And I'm going as Henk, tonight, not Helga." With that, he walked out, leaving Sam and I with Zöe, who smiled at us, apparently expecting some questions.

I looked at her, and asked, "Sex club?"

She nodded, "Sam told us about his policy of openness when we visited a few years ago, and also about some of his fetishes. We didn't want to say much about our own interests; Henk certainly couldn't disclose that he was a transvestite, and still keep his executive position. And, I'm into a few kinks, myself."

Zöe looked at me sweetly, "Sam introduced you via e-mail, and Henk thought this might fit in with your exploration of sex and fetishes." Sam had told them that we were exploring fetishes? I wondered how 'open' our openness should really be.

Zöe stood, and asked, "So do you guys want to visit one of our local saunas?" Sam and I looked at each other and nodded. It took Zöe another ten minutes to pack a large tote with towels, thin robes, slippers, and some bath supplies. We piled into Zöe's car, a relatively new Suzuki 'Alto', which I'd never heard of.

As we drove out of the village, Zöe explained, "We do have a nice fitness center here," she pointed to the left at some small buildings and a soccer field, "but not a sauna. Tomorrow, we're going to take you to our favorite sauna, not far to the East, but today we'll go to a local sauna, to our West, in a small planned community called Houten."

We got back onto the freeway, drove through an interchange, and got off, turning on to a curving road, which led into an industrial park. Zöe carried the tote, and we walked into the large building. Sam paid the admission, and Zöe led us into the dressing room.

We selected lockers and got undressed. Zöe was a big girl, especially on top; she also had big hips and thighs, but her middle was relatively trim. A silver bar passed through each of her nipples, and an abstract, lacy tattoo extended from one hip, across the small of her back to the other hip. She reached into her tote, and handed us towels and slippers, and we walked out into the huge central room.

The building was an ultra-modern design, with angular wood beams supporting a ceiling of glass panels. The spacious area had slate floors, hanging plants, and chaises, along with several jacuzzis – each tiled in a different color, an indoor-outdoor pool, six different temperature saunas, a steam room, two infrared saunas, and a special room for 'color therapy', with programmed LED lamps changing colors in a soothing pattern.

As per the ritual that I was now learning well, we started by taking showers. Then, we went into one of the jacuzzis. When that got too warm, we moved over to the indoor-outdoor pool, and swam through a small opening to the outside. It was a nice day again, and the grounds looked beautiful, the surrounding wall shielding our vision from the industrial park around us.

We had left our towels inside, but got out of the small pool, and walked over to the main swimming pool, where we floated around for a while. We went back inside, retrieved our towels, and went into the largest sauna I had ever seen, with a wall of glass enabling a view of the outside gardens and pool.

It was Saturday, and there were probably already more than a hundred people here, but Zöe explained that most people come later in the day, after chores had been finished. We tried a couple of other saunas, each set to a different temperature, taking cool showers in-between.

Carrying our towels, we walked outside, past the pool, and to a back area where another three sauna cabins were located.

Zöe asked if we were hungry, and told us that the sauna had a restaurant with some nice salads. It was already getting late, and we would be making dinner soon, so we opted to skip the food, and head out. It took twenty minutes for us to get showered and dressed, and another twenty to get back to Driebergen, where we stopped at the Albert Heijn market.

It was interesting to peruse the items and prices, which weren't much different from home. The market was modern and ultra-clean. Zöe picked up what she needed for dinner. The things in her basket looked more like American fare than some exotic Dutch specialty.

When we got back to Henk's house, Zöe suggested that we get settled, while she started dinner. We retired to our attic bedroom, and unpacked some of our clothes. There were hangers on an open rod along one wall, and we put the rolling cases underneath, laying out the items we would probably need for the weekend; basically, jeans, t-shirts, and one dress, for me.

I had a thin down jacket that had been wadded up, and I smoothed it and hung it up. Sam had said we might go skiing on this trip, and I hoped that the jacket, along with the silk long underwear Sam had bought me, and a heavy sweater, would suffice.

Sam suggested that we use the time we had wisely, and have sex, while Henk was out and Zöe was busy, but I had just taken a shower, and told Sam he would have to wait.

We went down the first flight of stairs, and found Zöe in a small room on the second floor, standing in her bra and underwear, ironing some clothes. Sam and I stood inside the doorway, as Zöe started to explain the sex club. They opened at nine o'clock, and expected everyone to arrive about that time. There was an hour of mingling, meeting people, and matching-up interests. There would be mostly couples, with some additional single females; single males weren't allowed in the club.

Assuming we could find a match for one or both of us, we would retire to one of the special rooms downstairs. Zöe said she hadn't seen them all, but they included several BDSM and dungeon-themed choices. There was a large open area that featured a small stage with a bed, surrounded by comfortable chairs. Zöe said that some people were more turned-on being more exhibitionistic, and others turned on by being voyeuristic; it was a perfect set up to satisfy everyone.

I asked if everyone was expected to have sex, and Zöe shook her head and laughed, "No. Actually most people don't have sex there, although it's fine if your partner consents. Condoms are provided, as well as lubricants, and a limited amount of supplies for each room, according to the theme, even including role-play costumes." Sam looked at me and arched his eyebrows, and I arched mine back at him.

"What are we supposed to wear to the sex club?" I asked, already having a good idea of what I would be wearing tonight. I didn't have that many choices, and although my usual dresses were cute, they were hardly sexy enough to wear to a club.

Zöe chortled, "Well, people come different ways. But most people try to dress in a sexy outfit." She reached over to the chair in the corner of the room and held up a corset, and a very short leather skirt. "I'll be wearing these tonight. But if you don't have anything special, you can just wear a simple dress."

I said, "Actually, Sam and I bought a couple of sexy things in Amsterdam. But I might have to wear a long coat, until I get inside." I tried to visualize how far down the jacket would go, and decided not far enough.

Zöe shook her head, "No, I usually bring a small duffel bag, and we change after we get to the club. They have a nice changing room, similar to the sauna." She looked at Sam, and said, "But men and women are segregated." Then, she added, "Although I have seen men in the women's changing room a few times."

That reminded me of something I wanted to tell Sam; I was surprised he hadn't already asked about it: My experience with Helga taking me to the restroom. I decided to mention it in front of Zöe, to get her take on it.

"When we were with Helga last night," Sam gave me a sharp look, and I turned to him, "What?" He held up his hands in resignation, and I continued, "Helga took me to the restroom. Didn't just *take* me there, but went in with me. We were in adjoining stalls."

I looked at Sam, his mouth now hanging open again. "It was pretty strange." I looked back at Zöe, who continued ironing, "When we finished, we stood in front of the mirror, and adjusted our makeup together. Although Helga uses a lot more makeup than I do."

Zöe laughed, casually, "Yes, I keep telling Helga that she has to go a little lighter on the makeup." She put down the iron, and looked at us seriously, "When Henk dresses up, he *is* Helga. He is a woman; at least he believes that he thinks like a woman and acts like a woman. It's more than an act; it's who he is, at least while he's dressed up and made up."

Continuing, Zöe explained, "But he still recognizes that Helga is not really who he is; only who he needs to be to get turned on. It's not schizophrenia, or multiple personality disorder, since he always knows who he is. But it turns him on to 'be' Helga occasionally."

Zöe shrugged, "But what do I know? I'm not a shrink. I can only go by what I observe, and what Henk tells me. And we have a very open relationship with each other."

We followed Zöe into the master bedroom, and continued talking, while she dressed for dinner. I pressed Zöe further, "Do you mind that he thinks of being dressed as a woman, while he's making love to you?"

Zöe buttoned her top, and said, "Not at all. Most people don't know what their partner is thinking during sex." She looked at Sam and back to me, "Do you know what Sam is thinking, when you're having sex?"

I laughed, "Probably about spanking me, or sticking needles in me. Or maybe spanking my friends."

Zöe spread her hands, her point made. We heard Henk come in, and walked downstairs to meet him. He was very apologetic, his face red. "Sorry guys. I couldn't get away any sooner."

Sam shrugged, and I offered, "We've had a good time visiting with Zöe."

Henk made a pitcher of frozen Margaritas, a taste he had acquired during his many trips to the U.S. We sat on bar stools at the counter, while Zöe made risotto. It was something I had never attempted, as it requires standing at the stove more than 20 minutes, always stirring the pot; in contradiction to the 'watched pot never boils' hypothesis.

Zöe explained that she was making a smoked Gouda and kale risotto to go with the steaks and asparagus. It was amazingly similar to the Labor Day dinner that Sam had made for Alex and I. I helped chop vegetables that Zöe made into a salad, and Henk and Sam took the steaks out to the patio, and put them on a gas grill.

A half hour later, we sat down to dinner. The meal was delicious. Zöe was a very good cook, and made it look effortless. Rather than wine or beer, Henk made another pitcher of Margaritas. When Sam looked at him questioningly, Henk said, "I didn't put much alcohol in them." Then, Henk smiled at Sam, "Unless you're afraid you won't be able to 'get it up' tonight?"

There were chuckles around the table, and Sam muttered, "I'm more worried about *staying* up tonight than getting it up." Now, we were all laughing.

As we sat around the dinner table, our plates empty, I asked Zöe, "Are you guys going to join us? In whatever we're going to do?"

Henk chuckled, and looked at Zöe, who said, "Probably not." She smiled, "We all have our 'thing'." Then, she added, "But let's see who we meet. I think there might be someone there I'd like to play with ... but I'll try to join you, for a while, if I can."

Henk added, "You guys can play with another couple, you can split up and play with halves of other couples, or you could even just play together, if you want to be antisocial." That was funny. With our bizarre lifestyle, it was getting difficult to tell what was 'social' and what was 'antisocial'.

Zöe and I sat at the table, talking about our respective interests, as Sam and Henk rinsed the dishes and put them in the dishwasher. As I explained my research project to

Zöe, I realized that I hadn't once looked at the literature I had collected, and downloaded to my phone.

Then, we went upstairs to get dressed for the club; or, at least, to dress for *going* to the club, where we would change into our 'sexy' outfits. I put on the black dress, black lace bra, and the G-string I would be wearing at the club, along with the leggings. We all looked nice, but not particularly sexy. I wasn't sure what Henk would be wearing, but Sam had selected his black underwear with the two strings holding the front and back at the waist. He also wore a silver tank top that he happened to have for running. Over those, he wore his standard dress shirt and black slacks.

We arrived at the club a few minutes after nine and, soon after, the doors closed, all 40 guests for the night having already arrived and checked-in. The bar opened, and there were light appetizers and desserts on round tables in the corners of the room. The lights were dim, and smoking was not allowed; hallelujah!

We mingled with several different couples, and got some ideas, but nothing specific was discussed. The four of us excused ourselves, and headed to the changing rooms. Zöe and I entered the women's side, and it looked like the dressing room of a strip club, women wearing all sorts of sexy – mostly skimpy – things.

As we got undressed, Zöe told me that she usually wore a full body suit of latex, but would be playing a slightly different role tonight.

In a couple of minutes, I had my dress on – the black halter lace dress that was mostly see-through. I was basically going into the club nude. Well, not exactly nude, as I wore the G-string, similar to a thong. And Sam had told me that women throughout most of Europe went to beaches topless, often wearing a thong. So I was just wearing beach attire.

But, as I looked in the mirror, it didn't *feel* like beach attire. Fortunately, Sam had instilled a lot of confidence in me over the past few months.

I reached for the door, but Zöe called me, from her locker. She was struggling to get into the corset – one, that I now realized had no bra top: Her huge breasts sat on a 'platform' at the top of the corset. I may have been wearing a see-through dress, but Zöe was going out there topless. I helped her tie the corset, and watched her put on stiletto heels. I almost expected her to put on a mask, and hold a crop or whip, but we exited the changing room with only the skimpy clothes, nothing in our hands.

Henk and Sam were waiting just outside the door, Sam in his black underwear and silver tank, looking altogether too casual for tonight's venue; and Henk, wearing tight leather pants, and a leather vest, open to expose his hairless chest.

There was a little chuckling, as we surveyed each other's outfits. I thought Sam would be shocked to see Zöe, topless, in the corset; but then, we'd already spent most of the afternoon together nude. We walked back into the main party room, and took champagne cocktails from a tray carried by a waitress dressed in a French maid outfit, and then started mixing with the guests.

A handsome gentleman in a tuxedo circulated around the room, handing out 'menu' cards, and short pencils with which to mark them. The menu listed a dozen types of rooms, including several devoted to BDSM, each listing specific equipment and supplies, such as ropes or spanking implements. There were several role-play rooms, each with a closet of outfits and accessories. And I noticed two 'medical play' rooms.

I nudged Sam, and pointed to the menu; his eyes opened wider, and he smiled – he looked like a cat with a bird in his mouth. There were other types of rooms that I wasn't sure I understood, such as 'wet play', and 'breath control'. And I saw an 'electrostimulation room', which had equipment similar to what Sam had tried on me, during our first long weekend together.

Most of the couples were younger than Sam, and all of them were older than me. We spoke with several of them, and realized that many of the fantasies were similar; but different people expected more or less, some insisting on 'real' sex, and others just wanting a simple dress-up role-play.

Somehow, we found a couple that seemed compatible: The guy, Max, wanted to role-play, which I would gladly oblige. Max told me that he was mostly interested in age play, in which his wife seldom let him indulge, and couldn't be done at clubs like this. But he would settle for being a teenage boy, and getting spanked for looking up my skirt. Of course, my 'skirt' was see-through, anyway.

Max wanted to be rewarded by watching me masturbate, and then having me get him off. Well, the role couldn't be more perfect for me. I just hoped that the room was soundproof!

And the woman, Brigitte, said she was willing to try a medical scene, including some spanking. That was close enough for our purposes, and we selected rooms, and filled-in the menus with our names. After he reviewed the menus, the gentleman in the tuxedo gave us room numbers, and we went downstairs, finding our rooms with our respective partners. I waved to Sam, as Max held the door of our assigned room open for me.

The room was small, but well thought-out, with a spanking bench, vertical rack, and ropes with carabineers hanging from the ceiling. On one entire wall hung dozens of spanking implements, from leather and wood paddles, to a variety of switches, and birtches, to a bewildering assortment of straps, belts, whips, and tawses, to a collection of canes, from very thin to very thick.

It looked like the BDSM equivalent of a mechanic's wall of tools. Max was looking around the room; he had evidently never been to this club before. I picked up a riding crop – longer, and with a much bigger 'slapper' than the heart-shaped toy we had bought at the sex shop in Amsterdam. I brought the crop down on the spanking bench, a loud 'WHAP!' echoing around the room, and Max jumped then looked at me wide-eyed.

"Standing position!" I commanded. Max looked at me uncertainly, and I said, "Feet apart, hands on head, eyes forward, stand straight!" Max complied, but looked very apprehensive, frightened. I asked, "Max, what is your crime, and how shall you be punished?" I was hamming it up but, perhaps due to the language mismatch, Max took me seriously.

He stuttered, "I've been a bad boy, and need to be spanked. I expect to be crying, my bottom red, before my punishment is over." Well! Max had told me exactly what he wanted. And I would certainly give it to him! As he stood there, waiting, I pulled open the small drawers of the chest in the corner of the room.

I smiled when I saw an incredible variety of butt plugs, lubricants, and accessories, such as clamps, a penis pump, and several small, sharp instruments, such as a Trachtenberg wheel – that Sam had used on me once: Sharp teeth bite into you, as the wheel is rolled along, like a pizza cutter. This was going to be fun!

"Are you in control of your body? Do you need to be bound?"

Max, looked confused, and shrugged, muttering, "I usually am cuffed, either to spreader bars, or to the ropes hanging from the ceiling. It's very uncomfortable."

I looked at Max, unashamedly. He had a hairy chest, and wore cream-colored canvas pants, tied at the waist with a narrow cord. His hair was long and ragged, and he had a two-day stubble of a beard. He looked almost how I would imagine a swashbuckling captain, fighting off pirates. Suddenly, my PC muscle clenched, as I remembered the pirate scene during my birthday party.

"You will not move, unless I command you. Do you understand?" Max nodded tentatively. Sam had taught me a little about building tension. I untied Max's makeshift belt, and let his pants drop to the floor. I nearly cracked up, as he wore underwear almost identical to Sam's, just one string, instead of two. I commanded loudly, "Turn around and bend over. Hold your knees!"

Max did so, albeit a tad slowly, and I selected the largest riding crop from the collection on the wall. I put the leather paddle of the crop against Max's bottom, and he flinched. "If you move, you will surely receive extra strokes!"

I thought that Sam had taught me well; at least this gentleman was submitting to me, and seemed truly frightened of what I might do. I gave Max four hard strokes of the crop, two on each side. Max was breathing hard, but hadn't said a word.

"There will be a 'corner time' after each spanking. I will insert increasingly large butt plugs into your rear." Max turned his head back, and I snapped the crop against the spanking bench again, and said, "You will face forward at all times!" Max snapped his head forward. I then asked, "Have you cleaned yourself out, already, or do I need to administer a couple of enemas?"

Max turned to face me again, and I snapped the crop loudly. When Max turned back, I gave him another four strokes, very quickly. I wasn't playing around. I laughed inside: Well, yes, I *was* playing around. But I had to be convincing, for Max to benefit from our session. *I* was benefitting already, and grabbed a tissue before my juices dirtied my new G-string.

I stifled a laugh, and said, sternly, "You're obviously not taking this seriously, so I'll give you five 4-liter enemas, and then we can get to your spanking." I watched, as Max reacted, whimpering, and moving his bottom slightly, but not complaining.

I hadn't seen any enema equipment in here, and I didn't feel like waiting while Max sat on the toilet, so I decided to begin his spanking immediately. I pulled his underwear down to his ankles, and tapped the insides of his thighs, Max understanding instantly, and spreading his feet further apart.

Without warning, I began spanking Max's bottom with my bare hand. This was a chance for me to try things, gain experience. I spanked Max very hard, learning to bring my hand up from below him, impacting his bum, and following through, just as in sports.

I chuckled as I thought how I was now using some of the sports lessons my adoptive father had taught me. And wondered what he would think if he could see me punishing this poor man. I continued the spanking, having lost count long ago. Finally, I stopped and gave Max a soothing butt massage. He wasn't crying, yet.

I let Max stay in position, as I selected a medium-size butt plug, lubed it, and inserted it roughly into Max's bottom. Max grunted, and whined at first, but quieted quickly.

Grabbing it from where it hung on the wall, I placed a tawse across Max's bottom. He made a squeaking sound, and then I began a barrage with the tawse, with a couple of dozen of strokes raining down on Max's tender bottom. Max was whimpering, now, and sniffling. His bottom was already quite red, but I was far from finished with him; and he knew it.

I instructed him to get onto the spanking bench, which separated his legs, and supported his chest against a slanted pad, positioning him facing a floor-to-ceiling mirror. I found fur-lined cuffs in one of the drawers, and figured out how to cuff Max to the spanking bench, using the rings provided in strategic locations. Then, I pulled the butt plug out of Max, and dropped it into the small sink in a corner of the room.

Surveying the set up, I saw that Max was fixed in position, ready for the rest of his spanking, while his middle was free – bridging the knee rests and the slanted pad against which his chest lay. His penis was hard, and pointing diagonally down. I reached under and stroked it a few times, and watched it bounce under it's own throbbing pressure, when I took my hand away.

Then, I selected a whippy switch from among the implements hanging on the wall, and stepped behind Max. I tickled him underneath with the tip of the switch, and then did a few light strokes, coming up from under him, the tip of the switch striking his perineum; when Max screamed and I realized that the switch had contacted his balls, I moved the switch up to his bum.

Max waited patiently, and I gave him time to anticipate my actions. Suddenly, I brought the switch down across his bum, and Max yelped; a thin red line traversed his already-red buttocks.

I asked, in a stern tone, "Do you like to see women masturbating themselves?" Max nodded, and let out a feeble 'Uh huh', as I placed the switch across his bottom again. "Then how many strokes of this switch will you take, to see me masturbate?" Max whimpered, and closed his eyes. I swung the switch, and snapped my wrist, the long, thin implement impacting Max's butt with a loud CRACK! Max's body convulsed, and he screamed. He was breathing heavily, now, but still not crying.

"I will ask you again: How many strokes will you take to see me masturbate?"

Max cleared his throat and, in a quavering voice said, "Six?" I gave him a cackling laugh, and an immediate six hard strokes of the switch. I had concentrated on making parallel lines on Max's bottom, and did pretty well, although the lines weren't evenly spaced. Max started to weep, and then stopped. I saw a couple of tears fall, and used a tissue to wipe his eyes, as his hands were cuffed to the spanking bench.

I took a handful of his thin hair, and pulled his head up. "Max, I thought you were serious. Do you think I'm *that* cheap? I was thinking more along the lines," I snickered, thinking of the red lines across Max's bottom, "of 40 strokes." I was laughing inside, and wondered how many strokes I would actually give him. As I had learned from Sam, the most important elements of the punishment were the anticipation and tension, not necessarily the amount of pain given.

Max looked imploringly at me, and croaked, "A dozen more?"

I pulled his head up harder, and said, quietly, "I'm going to give you *two* dozen more. I want you to feel the pain, as you watch me pleasure myself. We'll do the first twelve, and I'll give you a peak, and then another twelve, and I'll masturbate for you." Max just stared at me, then closed his eyes, and nodded once.

I let his head drop, and stepped behind him, and to his left. Holding the switch in the air, I instructed Max, "Prepare yourself, and say 'Now!' when you want the first set."

Max took some deep breaths, and released them slowly. Then, in a trembling voice, he said "Now."

The switch flew through the air, landing on Max's bottom with a CRACK! I continued the switching, with one stroke every second, until the dozen were delivered. Max bucked and yelped, but the cuffs held him in position on the spanking bench. When I put the switch down, Max heaved a few times, and groaned loudly.

I pulled his hair gently, raising his eyes to the mirror; and then, I pulled up the netted dress, removed the G-string, and sat on a wooden straight-backed chair that I moved next to the spanking bench, my legs widely apart, my hands going down ... and separating my labia, my pink inner tissues proudly displayed in the mirror for Max.

I moved the pointer finger of my right hand over my clit, then sucked it, raising my eyes to meet Max's in the mirror. He was still sniffling, but his eyes were glued on mine; then, he lowered them slowly, to watch, as I held my labia apart with my left hand, and inserted a finger into my wet cunt.

I was trying to act 'sexy' more than trying to get myself off, although I certainly planned to do that, after Max had taken the rest of his switching. I watched Max look at me hungrily, even licking his lips literally, as I moved my finger in and out of myself, occasionally gliding up my pink butterfly to the hardening knob of my clit. Then, I closed my eyes, continuing to move my finger, and started to actually get turned on.

Deciding this was enough reward for Max's first dozen strokes, I stood, and picked up the switch again, stepping into position behind Max. He looked beseechingly at me in the mirror, and let his head drop.

The door unexpectedly swung open behind me, and Zöe entered the room. I had asked her if she wanted to join us, but she had thanked me and politely refused, as she was smitten at that moment, up in the bar, with a punk-looking girl with blue hair. Evidently that hadn't worked out ... or maybe it had worked out very well? She smiled at me, and closed the door behind her.

Max's eyes were wide, as he looked up at Zöe in the mirror; I didn't know if it was the sight of her in the corset, her huge breasts hanging over it, or just the fact that another 'mistress' would join the fun. The expression on Max's face almost looked like terror. Perhaps they had 'played' together previously? Zöe leaned against the door, and I decided not to torture Max with any more waiting.

"OK, Max. It's time for your second dozen strokes. Let me know, when you're ready."

Max lowered his head, and breathed in deeply, quickly saying "Now." in a quiet voice.

I made this set short, but intense, letting the switch fly as quickly as I could, while still delivering reasonably hard strokes. The series of loud 'CRACK!'s sounded like machine gun fire. Max's body bucked, and he squealed, almost continuously, the pitch getting higher, as the last few hard strokes connected with his striped bum. Now, Max was weeping softly.

I assumed that he had received the pain he needed, and now I would finish 'doing' myself, and then masturbate him. It had been a relatively easy – and fun – experience for me, Max having been totally cooperative; not that he could have done anything else, being bound to the spanking bench.

Zöe looked alternately at Max and me, and said, "That looks like fun! Can I try it?" With that, she snapped the switch out of my hand, and began tanning Max's already-red hide. Max screamed and cried, but this only served to further excite Zöe.

I was getting ready to suggest to Zöe that Max had had enough, when she put down the switch, and lifted her foot, and addressed Max, "Suck my toes. Now!" She said it commandingly, but in a much softer tone and at a lower volume, than I had expected. Zöe was an artist: She was simultaneously soothing Max and humiliating him.

Max did as he had been bid, and I realized he'd done this before many times, taking much more pain and humiliation than Sam and I had ever dared to inflict. In fact, we *never* humiliated each other; embarrassed, maybe, but it was always civil, even dignified.

Zöe lowered her foot, and put the other one up for Max to lick, and he seemed to relish the opportunity to make her happy. I hadn't really discussed with Max his limits, assuming that he would let me know; and that was probably right. But had I never tested him the way Zöe was, now.

I whispered to Zöe that I had promised to masturbate for Max, after his last switching. Zöe stepped away from Max, and I sat on the chair, legs apart, labia separated, and started playing with myself again.

I was surprised – and suddenly excited, in a very sexual way – when Zöe turned to me, and chided, "You've been lax! I told you to punish your charge, and it looks like you were just playing with him." Zöe gave me a look that I took as meaning there was still a choice in whether I would 'play the game'. I stared at Zöe, and gave her a very slight nod. She smiled, and said, "And now you're playing with yourself!"

Louder, now, Zöe commanded, "Stand up, and bend over. Now!" I slowly stood, put my legs on either side of the chair, and bent over, holding the sides of the seat. Suddenly, I was the one being punished. As I held my position and faced forward, staring at Max in the mirror, Zöe carefully instructed, "I'm not going to bind you, as you've done Max. You should already know your job, and you'll take your punishment, as you deserve."

I was now a little worried, having seen the power of Zöe's strokes on poor Max's bottom. I felt the switch across my bottom, slowly sliding sideways, back-and-forth, then nothing ... and then I heard the 'swoosh', and immediately felt a burning pain across my bottom – like a hot knife cutting me. I screeched, but held my position.

Zöe whispered, "Good girl!" Then, she rubbed my bottom, somewhat dulling the searing line of pain. I heard her walking to the wall, and taking down another implement. I closed my eyes, and hoped it wasn't the cane. When I felt the tawse across my bum, I was relieved; I knew I could take a good tawsing, as Sam had proven.

Without warning, Zöe swung the tawse, and it landed with a WHAP! on my backside. There was pain, but not nearly as sharp as with the switch. A few seconds later, there was another stroke; then another. I didn't count, but the tawsing went on for a long time, and my bottom was definitely sore now.

Finally, my bottom got a respite, as Zöe put the tawse down. I heard her moving around, and glanced over my shoulder to see her putting a condom on Max, who was still in position on the spanking bench.

Then, Zöe stepped behind me, and said, "Let's get this finished, and then we can give Max the caning he deserves." I was *shocked*! Both at the fact that Zöe was going to spank me more, and that she was going to cane Max. I thought he'd had enough, but he didn't complain upon hearing Zöe's pronouncement.

Zöe repositioned both the chair and me, so that Max could see the tawse against my bottom. Then, Zöe began tawsing me, again taking her time, and thoroughly covering my bum and upper thighs. When it was over, she hung the tawse, and said, "That's 40 strokes. I hope you have learned your lesson!" Then, "You may get up, now."

I slowly stood, turned to face Zöe, and assumed the standing position. "Thank you, mistress! For the spanking that I deserved." Zöe smiled, and I stepped up to her, and hugged her – my arms around her waist, as her large breasts squashed against mine. She made a small kissing gesture, and I nodded. Zöe's arms were now around me, and we kissed each other, mouths open, our combined heat now sizzling.

Zöe turned me around, and examined my bum. Laughing, she said quietly, "I realized, after that first stroke of the switch, that you might not be comfortable going to the sauna with us tomorrow with red lines across your butt. Hopefully, the one line will fade, as will the rest of the redness."

I turned, and looked over my shoulder in the mirror: My bottom was a deep shade of red, and it was still stinging. I briefly wondered how Sam was doing, and whether his partner for the evening also had a red bottom by now.

Zöe opened a drawer, and pulled out a strange-looking device, a ball with a bunch of straps and, when she noticed me looking strangely at it, she said, simply, "ball gag". She fit the ball into Max's mouth, and fastened the straps behind his head. Then, she went back to the chest of drawers, and searched, until she found another strange-looking device. As she stepped over to Max, she looked at me, and said, "C&B torture".

I gave her a shocked and quizzical look, and she explained, "Cock-and-ball torture". She stroked Max's already-hard shaft, and slipped the device over it, pushing it down to the base, and making sure his balls were held tightly in the second and third rings. She stood, and explained, "This will keep him erect." She looked at Max's pained expression in the mirror, and added, "Even if he passes out from the caning."

Zöe had to be joking, to increase Max's tension, but it had the effect of increasing *my* tension, as well. I had no idea what to expect, next. Zöe selected a heavy cane from the wall, pushed me aside to make room, and swished it through the air a few times. Just the sound of the cane flying through the air was intimidating.

She pushed the straight-backed chair against the wall, and pulled over a larger chair, with a curved, padded back. She turned it so the back faced into the room, and pushed it into the corner, where Max could see it. Then, she said, matter-of-factly, "I haven't had much caning practice lately. And I want to be sure we make each stroke count." Looking at me, she asked, "What did you guys decide? Twelve strokes?" Max whimpered through the ball gag.

Stepping to the side of the padded-back chair, Zöe carefully positioned herself, gauging where the tip of the cane would land. Then, she pulled the cane back, and put all her – formidable – weight and power behind a stroke that impacted the chair with a loud 'THWACK!', a deep crease now running across the chair back, and my knees instantly becoming weak.

Max screeched through the ball gag, as the stroke crashed into the chair, and he was now moaning, whimpering, and weeping, as his head fell. Zöe took another couple of practice strokes, Max screaming each time, as if he were the one receiving the force of the cane.

His body was shaking, and I stroked his back, and lightly rubbed the multiple red lines crossing his bottom. Zöe brightly held out the cane to me, and said, "Now, *you* try it."

I took the cane, and tried a couple of strokes against the chair. It sounded very severe, even though I wasn't putting nearly as much power behind my strokes. Max was whimpering again; I think we had been successful in building the tension in him. I looked underneath, and saw that his erection was being maintained – either because he was still turned on, or due to the effect of the cock ring which, Zöe explained, prevented blood flow back out of his penis.

Zöe pulled a blindfold from the drawer, and fitted it over Max's eyes, saying, "The twelve strokes will go easier, if he doesn't see them coming." I still couldn't believe that Zöe was going to cane Max that hard. Once the blindfold was in place, Zöe walked to the wall, and quietly exchanged the cane for a thinner one – *still* incredibly intimidating; I was glad – *I hoped* – that it wasn't going to be used on me.

Zöe stepped behind Max, and swung the cane. It landed on Max's bum with a "SMACK" and a scream. While it had been a solid, hard stroke, it had been nothing like our practice strokes on the chair. As Max wept quietly, Zöe handed the cane to me and pointed at Max's rear. I took my time to position myself, finally delivering a hard stroke that again caused Sam to scream.

Zöe pulled the cane out of my hand, and said, loudly, "Not like *that*! You're not challenging him, at all." She put the cane across Max's butt, pulled back, and delivered an incredibly hard stroke. Max shrieked, and was now crying for real.

Zöe handed me the cane, put her finger to her lips, and said, "I've got to check on the other rooms, now. You have another nine strokes, and I want them to be *hard*!" Then, she briefly hugged me, and exited the room. I put the cane across Max's bottom, and his entire body flinched. Then, I took off his blindfold.

"Max, I may get in trouble for this, but my arm is getting tired." I tried hard to not laugh, and continued, sincerely, "I wouldn't mind masturbating now, if that's OK with you." Max was already nodding vigorously. Then, I added, "But, I'll give you the rest of your hard caning, if that's what you want."

I stepped back into position, and put the cane across his bottom, which now appeared to have thin white weals on a dark red background. Max was shaking his head wildly, but couldn't speak, due to the ball gag. I reached underneath him, and stroked him, the condom still in place, and his erection as firm as it had been for the past twenty minutes.

Making an exaggerated sigh, I walked to the wall of implements, and hung up the cane. Then, I removed the ball gag, and dropped it into the sink. I opened the top drawer, and pulled out a large butt plug, similar to the 'Christmas tree' shaped one we had at home. I lubed it, and turned to Max.

"You'll need one more corner time, Max, which you can take while I masturbate." I smiled at him, sweetly, and said, "And, if you're a good boy, I'll take care of you." Max was nodding, so I inserted the plug, which took a good five minutes, and still made Max yelp, when the fattest part passed through his sphincter.

Then, I pulled over the wooden chair, and hiked up my dress, sitting down with my legs straddling the chair, leaning back, and taking care of myself, my eyes closed. This time, I really *was* masturbating, and it took only a few minutes to reach orgasm. I realized that I was fantasizing about Zöe spanking me, and then satisfying me, perhaps using a strap-on. I came, and then came again, as Max watched, quietly. Then, I continued stroking myself lightly, as my pulse slowed.

I turned the chair, so that I would have access to the important parts of Max's anatomy, and bent over, struggling to remove the cock-and-ball rings. I considered giving Max oral sex, as he was wearing a condom, but decided to get him off with my hand. Actually, *hands*, as I used both hands to stroke him. Max's orgasm was epic, his body convulsing and thrusting, the tip of the condom filling like a balloon.

At that moment, I thought about Sam, and realized that I had a lot to learn; *we* had a lot to learn. Like most other fields of endeavor, there were many layers and details to BDSM, and I knew that we were still near the bottom of a steep learning curve.

I took Brigitte by the hand, and led her down the hall to find the room that had been assigned to us: The club's version of an 'exam room'. It was done nicely, a simplified version of my own – no big instruments, syringes or hypodermic needles, but there *were* thermometers, vaginal specula and, in a cabinet, some acupuncture needles.

Brigitte hopped up on the table, and looked at me blankly. She wore a black vinyl bustier, that came down to just above her navel, and a pair of black vinyl short shorts, that would have shown pubic hair, had she not been shaved or waxed.

Sitting on a straight-backed wooden chair, I started by taking her history; at least *my* version of a 'history'. I asked her about her spanking experience – she'd had some, although always light and playful; about her enema experience – she'd had a few; and about getting shots – she just shrugged.

I was sorry that I hadn't brought my own supplies, but it occurred to me that there might be a club policy to only use their supplies. I wouldn't have had any place to carry stuff, anyway, as I had no pockets. I would have to make-do with the equipment and supplies that the club had provided.

Continuing the interview, I asked about her sexual history, number of partners, and preferences; and then, I asked Brigitte about her fantasies and turn-ons. Unfortunately, she wasn't very forthcoming – either having a distinct lack of fantasies or, more probably, being too shy to talk about them. I asked her about birth control – she was on the pill – and what she expected in tonight's session.

She shrugged again, and said, "I guess I can let you do what you like, and we can go down on each other, but I'd rather not have intercourse, tonight." I told her that was fine with me, and that I preferred that we just use our hands on each other, which seemed to please her.

Then, I decided to get into the 'role', and said, "Brigitte, your mother has brought you here because you're sexually active, but refusing to use your diaphragm."

Brigitte looked at me, and then realized her role, and answered, "But all the guys I sleep with use condoms."

I nodded, "That's good, but you agreed last time you were here that you would *also* use the diaphragm, along with spermicidal jelly. Your mother doesn't want to take any chances of you getting pregnant, and you shouldn't want to, either."

Brigitte just nodded, and I continued, "So, therefore, I'm going to give you a good spanking for not obeying me, and a thorough check-up to make sure it's not too late." Brigitte didn't respond.

"Get down here, young lady!" Brigitte hopped down from the exam table, and stood in front of me. "Get those pants down!" Brigitte quickly unbuttoned and unzipped the tiny shorts, but had a tough time pulling them down; I helped her, and soon she was standing in front of me in a black thong – very similar to the G-string Kelly was wearing; I wondered if she was *still* wearing it.

I pulled the thong down, and let it drop to the ground, my eyes focusing on what was in front of them – a tiny, black, pubic triangle, about the size of the space my fingers make, when I touch my pointer finger and thumb in an 'OK' sign.

I stood, and stepped to the counter, where I found a thermometer, lubing it before sitting back down on the uncomfortable chair. I placed the thermometer on the counter, where I could reach it, and then pulled Brigitte gently over my lap.

I instructed, "You will stay in this position, while I spank you. If you move, or try to reach back with your hands, you will receive additional punishment. Do you understand, young lady?" Brigitte nodded, her short hair shaking. "I don't hear you."

Brigitte looked back at me, over her shoulder, and said, "Yes, sir." That was better!

Looking down, I assessed Brigitte's body: She was a plain-looking woman; I hadn't seen her breasts, yet, but her hips were wide, and her bottom full. I rubbed her bottom, and shook her buttocks roughly. Then, I asked, "Are you ready for your spanking, now, young lady?"

This time, Brigitte remembered. "Yes, sir," she said quietly, her head hanging down.

I said, "OK!" Then, I gave her a medium spank on each side of her butt. Brigitte exhaled loudly, but didn't complain. So I began spanking her soundly, alternating sides. The individual spanks weren't very hard, but I would be giving her 100 as a warm-up. Then, we could decide what else she needed.

My hand slapped Brigitte's flabby bottom loudly and, after a few dozen spanks, she groaned – or moaned – and began rocking her body. I increased the force of the final dozen blows, and was impressed that Brigitte held her position well. What I needed was a more severe implement, like a hairbrush or paddle; there was a chest of drawers, and I would have to check out what they held.

Reaching up to the counter, I took the thermometer and, spreading her butt cheeks with my left hand, I touched the thermometer to her anus using my right. She flinched a little, but I could see that she was forcing her anal muscles to relax. I slid the thermometer into her, and moved it around for a couple of minutes. Then, I took it out, and asked Brigitte to get into the standing position, while I rummaged through the drawers.

There wasn't much in them, but a few items caught my interest. There were two spanking implements – a 12" leather paddle with a wooden handle, that could be used OTK (over-the-knee); and a school paddle, made of clear plastic, with a dozen holes drilled through it. Another drawer held a collection of vaginal and anal specula, and a set of rectal dilators – similar to butt plugs, but sized in gradual steps.

I turned to Brigitte, who was still in the standing position, watching me take out supplies and line them up on the counter. "You will be getting two more hard spankings. I'll give you the choice between taking one of them now, or getting your pelvic exam first; either way, you'll be getting both."

Brigitte shrugged, and said, "I guess you can examine me, now." I had her hop back up onto the end of the exam table, and I helped her take off the bustier. She was small on top, but still had the full shape and firmness of the 'typical' Dutch breasts. I guessed that Brigitte was fortyish, and I would call her a 'handsome' woman. I manipulated her breasts, squeezing her nipples, and then had her lay back for a 'real' breast exam.

I raised the stirrups, which didn't come above the level of the table, Brigitte's feet against them more like they were stirrups on a saddle, than stirrups in a gynecology office. Brigitte scooted down the table, without me having to tell her, and clasped her hands together on her stomach.

I did an external exam, then inserted a gloved finger, and finally inserted another finger in her rear. I pushed both fingers into their respective holes, and pulled them most of the way out, repeating this several times, before taking my fingers out, and reaching for the speculum.

Brigitte was quite cooperative, almost passive. I hoped I could find her turn on, as it was not that exciting for me to see her taking what I gave her, but not enjoying it, or showing much enthusiasm. I finished the speculum exam, and told her it was time for her second spanking. She nodded, and sat up, took her feet off the stirrups, and hopped down from the exam table.

I put her over my knee again, this time putting my leg over hers, to clamp them for the more severe spanking. I held the wooden handle of the paddle, letting the leather sit on the convex curves of her bottom. Then, I reached between her legs, under her, and slid my hand along her genitals, and up over her clit, pulling back the hood slightly, before sliding my hand back down. A shiver passed through Brigitte's body.

Leaning over, my head as close to hers as possible, I whispered, "If you're a good girl, and take your punishment well, I'll reward you ... if you like." Brigitte didn't say anything, or give any indication of what she would – or wouldn't – like.

I sat up, held the paddle, and asked, "Are you ready for your second punishment, now, Brigitte?"

Brigitte sighed, and said, "Yes, sir."

Clamping my leg over hers more tightly, I began paddling Brigitte's behind, moving the implement around to cover her entire bottom, hips, and upper thighs. I was focusing on giving her a thorough spanking, and realized that I had not counted the strokes – probably for the first time, since I had first spanked a woman.

Brigitte was panting, and rocking her body on my thigh, providing some good stimulation for me, as my penis was being held vertically, between her hip and my stomach. I continued spanking Brigitte, until she was whining, with a continuous 'Ooooowwwww'. Then, I laid the paddle on her upper buttocks, and put my hand under her again.

This time, she didn't flinch, as I moved my hand, very slightly, as if I were rocking a tiny baby in it; I slipped a finger between her lips, and did feel some moistness. Taking my hand out, I picked up the paddle again, "I don't think you're quite ready, yet."

Brigitte groaned (I was pretty sure it was a 'groan'), and I resumed paddling her, the leather slapping against her reddening cheeks, as she resumed her whining, now punctuated with some very distinct, louder, 'Ow!'s, and a couple of 'Aiyeeee's.

"OK, Brigitte, I'm going to give you ten more swats – very hard. And you'll count them out for me."

I heard no response, but after the first – extra hard – swat, Brigitte called out, "One, sir!" I rubbed her bottom, and then repeated the process – giving her a nice rub in-between each swat. When I was done, there was silence for a few moments, and then I heard a shy, "Thank you, sir."

Smiling, I said, "Thank *you*, Brigitte. You did very well." I reached up to the counter, and grabbed the medium sized butt plug. "I'll need to put this in you, so that you'll be ready for the final part of your exam." I placed the lubricated plug against her anus and, with a gentle push, it slid into her. I slowly pulled it out and pushed it back in several times, finally pushing past the widest point – Brigitte emitting a quick yelp – so that the neck of the plug held it in her.

I massaged her bottom, and asked, "May I please reward you now, for taking your spanking so well?" I didn't hear anything, but saw her head bobbing, so put my hand under her, and began working on her, where it counted. It took several minutes, but Brigitte finally did get excited. I slipped my thumb into her, as I continued massaging her hood with my other fingers. She thrust once, and grunted, and I felt her wetness coat my thumb.

I allowed Brigitte to get up, and told her to lie on the exam table, to finish her exam and treatment. She really was being cooperative. I decided to leave the butt plug in her, rather than play with the rectal speculum; I also decided that Brigitte had had enough spanking, and put away both the leather paddle and the Plexiglas school paddle.

I opened the box of acupuncture needles, and dumped a bunch of them on the counter. There was also a box of alcohol swabs, and I took a couple, and put everything else away, except the vaginal speculum that I'd used on her, which I dropped into the sink.

As I swabbed her bottom, Brigitte groaned, the alcohol stinging her spanked skin. I told her, "I'm going to treat you now, using acupuncture needles, that will be inserted in your bottom." I didn't bother with a story about energy points, or exactly what I was treating her for; I just wanted to see some of the long needles sticking out of her twin mounds.

I inserted the first couple of needles into the middle of each buttock– tapping the ends, sliding off the guide, and then slowly rotating the needle, as it went a small fraction of an inch into her. Then, I inserted the rest of the needles in her upper hip, a safe location, as I continued to push each needle in, until they were nearly two inches into her. Brigitte groaned a few times, but didn't complain.

When all the needles were protruding from her still-red bottom, I put my head near hers, and stroked her hair. "How are you doing, Brigitte?"

She smiled at me, and said, "I'm OK." Then, she followed-up with, "May I help you find your own release, now?"

I knew that was shorthand for 'can you please take the needles out of me' – or, 'can you please take the butt plug out of me', or both. So I nodded, and said, "Yes, Brigitte. Your cooperation has turned me on, and I'm ready for some of your attention."

Pulling the needles out of her, I dropped them into a trashcan – not nearly as safe as using a special 'sharps' container. Then, I pulled out the butt plug, and dropped it into the small sink. I helped Brigitte get up, and I hopped up on the exam table.

As I took off my underwear, I asked, "Would you like to examine me, or insert a butt plug?" I was ready to take whatever Brigitte wanted to do to me.

Brigitte shook her head, "Not especially. I don't like playing with people's butt holes; that's why I won't satisfy my husband's 'age play' fetish. I'm OK with diapering him ... but don't want to clean up any mess he makes." I didn't ask if she had kids who had needed diaper changes.

Brigitte took a condom from the pile on the counter, and held it up, "I would be happy to 'give you head', if you like." The Dutch not only were fluent in English, but they knew most of the slang expressions – at least, the important ones.

I nodded, and smiled, laying on my back, and putting my feet on the low stirrups, "I was only asking for your hand," that sounded funny, "but I won't turn down your mouth, if you use the condom." It was Kelly's fault: I *was* getting more lax in my older age.

Brigitte stood between my legs, and did a creditable job of stroking me, until I was hard enough for her to roll on the condom. Then, she surprised me – with, perhaps, the best oral technique I've ever experienced; and she actually seemed to be enjoying this part. I closed my eyes, and let Brigitte do her thing, and came in less than five minutes.

We dressed and walked upstairs to the bar, finding Max and Kelly already there. It took only a few moments to realize that Kelly wasn't wearing her G-string: She was now totally nude beneath the see-through net dress; I wondered where she had stashed the string, as it was quite obvious she wasn't carrying it 'on her'.

Max and Brigitte kissed, and smiled at each other, and Kelly and I did the same. A few minutes later, Zöe appeared, smiling at us, and walking over, her breasts wobbling on the corset platform. "Well? Did you guys have a fun time?" We all nodded.

Then, Zöe stepped up to Kelly, and kissed her, their breasts squashed between them. They smiled at each other, and I wondered what special connection they had made here at the club.

Henk finally appeared, with a smile on his face like the rest of us. We said our goodbyes to the people we had met, and changed back into our street clothes.

Henk suggested that we stop at another Belgian beer bar, and we tried some different – and more powerful – malty brews. By the time we reached the car, Zöe had decided that she would drive us back to Driebergen, with the two inebriated men in the backseat.

CHAPTER 10: SOCIABLE SUNDAY

On Sunday, we all slept late, and then Zöe put out a breakfast array of breads and croissants, meats and cheeses, Nutella and various jams, and a pitcher of fresh juice, along with strong Dutch coffee. Sam and I felt rested, and I hoped our jetlag was over.

It was late morning before we packed, piled into the car, and headed to Henk and Zöe's favorite sauna – not far from where they lived. We drove through the tiny town of Soesterberg, where there is a military camp that was the site of the trials of the Libyan hijackers who blew up a Pan Am flight over Lockerbie, Scotland.

As we pulled into a parking lot in a forested area, Henk told us that the sauna was to be torn down in the near future, as the government wanted to make a trail to allow animals passage from one preserve to another.

We checked in and went downstairs to the locker room. It was quite busy and, as we found our lockers and I looked around, I couldn't help but smile: We were watching an exhibition of contemporary male and female undergarments. I was surprised to see that most of the men had 'normal' sized underwear, which Henk told us were called 'slips', not the tiny ones that Sam wore.

We took our towels, and walked into the huge shower room, where we all bathed, along with a dozen other people just arriving at the sauna. There were a few grade school aged children, but they were well behaved, obviously having come to a sauna many times.

Walking out into the main area, I realized how small the Amsterdam sauna had been, and how few people had been there. We tried several sauna cabins, cooling off in-between in one of the showers, or under a huge misting-jet.

We went into the steam room for a while, and then into the 'herb' sauna – which was a small pool, with a fountain in the center, and room for a dozen people on the tiled benches around the pool. I couldn't determine exactly which herbs were being used, but the aroma was definitely distinct.

After some relaxation in the jacuzzi, we took our towels, and went outside. Sam had warned me that the gardens wouldn't be like they were in the spring, with flowers and fruits growing around the yard. But it was still very nice – a huge grass area with chaise lounges – now mostly filled with people sun-bathing; a gazebo in the back, with vines growing over it; and lush landscaping along the edge of the property.

There was a large swimming pool, with tables scattered around it on the deck, where people were ordering from the sauna's restaurant. We lay in the sun for a while, and then took a dip in the pool. Although there were at least a dozen children, there was no screaming, crying, or other commotion; the pool was relaxing, and relatively quiet.

We picked a table on the deck, wrapping our towels around our waists, as we sat down. The menu was nice – everything from fish and chips, to chicken satay, to traditional Dutch specialties, such as *bitterballen*. We all ordered salads, and they were very large and very good.

Once again, the weather had cooperated, and we enjoyed the beautiful day in the fresh air, with a few hundred of the locals. As I sat back, already filled after having eaten only half my salad, I took in the panorama of people: Better than a sidewalk café (except for fashion-watching), there were people of nearly every age and body type, with teenagers the only under-represented age group.

While there were undoubtedly people here not of Dutch origin, a large percentage of the females had similar body types, with rounded, large firm breasts, and porcelain white skin. Men were uniformly uncircumcised; again, Sam may have been the only circumcised male here.

There were shriveled-up old men and women, and beautiful young people; everyone accepting each other's nudity and bodies in the same way, for example, that Americans accept everyone's looks in a theater filled with variously-dressed movie-goers.

Sitting at the tables, people wore robes, towels wrapped around them, or went topless – with a towel wrapped around their waist. People in the chaises, and elsewhere were uniformly nude, sitting or lying on their towel, and perhaps carrying it in front of them, as they walked around the facility, in an unnecessary show of modesty.

Henk turned to me and asked, "So what do you think about *our* lifestyle?" I wasn't sure exactly what Henk and Zöe's lifestyle was, but I had been impressed with them in several ways.

"It seems to be somewhat of a reflection of the lifestyle that Sam and I have been developing: One of sexual freedom without conditions, jealousy, or guilt. Unafraid to be open about who you are sexually. And, I'm impressed with your ability to live together, committed in many ways, but not holding each other back."

I tried to organize my thoughts for a moment, while Sam, Henk and Zöe munched their salads, awaiting the continued disclosure of my opinions. "You guys are obviously 'open'," I waved at their nude bodies, and those of dozens of people sitting around us, "And you're 'tolerant' – as Sam had explained to me. Tolerant of each other, and of us, and all the people at the sex club."

Henk laughed, "Well, as you can see, most Dutch people are open and tolerant, in the ways you're saying. But most Dutch people don't actually have a fetish or go to sex clubs. And, as far as my relationship with Zöe, accepting each other and not holding each other back from our sexual preferences is an important element, as is the 'commitment without commitment'. We are certainly a couple, whether we're married or not."

Then, Henk glanced at Zöe, and gave her a knowing smile, "And, actually, Zöe and I do respect the limits we have agreed to. There aren't many of them, but not having unprotected sex, and not having sex with others without the knowledge of our partner, are two of them." Henk smiled at Zöe again, and added, "And each of us has limits on what we will do with each other, sexually."

That was surprising, as I had envisioned them as completely open, but hadn't factored in their preferences. I gave Henk an questioning look, and saw Zöe give a slight nod. Henk explained, "Well, Zöe won't do anal." He chuckled, "She loves to 'give' anal, with a strap-on, but she won't let me have anal sex with her." Zöe had a blank look, but was nodding slowly.

Henk added, "I'll 'take it in the ass', if Zöe wants to use the strap-on with me ... or Helga." We all chuckled, a bit uncomfortably, and Henk continued, "But, I'm sure you've noticed that Zöe likes to be the dominant. In fact, her biggest turn on comes from degrading men. But I'm not into being degraded, especially by my living partner."

I now understood a bit more, and nodded, "Yes, Zöe came into the room where I was whipping Max, and she made him lick her toes. I wouldn't have thought of it, nor would I have ever asked Max to do that ... but I can see the turn-on there."

Henk smiled, thinly, "I wouldn't mind sucking Zöe's toes, occasionally ... but I don't like her to pee on me."

In my peripheral vision, I could see Sam's jaw drop, and we were both a bit shocked. There was a long moment of uncomfortable silence, before Zöe said, "It's just one more fetish. Some men are turned-on by watching me pee up-close; and feeling the warm liquid run over their body. And, urine is sterile, when it first comes out, so there's nothing particularly 'dirty' or dangerous about it."

I could see that Zöe was trying to rationalize her fetish, but Sam and I were pretty much speechless. Although, once again, I could see the potential turn on, for both the 'pee-er' and 'pee-ee' ... if that's what they would be called. If I did it to Sam, it would just be another form of his submission.

Zöe broke my thoughts, when she added, "Of course, if the guy – or girl – doesn't like the idea of 'golden showers', I have many other ways to intimidate and degrade them."

Before I could ask, Henk suggested, "Now that we're finished with lunch, let's try the rest of the place." He looked at Sam, and said, "You may have a 'rain shower' at your house, but they have a tropical thunderstorm, here."

We walked into the building, and turned down a hall; at the end was a painted tile wall depicting colorful tropical foliage. It looked like a large shower, but with no door. Henk signaled for us to get in, and we stepped over the threshold, and admired the tile work, as the rumble of thunder sounded, getting louder and louder. There were some flashes of lightning – obviously strobe lights somewhere in the ceiling. Then, Sam and I were surprised when there was suddenly a tropical downpour: Hundreds of gallons of rain being dumped on us, as the thunder and lightning continued.

The rainwater was lukewarm, but we became chilled, and walked around the corner into a huge sauna room, with wide tiered benches on two levels around the periphery. We stood just inside the door, waiting for our eyes to adapt, the room silent, save for a few creaks of the sauna furnace. When we could finally see, we walked around the room, and up to the second level. At least a dozen people were quietly lying on the benches, enjoying the quietness and cozy warmth.

We lay down, and closed our eyes, my body relaxing into the towel and bench, visions from our trip flashing through my mind. Even the past 24 hours had been amazing, with the two saunas, dinner made by Zöe, and the sex club. I realized that we were only on our fourth day here, although it seemed like we'd been here at least a week.

We spent the rest of the afternoon trying the various sauna cabins, and other amenities, ending as we had begun, in the communal showers. It was late afternoon, now, and all of the showers were filled, everyone soaping up, shampooing, and rinsing in close proximity to a few dozen other bathers.

As I stood under the warm shower, I thought back to my birthday party: Spending much of the day visiting and lying around nude, and taking showers together, really didn't seem like such a strange or unusual activity, seeing how many of the Dutch relax at a sauna, where they can expect to see their neighbors. Literally.

I sat at the end of the bench in the locker room, Sam combing out my hair. Zöe was standing at a counter blow-drying her hair, and Henk was dressing somewhere behind me. None of us said a word, as we finished getting dressed and groomed for the outside world.

Henk drove us to another small town, many of the houses with ancient-looking thatched roofs. We parked at a quaint restaurant, with the same thatched-roof style, and were shown to a table in a large room, quite a few other people already eating, including many families with children. But the restaurant was relatively quiet, the décor quaint, and the aroma of exotic cuisine delicious.

I opened a menu, but didn't recognize the names of any of the dishes; I had never been to an Indonesian restaurant, before. The waiter came, and we ordered drinks – including an eclectic mix of beers, mango nectar, and wine.

Henk explained, "We're going to be ordering a *rijstaffel* – an Indonesian 'rice plate', which is like a mini-buffet for our table, with about 30 different dishes. Originally, they were served around a huge mound of rice on a large platter. Here, the different dishes will be arranged in groups over heaters, going from mild, to medium, to spicy, to hot, to super-hot. We usually eat them in that order, so our mouths can still taste the more delicate dishes."

Sam interjected, "Yeah, after the spiciest dishes, we probably won't be tasting much of anything." Henk laughed, and Zöe nodded, as she sipped her mango nectar through a straw.

The waiter set up five burners on the table, and set five 6-section dishes on the grates above them. We each took some of the mild dishes, and the accompaniments. They were delicious; not spicy at all! As we made our way toward the hotter dishes, I realized that Sam hadn't been joking. The remaining food filled the dishes higher and higher, toward the hotter offerings, but it wasn't until we reached the most extreme six dishes that the true meaning of 'hot' in Indonesian cuisine was revealed.

After the first small bite of the first of the super-hot dishes – some dark brown meat stew – all of the taste buds in my tongue had been burned out. We ordered more beer, but it didn't come quickly enough.

Trying not to insult the natives, I duly tried each of the selections ... cooling my mouth by holding a swallow of beer in it, as everyone else talked. One more bite, and I had the hiccoughs! At first, it was funny, and then it was embarrassing, but finally, it was exhausting; I couldn't stop. Sam suggested putting a small spoonful of sugar on the back of my tongue. And Henk and Zöe also suggested their home remedies.

Fortunately, by the time the fresh mango and 'pisang goreng' (fried bananas) arrived, I could taste again, and appreciate the flavors of the desserts.

Stuffed, and slightly inebriated, we returned to Henk's house, where he poured liqueurs. We sat on their couch, and Sam outlined our itinerary, as we would be starting the driving portion of our trip tomorrow morning.

Somehow, the subject of fetishes came up again, and Henk asked, "So you are still turned on by someone submitting? Is that the relationship you have with Kelly?"

Sam smiled, and said, "Yes, and mostly. Our relationship began with Kelly submitting to me ... and it still turns me on. But sometimes I submit to her. So, I guess we're each a 'switch'." Sam looked at me, and chuckled, "There's not that much new for us to submit to, anymore, as we've already done so many things. But I'm still turned-on by the same old things."

Henk looked at Sam for a long moment, and then asked, "Would you and Kelly be interested in demonstrating for us?"

THAT was a surprise! I glanced at Zöe, and she was trying not to laugh; I wondered whether they had orchestrated this together. Then, I looked at Sam, and he was smiling broadly; *now*, I was wondering whether they *all* had plotted this.

Although I was shocked at first, thinking of some of the inevitable ramifications of 'submitting' in front of Henk and Zöe, I calmed quickly, realizing that there was no point in worrying about what would happen, as I knew I would submit to Sam, regardless of what he asked of me. Also, I had been nude all day with Henk, and Zöe had played with Max and I at the sex club, so we were already closer than casual acquaintances.

I decided to pre-empt some of the tension, and quickly stood, walked around the large, sturdy coffee table, and assumed the standing position. Henk and Zöe were startled and, when Sam turned to face me, I could see that he was also surprised at my immediate action.

Sam cleared his throat, and asked, firmly, "Kelly, will you submit to me?" I started to nod, and Sam said, very softly, "You don't have to do this, if you don't want, Kelly. It's not a test – I know you'll submit, if I really ask you to."

I smiled at him and, as I felt a clenching down below, replied, "Yes, Sam. I love you. And I will submit to you."

I smiled at Kelly, and said, "Get undressed, please." Kelly responded immediately, undressing completely, folding and stacking her clothes neatly on a rocking chair on the other side of the coffee table. I hadn't expected Henk to challenge us this way, and had to decide exactly what kind of 'demonstration' we would be giving tonight. The first thing I would need to do would be to bring down some of our 'toys' from the attic bedroom.

I suggested, "Kelly, please use the bathroom. I'm going upstairs to change into something more comfortable, and perhaps Henk and Zöe would like to do that, also? Then, get back in the standing position, and we'll come back down in a few minutes." Henk and Zöe smiled and nodded, and the three of us headed upstairs, while Kelly headed to the downstairs half-bath.

When we all convened again downstairs, Henk and Zöe were wearing robes, Zöe carrying a beach tote in which I could see a few sex 'gadgets'. I was in my running shorts and tank, and carried my backpack, filled with implements and supplies ... still not exactly knowing what I was going to request of Kelly, who waited patiently, nude, in the standing position.

Henk left for a moment, to find a fake bearskin rug, which he threw over the coffee table, making it into a platform for Kelly's performance. Zöe leaned over and whispered something to me, and I nodded; she left for a few minutes, and Kelly and I were alone in Henk's living room.

Kelly smiled at me, "Sam, I'm OK with whatever you want to do." That was a great offer, but I wasn't sure how far I would take Kelly's submission demonstration. I nodded, as Henk and Zöe came back into the room.

We all sat on the couch, and I instructed Kelly to come over, and get into a knee chest position on the bearskin rug-covered coffee table, her feet hanging slightly over the edge closest to us. I was very impressed to see Kelly reach under and separate her labia, and then make sure her buttocks were well separated, before facing forward to await her fate.

I slipped a blindfold over her eyes, and stood behind her, my hand on her bare bottom. "You're going to receive 100 spanks from each of us, 25 at a time." Without delay, I began spanking Kelly, alternating sides, and giving her relatively hard spanks, so that Henk and Zöe would see what she could take, and not be inhibited.

Kelly held her position, and didn't make a sound, as I finished the last ten spanks extra hard. I pointed at Zöe, and she took her turn, if anything giving Kelly harder spanks than I had. Then, I pointed at Henk, and he spanked Kelly, who was now making grunting sounds, her bottom swaying slightly. Zöe was next, then me, then Henk twice, then Zöe twice, then me twice, and then Henk for the final 25 spanks. By the end, Kelly was whimpering quietly, and her bottom was a nice light red color. I smiled at Zöe and nodded.

She walked over to the hall, where she had stashed it, and retrieved a 36" long rattan cane. I would have to ask Zöe to give me a 'tour' of her spanking and BDSM implements. She said loudly, "Kelly was acting like a wimp when we were at the sex club, barely making a mark on Max's behind. So I had to take things into my own hands for a while. Now, Kelly is going to get a taste of what a *real* caning feels like."

With that, she swung the cane in the air, a loud 'Swoosh!' making Kelly flinch. Zöe swung the cane again, and Kelly flinched again, this time emitting a high-pitched whining sound.

Then, Kelly quieted, and said, with confidence, "Sorry. I'm ready for my caning now, Zöe." Zöe had brought the cane out for 'impact' only, and it had worked initially to scare Kelly, but she had recovered, and Zöe knew that Kelly would submit to a caning.

I interrupted the action, and said, "Zöe, I'd like to suggest that you don't cane Kelly, as we have another sauna to visit in 24 hours, and I would rather she not be marked too badly."

Zöe said, "Sure, Sam."

I then said, "I think it's time for a rectal insertion, now, before we give Kelly her next spanking." As I said this, I lubed a medium-size butt plug, and handed it to Henk. He sat on the couch behind Kelly, and worked the plug into her, everyone silent, save a few deep breaths from Kelly. When the plug was in, I handed Zöe my heavy leather belt, and held up both hands twice, indicating 20 strokes; Zöe nodded, and I said, "OK, Kelly, let's demonstrate the strap. I think 50 strokes should be enough."

Kelly voiced a tiny, "Yes, Sir. I'm ready, Sir."

Zöe stood, and put the belt against Kelly's rear. Then, she pulled it back, and let it swing; the belt struck Kelly's buttocks with a 'Whap!', and her flesh rippled outward from the impact. Zöe continued the strapping, giving Kelly respectably hard strokes, until the full twenty strokes had been given, and Kelly was whimpering. Most of her bottom was now a deep shade of red. Zöe sat back down on the couch, and we watched, as Kelly shook her bottom, but didn't attempt to reach back to rub it.

"I think Kelly's had enough, for the moment." Kelly's head was nodding up and down, but she remained silent. I turned to Henk, and said, "Henk, you may ask Kelly to submit to one thing."

Henk replied, "I'd like to see one of your 'medical procedures'." I nodded, and pulled supplies out of my backpack, assembling a shot, and readying alcohol swabs and gauze pads. When the shot was ready, I uncapped the needle, held it up, and squirted some saline from the tip of the needle. Henk looked curious, while Zöe's eyes were wide, as she looked intently at the syringe and needle. I announced to Kelly, "You'll be getting four cc's; which side would you like it on, Kelly?"

She immediately responded, "I'd like the shot on the right side, Sir."

After swabbing her right hip, I inserted the needle. Then, I checked for blood, and let go of the syringe, which stuck out of Kelly's hip, wobbling a little, as she breathed.

I sat back on the couch, and explained to Henk and Zöe, "I'm using a small needle, which really doesn't hurt much. Kelly's used to getting needles stuck in her bottom, so this isn't too big of a deal for her." Then, I sat forward, and injected the saline into Kelly. I left the needle in another few seconds, and then pulled it out.

I told Henk, "Sorry, but I don't have many supplies with me; we'll have to give you a 'rain check' for a few more medical procedure demonstrations."

Henk laughed, "That's OK. Kelly's been a brave girl. It was a good demonstration."

I turned to Zöe, and asked, "What would *you* like Kelly to submit to?"

Zöe stood, and said, "Well, if I can't cane her, then I want to fuck her in the ass." We heard a sharp intake of breath from Kelly. Zöe removed her robe, and stood next to me in a very small thong, and very large bra. She took off the thong, and pulled something from the tote she had brought down to the living room.

It was a strap-on. This one was similar to the one Kelly had purchased at the sex shop in Amsterdam, having a phallus for insertion into the person wearing the strap-on, as well as a large dildo for the recipient of the device. When Zöe had the thing strapped onto her, she pointed at the butt plug still inside Kelly.

I pointed to Henk, and said, "OK, Kelly, give a push, so we can pull the butt plug out." Kelly pushed, and Henk pulled, the plug coming out of Kelly easily.

Zöe carefully guided the dildo into Kelly, and began slow back-and-forth movements, holding Kelly's hips. The movements became more forceful, and soon, Zöe was slapping against Kelly, the dildo entering her fully before being pulled out and thrust forward again. Zöe reached around, and stimulated Kelly, and they humped for several minutes, both getting more excited, but neither ready for release. Zöe looked over her shoulder, and said, "You girls should start getting yourselves ready!"

I wasn't sure what she meant by 'girls', but my question was answered, when Henk walked around the coffee table, and Zöe removed the blindfold from Kelly. As Kelly looked up at Henk, he opened and dropped his robe ... revealing the sexy women's underwear and lace bra that he was wearing.

Kelly gave one loud chuckle, and Henk began stroking himself, his swelling manhood tenting the skimpy feminine panties, his penis finally emerging from above the waistband. Henk pulled the underwear down, under his balls, and Kelly reached up to stroke him.

At the same time, I removed my tank and shorts, and stood next to Zöe, who stroked me, while still moving in and out of Kelly's rear. Henk and I both responded rapidly, and then Zöe took control. "OK, boys, move the table, and then take the standing position, over there."

She pointed to the wall, and Henk and I dragged the coffee table out of the way, and put the bearskin rug on the floor; then we stood against the wall, hands on our heads, our erections bobbing. Zöe pulled a huge dildo from her tote; it must have been more than two feet long, and at least three inches in diameter.

She and Kelly then positioned themselves on the bearskin, butt to butt, in knee chest positions, and Zöe inserted the huge double-ended dildo into her vagina, as Kelly inserted the other end into herself. A dildo bridge now connected the two women.

Zöe looked up at me, and said, "I'm ready for you, now." Again, I wasn't sure what Zöe meant, and I looked at Henk for confirmation.

Henk chuckled, "Well, Sam, we usually don't have sex with other people; although I guess Zöe has had oral sex with some of her friends. This is the first time since I met her that Zöe has actually offered something sexual to a man ... other than me. At least, as far as I know." He laughed, and Zöe was now chuckling.

"You know everything, dear," Zöe said in a mock scolding-wife tone.

I knew that I should be able to relax and enjoy what my hostess was offering so graciously ... but it seemed like we were suddenly becoming more promiscuous. Although I guess it wasn't that sudden: Kelly and I had already had oral sex with her friends; and Kelly and Fiona had made out. But I would still feel more comfortable if Henk and I let our own partners go down on us ... or, at least, we should wear condoms.

Henk was stroking himself again, and I would need to make a decision quickly, or everyone would be turned-off. "I'll leave it up to Kelly – whether we should wear condoms, or just play with our own partners."

Kelly shook her head, "Sam, I would like to give Henk a treat." She chortled, "Anyway, I'm turned on by his sexy bra and underwear." We all laughed, a bit uncomfortably. Then Kelly added, "And I don't want to suck on a condom."

Well, that was clear enough. Henk got down and crawled onto the bearskin rug, lay on his back, and positioned his throbbing member under Kelly's head. Kelly took Henk in her right hand – balancing on her left – and stroked him a few times, then pulled his foreskin down, licked him, and swirled her tongue over the pink head beneath. Kelly then took Henk in her mouth, making long strokes, bobbing her head and, at the same time, rocking fore-and-aft, so that the dildo connecting her with Zöe was pounding into both of them.

I shrugged, and got down onto the rug, and positioned myself under Zöe, my head and legs in the opposite direction to Henk's. As Zöe took me in her mouth, I lifted my head and surveyed the scene: Zöe and Kelly were butt-to-butt, and I could see a few inches of the dildo connecting them. Kelly's hair obscured any view of Henk's privates – which was fine with me. I put my head back down on the rug, and closed my eyes.

The room was quiet, save for some heavy breathing, and the sounds of our motions. I began to thrust upward, Zöe fellating me expertly. I felt Zöe take my hand and move it upward, and I opened one eye to fine-tune my proprioception of our joined bodies, now realizing that I could reach Zöe's clit. I noticed a hand under Kelly, and assumed it belonged to Henk.

I closed my eye, and moved my fingers through Zöe's small patch of pubic hair, and down over her hood. My three middle fingers pushed upward, against Zöe, moving in a slow, circular motion over her hood. I occasionally moved my middle finger in a 'come here' motion, lifting her hood, and flicking against her clit.

We were all breathing more heavily now, and my hand continued its duty autonomically, as my mind whirled, random images of the past few days flying by: Seeing Henk as 'Helga' for the first time; Kelly modeling the outfits from the sex shop for me on the hotel balcony; our multiple sauna visits, the two most recent with Zöe; and my experience with Brigitte at the sex club.

I heard Kelly grunting, and felt Zöe being pushed forward each time Kelly thrust back toward her. I advanced my hand, and then pulled it back slowly, lifting Zöe's hood, her clit sliding between my fingers. I knew Zöe was close, and realized that I wouldn't be able to hold out much longer.

Kelly squealed, and within a few seconds Zöe took her mouth off me, and thrust her body on the dildo; I heard a long intake of breath, and I squeezed her clit between my fingers. Zöe thrust quickly several more times, and I heard a quiet 'No', as she took my wrist in her hand, and pulled it down to the rug, away from her clit.

It suddenly occurred to me that Zöe was having a very 'real' experience, unabashed, nearly feral – and I was suddenly incredibly turned on, watching – and feeling – Zöe in her throes of masturbatory passion ... just as Kelly and I had been turned on by Julie's performance, many months ago.

Zöe's mouth was on me again, and my orgasm emptied myself into her, as my mind's eye saw Kelly – herself feral, as she masturbated on top of me during our first experience. It seemed like long ago; that I had always been with Kelly. I realized that I was still thrusting, Zöe 'finishing me', as I lay there thinking of Kelly.

While I could get turned on by many different experiences or scenes, and could get off by the hand – or mouth – of various partners, Kelly was the only one I wanted; the only person who turned me on, irrespective of what we were doing – sexual, or not. I felt beads of sweat on my forehead, as I saw – with perfect clarity – that I wanted to be with Kelly forever.

Then, a strange thought popped into my head. I remembered what it was like, when I was a small kid, with my grandfather, sitting on the back steps after doing some yard work. He would hand me a Coke that he had put in the freezer, one of the old-style thick glass bottles. I would take a swig, and hold the bottle near my nose, letting the tiny bubbles pop against me, both providing a tickling sensation ... and an indescribable 'satisfying' feeling. Perhaps it *was* 'coke'? But I had the same feeling now, thinking about Kelly; thinking that I was *with* Kelly. Being with Kelly.

There were some movements, and I felt hands on my face. "Sam? Are you OK?" It was Zöe, looking concerned about me. She was on all fours, her head above mine. Behind her, I could see that Kelly and Henk were extricating themselves from each other and from Zöe.

I don't think I had passed out, just been daydreaming. "Yes, Zöe, I'm fine. Thank you for the nice experience." She lowered her head, and kissed me on the lips. As I sat up, I had to add, "Even though I'm a *man*."

Zöe chuckled, "I told you, Sam, a long time ago – when we visited you and Sarah – that I'm bi. I get off on some men ... but find more women I want to play with, than men. Henk and I have a good relationship, including sex ... and it's *not* because he's a cross-dresser!"

We were all sitting on the bearskin rug, now, and Henk laughed, "I *hope* not!" He continued to laugh, but glanced at Kelly, and turned to me, "Actually, our relationship is quite straight – Zöe likes me as a *man*." Zöe was nodding.

The laughing was contagious, and I just had to say, "But if Henk ever decides to get a sex change, you guys can share that huge dildo! *And*, there's always the strap-on." Everyone was laughing, but both Henk and Zöe were shaking their heads.

"Sam, I think you know – that's not what it's about. I like being a man ... but sometimes get turned on by *imagining* myself as a woman."

"Well, it was pretty good imagining, because I didn't recognize you, when I first saw Helga."

Zöe stood, and reached for her robe. "Have you guys had enough 'sex play' tonight?" Then, as a sadistic-sounding afterthought, she added, "Or, maybe Kelly wants to feel a 'real' caning? As you've said, the Dutch are very tolerant – especially the ones who go to saunas. But you probably would get a few chuckles, as people noticed your striped bottom."

Kelly was shaking her head, "No, Zöe, I think we've had enough for one night." She was looking at me for confirmation, and I nodded. Then, she said, "Actually it was enough for two nights!" We were laughing again, as I put on my shorts and tank, and Henk and I moved the rug out of the way, and the coffee table back into position.

Kelly picked up her clothes, and ran upstairs, coming back down a few minutes later, wearing the satin nightgown I had given her for her birthday. Zöe poured a Diet Coke for herself and Kelly, and Henk poured couple of Belgian beers for the men. Well, at least *one* of us was dressed like a man – Henk still wearing a bra and women's bikini underwear under his robe.

As we sat around the couch sipping our drinks, Henk asked, "So I guess you're getting a little more accepting of other people's 'germs', in your old age?" Then, before I could respond, he added, "Or maybe Kelly is having a good effect on you? When we visited five years ago, you were fixated on *non-sexual* things that two people could do together."

I nodded, "Not really to the first, and definitely to the second. I'm still not comfortable with multiple 'sex' partners, and I probably would have been satisfied with a hand-job ..."

Zöe looked indignant, and said, "You mean I swallowed for nothing?"

I laughed, "Actually, it was a wonderful experience ... and I wouldn't have known what I was missing." She seemed satisfied with that. I continued, "But for more than two decades, I respected my married life – at least to the point of not having 'sex' outside our relationship, even though Sarah and I were open to 'playing' with other people."

I thought a little, and said, "And, now, if I 'catch' something, it's only me at stake ... and Kelly. And Kelly is the one pushing for more 'open' relationships *including* having sex with other people."

I slid down the couch, next to Kelly, our hips pressed together, as I took her cheeks in my hands, and kissed her gently. "I have realized – even more tonight – that I love Kelly, and want to be with her." I looked into Kelly's eyes, "I won't hold her back – either professionally, or relationship-wise ... but I hope we can be together ... for a long time." I could see a tear forming in Kelly's eye, and she kissed me passionately.

Looking at Zöe and Henk, Kelly affirmed, "I love Sam, too. I've known it for a while ... but he keeps harping on our age difference, and how I should find someone my own age to play with." She smiled at me, knowing that wasn't exactly what I had said.

Then, she turned serious, "I don't know how long our relationship will last ... or exactly what our relationship will be ... but I hope we're together a long time, too." She gave me a peck on the cheek.

CHAPTER 11: DIKES, DIJKS, & MORE DYKES

Monday morning, we packed our things, and said our goodbyes. As we sat around the breakfast table, Zöe stood, and opened her robe: She wore blue jeans, a dress shirt with rolled-up sleeves, and a vest. She reached over and put on a cap, and the effect was complete. She said, "This morning, I'm a 'butch dyke'. I have a friend who likes me to get a little 'rough' with her. I don't have to go in to work until after lunch, and I can take off the cap and vest, and look reasonably presentable."

Kelly smiled, "So you're a 'cross-dresser' in a way, also."

Zöe shrugged, and sat down at the table, not bothering to put her robe back on. "In a way. But I don't try to pass for a man. And, I don't get sexually turned on by wearing these clothes. They just go with the dominant role that I'm playing today."

Then, she turned to me, "And most of the time, *my* playing doesn't involve sex, either. This partner, for example, will get herself off after I leave – and after I've ripped her clothes off, stuffed her panties in her mouth, and tied her loosely to the bed. I may fuck *her* in the ass with the strap-on, also ... I haven't decided. Mostly, she just likes to be slapped around, a little."

It now seemed that my fetishes were rather tame, compared to those of Henk and Zöe; but very extreme to most other people. Everything was relative.

We kissed Zöe goodbye, and Henk drove us to a rental car agency in Utrecht, where we picked up a BMW sedan. Not only would it be comfortable for the long driving section of our trip, but it would also be able to keep-up with traffic on the Autobahn; and, it would handle the mountain roads well.

When we had transferred our backpacks and rolling cases, we said goodbye to Henk, and headed west. Kelly said, "I thought we were going to the south of Holland?"

"We're going to the far south of The Netherlands. Actually, 'Holland' refers to only two provinces along the coast – roughly from Amsterdam to Rotterdam; everything else is The Netherlands. But before we head south, we're going to visit 'Madurodam', a park with a miniature model of the country – with most of the major things you'll see here – Schiphol airport, container ships, and even the Delta Works – where we'll be going this afternoon."

As the car smoothly accelerated, I explained, "Then, we'll drive through Rotterdam – probably have lunch there – and over the huge Delta Works, which was a decades-long project. If we have time, we'll drive to Eindhoven, where my company has offices. Then, we'll head south to Maastricht, and finally to the Valkenburg area, where we'll visit one of the largest spas in the country."

Kelly shook her head, "That sounds like a lot of driving!"

"Yes. If we went directly to Maastricht, we could get to the spa in less than two hours; so we would be there before noon. But my itinerary will take about five hours of driving, plus time for the stops – so we should get to Thermae 2000 around 5PM. Enough time to get settled, maybe go in the pool, and then have dinner. We'll be there all day tomorrow, enjoying the pools and saunas."

Kelly looked out the window blankly, "It sounds like a long day." Then, "Maybe we could skip the dikes, since we already got that in Driebergen." That was funny; I guess Zöe was a 'dyke' sometimes, a bi other times, and a committed partner with a home life. Kelly added, "I think I still have some jetlag." She continued to stare out the window.

Now, I was concerned, "Kelly! It's been six days – you can't still have jetlag. But you *can* be very tired, since we've had some late nights with … some excitement. Or, are you feeling ill?"

Kelly looked at me and smiled, "No, Sam, I'm not ill. Just tired. I'll be fine."

I hadn't seen Kelly this cranky before. We had a lot more driving to do on this trip, and we had just gotten started. But I couldn't fault Kelly for being tired; we had done a lot during our first week in Europe. This week would be another whirlwind.

Kelly liked Madurodam, an amazing caricature of a Dutch town and the country of The Netherlands; it was cute, but perhaps better for young children. We drove a short distance to the beach at Scheveningen, and I offered Kelly another run. "There are dunes north of us, like the dunes we saw in the national park by Zandvoort."

Kelly shook her head, "I think I'll save my energy for the sauna." She looked at me questioningly, "How do you pronounce this place?"

I laughed, "Ha! I can say it for you," and I did, making a guttural sound, "but it's not likely that I can pronounce it correctly. During World War II, the Dutch resistance tested people to see if they were really Dutch by asking them to pronounce this place. It's virtually impossible, unless you're really Dutch."

We drove south, skirting Rotterdam, and only stopping for a snack before our 40-mile drive through the Delta Works. I informed Kelly, "This was a decades-long project, to protect this part of The Netherlands, where several huge inlets of water bring the North Sea well inland. In 1953, nearly two thousand people died, and 70,000 lost their homes, when a storm surge flooded this whole area."

We drove over several connected 'dijks', and I explained to Kelly, "These aren't really dikes or dams. The Dutch government was going to build dams, but eventually realized that they would alter the entire ecology of this area ... so they built huge sluice gates, instead. They are usually open, but can be closed when a big storm coming from the north threatens high surges."

We made several stops along the way, including the Delta Works museum, which chronicled the incredible engineering project. "This is sometimes called one of the wonders of the modern world." Kelly was only moderately interested, and perhaps we should have saved a couple of hours by driving directly to the spa.

After the Delta Works, and given Kelly's interest level, I decided to drive directly to Maastricht. "We'll be driving through Antwerp – that's in Belgium, and across northern 'Flanders', which is a Dutch-speaking part of Belgium, and the home of the 'Flemish' artists."

Then, I thought of some of the other travel possibilities in the area. "Actually, if we'd had a few more days, we would have driven to Bruges: It's called the 'Venice of the North', as it has many beautiful canals. And, we could have driven through Ghent, and seen the famous cathedral there. Of course, Brussels is a neat place to visit, also – even though it's a big city. We just don't have time to do it all." Kelly nodded, but I think the trip was already becoming a bit overwhelming for her.

Now that I thought about it, Bruges would have been a nice place to spend the night; we could have taken a romantic canal boat tour, and eaten at one of the many great restaurants. I laughed, "Belgium has some great food – similar to what we think of as 'French' food. I think they have the best sauces ... heavy with butter and cream, as they have some of the happiest cows."

Kelly chuckled, but I wasn't kidding. I guess I was starting to get hungry, as my mouth watered and stomach grumbled, just thinking about the Belgian food.

I was startled from my thoughts when Kelly asked, "What did you think about our sexual experiment last night with Henk and Zöe?" That was a good question; one that I had been pondering all morning, but hadn't wanted to discuss with Kelly, until I could gather my thoughts. I guess I would give Kelly the unedited version.

I glanced at Kelly, and back to the road, as I tried to put my thoughts into words. "Well, I thought your performance was fantastic – every part of it. I know that Henk and Zöe were impressed ... and, obviously, you were a big turn on to Henk."

Kelly laughed, "You don't know what he was fantasizing about. And, he was wearing women's underwear." We laughed, and I wondered what *had* excited Henk, last night.

I drove a few minutes, thinking about the evening, and finally had to admit my discomfort. "Kelly, I wasn't comfortable with all of us having unprotected oral sex. I'm still not. And it appears that Zöe has several sex partners." I shivered, wondering how we could have shifted our perspective so far, from playing non-sexually with each other ... to actually having sex with multiple partners.

Kelly was shaking her head. "I'm sorry, Sam, if I pushed you too hard, last night. I knew you would have preferred that Zöe and I had gone down on our own partners."

"It was exciting for me to have Zöe give me head, but I would have been much more comfortable, had I been wearing a condom; and, of course, with Henk wearing a condom, as well."

Why hadn't I lobbied harder for that? Nobody was forcing me to go through with it, but there was social pressure, with everyone else being easy-going, except for me.

I sat back in the car seat, as I realized how little social pressure it had taken; and, how easily my relationship with Kelly had turned sexual. While I had been quite serious about my definition of sex, I had used the mix-up of our drinking glasses as an excuse ... to go farther. If I could be this weak, it seemed amazing that STDs weren't an even more serious epidemic.

Kelly had been watching me, as the tortured thoughts rambled through my mind. "Sam, I'm proud of you for letting us have that experience without making a scene. Both Zöe and I were pushing you. As you know, I like finding your 'weaknesses', and pushing you to overcome them, as much as you do with me. But if you are that upset about it, I'll be more sensitive and supportive."

Kelly looked out her side window, and back to me, "And what about friends? What about Julie? You could have used a condom with her, and all of my friends have gone down on you." Suddenly my stomach rumbled again ... and it might not have been because I was hungry.

Kelly looked out the side window again, and we drove in silence ... for 30 seconds, before she turned back to me, "And, what about Fiona?" My stomach rumbled again.

"I don't know, Kelly; I really don't. Using condoms seems to be the best answer; and maybe they should be rolled over the tongue for oral sex?" It wasn't a very satisfying answer. If only there weren't STD's, or at least if there were cures for all of them ...

I looked over at Kelly; she was looking out the side window, slowly shaking her head. Perhaps I was being the hypocritical one, talking about non-sexual play and using condoms, after allowing Kelly's friends to have oral sex with me? When I was married to Sarah, it had all been so simple: I could play intimately with female friends, but there would be no sex ... so protection from STDs was never anything that I had to think about.

It took another two hours of driving to get to Maastricht, and we arrived in mid-afternoon. I parked near the main square, the *vrijthof*, and we had a snack at one of the few restaurants that had tables and chairs outside this late in the season. The *bitterballen* were different here, even more delicious, and the beer took the edge off the hours of driving I had done.

We were only 20 minutes from the spa and hotel, now, and I thought we would walk around a little, and visit the *Vrijthof* Museum, but it was closed on Mondays. I heard a sigh of relief from Kelly; we were both ready for a little relaxation.

We drove across the Maas River, for which the town had been named, and continued through a beautiful area of rolling hills and quaint villages, arriving at the spa at 4:30 – plenty of time for some relaxation before dinner.

As we checked in, I perused a pamphlet on the spa, and saw that the saunas – usually taken nude – required bathing suits two Mondays per month, and the pools – which usually required a suit – were nude two Mondays per month. And today was one of the nude pool days. I had been here twice before, and always had to wear a suit in the main pool area.

Our room was nice, but not opulent; it featured a small Japanese garden area, and sliding doors led to a patio that overlooked the forest. We got settled, and changed into the robes provided with the room, then walked down to the main indoor pool area, taking towels from the small reception area, after flashing our room key.

There were a few dozen people in the huge space, and it was very quiet – perhaps at this hour most people were already back in their rooms? Or, perhaps everyone was in the sauna areas?

The place seemed different than when I had been here before, and I finally realized why: There were no children. While most sauna and health spa patrons were 25-85 years old, and there seemed to always be a deficit of teenagers, there were always some young children that parents had brought with them. I guess on the 'nude only' days, there were fewer people, and fewer children, at the resort.

We could have enjoyed a quieter and more relaxing day today in the pool area, had we come directly from Utrecht. But the younger children weren't seen often in the sauna area, so at least that part of the place should be relaxed, tomorrow.

As I took off my robe, and hung it on a nearby wall hook, I looked at Kelly: She was staring into the open space, her mouth agape, and eyes large. And I couldn't help staring at those beautiful, hazel eyes, now sparkling from the bright light entering the space, and from her evident enchantment with the beauty of this place.

"Wow! I had no idea it would be this big. And, what neat architecture!" Sam hadn't told me much about this spa, except that it was a popular sauna destination in the south of Holland. As I looked around, I was enthralled with the openness, the modern look, and the relaxed feel of the place; while it was already getting chilly outside, it felt quite warm and humid in here – like a sultry rainforest.

I couldn't stop looking around: There were huge, angled, laminated wood beams, rising from the glass walls, supporting angled glass skylights, to a very high, beamed ceiling. The pool was gigantic, curving around the room, with inlets that led to whirlpools, and a multitude of tropical plants making this seem like an island paradise.

I followed Sam's lead, and slipped off and hung my robe and towel. Fortunately, Sam was correct – all of the people were nude; it was a good thing, because we hadn't worn anything under the robes. We walked around the curving deck, and down the wide steps into the warm pool; the water was luscious.

I floated, my body tingling, probably from the lack of sleep, and looked up at the wooden beams high above. I closed my eyes, my mind boggled at the insight I'd had over the past few nights; not insights into Sam, or sex ... or sex with Sam, but where my Ph.D. dissertation project could lead. It had taken a lot of research, but I now had a clear vision – a vision of the future, potentially revolutionizing the process of drug discovery; and, hopefully, discovering some important new drugs, in the process.

I opened my eyes, and treaded water, rotating slowly, as I looked around the huge space. When I had turned nearly 360 degrees, I saw Sam, sitting on the edge of the pool by one of the inlets, and smiling at me. I swam over to him, and we continued into the whirlpool, which was surrounded by tropical plants and, fortunately, being unused by anyone else.

The jets weren't turned on and, without a lot of other people around, it was very quiet, only the sounds of flowing water, and water from a nearby waterfall reaching my ears.

Sam and I sat on the bench of the private, circular pool, and he leaned over and kissed me. "I'm sorry you haven't been sleeping well, Kelly." He stroked my hair, as he looked at me with concern.

I had been planning to tell Sam soon, but now the time had come for me to share my thoughts. "Sam, I'm not sure how to tell you this," I tried not to laugh, as this was a serious subject ... except for the introduction that I had just thought-up spontaneously, "but I've been cheating on you."

There was a slight delay, before Sam cocked his head, and said "What?" Then he put a finger in one of his ears, and said, "I must have gotten water in my ears; I don't think I heard you correctly."

I chuckled, "You heard me. I haven't been all yours on this trip. I will give you an apology ... but I'm more excited about telling you what I've discovered." Sam shook his head abruptly, as if trying to rid his mind of an ugly thought. He said nothing and, as I smiled at him, his face relaxed, the furrows in his brow nearly disappearing, and a slight, mischievous smile forming on his lips.

I said, "As you predicted, I felt jet lag mainly on the second and third afternoons. By the time we got to the sex club, I think I was over the jet lag, but I had a gnawing thought ... about my research project. And that night, after you were asleep, I used your tablet to do some research." I realized I was looking down into the swirling water, and glanced back up at Sam, "And I was awake most of the last two nights, also – doing more research, and checking my idea. And I think it will work!"

Sam was slowly shaking his head, "*What* will 'work', exactly?"

It took twenty minutes, but I described my thought process in detail. I reviewed the concept of my project – automating the current generation of DNA sequencers to check hundreds, or thousands, of genes that are responsible for making chemicals or their receptors that are used in various biochemical pathways throughout the body.

It was a work in progress, and the goal was – initially – to facilitate research on 'mechanisms of action' – the biochemical pathways that underlie the detailed workings of the body, and its responses, including why we get certain diseases.

The lay public often thinks that one gene is responsible for one characteristic, for example susceptibility to a disease. However, few diseases are caused by a single mutation; more often, there are several – or dozens – of genes that are related to a particular illness. By sequencing these genes – analyzing the coded message – and determining what proteins the genes produce, it may be possible to determine what mechanisms of action are involved for each disease.

So my automation of the DNA machine would help researchers to trace the biochemical pathways to a disease, which could then enable development of drugs that would interrupt those pathways. There are often multiple pathways, so this process can be very complex and tedious.

My breakthrough was to think backwards: Take the known DNA sequences of viruses and knowledge of the human genome, and develop a computer program that would predict, and then test every possible mechanism of action – like thinking many steps ahead when playing chess – for a very specific disease. Then, the computer would direct a DNA machine to sequence the various antibodies and receptors, and these would be used to determine the proteins, for example the enzymes, involved.

This information could then be used to design a drug that interferes with the protein production, or binds to the receptors, or otherwise interrupts the pathway, thereby preventing the disease. It seemed like a long shot, but it was perfect for a creative Ph.D. dissertation topic.

Sam was initially very skeptical, "I think you're looking at this too simplistically. Many pathways are already known, but that doesn't mean we can easily develop drugs to modify them. And there are many parallel pathways, so interrupting one may not prevent others from causing the disease."

Sam put his head back on the edge of the pool and looked up at the ceiling for several minutes. Then, he smiled, and said brightly, "But if you could really do what you're thinking, you would have a blockbuster technology on your hands." He chuckled, the implication being that I had come up with a good idea, but Sam didn't think it likely that I could really pull it off. I would have to discuss this with my advisor at the university.

We swam across the pool, and retrieved our towels, then Sam led me through the building. We passed through a curtain into another section, where there were several sauna rooms, another jacuzzi, a steam room, and line of showers open to the room.

We entered the first sauna, spread our towels, and relaxed in the heat. There were a handful of other people in the sauna with us, one much older couple (in their 80's?), and several middle-aged men and women. I lay down on the upper bench, my towel spread over a wooden triangle – just like in Sam's sauna – where my head rested, my feet on the towel, and my knees up, only a few inches from the sauna ceiling. It was quiet in here, only the creaks of the sauna furnace punctuating the otherwise silent ambiance.

After our typical ten-minute sauna session, we took quick showers and, carrying our towels, walked through a side-door and found ourselves on a winding path through the outdoor gardens. There was a large swimming pool, and I put my toe in the water, but it was freezing.

Sam put the towel around his neck, and I wrapped mine around my waist, and we continued walking around the grounds, holding hands. Our bodies were steaming, but it didn't feel cold; it was now dusk, and thin orange clouds striped the horizon, beyond the forest and fields.

We circled around the building, and walked back inside – now again in the main pool area. Walking up some steps, we entered a small, ultra-modern bar; Sam wrapped his towel around his waist, and we sat at a small circular table. The bartender came over – fully dressed, and looking a bit out-of-place in this '*naturiste*' environment, but he took our order efficiently, without a single glance at my bare breasts.

As Sam sipped his Belgian beer, he suddenly remarked, "It *might* work. But I think you're missing a critical element: It's not just the composition of the proteins, but their detailed structure – how they fold to make three-dimensional objects that fit together like a jig-saw puzzle." He took a swig of the dark golden liquid; I recognized the tulip-shaped glass, and then saw 'Duvel' in gold letters.

I nodded, "There is software that can predict the folding of proteins ..." And then, I realized that Sam had a point: Things were more complicated than I had realized ... as usual. My thoughts turned to how I could incorporate protein-folding algorithms into my software. We finished our drinks, thanked the bartender, and made our way back downstairs to retrieve our robes. Then, we went back to our room to dress for dinner ... after a little tension release that I knew both Sam and I needed.

The restaurant was filled; it was a good thing that Sam had made dinner reservations when he had reserved our room. We had eaten a light lunch, and were famished. The menu was in Dutch, English, and French, and featured gourmet fare – most of which I didn't recognize. I closed the menu, and suggested that Sam order for both of us.

In his usual style, he went a bit overboard, first ordering a special appetizer – Zeeland oysters with a thyme-potato flan, then the smoked eel soup, and finally the chateaubriand for two. He then decided to go with the restaurant's wine-pairing menu. We would have four wines, especially selected for our menu choices ... and the dessert, which I wasn't sure we would get to, or need, by the time we were finished with the food that Sam had already ordered.

Without delay, we were poured glasses of a sparkling wine from the vineyards along the Moselle River; Sam informed me that we would be sampling many more of these wines in a couple of days.

The oysters came, and I tried one: It was delicious! We held our glasses high, as Sam toasted: To our trip, and to my 'breakthrough' idea. After a sip of wine, I put my glass down, and looked around the room: It looked like any normal gourmet restaurant, with people well-dressed, many women in beautiful dresses, and men in a jacket and tie. Sam was wearing a sport jacket, and looked quite dapper – much younger than his years would suggest.

The lights were low, and candles on each table flickered. I irreverently touched my knife against the wineglass, and it 'dinged' with a perfect tone, that carried much farther than I had expected, as I saw a few glances from nearby tables. The patrons of the restaurant were mostly middle-aged, with a few older couples, and one or two 'younger couples' – probably in their late 30s or early 40s.

I recognized a few of the people from the pool or the sauna, and I realized that – despite all the formality and fine dinner wear here at the restaurant – all of these people had been nude with each other just a few hours before; and we would undoubtedly see many of them nude tomorrow.

The soup came, and I wasn't sure what to expect, although I had tried smoked eel in Amsterdam; it was outrageous – probably the best soup I'd ever tasted. It had a thick cream base, and I was already getting full ... and feeling the wine. We were now on our second wine, a Gewürztraminer, that was light and fruity.

Sam said, "I think you're getting a decent perspective on The Netherlands; we didn't drive to the north, missed Rotterdam, and I would have liked to take you to Eindhoven, and maybe a few other places ... but we did see a lot of the country, and the culture." I smiled, thinking of the 'culture' we had experienced in the past couple of days ... and nights.

Sam continued, "But tomorrow will end our first week in Europe – and we've only seen one country so-far. And we have several days planned in London and vicinity at the end of the trip; so we only have another ten days to see Germany, Switzerland, and France. We could easily spend two or three weeks in Germany; even seeing a decent amount of Switzerland would take ten days; and ten days is barely enough to get a feeling for Paris!"

I took another sip of the fragrant wine, "So are we going to skip the rest, and go directly to Paris tomorrow?"

Sam stopped suddenly, his spoon in mid-air, and looked at me questioningly. I shook my head, and he said,

"We can do anything you want, Kelly. But you'll see a lot on our drive, and there are a few more things I'd like to share with you. For example, sitting on the deck outside our room, with some wine," he lifted his glass, "watching the Matterhorn." He put down his glass, and sipped the soup from his spoon.

"I'm happy doing anything, Sam. I'm just glad to be here. With you." The waiter cleared our table, except for the latest glass of wine, and brought the intermezzo: A lemon-ginger sorbet inside a sugared lemon.

Sam stood, walked around the table, bent down, and kissed me. Then, he walked back, sat down, spread the large cloth napkin across his lap, and tasted the sorbet. This man may be an over-analytical, clinical, nerd ... but he had a nice romantic streak somewhere within him. Sam continued to be thoughtful and kind.

Somehow, that thought triggered a strange image: I was seeing myself, as I had been last night, in a knee-chest position on the coffee table, Henk and Zöe seeing my privates, and Sam spanking me; and then, Zöe strapping me. My muscles clenched, and I wondered why I had thought of that image rather, for example, than the image of Henk opening his robe, showing us his bra and panties; or the image of Zöe and I butt-to-butt, connected by that huge dildo.

The main course came, and the steak was carved tableside, the entire platter being unloaded onto our plates. There were scalloped potatoes, a mound of wild forest mushrooms, asparagus, and a black truffle aioli. A French Bordeaux was poured, and Sam explained the region, and where this winery sat, relative to the more famous Chateaux.

The plate looked beautiful, and tasted even better; I had never tasted anything like the mushrooms, which had been cooked in wine and butter. We were enjoying our dinner at a slow pace, and some of the other tables were now empty. The waiter asked how we were doing, and left the bottle of wine, telling Sam that there weren't many 'takers' on the wine-pairing, and that we could have the rest of the bottle – which was at least half filled.

It had been a romantic dinner, and I was ready to retire for the evening – and *not* do any research ... but Sam insisted that we continue to the dessert course, with the wine pairing, of course. We sipped the luscious red wine, and Sam explained our driving itinerary Wednesday and Thursday. Then, on Friday, we would be arriving in Munich, Germany.

I sat back, and marveled that I was actually here, visiting these historic cities, seeing the countryside, and tasting the foods. My eyes closed, and I heard 'Kelly?'. I must have drifted off, because the dessert was now in front of us: It was a chocolate box, with a lavender crème brulée, surrounded by a design of fresh mango and blueberries, and drizzled with a fig-balsamic reduction.

It was like a dream; but I was now awake, and I tasted a piece of mango with the balsamic drizzle: My eyes rolled to the back of my head, and I knew I must be in heaven! This was an incredible dessert! How did they 'fire' the crème brulée in that hard, dark chocolate box?

Then, the waiter poured the wine, and left this bottle, also. Sam explained, "This is a *Beerenauslese*, a sweet dessert wine, from the Rheinhessen area of Germany. We'll be driving near that area – on the other side of the river – on Thursday. The grapes are allowed to over-ripen, so there is a high sugar content."

I didn't care about the details, but one sip of the wine, and I was in heaven again: It was almost like honey, with a slight apricot aftertaste. The sweet wine paired with the rich dessert incredibly well, and somehow I was awake again. Sam smiled, as he watched me enjoy the finale of our dinner.

We managed to make it all the way back to the room, and Sam helped me undress, and tucked me into bed. He turned off all the lights, except a nightlight in the bathroom and, as he unbuttoned his shirt, he leaned over and kissed me. And that was the last thing I remember.

I woke Tuesday morning, feeling much more refreshed; I had not done any research last night, as my body and my mind needed the rest. I sat up, and realized that I had slept in the nude, and wondered whether I had even brushed my teeth, before Sam put me to bed. Sam was sitting on the patio, studying his tablet. I spent a few minutes in the bathroom, washing my face and brushing my teeth, then stepped into the sandals provided by the spa, and opened the sliding door.

It was another beautiful day. Although there were more clouds than we'd had in Amsterdam, the forest was a deep green color, and the sky – in-between the clouds – was a deep blue. It was nice that the patio was totally private, so I could walk out without clothes. Then, I realized how funny that was, considering that everyone here would be seeing each other without clothes all day.

I straddled Sam's left leg, and leaned forward, taking his head in my hands, and giving him a good morning kiss. We hugged, and I felt a stirring, amplified by the pressure of Sam's leg against me. I began moving, as I kissed Sam again, and put my head on his shoulder. His arms around my back, I opened the top of his robe, and pressed up against him, my breasts against his chest.

For some reason, this position – at this moment – was an incredible turn on. I humped Sam's leg, and rocked against him, as he held me tight. As I reached a heightened state of sensitivity, I lifted my head and looked at Sam; I knew he would want to make love to me, and it might be selfish, but I really wanted to get off here, and now. Sam smiled and nodded, innately understanding my desire, and I put my head back on his shoulder and closed my eyes.

My legs squeezed around Sam's thigh as I rocked forward, then down, my hips moving in a circular motion as I relaxed all of my weight onto him. His hands dropped, and squeezed my bum, nicely, massaging in synch with my increasingly rapid motions. Letting my own hands drop to Sam's bottom, I grabbed, squeezed, and pulled him up to me, willing his help as I sought my release.

Sam responded to my mental request, his leg tensing and relaxing, and then coming up against my sex, repeatedly, pounding, as I dropped onto him with furious desire. I pulled Sam to me, as I tensed every muscle in my body in one last spasm of agony, and found my glorious release. Then, I came a second time. I held Sam's head and kissed him, coming a third time as Sam slowed the motion of his leg, and I finally collapsed against him, breathing heavily, fully spent.

Sam gave me a few moments to calm, our cheeks together, my breasts pressed into his chest. Then he asked, "Was that as good as it looked?" He chuckled, and I pinched his bottom, then slid off his leg.

"Thank you, Sam. It was great." I bent down and gave him a peck on the lips. As I pulled open the sliding door, I turned to Sam, and added, "And I won't make you go all day, seeing those beautiful nude women, without having an orgasm. So I'll satisfy you any way you want. Sir."

Sam understood that I wasn't asking for a spanking, but that I would submit to him … yes, even if he wanted to spank me. My body was high on the endorphin rush from my orgasm, and I didn't care what Sam requested.

Sam loudly commanded, "Then get back here, young lady! Where do you think you're going?" Uh oh; maybe Sam thought I *had* asked for some discipline?

As I slowly walked to him, I answered, "I was going to get into bed, and wait for you."

Sam stood, and turned the chair around. "Front of chair position, young lady!"

I stepped in front of the chair, put my feet on either side of the legs, and bent over at the waist, holding the thin arms of the chair, dropping my head, and trying to relax my butt. I was still tingling, and Sam's hand on my left buttock sent an electric jolt through me.

I awaited my fate, whatever my lover had decided; I had given him full power over me. I looked up briefly, out into the forest, and then dropped my head again, and closed my eyes. "I'm ready, Sir."

A few tense moments passed, and Sam's hand left me; then I felt his front against me. He lifted his dick – it was already hard – onto the top of my butt crack, and rubbed himself against me. It didn't take long before Sam was re-positioning himself, and I reached under, taking him in my hand, and inserting him into my wetness.

I held his balls in my right hand, as I held myself up with my left. Sam held my hips, and I probably would have fallen into the chair, had he let go. No words were spoken: Sam pounded into me, as I continued to hold his balls firmly. I knew Sam was ready when he suddenly slowed down, taking long strokes, plunging deeply into me.

Then, his body tensed, and he shot his load into me, our bodies conjoined and motionless for an instant, before Sam began thrusting quickly, almost vibratory, as his orgasm subsided.

Sam's body relaxed, and he bent forward, his chest on my back. He reached around and held my breasts, gently kneading them, and I had to support myself with both hands on the arms of the chair. I expected him to come out of me at any time, but felt a throb, and then Sam started moving again, slowly, pushing himself into my depths. I couldn't believe it: Was he going to try for a second orgasm, so soon after the last one?

Then, I felt Sam's body heave on top of me, and realized he was laughing. His shrunken manhood slid out of me, as expected, and he pulled me up, turned me around, and kissed me. Then, he pushed me toward the sliding door, gave me a good slap on the bottom, and said, "Get the shower going, young lady."

We ate in the restaurant, which offered a typical Dutch breakfast buffet – breads, cheeses, meats, jams, fruit, and made-to-order coffees. I knew that I must be already gaining weight, so limited myself to a flaky croissant, and a cappuccino. Then, we went down to the pool area.

We wore our bathing suits and robes, but there were already quite a few people in the pool, including a few kids, so we decided to skip the pool, and continued to the sauna side of the building. We stopped at the entrance, took off our suits, and shoes, and put them in a little 'cubby', then took our towels, and walked through the curtain into the sauna area.

We spent the day enjoying the various options – dry saunas, wet steam baths, cold pools, and hot jacuzzis. The facilities were much bigger than I had realized. An outside pool was shaped in a spiral, and had a fast-flowing current that pulled everyone along, and spat them back out at the wide end of the spiral. Sam tried swimming against the current ... but went backwards through the spiral, despite his valiant effort to maintain his position.

We walked, nude down the meandering paths, trying out the various sauna cabins – each one having some special feature.

In one cabin, we were fortunate to enter just as a special ceremony was beginning. All of the benches were filled, with probably more than 40 bodies in the small room, but people squeezed together and made room for us.

There were some cute girls across from us – probably my age, or perhaps a couple of years older – quite the beauties. And, sitting next to me, our flesh squeezing together, was also a young woman – certainly not over thirty years old; but she must have weighed at least three hundred pounds, each of her breasts bigger than my head, and her private parts well-hidden by rolls of fat.

Now, another girl about my age, quite fit and - if anything - too lean, entered the sauna, carrying an armful of branches and leaves. She looked like a triathlete, as she bent to put her load on the sauna tiles. Then she stood, and clapped her hands together.

Over a ten-minute period, eucalyptus branches were waved, and brought down onto the sauna rocks. The scent was unmistakable, and everyone was focused, as if in a trance. I didn't understand exactly what was being said, but got the gist of it – the eucalyptus part of an ancient rite of health.

By the time the ceremony was over, everyone was dripping; I probably lost several pounds in that sauna. We all filed out, and headed to the nearest showers, and the outdoor heated pool. Sam leaned over and explained, "That ceremony is similar to the old Russian 'banya' – which is the closest relative to the Finnish sauna. They used to hit each other with eucalyptus branches, supposedly to improve the circulation. Now, it's just an aromatic ceremony."

We went into the building and stepped up onto the shower platform – which had at least a dozen showerheads in a row. I did a quick rinse, and stepped into the room, drying my eyes with my towel, and watching Sam bathe. At the end of the row of showers was an old woman – probably an octogenarian, who was stooped over, and had trouble making it over the six-inch step onto the shower platform.

But, next to Sam, a true beauty started her shower: She was a very dark black woman, probably a model or actress – with a perfect Playboy-type body, and personality to match; even though she wasn't interacting with another soul at the moment. It's funny how we can 'tell' people's types, by looking at them, sometimes even when they're nude. Maybe I was unconsciously 'profiling'?

Then a woman, probably fortyish, stepped into the position on the other side of Sam. She was stout – actually, quite similar to Zöe's body shape, but smaller, and with much smaller breasts. Her hair was in a short, severe style, and she had a bar through each of her nipples, and obvious genital jewelry, as well.

From her look, her stance, her personality, she was obviously 'butch'. None of my friends was gay – as far as I knew – and I really didn't know what the 'other' partner, to a butch lesbian would look like. I guess I shouldn't try to generalize ... but I wondered if the counterpart to a butch female is a 'girlie' female?

I surveyed the central area, around which were arranged the saunas, and other facilities, and saw more than a hundred people – perhaps two hundred. It was getting 'crowded' here. And my one standout thought: We're all the same. Everyone here, walking by me, nude, looks just like everyone crossing a major street in any big city.

In fact, I suddenly realized that I had entirely forgotten about the fact that everyone was nude; we were just people, all different, and all the same. A shiver went down my spine, and I was glad to see that Sam was finally out of the shower. "Can we get into a sauna or jacuzzi, now? I'm getting chilled."

Sam responded instantly, "Of course, Kelly. How about the steam bath? We haven't been in that, yet." I nodded blankly, not sure exactly what a 'steam bath' was, but happy, if I could get warmed up, again. We walked across the space, and left our towels on a hook outside. Sam held the door open a crack, and we both slipped in. Into the fog – a hot, wet, thick, moving fog, that blinded us from seeing anything.

Sam took my hand, and led me across to a bench. We sat down directly on the bench – the first time our bottoms had touched anything but air, water, or a towel – and we started to warm. The steam hissed from a pipe somewhere, and swirled in front of us. I could barely see another couple, sitting farther down on the same bench. We were dripping.

I squeezed Sam's hand, and looked at him, through the fog; I could barely see him, a foot away, but he nodded and stood. Then he reached over and picked up a squeegee ... and wiped the bench, before leading me back through the door into a much more comfortable world.

"You didn't like that?" Sam asked, chuckling, and wiping his brow with the corner of his towel.

"Not especially. Can we just go in the jacuzzi, for a while?"

Sam laughed, and said, "Sure." Then he eyed the showers and, seeing another gorgeous woman, this time with waist-length blond hair (probably a Swede), he headed that direction, saying, "We need to get a quick rinse-off, first."

It really was a relaxing day – something I needed, and that fortified me, even after the good sleep I'd had. Sam offered to pay for a massage, and even a full spa treatment, but I declined, preferring to relax with everyone in the saunas, and around the pool.

In the late afternoon, we went back to the room, showered again, put on our jeans and long-sleeve shirts, and carried our jackets out to the car. Then we drove down the hill, around the dale, and whatever, to a small village, which was at the base of a castle.

Sam and I walked, hand-in-hand, and then – as I got chilled, and put on my jacket – with his arm around me. We visited small shops and art galleries. It was cute, but touristy. But it did feel 'old world', and I again realized how special this was – being in Europe, being with Sam.

We ate at a small café, with probably only a half dozen tables. The food was amazing, again. This was basically a 'hole-in-the-wall' place, and we were having a dinner that was more incredible than at the French restaurant Sam had taken me to – when my friends had first discovered Sam and I ... when I had been jolted by the vibrations from Sam's little remote-controlled vaginal vibrator.

We got back to the room not quite as inebriated as we'd been last night, and made love slowly and passionately. Sam spooned me, his body curving around mine, our heat combining, a deep sleep finally overtaking the day's events. It had been a very surreal day – relaxing and stimulating, seeing a slice of humanity, and experiencing a lifestyle that I'd never seen in the U.S.

Except at Sam's house.

CHAPTER 12: RIVERS OF WINE

We checked out of the hotel, and were on the road by eight in the morning, heading south, toward Luxembourg. I felt rested, and ready for the next part of our trip. We entered Belgium, and drove along the river – it's name now morphed from the Dutch 'Maas' to the French 'Meuse', and through the picturesque town of Liège.

Then we were in the countryside. I watched the landscape go by – fields, and trees, and more trees, with huge puffy clouds dotting a deep blue sky. We drove through small villages and, after nearly two hours, I pointed at a sign, which welcomed us to Luxembourg.

I commented to Sam, "Their flag is red, white, and blue, also."

Sam laughed, "Yes – there are a lot of country flags with those colors. The Luxembourg flag is basically the same as the Dutch flag, only with lighter colors. And the French flag is similar to the Dutch flag, but with the colors striped vertically, instead of horizontally."

Sam continued his lecture. "After Napoleon came through here, the country became a 'Grand Duchy', and was owned by Germany and The Netherlands. I'm not exactly sure how that worked ..."

I had to ask, "So what is a 'grand duchy'?"

Sam smiled, and replied, "It's a small country headed by a 'Grand Duke'." Very helpful! Then he explained a bit more, "Luxembourg has a constitutional government, but is headed by a monarch – sort-of like the U.K. And, also like The Netherlands, which calls itself a 'kingdom'." Sam was a fount of information, more than I needed.

We drove through Luxembourg City without stopping, and headed back into the countryside, which was now becoming more hilly. I looked over at Sam, and he explained, "We're going to the East side of Luxembourg – the 'Mullerthal' region – to visit the so-called 'Little Switzerland'. It's an area of mountains and streams, rock formations and boulders, and nearly 70 miles of hiking trails."

In less than thirty minutes, we entered the small town of Echternach, and Sam pulled over suddenly and parked. I asked, "Are we here?" We were in the middle of the town, and I didn't see anything resembling a hiking trail, only small shops, and plenty of cars driving by.

Sam replied, "No, we're just going to pick up some items for a picnic." We locked the car, and I followed Sam down the street, where we stopped first at a *boulangerie*, a bread and pastry shop, and then at a meat shop, where there was an incredible array of sausages, fowl, and animal parts hanging from the ceiling.

We made a selection from the glass cases, and the meat was sliced and packed for us. Sam inquired, and we found a cheese shop a few blocks away, and Sam made a selection. Once again, we had bought way more food than the two of us could eat.

We hopped back into the car, and drove a short distance, entering a beautiful hilly area, with tall trees and huge boulders. Sam parked in a small lot, and loaded the food into his backpack. Then, we headed down one of the many trails. Sam apologized that we didn't have time to walk very far, but was satisfied when we soon found a nice stream, and some flat rocks on which we could sit and have our picnic.

This was another picture spot, and Sam took some shots of the beautiful surroundings with his camera, and then we took a few selfies with his phone. It was truly an idyllic setting – much more beautiful than the small stream near Sam's house.

After our lunch, I felt the water temperature, but decided it was too cold to even bother finding a pond in which we could swim. We packed-up, and walked back to the car to continue our drive; thirty minutes later, we crossed a large river, and entered the outskirts of the ancient town of Trier.

Sam informed me, "Trier is probably the oldest city in Germany – dating from before the Roman Empire. There are quite a few things to see here, including the Roman baths."

I joked, "Oh, are we going to go to a sauna here, too?"

Sam laughed, "No, Kelly. All that's left of the Roman baths are a few walls, and brick archways. We'll just have to come back to Europe a few more times, to explore some of these places in more detail."

We drove along the river, and Sam explained, "This is the Moselle River – called the 'Mosel River' around here, since they speak German, not French. It's a famous wine region, so we'll stop at a few wineries to do some tasting."

Sam glanced at me as he drove, "That's why I wanted to be sure we had eaten something; I'm not sure how many tastings we'll be doing, but I've planned for us to spend the night in Koblenz, which is only about an hour's drive from here. With all the wine tasting stops, we'll probably get there in three or four hours."

Ten minutes later, we were pulling in to the first winery. The sky had clouded-up, and it felt cooler, but the view of the vineyards and river beyond was spectacular. I insisted that Sam take a few more snapshots, and he set his camera on the hood of our car and set the automatic timer to get a great shot of us standing next to the winery, with the river and vineyards behind us.

We were given a private tour, and tasted some of the local Rieslings. I learned that the cool weather in this region, along with the coarse soil and the slopes of the vineyards, was ideal for the varieties of grapes grown here, providing drainage and keeping the frost off the vines.

We also sampled some other varieties, including Gewürztraminer, Müller-Thurgau, and the rustic wine made from Elbling grapes, which Sam said would be the base for the sparkling wines we would be tasting a bit farther down the river.

At the second winery we took another tour, seeing the huge fermentation tanks, and sampling some wines directly from the barrel. I learned about the *prädikatswein* designation that Germany gives to quality wines, and about the varying categories of wine according to sweetness: *Spätlese, Auslese, Beerenauslese, Trocken-beerenauslese,* and finally *Eiswein.*

We tasted a sample of Eiswein, which was even sweeter than the dessert wine we'd had last night. Sam explained that for this special wine, the grapes were allowed to ripen, becoming higher in sugar content, until the first frost; that morning (and no later), the grapes are quickly picked, and the sweetest-possible wine produced.

We continued our drive, winding along the bank of the river. The third winery was famous for its *champagne methodoise,* a way of making sparkling wine. It was 'champagne', but it cannot be called that, unless it was made in the Champagne region of France.

We tasted several different versions of this wine, which is made from the Elbling grapes, and learned that smaller and more bubbles are desirable. By this time, I was definitely feeling the alcohol, and I could tell that Sam was in the same condition by some slurring of words, as he educated me further about the region.

We stopped at one more winery, and tasted more sparkling wine. Getting back into the car, Sam asked, "Would it be OK with you, Kelly, if we headed directly to our hotel in Koblenz? Otherwise, after one more wine tasting, you might have to do the driving."

I chuckled, "Sure, Sam. That sounds fine. I think I've had enough wine, also. And I'm not sure I could tell a Riesling from a Merlot, right now." Sam glanced over and gave me a 'look'; of course, I could tell the difference between a red wine and a white wine. But that was about it. I was ready to take a break from our hard day of touring.

The hotel in Koblenz sat at the confluence of the Mosel and Rhine rivers, and our penthouse suite overlooked both rivers. We sat on the narrow balcony, watching ships pass by in every direction. It was still early, so we decided to walk around the area.

Across the street was a small museum with 20th-century art, including a few Picassos, and a short distance further was the sprit of land at the confluence of the two huge rivers. There was a giant equestrian statue, and we walked to the tip of the plaza, which looked like the bow of a ship. Sam had to take quite a few shots – of the bridges down the river, and of several ships passing by. We also took a few selfies to add to our collection.

We walked back, past our hotel, and into an area filled with art galleries. We did some window-shopping, and came upon a huge, indoor mall, with ultramodern shops.

There were shoe stores and dress stores ... and I could have spent much longer shopping, but knew that Sam was getting antsy.

However, we both noticed some beautiful jackets in one of the windows, and Sam insisted that I try one on. They were Bogner jackets ... but when I glanced at the prices – more than $2,000 – I decided to not even try them on. I knew that Sam would buy me anything I wanted, but I didn't need something that over-the-top.

However, I did find a very stylish down jacket – grey with a faux fox fur collar. It fit perfectly, and would be much better than what I had brought for skiing. It would also be nice for walking around the cities, now that it was getting cooler.

Sam paid for the jacket, reminding me twice that I would need to either stuff it into my rolling case, or to carry it on the plane. That wouldn't be a problem. I put the jacket on as we walked out to the street, and then I turned, and gave Sam a big kiss. We walked a while longer, holding hands, and then headed back towards our hotel. We passed several nice-looking restaurants, Sam reading all of the menus posted in the windows.

Then, he turned to me with a pained expression, and asked, "Kelly, there are lots of good restaurants around here ... and we can eat whatever you want," he smiled at me, and put his arms out with his palms up, before he continued, "but what would you think about eating at the beer garden that we saw, back on the point?" I could tell that he really had his heart set on eating there.

"Well, Sam, now that I have a nice jacket to keep me warm, that would be fine. But I'm not sure how much beer I can drink, after all that wine we imbibed during our drive."

Sam laughed, "I won't force you to drink beer. But the menu looked good, and they'll only be open for another two weeks this season." We walked back to the point, as the sun set, the clouds becoming pinks and purples, and reflecting off the rivers. Ships continued to ply their way upstream – which Sam said was to the south, or downstream – to the North Sea; it seemed backwards.

There were lots of wooden tables and chairs, and Sam said that during the summer they would be packed; but it was still early in the evening, and late in the season, so there were only a few people in the *biergarten*. We found a couch, and sat together, facing the rivers, as the sky darkened, and a light breeze rustled the trees.

I ordered the pork schnitzel with fries, and was astounded when the order came, and it covered the plate, hanging over the edges. Sam ate homemade sausages, with wine sauerkraut. Sam ordered a dark beer, and then – after our plates were cleared – ordered the 'flaming' cake, a specialty of this *biergarten*.

I zipped my jacket, and was toasty, as we shared the dessert, and watched ships – now brightly lit – pass by, one after another. We walked back to the hotel, and sat out on the balcony for a while, unable to take our eyes off the river scene. Sam stayed out there, doing some research on his tablet, while I went inside to get ready for bed.

This morning, I had been a little selfish, but I had offered Sam anything he wanted – and he pretended that he was going to spank me; then, he had made love to me from behind, both of us enjoying the forest view.

It was getting cold on the balcony, so I walked back into the room and put my tablet down. I turned the corner into the bedroom, and found Kelly, sitting on the bed – and looking very sexy – in her satin nightgown. Her deep auburn hair fell around her onto the bed, and her eyes sparkled, despite the dim light. She pulled her knees to her chest, her swollen lips peaking out from between her legs, and she exhaled loudly.

"I was getting lonely in here, big boy ... and want a little action. How about it?"

That was funny; but a good offer. "Of course, Kelly! Have I ever been known to turn down an offer like that?"

Kelly chortled, "Not that *I* can remember." She got off the bed, stood in front of me, and suddenly looked serious. "Sam, I offered you what ever you wanted, in the way of sex ... or other activities, as compensation for my selfishness this morning. And you didn't take advantage of my offer ... but it still stands. What would turn you on tonight?"

I pulled Kelly close to me, and kissed her nose. "Kelly, it was great that you were so turned on this morning, and I was more than happy to help ... and wait my turn. Please don't feel *bad* about it!" I kissed her nose again, and continued, "And you *did* make me a great offer. But I'm mainly turned on by *you*, and I don't feel the need to make you submit to anything, or take any pain. I just want you to be happy."

Kelly put her lips to mine, and we kissed, Kelly attacking my mouth with ardor, as my muscles struggled to respond, almost as if in quicksand. Then, Kelly pushed my chest and took a step back. "OK, Sam. Then I would like *you* to submit to *me* ... and let me take the responsibility for making the decisions on how to please you." Kelly put her hands on her hips, and I could imagine her as a drill sergeant in the army, issuing instructions, and not taking any guff from her recruits.

All I could do was voice a weak, "Yes, ma'am." Then I got into the standing position.

Kelly snickered, "This isn't going to be a punishment, Sam. So why don't you get undressed, and just try to relax." As I undressed, Kelly took a bath towel and walked into the living room area of the suite. I heard her turn on the wall-mounted television, and start flipping channels. She looked through the bedroom door at me, and commented, "There sure are a lot of 'talking heads' on TV here – it seems like they're on almost every channel!"

I finished undressing and told her, "Keep clicking; there should be more." She clicked through old serials, some bizarre game shows, and then to a few channels apparently devoted to porn.

Kelly said, "Sam, can you take out the 'toys' we bought in Amsterdam, and lay them out on the coffee table?" I had stashed most of the things in my rolling case, but there were a few in my backpack, also. I lined everything up, along with the tube of KY.

When Kelly saw the medical items, she said, "You can put those away; we won't need that stuff, tonight. Unless you insist." She stared at me, and I shrugged and shook my head. Then, Kelly said, "OK, Sam. Get in the chair position in that large chair I've put the towel on and turned around. You can watch TV ... as long as you keep your head down, and your butt up." She smiled at me, but I knew she was serious.

I followed her instructions, and was already getting turned on, even though I had not touched myself. I folded my arms, put my head down on the low-back chair, and arched my back, sticking my bottom as high up as possible. An unseen breeze tickled my anus, and I had to make an effort to keep it relaxed.

Kelly rubbed my back, and massaged my buttocks. "Just relax, Sam. I think you'll enjoy what I've planned." I felt something cold against my anus, and Kelly said, "We'll start with your new prostate stimulator gizmo." I relaxed my muscles, and the device slid into me. Kelly twisted it around a little, and I suddenly felt the pressure against my prostate. I guided her to the target with my 'Mmm's' and 'Aaah's', and Kelly quickly learned how to tilt the handle, so that the bulbous angled tip would press against me to maximum effect.

We watched the porn movie as Kelly slowly moved the stimulator around, and lightly stroked my bottom and hips, and the backs of my legs. Then, she held my balls, moving her hand very slightly, prolonging the feeling, for several more minutes, as she continued to move the tip of the stimulator inside me.

There was a dull part of the movie, so Kelly flipped channels, and found a great girl-on-girl scene, the only problem being all of the fake sounds the girls were making. Kelly turned the volume down to barely audible; problem solved. I heard some things on the coffee table move, and a minute later felt the prostate stimulator being pulled out of me. Then, the rounded tip of one of the glass butt plugs was against me.

Kelly took her time, moving the plug in slightly, then back out, pushing in farther each time, until the glass bumps had moved into me, and my anal muscles were holding the waist of the plug. The thickness of this plug put pressure on my prostate also, and only slight motion of the protruding disc by Kelly was enough to escalate my excitement. Kelly massaged my backside for a while, and then put her hand under me and stroked, until I was hard.

"Please get out of the chair now, Sam. We need to make a few adjustments." I got out of the chair, feeling the large butt plug unmistakably inside me, and watched, as Kelly turned the chair around, facing the television. Then, she adjusted the towel, pointed, and said, "Sit!"

I knew that I might bring on Kelly's wrath, and end-up taking a spanking tonight, but I had to do it: I put my arms up with my hands pointed down, stuck out my tongue, and panted loudly. Then I 'wagged' my butt, barked once, sat on the chair, and said, "Yes, ma'am!"

Kelly laughed, "Good boy! Now, sit back, Sam, and get comfortable." It was a comfortable chair – at least this way; but not as comfortable when on my knees in the 'chair' position. Kelly stood in front of me, and shimmied out of her satin négligée. She stepped in front of me, and rubbed her breasts in my face, and then swung them against me. I put my tongue out, and got a couple of good licks in, before she turned around, swung her right leg over my legs, and sat on my lap.

I grabbed her, and pulled her back to me ... causing a dramatic sensation from the butt plug against my prostate. Kelly lifted herself, using the armrests of the chair, and sat back on me. I held my shaft against my stomach, as she sat back, pressing her butt into my groin. Then, she reached over to the corner table, picked up the television remote, and started clicking. She found the MTV channel, and turned up the sound of the music, her hips now moving against me with the strong drum beat permeating the room.

It took Kelly a few minutes to perfect the lap dance ... and it took me a few minutes to realize that's what she was doing. I relaxed back into the chair, the slight motion again shifting the butt plug inside me, and I put my head back and closed my eyes.

I saw vineyards and rivers, the beer garden, and artwork. Then, the images blurred, as my senses focused on the music. The beat. Kelly's motions increased, her butt moving against me, stroking, as my tactile senses took over. I reached around, and held Kelly's breasts, putting my head against her back. Kelly's motions slowed, and she lifted herself, again using the armrests of the chair.

"Put yourself in me, please," Kelly said, softly. I gladly did as she asked, and now Kelly was sliding up and down on my shaft, her hips still gyrating. She lowered herself fully onto me, and then slid back up, squeezing her pelvic muscles, grasping me like lips sucking a straw, then lowering herself again. The feeling was incredible.

Holding Kelly's breasts, I gazed down, and watched her hips and buttocks wobble, as she slammed down on me with each stroke. A guttural sound emanated from deep within me, as I crescendoed to a stupendous climax. Kelly kept moving on my shaft, and I reached around, and fingered her clit. Holding my wrist, she lifted my arm, and said, "This is for you, tonight, Sam." She chuckled, adding, "I'm getting pretty tired."

I put my head against her back again, and held her. "Well, at least *you* tell me you're tired *after* I've had an orgasm. That's a great improvement on the usual situation." Kelly laughed, and I asked, "You don't have a headache, do you?"

Kelly lifted herself off me, stood up, and turned around, bending over, her arms on my shoulders, and her breasts hanging pendulously in front of me. "No, Sam. But I might take some aspirin, anyway, because after all that wine, I might wake up with a hangover tomorrow."

I hoped not, as we would be driving one of the most romantic routes of our trip.

Sam and I got another early start, driving south along the Rhine River. We saw cruise ships on the river and castles – or remains of castles – in the hills above. In-between were vineyards, curving around the hills, the sky above clouded now.

We visited several wineries, even going down into their cellars, and tasting wines decades old, as well as 'fresh' vintages. We learned about *kabinett* wines and the quality system, and how to discern the color of the wine by candlelight. There were dozens of wineries, but Sam was selective, and we only stopped at three ... or perhaps four. And that was just in the morning!

We stopped on the outskirts of Heidelberg for lunch, Sam and I splitting a giant *brezel* (pretzel) with *senf* (mustard), and a plate of delicious 'black forest' ham. My mind was muddled from the wine as we turned east, and drove into the Neckar Valley.

Sam explained, "We're driving on part of the *Burgenstrasse*, or 'Castle Highway', but we'll do only the Neckar Valley portion. Then, tomorrow, we will drive down the *Romantische Strasse*, or 'Romantic Road' into Munich."

It was beautiful: We drove along the winding Neckar River, castles perched high above us on both sides. The sun was behind us, and the view of the valley was spectacular – terraces of vineyards steeply descending to the slow-flowing river, old bridges punctuating its stretch ahead, and tiny villages – church steeples rising above all – dotting the valley as far as we could see.

We turned onto a small road, and wound up the mountain toward an old castle with high walls and a tall, octagonal turret. The river was now far below, the vista opening up as we drove into the small, gravel-covered parking area in front of the castle."

"Are we taking a tour of this castle?" We hadn't actually seen the inside of any castles, yet.

Sam smiled, and put his arm around me as we walked up to the huge door. As he held the door open for me, he said, "We'll probably see a lot of this place ... we're staying here tonight." As we walked inside, I turned to Sam and hugged him.

He explained, "There are a lot of '*schlosshotels*' here – old castles that have been renovated, and now available for a small number of guests to stay. Some of them are pretty run-down ... but this one should be good; I've never stayed here, but read a lot of reviews, and this is supposed to be one of the really high-end *schlosshotels* in this area."

We checked in and were shown to our room – one of only six in the entire hotel. When we opened the door, and walked into the room, Sam and I had to stop and gawk: The huge room – with an incredibly high ceiling – was the model of opulence. It was truly over-the-top, but I guess the hotel wasn't taking any chances that the guests might not be impressed.

One wall had a line of very tall, leaded windows, looking out over the valley, with dark blue pleated curtains held to the side by thick gold cords. A finely patterned blue wallpaper covered the walls, dark wood built-in cabinets lined one wall, and heavy furniture, including a seating arrangement and a four-poster bed filled much of the room. The parquet floors were covered in several places by beautiful rugs, and a very old tapestry, at least ten feet on a side, covered one wall.

I walked into the bathroom and turned on the light, and was a amazed again at the glittering of the gold fixtures, crystal knobs, and ornate tile work. I sat on the toilet to pee, and a few moments later Sam came in to arrange his toiletries on the counter.

He looked around and whistled, "Boy, this really *is* a fancy place!" Then he added cryptically, "Now, we just need to find some rope." When I looked up at him inquisitively, Sam shrugged, and explained, "Well, we *do* have a four-poster bed ..."

We walked downstairs, and explored the hotel, which was smaller than it had appeared from the outside. There was a formal dining room, a small gym, and even a sauna. Then, we walked around the grounds, which included a small vegetable garden, terraces of vineyards, and a gravel area, with tables and chairs, bordered by a waist-high block wall at the edge of the steep drop-off down to the river.

In the distance, a bridge crossed the river, and we could see a church steeple rising above the fields and trees on the other side. We sat at one of the tables, and one of the staff asked if we would like some wine; we both declined, taking mineral water (no gas), instead. It was a very idyllic and pastoral setting, very quiet. I realized that I could not hear or see any cars, anywhere in the valley.

We decided to try the sauna, and went directly to the facility without going back to our room. There was a small changing room with perhaps a dozen lockers, and a stack of towels near the door to the sauna area. We walked in, and surveyed the small space; it was tiny, compared to the spa we had just visited – as well as all of the other saunas we had seen in Europe – but it was still larger than Sam's home sauna.

We showered, and then grabbed our towels and entered the sauna itself. It was a shock to see a couple already inside the sauna – probably in their late 40s, and already dripping with sweat. The woman was very good looking, and obviously kept herself in shape; she looked 'classy', despite the fact that she was nude. Her husband, on the other hand, was huge – he had to weigh more than 300 pounds, his overhanging stomach so large that his genitals were completely hidden.

Spreading our towels on the middle bench, Sam and I sat quietly, enjoying the warmth. Almost immediately, the overweight gentleman made a gruff remark, in German, to the woman, got up, and exited the sauna. Sam moved to the upper bench, and lay down, and I sat cross-legged, facing the sauna furnace.

A few minutes later, the woman stood, picked up her towel, and walked past me, and out of the sauna. She had a beautiful body, her breasts still firm, and perfectly formed, and her stomach flat. Her pubic hair was trimmed in a large triangle of black, and I couldn't help but notice her pedicure, as she walked by.

I lay down on the middle bench, and closed my eyes; it appeared that we would have the sauna to ourselves. I heard the shower going outside, and then being turned off; we were left in silence, broken only by the occasional creaking of the lava rocks on the furnace grate in front of me.

I was surprised to hear the door open, and looked up to see the woman re-entering the sauna. I began to sit up, to make room for her, and she made a brief remark in German. I casually said, "Sorry".

As she arranged her towel, and sat near the end of the bench, she looked at me, and asked, "Are you American?" I didn't realize that my 'sorry' carried so much information. Nor, that I had an accent. I nodded, and sat up, and the woman moved over a bit so that we could talk comfortably.

I asked her, "Have you been to the U.S.?"

She laughed, and said, "Oh my, yes! We've seen most of the big cities – New York, of course, Chicago, Miami, Los Angeles, and San Francisco. And we've toured many of your beautiful national parks. One of our sons is in the financial sector, and spends a lot of time in New York, so we use that as an excuse, if we want to try some of the new restaurants, or see a couple of plays." I realized that she had probably seen much more of the U.S. than I had.

I asked, "Where are you from? Are you on vacation, touring Germany?"

She shook her head, "We live in the north, in Hamburg. My husband is on holiday, and we had never been to the Neckar Valley, so we're exploring the area." She lifted a corner of her towel, and wiped her face, then asked, "Where have you been so far on your trip?"

I saw Sam stir, but he didn't volunteer to join the conversation, so I answered, "We've mainly been to The Netherlands – Amsterdam and the Utrecht area, and then we went to a spa in the south, near Maastricht. Tomorrow, we're driving the 'Romantic Road' to Munich."

The woman nodded, and smiled, "Yes, I've heard about that spa ... and would like to try it sometime." Then she looked at me seriously, and warned, "I hope you have reservations in Munich, or you'll have a problem: The Oktoberfest celebration started two weeks ago, and runs through the weekend, so the town will be packed." She smiled, and added, "But it can be a fun experience, if you haven't been, before."

I assured her that we had hotel reservations, and let her know that it was my first time in Europe. Her eyes went wide, and she smiled, "It should be an interesting trip for you; there's a lot to see."

Sam sat up, and stretched his arms. We all introduced ourselves to each other, and then Sam and I stepped out of the sauna and into the showers. After a brief cool-down, we went back into the sauna for a short session; this sauna really didn't have much to offer – no jacuzzi or pool, and only a single sauna cabin.

We visited with our new companion for a while, then we all decided we'd had enough. We took showers together, and as we dried off, I asked the woman whether they would be eating in the hotel dining room tonight. She replied that they were trying a Michelin-starred restaurant in Mannheim, but that they had eaten in the hotel last night and had a very good meal.

We walked into the changing room, and opened our lockers. As the woman was putting on a sexy thong and white lace bra, I asked, "Isn't Mannheim far to drive for dinner?" It seemed silly to leave this peaceful valley and drive to a big city, just for dinner.

She laughed, "We've wanted to eat there since it opened a couple of years ago, but they have a four-month waiting list. One of the reasons for our visit here is that we were finally able to secure reservations." As she put on a beautiful white silk blouse, she explained, "It would be a six-hour drive – each way – from home. So it's not a big deal to drive an hour each way on our holiday to have a special dinner."

As she put on a medium-length black skirt and tucked in her blouse, I donned my black jeans, and the same t-shirt I had worn all day. Sam was taking me to some elegant places, and I had brought mainly casual clothes; I did have one nice skirt in my rolling bag, and I could steam the blouse in the shower. I resolved to dress better, although people had been very accepting so far of what I was wearing ... or not wearing.

We had a 'quickie' up in the room, and I got into a hot shower to wash my hair properly, and hopefully steam some of the wrinkles out of the blouse. I washed several pairs of my underwear in the sink, and hung them over the towel rack. After spending more time than usual with makeup, I put on a pair of purple panties, and matching bra – the ones I had modeled for Sam the first time I went over to his house.

Then, I took the hairbrush, and walked into the bedroom, where Sam was sitting on one of the huge chairs, doing more research on his tablet. I stood in front of him, and he looked up expectantly. "Would you? Please?" I handed him the brush. Then, I realized that I hadn't been clear: I had only wanted Sam to brush my hair, and then put it in French braids.

Sam pulled me over his lap, and I decided to humor him. I wiggled into position, and let my head drop. When I didn't hear anything above me, I said, "Ready, Sir."

Sam coughed, and asked, "How many?"

I was made-up, ready to go to a nice dinner, and didn't want a serious spanking experience. "As you wish, Sir ... but perhaps a dozen hard ones would redden my cheeks just enough?"

Sam laughed, and I felt him pulling the high-back underwear even higher on my bum. "These are very cute panties." He ran his fingers under the pink waistband, and then patted my bottom. He said, "Prepare yourself, girl!"

I wondered whether he would build my tension, and then let me off the hook, so we could finish getting ready for dinner. But I found out soon enough that he was going to honor my 'request'. The back of the brush impacted my left butt cheek, and a moment later, I felt a searing pain. Before I could assimilate that, the brush landed on my right side, creating another flaming rectangle.

Then, he proceeded to administer ten medium strokes of the brush very quickly, alternating sides, and covering all of my lower bum. The last two strokes were harder, at the top of my thighs, and I had to concentrate to stay in position. Sam laid the hairbrush in the small of my back, as I took some deep breaths; my bottom was stinging.

I turned my head back and, through a curtain of hair, said, "Thank you, Sir." Then, I added, "Sir ... maybe you could rub my bum a little, and then brush my hair and braid it … as that's why I came in here to you."

Sam rubbed my sore bottom, and the pain quickly dulled. He was very apologetic, "I'm sorry, Kelly. You should have clarified what you wanted … *before* you got over my lap." He gave me little kisses all over my bottom.

"That's OK, Sir. It's been a few days, and I thought that we could both use a little practice." I rubbed my bottom, and chuckled, "And I'll certainly be feeling this during dinner … and waiting patiently until we get back up here to see what you're going to do to help me forget about the pain."

I got up, smiled seductively at him, and then sat on the huge, rounded arm of the chair, throwing my hair back so that Sam could begin; it was going to take a while, now that my hair was nearly dry.

We went downstairs to the restaurant, and were seated at a window table in the dining room, where we could see a few scattered lights down in the valley. The room was very dim, and candles flickered on all the tables. There was only one other couple seated already, across the room.

A tuxedoed waiter handed Sam the wine list, filled crystal glasses with bottled water, placed a steaming basket of bread on the table, and poured olive oil and balsamic vinegar on our bread plates.

Sam perused the extensive wine list – I could tell because it was as thick as a book, and Sam kept turning pages – finally closing it and looking up at me. "Well, Kelly, you've learned about German wines," he reached around the side of the table, and handed me the wine list, "so why don't you make the selection?"

I wasn't sure I could even drink any more wine, didn't want to spend time reading a long list, or taking the responsibility for selecting a nice one. Although I doubt if there could have been any 'bad' wines offered here. I pushed the wine list back into Sam's hand, and he shrugged, and opened it again. I had eaten two pieces of the crusty bread by the time he had made a tentative selection.

"Let's decide what we're going to order, and I'll make sure the wine will work with the food – although I'd like to get something local."

I nodded, swallowed the last morsel of bread, and said, agreeably, "Whatever."

The waiter came, and we ordered our dinners, and appetizers. I heard a clink of glasses, and realized it was nearly silent in here, except for the murmurs and toasts of the other couple. The wine came, and we made our own toast, Sam wishing that we would be able to do things like this together, forever. It was a nice wish, one that I shared.

The meal was incredible and, once again, I told myself that I would have to cut back soon, or not be able to get into the clothes I had brought on the trip. The service had been on European-time, slow and stately, giving us plenty of time to savor the flavors, drink the wine, and have some nice conversation, before moving on to the next course.

We had already been here close to two hours, and had discussed diverse topics from Sam's stories of his European ski experiences to my dissertation research project. Sam had been intently researching my idea, even searching the patent databases; now, he was surprisingly positive about the possibilities, and offered his full support. The other couple had left, and an older couple was now seated in the corner table, looking at the menus.

The waiter came and took our coffee orders, handing us the dessert menus, and placing a three-layer carousel of sweets on the table. There appeared to be small cookies, petit fours, and fruit-filled pastries, along with several different types of chocolate truffles. I had never seen anything like it. What a nice dessert!

As Sam perused the menu, he suddenly said, "Oh!" It was loud enough that the other couple turned to look. He smiled at me, and said, "Kelly, I know we've eaten a lot already," Now *that* was an understatement! Sam continued, "and drank a lot, already," Oh my! I don't even know how much I'd had, although I was feeling pretty good at the moment.

Sam announced, "but they have something very special here. Something that I would have liked to share with you, had we been able to visit Salzburg."

I was shaking my head already, but Sam persisted, "It's Austrian, and not usually on a menu in Germany ... but it goes very well with the romantic castle atmosphere." He paused again, and then explained, "It's called a *Salzburger Nockerl*. It's very light – just a soufflé of egg; but it's impressive to look at, and delicious." I nodded, and had to stifle a burp. Sam could order his dessert, and I'd have a taste of it.

But Sam wasn't finished. He smiled, "*And*, they have a half-bottle of a *Trockenbeerenauslese* – one of the really sweet wines, the next grade up from the wine we had at the spa. I would have preferred an *Eiswein*, but they don't seem to have it on their dessert menu. Sam ordered, and it took another twenty minutes before our dessert was served.

When I saw it, my eyes almost fell out of my head: It was a large, oblong dish with meringue formed into three huge peaks, baked to a golden color, and sprinkled with powdered sugar.

The waiter then spooned a thick red sauce from a small bowl over the peaks, and put the bowl on the table. The waiter left, and a moment later was back with the wine. He opened it, and poured it into crystal glasses. *'Guten appetit'* he said, and he disappeared as quietly as he had appeared.

Sam raised his glass, and examined the color of the wine by candlelight. He explained, "This style of glass was designed to enhance the acidity of the wine, balancing the sweetness of the dessert." He took a sip, and smiled broadly, "It's almost like 'Mead', the English honey-wine." I tasted it, and it *was* delicious. With all the wine we'd had in the past two days, this was still something special.

Then, I tasted the *Nockerl*: It was unbelievable! It was light, as Sam had said, but incredibly sweet, especially with the raspberry sauce. And Sam was right – the wine was matched perfectly to the dessert. I couldn't help myself – I had to keep tasting it, letting it melt in my mouth, spooning up the sauce ... and washing it down with the rich, sweet wine. Heaven!

When we got back to the room after our three-hour dinner, we were both spent. I told Sam I would take a 'rain check' on his reward for my submission to the hairbrush. He whined that he had hoped we could 'try out' all the furniture; he said that if we made love five or six times, we could try the best of it. In his mind!

Then, he whined that – although he was a 'boy scout' – he couldn't find any rope ... and he didn't want to waste the opportunity with the four-poster bed. He stood by the drapes, fingering the decorative gold cord. He was slurring his words, and I doubted he could get it up, anyway. I finally convinced him to just snuggle with me, and that we would have plenty of time for lovemaking.

That wasn't a very satisfying answer for him, but he finally conceded, and we undressed, dropping our clothes on the floor, and climbed into the massive bed and under the covers.

As we sunk into the most comfortable mattress I had ever felt, we both let out an 'Aaah'. There were no sheets or blankets – only a thick, down comforter. We pulled it over us, and snuggled together. Heaven, again! I was discovering new ways of living, and had no doubt that I was being spoiled. I kissed Sam lightly on the lips ... and heard a snore. We were both really tired. Again.

I woke to a nearly pitch-black room, at first forgetting where I was, until I felt Kelly next to me, and pulled my arms out, letting them drop onto the *Federbett*. My mind filled with images from last night's dinner – the candle-lit tables, crystal glasses refracting the flickering light, beautiful food, the *Salzburger Nockerl* ... and the dessert wine. But I couldn't remember anything after getting back to the room.

Lifting my head, I glanced at the digital clock next to the bed, then let my head drop, disappointed that it was already past seven; I had hoped to get an early start, so we could get to Munich early in the afternoon. I sat up, and Kelly stirred. I leaned over and kissed her, and her eyes blinked open. "Good morning, starshine." Kelly smiled.

We spooned, and when she was fully awake, I suggested that we make love quickly, take advantage of the included breakfast, and hit the road. It would take about five hours of driving, assuming the traffic cooperated. Although it was mainly a scenic drive, and we would be making only a couple of stops, it would be a long day.

Kelly agreed, and climbed on top of me. She took me in her hands, and expertly readied me, then inserted my throbbing manhood into her warmth. As she lowered herself onto me, her breasts against my chest, I stopped moving for a moment, and asked, "Do you remember what happened, after we got back to the room, last night? I seem to have a lapse of memory."

Kelly laughed, and we started moving again. She lifted her head, and whispered, "I put you to bed, darling."

After our lovemaking, we took a quick shower together, and got dressed and packed. We went to the restaurant, and were surprised when they served a full made-to-order breakfast. I hated to delay our start any longer, but tried to relax, and enjoy the last of our Neckar Valley *schlosshotel* experience. It was almost nine, by the time we drove down the hill, and turned onto the winding road along the river.

Two hours later, we crossed the Main River, and turned south on the *Romantische Strasse*. We drove through many small villages with picturesque houses, crisscrosses of dark wood over multi-hued walls, large shutters, and planter boxes with colorful flowers outside each window.

Around noon, we drove into Rothenburg, one of the classic old-German towns, now quite touristy, but still worth seeing. We parked near the center of the town, and walked around, admiring the architecture and the perfect condition of the houses – looking almost like Disneyworld.

We visited one of the most interesting, but least romantic, of the museums we would visit on this trip: The Medieval Criminal Museum – an incredible collection of weapons and instruments of torture. Several of the tortures involved the genitals, and although they fascinated Kelly, they hurt too much – just looking at them – so I wandered to a different area of the museum where there was a collection of medieval armor.

I offered to take Kelly to a typical German restaurant for lunch, but we'd had a big breakfast, so decided to have a snack later and save our hunger for Munich.

Continuing south, we stopped again at the picturesque town of Dinklesbühl, a 700-year old city that probably hadn't changed much in that time. We parked and walked up the small hill to the central church, and then circled back through narrow streets, stopping at a würst stand for a snack, before our last leg to Munich.

CHAPTER 13: OKTOBERFEST LOVEFEST

Two hours later, we entered the outer ring of Munich, and continued around to the Westpark area, where our hotel was located. We had been very lucky getting a room there, as the hotel was within walking distance to the Oktoberfest, and had direct access to a U-Bahn station, where we could take the underground train quickly to the center of the old town.

It was already too late to visit the Nymphenburg Palace, and too early for dinner, but perfect timing for a little walking tour of *München*.

As we walked down to the U-Bahn, I explained that Munich had built its subway system for the 1972 Olympics. Unfortunately, the games had been overshadowed by the 'Munich Massacre', in which the Black September terrorist group had murdered nearly a dozen Israeli athletes and coaches.

It was only three stops to the *Hauptbahnhof* (main train station), and I took Kelly out to the tracks to show her all the trains leaving for destinations around Europe. Then, we crossed the busy intersection to Karlsplatz, passed through the medieval *Karlstor* gate, and began our walk down *Neuhauser Strasse*, the pedestrian thoroughfare.

We passed clothing stores, toy stores with incredible miniature train sets, and many fast-food restaurants. There was a crowd of people, as usual – mostly tourists –

and much entertainment along the way, including jugglers, a horn player, and a full Argentinean street band.

We took a short detour, and entered the *Frauenkirche*, one of the largest and oldest churches in Munich, having been built more than 800 years ago. When we exited, I pointed out the dual domed towers that literally tower over Munich. We continued our walk, finally arriving at Marienplatz, a large square, dominated by the *Rathaus*, or city hall.

I glanced at my watch, and realized we had another ten minutes until the show, so we sat at one of the outdoor tables, and ordered beers. It truly was a 'sidewalk café', watching the wildly different people walk by. I tapped Kelly on the shoulder, and pointed out the Middle Eastern woman, in full Burka with veil, who was following close behind a teenage girl who was wearing a micro-miniskirt, and sporting tattoos and body jewelry. What a cultural chasm!

We were halfway through our beers when the hourly show began: The *Glockenspiel*, the large clock on the Rathaus tower, suddenly became animated with figures coming out of doors, and dancing around. The same show had been going for the past century, but there were always large crowds of tourists watching – and photographing – the spectacle.

We finished our beers, and walked around a while longer, passing through the *Isartor*, and walking across the bridge over the Isar River. I pointed out the Deutches Science Museum, which we would hopefully see tomorrow, or the next day. It had an incredible collection of real trains, planes, and boats, in addition to a model coalmine, and many other attractions. It sat on an island in the river.

On the other side of the bridge, we turned onto a dirt path, and walked through a beautiful treed area on the banks of the river. I pointed out the large public swimming hall – that featured nude swimming a couple of nights a week, and then we walked down the bank on to a gravel beach. We sat down and relaxed, watching people cross the bridge above us, and ride their bikes on the trail through the park behind us.

"This is actually a 'nude beach' during the summer. I've seen women ride down here on a bike during their lunch break, dressed to the nines – perhaps from working in a department store – and then undressing and laying out in the sun, before they had to get dressed again and return to work. People play all day, nude, on the beach and in the water, in plain sight of thousands of people crossing over the bridge, or driving on the street alongside the river."

We headed back across the bridge into the old town, and I led Kelly to another tourist attraction, the Hofbräuhaus – a huge beer hall, frequented by kids on their first trip to Europe, families touring the area, and old men who are regulars, their large steins hanging on hooks behind the bar. It was early on a Thursday evening, and the place wasn't packed, but there was still quite a bit of action, with an 'Oom-Pah' band playing German music, and people swinging huge steins of beer.

I explained to Kelly, "The 'normal' size beer here is one liter – a little more than two pints; they call it a *Masskrug* or '*Mass*', for short." I pointed out one of the beer maidens, dressed in her *dirndl*, a traditional, German dress worn over petticoats. "They can carry as many as six *Mass* of beer in each hand. That's real weightlifting! Two pints of beer weighs about two pounds, and the glasses weigh two or three pounds ... so they are carrying 60 pounds – that's like lifting a 30-pound barbell in each hand!"

Kelly wasn't up for a liter of beer, so we walked through the Hofbräuhaus, and out to the road. Nearby, we looked in the window of one of my favorite restaurants in Munich, the Haxnbauer: There were spits with about 50 'hocks' – ankles of pigs. Unhealthy, but delicious, the skin is left on, and crisps to an incredible flavor. I hoped we would eat here, whichever night we weren't at the Oktoberfest ... but we'd had too many big dinners lately, and had to take a little break, before coming here.

We walked back past Marienplatz, and down the stairs to a *keller*, or cellar, restaurant. It was jammed, and hot in the main room, but I maneuvered us around tables, and past wait staff to a back door, where there was a small patio. As I had hoped, and being incredibly lucky, there was a table available, and we sat down.

We picked some traditional German fare, and ordered a couple of beers – available in 'small' pints, here. "In the spring, Bavaria celebrates the white asparagus harvest, and this place has the best white asparagus soup I've ever tasted." I smiled at Kelly, "We'll just have to come back again." Kelly nodded, as she munched on a slice of *leberkäse*, literally 'liver cheese', one of Munich's culinary specialties.

We didn't order main courses but, once again, I wanted to share with Kelly a special dessert – one typical of Germany, called *Rote Grüze*. I explained to her, "It's basically a very sweet, red gelatin of various berries, like red and black currants, served over ice cream with *schlag*, rich, house-made whipped cream. It was as good as I had remembered

After dinner, we walked down the pedestrian shopping street – most of the stores still open, and entered one of the larger clothing stores, the size of a small department store

– squashed between the other shops, but having several floors accessible by escalator.

We went up to the fourth floor (actually, the 'third' floor, if you counted, as they do in Germany, starting with the 'ground floor'), and looked at a huge array of German *Trachten*, or traditional outfits. It wasn't really necessary for us to wear these kinds of outfits to Oktoberfest, but I suggested to Kelly that they would get us into the spirit of the festival.

Kelly picked out a beautiful *dirndl* and tried it on: She looked like a typical Bavarian beer maiden, and I suggested that she consider putting her hair in pigtails or braids, which would add to the effect.

I bought a pair of traditional *Lederhosen*, suede leather shorts with suspenders, and suede vest, along with a checkered red dress shirt. When I walked out of the dressing room, Kelly squealed with laughter. It would have been embarrassing wearing this to a party in the U.S., but we would feel perfectly dressed tomorrow at the Oktoberfest.

I decided to change back into my original clothes before paying (the bill was more than 300 Euro), and carrying the large shopping bags back out to the street.

Although in my research I had found a fetish club in Munich, I hadn't contacted them, or made arrangements, and decided to show Kelly more of the 'normal' tourist sights of Munich.

We went down to the U-Bahn, and took a train back to our hotel, where we dropped our jackets and shopping bags in the room, and went down to the hotel sauna. It was beautiful and modern, with curving tile walls, a nice swimming pool, and compact but complete sauna facilities.

We entered the changing room, where a surprising number of people were getting dressed or undressed. We stashed our clothes in a locker, took a towel, and walked down a winding hallway, stopping to shower in a small circular alcove; we had to share a shower, as the others were already taken. We noticed that most of the people here were younger – mostly business-types in their thirties and forties. There were several very cute girls in the showers with us, and we found even more in the sauna.

We spent an hour relaxing in the sauna and the pool, and then returned to our room, where I did some research on other saunas around Munich. I was surprised to see one advertised in the Arabella Park area, across the river from the *Englischer Garten*.

It looked nearly identical to a sauna that I had visited in Berlin – on the top of a skyscraper, with cute Bavarian 'cabins', and an indoor-outdoor pool. Perhaps we could visit that sauna ... but I didn't know when it would be, as we would be here only another three days, and I had many activities already planned for us.

Then, Kelly 'borrowed' my tablet, and continued her research. I turned off most of the lights, and sat on the bed in the hotel robe. Kelly put down the tablet, and came over to the bed, sitting on the edge next to me. She was still completely dressed.

"Sam, I'd like to do some research tonight." She smiled at me, and reached under my robe. "But I'd be happy to help you get to sleep, if you like." I didn't want to dissuade her from pursuing her research – quite admirable in the middle of a European tour; and I would take whatever she would give me, in terms of sexual satisfaction. Kelly was a very 'satisfying' woman.

I nodded, and lay back on the pillow. Kelly undid the sash of my robe, and laid it open, then stroked me with both hands, using every technique that I had taught her, as well as a few of her own moves. When I was hard, she went down on me. I closed my eyes, and let Kelly perform her magic.

As she sucked me, she poked the tip of a finger into my perineum – the small area between my anus and the base of my penis. That had an effect similar to inserting a finger into my rectum: Stimulation of my prostate. She continued with her mouth and her finger, until I came, with a few violent thrusts. She hummed, as she swallowed, and sucked again, finally swirling her tongue around me, and taking me out of her mouth with her hand clasped tightly around the girth of my flagging erection.

She leaned over and kissed me – a nice ending to the evening, but it was still a bit challenging for me to taste my own semen. Then, she covered me with the fluffy comforter, and walked back to the sitting area, where she picked up the tablet, and continued her research.

I closed my eyes, and drifted off. My last thought was how I was now retired, and able to take the time to do whatever I wanted, while Kelly was just beginning her career, and would have many years – perhaps decades – of hard work ahead of her. I hoped that we would be able to make some time for ourselves, along with her career.

Sam and I took the U-Bahn three stops to the *Hauptbahnhof*, and three stops north, then took a tram to Schloss Nymphenburg. It was a beautiful palace, with magnificent grounds. We were early enough that it was fairly empty, busloads of tourists starting to arrive just as we were leaving. We then went to the Olympic Park, where the infamous Munich Olympics of 1972 had been held.

After visiting the BMW museum, we took the U-Bahn to the Munich *Residenz* – the old palace, situated near the state theater – where we toured the *Schatzkammer*, the royal jewel collection. That was really impressive, with the jeweled crowns, scepters, swords, and other priceless pieces. Then, we visited the *Alte Pinakothek, and Neue Pinakothek*, the so-called 'old' and 'new' art museums, which house one of the world's largest collections of paintings by the 'masters'.

We walked toward the Bavarian National Museum, and still another art museum, which were both on the southern edge of the *Englischer Garten*, or 'English Garden', a huge city park which, Sam informed me, was known for open nudity – at least on the warmer days.

Before we reached the museums, we stopped on the side of the road, and looked north, into the park; a small stream flowed south, and under the street, disappearing somewhere under Munich. But a few hundred feet upstream, kids were surfing on a wave that remained in place due to the rocks underneath. The surfers were quite good, and it was very surprising to see them in wetsuits, surfing right in front of us, while traffic was backed-up on the road behind us.

As we walked up the steps of the next museum, I told Sam, "I think I'm 'museumed-out' for the day; I was up pretty late last night." We sat down on the steps, and Sam thought a moment.

"I had originally thought of going to the Oktoberfest this evening, but maybe it will be more fun starting fresh tomorrow, and spending the day." Sam smiled, "So maybe we could go to the Haxnbauer for dinner, and try out that new sauna I found, afterward?" He looked at me, and reasoned, "Why don't we go back to the hotel, and take a short nap; then, we'll be fresh for the evening?"

My feet were hurting, and I felt gritty, so readily agreed to Sam's plan. We walked across the street and down the stairs to the *Odeonplatz* U-Bahn station, and in five stops, we were back to the hotel. We went up to the room, and got undressed. Sam had a bobbing erection, so I bent over the corner of the bed, and he made love to me, coming before I had a chance to get turned on; perhaps I was too tired to get turned on? We took a quick shower, and climbed into bed.

Sam kissed me, and my eyes flew open. He smiled, and announced that it was past seven, and that we should get going. I saw that he was already dressed, and he informed me that he had made reservations at the *Haxnbauer* for eight o'clock. I got going, and we were out of the hotel within twenty minutes, and made it to the restaurant on time. We were led to our seat through a huge room, with a painted arched ceiling, and packed with people. It was bustling and noisy, but was filled with German ambiance.

Sam ordered, and our beers and a plate of food were delivered efficiently to us. Sam explained that there were many typical appetizers in Bavaria, the southern region of Germany, including this plate of buttered brown bread, and a huge, spiral-cut white radish. I followed Sam's lead, and broke off some of the radish, putting it on the bread.

Then, our main course arrived: A whole *haxe*. It was a spherical ball of meat, with a crisp brown skin on the outside. Sam sliced some sections for each of us, and scooped hot potato salad, and sauerkraut from bowls onto our plates. It smelled delicious, but it looked very heavy.

After my first bite of the luscious meat, I realized that the dish was so rich that I wouldn't be able to eat much, and hoped that Sam was really hungry. The dinner was slow, but my food didn't go down fast enough to enable me to make a dent in the food on my plate.

But we did pretty well, finishing the sauerkraut and potato salad, and a good portion of the *haxe*. I hadn't stuffed, but wasn't sure I could move, with the heavy meal inside me. We paid the bill, and walked out into the air, which felt cool and fresh, after the hot stuffy atmosphere of the packed restaurant.

We took the U-Bahn to the Arabella Park area, where there were some big hotels, and tall bank buildings. It was across the river where, Sam told me, the building height restrictions had been relaxed. We found the address that Sam had obtained on the Internet, and took the elevator to the top floor. We exited into a rather commercial cashier's area, which also had some spa supplies for sale. Sam paid, and we were given towels and robes, and directed toward the changing room.

Sam explained that, whereas the sauna in Berlin had separate men's and women's locker rooms, this sauna had a single 'mixed' changing room, like all of the Dutch saunas we had visited. I was used to the procedure, by now, and we found our lockers, and got undressed. We left our robes in the lockers, and carried our towels through double doors into the main area, which spanned the entire width of the office building.

The interior was styled like we were in the Black Forest, with faux log sauna cabins surrounding a large, round central pool. On each side of the building, along with the saunas, were jacuzzis, cold pools, steam rooms, footbaths, and showers. Around the pool, in a radial pattern, were rows of chaises, nearly all filled, and mostly with younger women – probably my age or younger.

Sam walked by, focusing on the pool, and not even glancing around, but I spent a moment surveying the rows of nice-looking bodies. My 'style' was quite appropriate, as most of the girls had either removed all their pubic hair, or sported a thin 'landing strip'. Only the middle-age women (and older) had a full bush.

Sam wanted to try out the pool, so we hung our towels, and waded down the steps into the warm water. My breasts were bobbing on the surface of the water when Sam turned around, and gave me a thumbs-up signal. I didn't know what he was saying; he turned, did a surface dive, and disappeared from the pool. I pushed off the steps, and sidestroked around, looking for him, but somehow he had disappeared into thin water.

Then, I noticed the hanging plastic strips, and swam up to them ... and through them ... ending-up in a beautiful, lit, outdoor pool that circled around half of the building. I spied Sam around the bend, floating, and looking up at the sky; I glanced up, but couldn't see a single star.

"Isn't this nice?" Sam asked, when I had swum up to him. I nodded, and followed Sam to the far end, where we walked up the steps, onto the stone deck that overlooked part of Munich. It was spectacular: We could see several other tall buildings nearby, and the lights of Munich across the dark line of the river. Sam pointed to the huge dark area; it looked like the power had gone out in a large part of Munich.

Then Sam explained, "That's the *Englischer Garten*, the huge city park. We watched the surfers at the left end, over there." He pointed. We slowly walked the perimeter of the building, nude, in the moonlight, and above all of the neighboring skyscrapers. Sam pointed: Looking about ten floors below us, into the building across the street, we could see a kitchen, and people being served at a counter – perhaps a sushi bar. It was getting chilly, so we swam back into the building, grabbed our towels, and entered the nearest sauna.

It was dark and very hot. After I pulled the door closed behind me, I looked up, and was startled to see nearly forty people, squished together on three benches. Many of them looked up at us, and several men – and women – smiled and nodded, as we made our way across to the far bench, where a couple of middle-age women moved over to make room for us. We arranged our towels, and settled in to the darkness, the heat, and the quiet.

If I closed my eyes, it was hard to imagine three dozen nude people nearly within arm's length, but when I opened my eyes, they were there: So many bodies that it was difficult to discern any particular body type; there was a panorama of breasts, and penises, and bulging stomachs, sagging skin, and bald heads. There were a few cute, younger couples in here, but the mix wasn't much different from the people we saw walking around the town.

The sauna door swung open, and a very large man entered, his stomach protruding, and hanging over any genitals that he might have had. He was carrying his towel, and stepped from side to side, a bit like the movies I'd seen of a sumo wrestler. He ladled some water onto the sauna furnace rocks, and there was a loud sizzle, and a billow of steam.

Most people hunched over, trying to get a little lower, as the scalding air rose above us, and settled onto our backs. I was really hot already, and the guy was now ladling more water over the coals. More billows of steam, and another searing wave of heat; it felt like it was blistering my back. We hunched down farther, and I wished that he would ladle some cool water over my burnt back. There were a few murmurs in the sauna, but everyone went with the flow – the entire experience now under the control of the fat guy now taking his towel from around his neck.

As I watched, mesmerized, by the scene unfolding (literally, as he was extending the towel) before me, I realized that I wasn't the only one; Sam, and many other people were watching, and waiting. A couple of people stepped down to the bottom bench, and squeezed between the bodies that were already there. I was glad we were only on the middle bench; I don't think my back would have taken any more heat, from that steam.

Now, the guy looked around the sauna at all of us, and smiled. He mumbled a few words – I'm not sure if I would have understood them, even if I spoke German – and began twirling the towel above his head. I recoiled, as there was an immediate effect, the blast wave of heat rolling over my body, which actually *shivered*, perhaps confused by the sensory overload. As Sam had said, hot and cold, pleasure and pain, could be very close feelings.

The guy was twirling the towel expertly, and the increase in heat was apparent. I bent over, my face almost to my knees, and Sam rubbed my back lightly. The towel twirling stopped, and I was glad we had survived the ordeal. But then the fat guy ladled more water onto the rocks, and began twirling again. Now, the vortices of air hitting us were exponentially hotter, and I realized that the prior experience had been just a warm-up. In a manner of speaking.

It *was* an ordeal, but it was over after only a few minutes had elapsed – although it felt like I had descended into a fiery Hell some time ago. The fat guy walked back and forth inside the sauna, then nodded at everyone, and exited the still-quiet space. Immediately, everyone else in the sauna rose, and we all filed out, to the showers, to the cold pool, or to walk around the outside deck in the cooling atmosphere of the night.

Sam and I did all three: We first rinsed off under some showers that had wide heads creating sheets of lukewarm water over our bodies. I wondered whether I should ask Sam to examine my back, and let me know if it really had been scalded; but everyone else had – I guess – survived, so I savored the coolness of the water, and then we walked out onto the deck.

The moon was low, between two buildings, as we stood together – our bodies sending swirls of steam into the night – and took in the scene before us: Most of the town of Munich, the twin domed towers of the *Frauenkirche* clearly visible, rising above the rooftops, the darkness of the winding Isar river and the park on the other side, and a few high clouds, now silver from the moonlight.

I shivered again, not from cold, but thinking that our experience was real – it wasn't a dream; we were in Europe, looking at structures that were many centuries old, seeing the people (boy, did we *see* the people!), and even smelling the aromas wafting from the ethnic neighborhoods below.

Sam turned to me and kissed me tenderly, putting his hand on my cheek; then he stood straight, held my hips, and looked into my eyes. "I love you, Kelly. I hope you're having a nice time on this trip." I was about to respond, when he chuckled, and added, "We may be at a commercial sauna, in a tall, modern building ... but it still seems romantic to me." I couldn't have agreed more, and let him know by putting my arms over his shoulders, and kissing him deeply.

"Sam, I'm enjoying the trip very much. And I agree – it's very romantic."

Sam spoiled the atmosphere by whining, "I'm sorry we aren't going to see more, Kelly, but we just don't have the time. I tried to pick places that I enjoyed, that were representative of some aspect of Europe, and where you could see some of the culture," he laughed loudly, "even if it is the culture of the sex clubs."

We walked back inside, and spent another couple of hours enjoying the various pools and saunas, and even a 'color therapy' room, with colored lights that lit the room in an ever-evolving hue. We went back to the changing room, and grabbed our robes, and then walked up to the next level behind the pool, where there was a small bar and restaurant. Sam ordered a dark beer and a slice of apple strudel, and I drank a Fanta orange – too sweet, but it brought back memories from sometime in my childhood.

It was nearly midnight when we walked down to the U-Bahn station, our bodies still steaming. We rode the train back towards our hotel, the loud clacking of the wheels on the tracks, and reverberation inside the constricted underground space making a racket and jostling us, as the train picked up speed. Perhaps the driver was longing to be done with the day's duties, and return home to his family?

As we waited for people to enter and exit at the main train station stop, Sam asked, "I think we're both wide awake, now ... and it's still early on a big Friday night in Munich. I could still look-up the address of that sex club, and we could check it out, if you like?"

I shook my head, "I'm feeling good, Sam, but I'm still pretty tired. Maybe we can catch that on our *next* trip to Europe?" The train lurched forward, and we both held a shiny chrome pole that was marred with greasy fingerprints, as Sam chuckled and nodded.

I woke on Saturday morning, Kelly snoozing beside me, and stared at the ceiling, deciding to modify our itinerary, slightly. If it had been warmer, I would have liked to have a picnic in the park on Sunday, perhaps getting some rays, and eating at one of the many outdoor restaurants serving rotisserie chicken that seemed more 'real' than anything we could get in the U.S.

Or, we could spend part of Sunday on a beach on the Isar River. There were many other things we could do here in Munich – such as go to the theater; and there were also plenty of sights nearby, such as the Dachau concentration camp. While that would be an important experience for Kelly, I wasn't sure I wanted to put us both through those emotions, in the short time we had in Europe; I hoped to keep the trip up-beat, as much as possible.

I decided that we would leave tomorrow, and visit a few sights in the countryside, before heading to Zurich. Our hotel here could easily fill our room, and the hotel in Zurich would take us a day early.

As I stayed at this hotel often, the management knew me, and I managed to wrangle an Oktoberfest VIP pass, which would gain us priority entrance to some of the tents – although I knew that we would still need to pay for the beer (10 Euro per *Mass*), and the food. Kelly woke, and we showered together, and then dressed in our traditional German costumes.

I was determined to be at the Oktoberfest gate by 8:30AM, and knew that by noon, the entire festival grounds would be packed. We walked the few blocks, and I explained to Kelly, "The locals call this the *Weisn*, or lawn. The Oktoberfest was originally to celebrate the marriage of Prince Ludwig I to Therese; the so-called 'Oktoberfest meadows' is actually named the *Thereseinweisen*."

We walked a few more blocks, cut through a small park, and were at the Oktoberfest gate within ten minutes; there was already a crowd, but the gate opened promptly, and we filed in – our passes having been printed out at the hotel from my Internet confirmation.

We walked down the main 'drag', similar to a huge carnival or, perhaps, state fair; except for the animals. But as we walked down the row of concessions, we saw plenty of animals – chickens and ducks hanging, pigs feet, and many other foods, ready for today's crowd – the average daily attendance totaling nearly 400,000 hungry and thirsty people.

Kelly pointed, and I bought a huge pretzel, which we broke in half – each of us still having a huge, browned knot of dough in our hands, which we dipped into traditional mustard, *senf*. I knew we would be thirsty soon, and explained to Kelly, "There are places to get beer out here, as well as fourteen huge beer tents, sponsored by the major breweries; some of the 'tents' are actually huge buildings, that hold 5,000 people."

As it was still early, we managed to get into the tent of one of the major breweries, and sat at a long table, already filled with people toasting with huge steins of beer. By the time our beers arrived, an 'Oom-Pah' band had started playing, and people were swaying and waving their steins. Fortunately, the band was at the other end of the tent ... but there was plenty of loud singing and toasting all around us.

I drained the last of my liter of beer, holding the huge stein with my hand through the handle, and surrounding as much of the glass as I could grab. Then, I plunked the stein down on the wooden table, and regarded Kelly: She was lifting the stein using both hands, and her face was hidden from view. She set the stein carefully down on the table, and I saw that Kelly had only finished about half. I jokingly said, "What, you don't like the beer?"

Kelly laughed, and shook her head, as she wiped a bit of foam off her upper lip using the back of her hand. "I'm feeling the alcohol, already. And, who can fit all this in their stomach? One more of these, and we can skip lunch and dinner."

I was about to hold up my empty stein in answer, when the crowd erupted in laughter and applause. We looked around, and saw a middle-aged man standing on a table, lifting his full *Mass* of beer, and then tilting his head back, and chugging the entire stein; it couldn't have taken more than thirty seconds!

"That's incredible," I heard Kelly yell, her voice reaching me through the applause of the crowd only because I was sitting next to her on the bench. I nodded, and again was going to comment, when another guy stood on the table next to ours; it was an effort for him to clamber up, and he had to bend over to take the beer that was handed up to him, with his gigantic stomach spreading open his lederhosen vest.

I glanced at Kelly, and had to snap a quick picture – her head turned up, twin long braids hanging over the ruffles of her dirndl, cheeks reddened, eyes sparkling, and a smile that would melt any man ... and, I now realized, quite a few women. Kelly's mouth fell open, and the crowd roared as I turned back around. The stein that had held a liter a moment ago was now empty, and being held high in the air victoriously. I turned to Kelly, and shrugged, and she explained, "He drank that entire beer in less than ten seconds!"

I thought that was probably an exaggeration, when a guy at *our* table climbed up, with his beer. He was solid, but not fat, and was wearing some very stylish lederhosen – you could tell that this was not a costume for him: It was normal attire. We watched as he lifted the stein, and tilted it, the beer level visibly lowering, and the Adam's apple of his throat pulsing, and then taking the stein from his mouth, turning it over his green felt hat to prove that it was empty, and doing a quick tap-dance on the table.

Everyone applauded, and Kelly took my arm, "How can they *do* that? Maybe the fat guy, but this one wasn't heavy, and he still drank a liter in only a few seconds. I'm still working on my first liter, and I'm full, already."

We walked back outside, and continued our way, passing shops with giant, decorated gingerbread hearts, candies, and a huge variety of *würst*. "Kelly, let's keep eating along the way, so that we can keep up with the alcohol." I walked over to a stand that had fantastic-looking *würst* on the grill, and bought a *weissewürst*, or white sausage, that is traditionally eaten as a snack in the morning. It came with a spherical, hard-crusted roll and, of course, mustard.

Standing at barrel-tables with umbrellas in front of the *würst* stand, we enjoyed the food and the ambiance. Kelly munched on her sausage, and I broke open my bread, showing Kelly the airy, fluffiness inside. I wished that we could get *würst und brot* like this at home!

We left the long line of shops and food stands, and passed various carnival rides – roller coasters, carousels, the Ferris wheel, spook houses, and thrill-rides, such as the 'Top Spin', which Kelly and I watched for a while, people lined up in seats being repeatedly thrown in an inverted circle. We went into one of the smaller rides, and I suggested that Kelly try it: Everyone sat on a large disk, and it was rotated at high speed until people flew off – hitting against a foam barrier. Something that would never be allowed in the U.S., considering the liability, and our legal system!

Kelly complained that she was wearing the dress, but I really wanted to see her do it. I then made a mistake: I asked whether she would submit to me. When the 'barker' called out for women in dirndls, Kelly boarded the disk, along with at least a dozen other women dressed similarly, and sat facing outward, her legs pointing to me.

The ride started, spinning the wheel up to an incredible number of revolutions per minute. The women started losing their frictional hold, and began flying outward off the disk and against the barrier. It was hilarious. Kelly maintained her position, until there were only a handful of people still on the disk, when she suddenly flew off, her skirts and underskirts flying all around her. The ride slowed, and all the women arranged their clothing.

Kelly walked unsteadily toward me, smiling, and then falling forward, her arms over my shoulder. I held her as her dizziness passed, and we continued our walk down the row of rides. I told Kelly, "That looked like fun!" She gave me a sour look, then smiled.

Suddenly, Kelly stopped, turned in front of me, and held me by the waist. I wasn't sure what was wrong, but she looked sincerely into my eyes ... and said, "Sam, will you submit to me?" Uh oh! What had she thought of, now? And what choice did I have? I *wanted* to submit to Kelly ... but I wasn't sure I wanted to do whatever Kelly was going to ask. But she had just submitted to me ...

"Yes, Kelly," I said apprehensively, glancing around, "I will submit to you."

Kelly smiled broadly, jumped up and down, and clapped her hands. Then, she put her arms around my neck and kissed me. Well, whatever it was, it had already earned me a nice kiss! And these were just kids' carnival rides; although the 'Top Spin' and the 'Hammer' both looked pretty challenging. I wondered whether I had ever shared with Kelly my fear of heights? I'm fine in a plane, or in a tall building ... but I nearly pass out when looking over the edge of the balcony of a tall building, or over a ledge on a mountain.

Then, Kelly spun around twice, smiled again, and pointed upward. There was already such a crowd of people that I realized I had only been looking around our immediate vicinity. Now, I looked up, and my knees were suddenly weak: An incredibly tall tower loomed above us, its base just ahead, and as we maneuvered between the people, I saw the neon-lighted sign of the ride: Sky Fall.

Sam was so easy to tease! He had asked me to go on that spinning disk – wearing a dress – so it was only fair that he have a new 'experience' here at the Oktoberfest. I pulled his hand, as we walked through the crowd towards the ride. When we got to the ticket booth, Sam gave me a pleading look. I shrugged, and smiled at him innocently; he *had* said that he would submit to me …

Sam resignedly asked, "Shall I buy one ticket, or two?"

I smiled sweetly at him, "It's just for you, silly!"

Sam's eyes closed, and his face was pale. A wisp of a smile crossed his lips, and he bent over and asked, "Am I supposed to throw up *before*, or *after* I get on the ride?"

I took his arm, and we walked up to the ticket window. Sam gave me another pleading look, and I softened, "OK, Sam. If you're going to act like such a baby, I'll do it with you, if you want." Sam still didn't look too pleased, as he bought two tickets. We filed into a 'holding' area, as people from the previous ride exited in another direction.

Sam started coughing, and pointed to a sign, "80 meters? That's more than 260 feet!" I had seen the sign before he had bought the tickets; it really was an impressive ride. I smiled and nodded at Sam. Then, the gate opened, and we took our seats, pulling the harness against our chests. I looked over at Sam, and his face looked a light shade of green – maybe chartreuse – and now I wondered whether he might actually throw up on the ride. He mumbled something about heights, but I couldn't understand him.

Then, we were rising rapidly, the park receding below us. It was an incredible sight: Many acres of rides, and food concessions, and beer halls ... and a virtual sea of humanity, tens of thousands of bodies, like ants, moving slowly along the wide walkways of the fairgrounds. We kept rising – higher and higher – and the view was spectacular. I glanced at Sam, and his eyes were closed. "Sam! You have to see this! The view is incredible, and your 'submission' requires you to keep your eyes open."

Sam whimpered, and opened his eyes. Our feet were dangling, now more than two hundred feet above the crowd. We could see trains entering and leaving the main station and, in the far distance, I could make out the grounds of the Nymphenburg Palace to our left, and the English Garden to our right. Sam whimpered louder, and I reached over and held his hand.

There was a loud clunk, and our motion stopped. We hung motionless, our legs dangling, and I squeezed Sam's hand. Then, suddenly, we were in free-fall, accelerating toward the ground, the wind tearing through us, our stomachs being left at the top. Sam screamed, and we suddenly slowed, the ride now floating down the last twenty or thirty feet. I squeezed Sam's hand, and looked at him: His eyes were closed again, and I saw beads of sweat on his brow.

The harnesses released, and I helped Sam stand and walk back to the main thoroughfare. We stopped, a continuous stream of people passing around us, and I gave Sam a peck on the lips. He opened his eyes, and said, "I must not have told you about my acrophobia." I guess there were still things I needed to learn about Sam.

We walked much of the grounds, and were able to find a table at one of the outdoor beer gardens. Sam returned with two huge mugs, which he held in one hand, and a plate of roasted chicken, *hendl*, in the other. Before, I could comment on the gigantic beers, Sam explained, "Mine is the special *märzen* they brew for Oktoberfest, and yours is a '*Radler*' – beer mixed with lemonade and soda water. Let me know what you think."

We clanked our steins together. I knew that he was eliciting my opinion of the drink, but I responded, "Sam, I think you're a good sport for submitting to me, even though you were deathly afraid." Sam looked at me cautiously, and I continued, "Yes, Sam, I could certainly tell that you weren't bluffing about your fear: Your face was green, and I really was worried that you might give up your *weisswürst* on that ride."

Sam nodded, and pulled a wing off the tender, juicy chicken. I pulled some meat off the bird, and tasted it: It was one of the best roasted chickens I'd even eaten. We took our time, grateful to have a table and be able to sit down for a while. We watched hordes of people moving past us – groups of Italians in soccer uniforms, some Austrians in even fancier lederhosen, and plenty of Americans.

It was still early in the afternoon, but the volume of the singing and cheering increased, and most people were tipsy, if not full-on drunk. Sam and I squeezed through the crowd, finally making our way to one of the larger beer tents. There was a long line, but also a handful of people gaining admission immediately. Sam showed our VIP pass, and handed a twenty Euro note to the guy guarding the door, and he let us in, pointing to some stairs.

The ground floor was mobbed, and we made our way up the stairs, where Sam had to show his VIP pass again. A cute girl in a dirndl showed us to a wooden table, where we sat near the rail, overlooking the packed floor of this 'tent'. I stared, mesmerized, by the enormity of the place: There had to be several thousand people in here, and the sound level was incredible.

Another maiden in her dirndl set the beers in front of us, and we toasted, barely able to hear each other over the roar of the crowd. Sam put his mouth near my ear and yelled, "Let's stay here for a while, now that we have a good seat." I nodded, but didn't bother trying to respond verbally. The band began playing, and everyone was singing and swaying their beer steins with the music. I could see several people standing on tables, chugging their liters of beer.

Sam handed me an aspirin – not a bad idea! – and we 'toasted' by clicking our aspirins together, before washing them down with the beer. We listened to the music, and watched the antics on the various tables inside the tent. Sam had to pee, so I saved our seats, while he disappeared for ten minutes. Then, it was my turn. The women's WC had a long line, and I didn't return to the table for more than half an hour.

We spent another hour in the tent, and then Sam suggested we try to get into another tent listed on the VIP pass. We exited the tent into the thick crowd, and made our way to our next venue, which specialized in oxen dishes. In front of the tent, there were huge vertical spits rotating with a model of an oxen skewered on each of them. Inside, it was standing room only, and we had to wait a for a table.

Eventually we were squeezed between other couples who were obviously already having a good time. Sam ordered ox-tail soup for both of us, with thick dark bread, and a plate with an array of pickles and other accompaniments. An hour later, we were outside again, making our way through the crowd to the tent that Sam had selected where we would have dinner, and camp out the rest of the day.

Fortunately there was a VIP section, and we were seated quickly. We ordered beers – there were half-liters here – and Sam perused the menu. I was hungry again by the time our food arrived, nearly an hour later. Sam had finished another *Mass* of beer, and I don't think he cared about the food, or anything else, for that matter.

Sam had decided to order only one dish for the two of us, the theory being that we could share another 'dinner' later, at still another tent. I wasn't sure whether Sam could even walk to another tent, at this point. A platter arrived, with *spannferkel* (suckling pig), two huge, softball-size, round dumplings, and a mound of sweet-and-sour red cabbage. There was a brown juice covering the platter, and Sam cut into the dumpling with his fork, and scooped up some of the gravy.

I tasted each of the dishes – the cabbage being my favorite. The pig was delicious, but so rich that I could only have one bite. I drank another *Radler*, and now I was definitely feeling tipsy.

When we could stand the loud music no longer, we exited the tent into the densest crowd of people I'd ever seen. Sam suggested we visit the small tent offering wild animal dishes, or one of the tents specializing in roast duck. "Sam, I think I've had as much food as my stomach is going to fit for one day. And I think you've probably had as much beer as your brain will fit."

Sam gave me a sharp look, and then smiled, "You have a point, Kelly. But there is so much more to see, here." He pointed in the distance to a ride we'd walked past earlier: The Frisbee. It was a whirling disk of seats at the end of a long arm that fell back and forth like a pendulum. "And we still have a lot of rides to try."

I laughed, and replied, "I'd like to go back to our room and ride you ... but you would never get it up, after all that beer." Sam didn't argue, just shrugged. The sun was below the tents, now, and lights were coming on all around us. We jostled our way through the crowd, heading toward the rides.

Sam pointed at a large tent, "This is the only tent that doesn't serve beer – the *Weinzelt* – it only has wine." The building looked like the ones we saw on the Romantic Road, with crisscrosses of dark wood over lighter-color walls. Music was coming from all around us, as was singing, yelling, and the general noise of the crowd.

I was starting to get a headache from it all, despite the aspirin we'd taken. Sam kept pointing out various tents, and some of the specialties that we would undoubtedly miss this time around. And I wasn't sure that the Oktoberfest would be my top priority for a return trip.

We kept walking, at the pace of the thousands of people around us, and Sam took my hand as we made a jog to the right, then to the left, finally arriving at the huge Ferris wheel. He bought tickets, and spoke quietly to the man controlling the ride, handing him a folded bill.

Then, we entered one of the cages – alone; it was the only cage not packed with people. As soon as the wheel moved, and our cage rose above the crowd, Sam, in a slurred voice, said, "Please take off your underwear." I was happy to humor Sam, as it was clear that nothing was going to happen, with him in this state.

Fortunately, the ride was slow, without too much rocking, as my entire body was rocking, now. As we reached the pinnacle of our once-around, we watched the sunset over the forest. Lights were on everywhere, and Sam snapped a few pictures. It really was an incredible sight – both the number of lights, and the number of people.

Then, Sam knelt on the metal floor in front of me, and stuck his head up my skirts. I separated my legs, and felt Sam's head moving up them, kissing my inner thighs, then – literally – 'going down' on me: He lowered his head, and I felt one slobbery lap from his tongue ... and then his ear was against me (playing me 'by ear'?), and Sam's motion stopped, except for his slow breathing that made my skirt rise and fall, as I gazed at the lights of the Oktoberfest far below.

I assumed that Sam was playing around, and let him root around under my skirts; I slowly stroked his back, and his deep breathing continued. Our cage was almost down to the bottom, and we would have to get off the Ferris wheel soon. I quietly said, "Sam – we have to get off soon." The only response was a couple of loud snores. "Come on, Sam, stop playing around." More snores. I put my hands under my skirt and petticoat, and shook him by the shoulders, "Sam!"

Finally he moaned, and pulled his head out. "Are we there, yet?" His words were slurred, and it appeared that he really was out of it. He had put my panties in his pocket, and I didn't bother trying to retrieve them. I helped Sam onto the seat just about the time our cage came to the bottom, and the door opened. Sam and I stumbled onto the boarding platform like a couple of drunks; well, at least *one* of us was drunk!

We walked a short distance, out of the most crowded thoroughfare, and found an adjacent field, filled with 'dead bodies' – others also overly inebriated. We sat down on a small patch of uninhabited grass, and Sam lay back, and closed his eyes. I reached over and grabbed his phone, sat cross-legged, and continued my research. It was nearly an hour later when a hand held onto my thigh, and Sam pulled himself into a sitting position. I smiled sweetly at him and asked, "Are we having fun, yet?"

Sam shook his head, and replied, "I guess I might have had one *Mass* too many."

I laughed, "Or two, or three too many! I don't even know how many you had. Shall we head back to the hotel? Are you *capable* of getting back to the hotel? Or will I have to carry you?"

Sam harrumphed, and managed to stand up, albeit a little wobbly. As we walked through the crowd, Sam complained, "But we haven't had our *other* dinner, yet." We passed a würst stand, and Sam pointed, "How about one of *those*?"

It wasn't difficult to read the German on the sign: They were making 'hot dogs', with a half-meter of würst – six inches sticking out of each side of the bun. I took Sam by the arm, and pulled him along. We nearly made it out of the fairgrounds, when he suddenly pulled me to one of the stands, "At least, we can have cotton candy. That doesn't take up any room."

He paid for a huge, blue puff of cotton candy, and we walked a few blocks – the atmosphere morphing from zillions of rowdy people at the Oktoberfest, to a quiet residential neighborhood in Westpark.

Sam managed to get back to the room without getting sick, and suggested that we go down to the sauna. I just shook my head, "I'd be too embarrassed." When Sam's eyes narrowed, and his brow furrowed, I added, "Too embarrassed to be seen with an Oktoberfest drunk."

He laughed and nodded, and then Sam looked at me seriously, "I'll be OK, Kelly. Maybe the sauna will sober me up, a little?" I was doubtful, but Sam helped me out of the dress, we put on running outfits, and went down to the hotel sauna. It was crowded, and we found the only lockers left.

We went out to the pool area, and nearly all the chaises were occupied, mostly with couples, several of the men being rather loud ... or being asleep. I surmised that we weren't the only ones in this condition, tonight. People were polite in the saunas, and the heat seemed to dissipate the alcohol – both in Sam and in me. We went through a couple of sauna cycles, and then stepped out onto a deck that faced towards the *Theresienwiese*. The noise could be heard from here as a rumbling, and colored lights lit the grounds, and reflected from the low clouds now dotting the dark sky.

Sam did sober up enough to make it back to the room, and get into bed – but not enough to get it up. I hadn't expected it, and also rejected his offer to go down on me: I didn't need him falling asleep with his nose in my privates, again. I spooned Sam, and he was instantly asleep.

The alcohol had tired me out, also, but it was still early, and my mind wandered, recalling a few of the images from the Oktoberfest – seeing Sam's face, as the Sky Fall ride lifted us high above the thronging crowd; looking down over 5,000 people all waving their beer steins in one of the tents; and the half-meter hot dog that would surely have led to Sam giving up everything he had eaten.

Then, I thought about what I'd found on the Internet, while Sam had slept on the grass. It was exciting: I knew I was onto something big; which would have described Sam's cock right now, had he not been drunk.

CHAPTER 14: ZÜRICH LAKE VIEW

We were up very early, and on the road by 7AM, with me driving, as Sam had the predicted hangover. On the outskirts of Munich, Sam asked me to pull over, and we went into a *bäckerei*, where we made a selection of some incredible pastries, and bought a couple of coffees to drink in the car.

I munched on a *mohnscnitte*, a delicious poppy seed pastry, as Sam guided me using the GPS on his phone. We drove west, then south, through beautiful countryside, passing through small villages with cute houses, flowers in the windows, and well-manicured lawns in front. As we drove down a long valley, Sam asked me to pull over again, and we got out of the car, and walked across the street, where he snapped a few shots of me ... with a fairytale castle in the background.

"That's our destination this morning: *Schloss Neuschwanstein*, the castle of King Ludwig II, 'crazy King Ludwig'."

When I glanced at him inquisitively, he explained, "It's quite a story. Ludwig II was King of Bavaria, although it was taken over by Prussia, and then the German Empire. But Ludwig was only interested in commissioning art and architecture projects. He built two palaces, and this castle, taking elements from many others he had researched."

Sam continued, "He spent all the royal money of Bavaria, as well as his own fortune, and kept borrowing to support his building 'habit'. The Bavarian cabinet tried to stop him, and he threatened to get rid of them. His ministers ginned-up information – most likely false – that showed that he was insane, and he was deposed, but not before making a stand here at Neuschwanstein."

We drove up to the castle, and bought tickets for the first tour at 9AM, but had half an hour to wait, so I drove back down the hill to where there were several hotels on a small lake. We had coffee in one of the cafes, and watched the swans on the lake, before driving back to the castle for the tour.

The castle could only be described as a 'fairytale' castle – in fact, the one after which the castle in Disneyland was modeled. After the tour, we walked across a wooden bridge to get a better view of Neuschwanstein, with the valley in the background. The photos would be a touch anachronistic, as there were hang gliders flying in the distance.

I continued driving, and Sam informed me that we should be in Zurich in a little over three hours. Sam complained, "There were a lot of compromises to be made in designing the itinerary for this trip. We could be in Innsbruck, Austria in less than two hours, and get in a half-day of skiing this afternoon. Or, we could stay another day in Zurich, and drive to a ski resort – like Engelberg or Andermatt. There are so many possibilities." I smiled inwardly: Yes, there were!

Around lunchtime, we drove into the Principality of Liechtenstein, and its capital city Vaduz. Sam became the tour guide again. "This tiny country – only about twice as big as Manhattan Island in New York – is the richest country per capita, and has one of the highest standards of living, in the world."

We were quickly out of Vaduz and driving through a beautiful valley, with fields, trees, lakes, and spectacular mountains on either side. We passed tiny town of Flums, and Sam pointed to the left, up the mountain. "There's a ski resort up there, called Flumserberg. It has an incredible view of the lake."

A while later, Sam pointed to the right and below us, "That is the *Zürichsee*, Lake Zurich. The town of Zurich is at the other end of the lake." An hour later, we entered Zurich and drove to our hotel, which was up a winding mountain road.

As we took our rolling cases and backpacks out of the car, Sam explained, "We could have stayed on the lake, but this hotel has a great view of the city and the lake, and we can take the funicular down, and walk from there ... or take a tram."

The room was stark, but modern, with wood everywhere – the floors, walls, and a full wall of closets and cabinets. There was a small patio that had a magnificent view of the city and lake. We left our bags, and took the funicular down, and then a tram to Bellevue.

Sam looked at his watch, and announced, "Well, if I couldn't have the half-meter *würst* with you, last night ... at least I can have a late lunch at my favorite *würst* stand." We walked a couple of blocks, and stood in a line, then Sam got his *bratwürst* and mustard with a huge, spherical ball of bread. I took a bite from the end of the *würst* – it was great, but I still felt full from the rich food we'd had yesterday at Oktoberfest.

Sam led me through the 'old town' of Zurich, where there were art galleries, bookstores, many small shops, and restaurants. It was quaint, but a little touristy. Then, we crossed the bridge, and walked to Bürkliplatz, where we could look down the length of the lake, to the snowy mountains beyond.

Sam pointed to a statue: A bronze of a young man, one hand to the sky, and the other reaching for an eagle. "The eagle is Zeus, come to abduct Ganymede, whisk him away to Mount Olympus, and take him as a lover. It represents gay rights, which have been part of Swiss law since before World War II. Zurich is a very tolerant and progressive city; the mayor for the past five years has been a lesbian woman."

We continued our walk, entering a park along the lake, huge trees raining multi-hued leaves: Bright reds, yellows, oranges and browns, making the walkway a kaleidoscopic progression of colors. We passed small sailboats on our left, bobbing in the chop of the lake, attached to white buoys; and, on our right, was a large expanse of lawn.

Many people were enjoying the beautiful Sunday weather, throwing Frisbees, having picnics, and making out. We walked down a path near the water, and Sam led me onto a dock, past rows of sailboats, and onto a barge-like structure, where we went through a curtain, and walked into a small reception area, with a few tables, where they served simple snacks. Sam paid, and handed me a towel and a robe.

Descending stairs that led to an underwater 'basement', we found our lockers and got undressed. There was nobody else down here, and I wondered if we would be the only people in the sauna. Then, we went upstairs, and into a glassed-in area, with chaise lounges, and multiple saunas. It was packed!

We hung our robes and towels, and took a quick shower; then, grabbing our towels, we entered one of the saunas. It had windows high on the walls behind us and in front of us, giving a view of the park, and the lake. Almost all of the people here were from my age to perhaps 40; they were all younger than Sam.

When we exited the sauna, Sam took me out to the lakeside deck, in which a rectangular opening in the middle served as a 'swimming pool'; but I noticed that the water temperature was only 5 degrees Centigrade – that would be about forty degrees – a bit cold for swimming. There were people lying on chaises, and some even dunking themselves in the cold water. Standing at the end of the deck, we had a 360-degree view of Zurich.

Sam pointed west, "The sun is setting over the Uetliberg – Zurich's 'mountain'. We have a similar view from our hotel room."

We went back inside and took another sauna, rinsed, and then repeated with a third sauna. Sam smiled at me in a certain 'way', and I knew he had something planned. People were coming into our sauna cabin and leaving it, but we were in there for a very long time – it had to be 15 minutes.

When we were both too hot to stand it any longer, we exited the sauna, and Sam took me by the hand. We quickly walked out to the end of the deck, where Sam hugged me tightly. Then, he put his towel on a bench, and stepped down the ladder into the freezing lake water. He let go, and treaded water, then signaled me to come in.

He had not asked me to 'submit', but I would do as he asked. As I lowered myself into the water, my legs felt a shocking cold. But, somehow, the accumulated heat of the sauna allowed me to get fully in, before quickly climbing back up the ladder and putting my towel around me.

Sam swam a leisurely lap across the deck, and climbed up the ladder on the opposite side. "Well, that was refreshing!" Sam laughed, "I've been in the lake when it's only two degrees – about 35 degrees Fahrenheit. But in the summer, it can be quite pleasant, and I've swum around the fountain out there in the lake.

We spent the early evening playing around at the sauna, and just before we were ready to leave, Sam walked me out to the end of the deck again. Now, the sky was dark, with only a thin orange band over the Uetliberg, and a few stars already visible to the east. Sam held me, and we spun around slowly, taking in the vista of this historic town. Then, Sam turned me to him, and kissed me deeply.

After dressing at the sauna, we walked down the elite Bahnhofstrasse – the street running from Zurich's *Hauptbahnhof* to Bürkliplatz. We looked in the windows – Cartier, Louis Vuitton, Gucci, Bulgari, Chanel, Dior, and even the Apple Store resided on this boulevard. We did enter one store – where Sam bought a couple of chocolate truffles for a dessert, as we walked back to our hotel.

Then, we walked past the largest clock face in Europe, turned into an alley, and entered a huge restaurant – the *Zeughauskeller*. It had the atmosphere of the *Haxnbauer* in Munich, but I noticed that nearly all the diners were families on this Sunday evening. Sam suggested the *Züricher Geschnetzeltes*, pieces of veal in a mushroom cream sauce, with *spätzle*. Sam explained that this building used to house an armory, among other things, in its 500-year history.

When we walked out of the restaurant, we turned away from the lake. "Isn't our hotel in the other direction?" I inquired.

Sam responded glibly, "Yes. But I thought we would go to a club tonight."

I reacted, "Sam, I can't go to a club, dressed like this!" I was wearing black jeans and a sweater, clunky touring shoes, and no makeup, as I hadn't applied any after the sauna.

Sam smiled, "I don't think that will be a problem. When I checked on the Internet, I found lots of 'gentlemen' clubs, massage parlors, and brothels. But there were a few BDSM and fetish clubs, also. This club has some kind of training session every Sunday night – so I thought it might be interesting." It was *always* interesting with Sam!

We entered the club, and I guess our attire was appropriate; there were probably a dozen young couples mingling, and we sat around a small circular 'stage'. A woman came out, wearing a shiny PVC (rubber) corset, similar to the one Zöe had worn at the club in Amsterdam. She began her talk in *Schweitzer-Deutsche*, the Swiss-German dialect spoken here, but then she thankfully turned to English.

This was, evidently, a class on latex clothing. She modeled the corset, and then opened a large trunk, and pulled out a shiny black outfit. She called for a male volunteer, and a guy stepped onto the stage. The woman took the guy by the arm, and walked him behind a small privacy screen.

A minute or two later, they came back out: He wore latex pants, and had a bare chest. He couldn't stop laughing, as the woman spun him around, and we saw that the latex left his buttocks exposed. Everyone clapped.

There were several more outfits – a policewoman's uniform and hat, and even a medical outfit and hat, all in latex rubber. The evening was heating up, and now several different latex lingerie were modeled by women from the audience. One was a short-legged body suit, with cut-outs for the breasts. There was applause and laughter, everyone having a good time. The woman pulled out the last outfit, and called for volunteers; nobody responded immediately, so she pointed at me, and crooked her finger.

I looked at Sam, and he smiled and shrugged. I stepped up onto the stage, and the woman applauded, then held up the outfit for everyone to see: It was a full body suit, which the woman announced was an 'open breast cat suit'. She pulled my hand, and we went behind the narrow screen.

She whispered to me, and I undressed down to my underwear. Then, she helped me into the suit. My thoughts became a haze, as she pulled me to the center of the stage, my body tightly enclosed in the shiny red bodysuit, my breasts bare as they protruded through the openings in the outfit. Everyone applauded, and Sam made a couple of catcalls.

I got into the spirit and modeled the outfit, bending over, and letting my breasts swing over the first row of patrons. There was more applause, and the woman sent me behind the screen to change back into my street clothes.

When the show was over, the woman came to us, and handed me a box. "The participants take home the things they wear, so this is yours. You were a perfect model for this outfit!" We hugged, and she disappeared behind the curtain.

We ate the truffles, as we walked back to the funicular and took the slow, steep ride up to our hotel. Then we took some time to view the expanse of nighttime Zurich from our patio. Looking over the incredible view, Sam remarked, "There's so much more to see here."

I held his arm, and commiserated, "I know."

Sam turned, and gave me a wet kiss. Then, he asked, brightly, "So how would you feel about sailing tomorrow?"

That sounded great! "In Lake Zurich?"

Sam shook his head, "No, in Interlaken – near the middle of Switzerland. We'll stay there one night, which might also allow us to ski the next day."

It was nice that we were participating in many activities, here in Europe, not just touring; activities in which the 'locals' – at least some segment of them – were also involved. I was getting a sense of the history, but also a glimpse into the lifestyle of some Europeans.

Then, I realized how many different 'lifestyles' there were in the U.S. – I had to be careful not to generalize. I was getting a very distorted view of Europe, focused on the areas that Sam wanted to share.

Early Monday morning, we ate in the hotel restaurant – wonderful breads and jams, meats and cheeses, and made-to-order omelets. Then, we drove through beautiful valleys, bordered by sheer mountains, arriving at Interlaken by mid-morning. We drove directly to the lake, and Sam rented a small sailboat.

It was a beautiful day, with blue skies and wispy clouds, as we pushed off the dock, and Sam guided our boat across the lake. There was a brisk wind, and the boat heeled over, both of us leaning out the other side of the cockpit to keep the boat stable. We made a few tacks, and Sam sailed us near the mountain that rose from the lake.

A few minutes later, I saw that we were sailing towards a waterfall. We tacked less than a hundred yards from the waterfall, and headed back across small chop, jibing a few times to make our way back to the dock.

We drove to our hotel and checked-in, spending the afternoon 'playing around' in the well-appointed room. We dressed in the early evening, and walked around the small town. Sam asked if I would be interested in visiting the casino, but I declined; I wasn't much of a gambling person; although my gamble with Sam was paying off nicely.

Sam picked a fondue restaurant, and ordered *fondue bourguignonne*, which came with a platter of filet to be dipped in the hot oil, along with a half dozen different sauces. We drank red wine, and had a very romantic dinner, by candlelight. As usual, Sam went overboard, and ordered the dark chocolate strawberry fondue, which was fabulous. I felt like I really had died, and gone to heaven. My next thought was, 'after this kind of eating, I'm going to be dieting for the next year!'.

The next morning, we drove up to Grindlewald, below the Jungfrau summit. We rented equipment, and skied together for the first time. My new jacket worked well, and I was toasty on the slopes. The views were magnificent; I had never seen mountains like this before – an expanse of jagged white peaks, towering over beautiful green valleys.

Sam surprised me with his skiing skills; our family had taken ski trips every year, and my sports jock father had made sure his children were proficient in every sport we tried. We ate lunch on the mountain, and Sam commented, "Kelly, if I'd known you were this good of a skier, I would have taken you to the Schilthorn; we could have skied down from 10,000 feet."

We ate dinner in Grindlewald, and drove down the mountain in the dark, the lights of Interlaken far below. That evening, we made use of the hotel's sauna and pool, which was very mellow with only three or four other couples; quite a change from the mobs we had seen at Oktoberfest.

Wednesday morning, we drove along the lake we had sailed, the *Thunersee*, and headed south. Sam explained that we would have to cross one of the main mountain ranges cutting through Switzerland ... and that the most efficient way to do that was on the 'car train'. About an hour from Interlaken, we drove the car onto a special train with a line of other cars. It was weird: We sat in our car, as the train took us through some incredibly long tunnels under the mountains.

Sam looked over to me with a devilish grin. "How about some 'car sex'?" I looked at him as though he was crazy, and he said, sheepishly, "We have forty minutes ... that's plenty of time."

I gave him a 'look', but at that moment we entered a tunnel, our car now in instant darkness. "I could just give you a blow job," I offered, raising my voice to be heard over the clackety rails echoing in the tunnel. I thought it was a pretty good offer, but Sam crawled awkwardly out of the driver's seat, and over the console into the backseat. I followed him, feeling my way, as we entered still another tunnel.

Sam lowered his jeans, and I took mine off, smacking Sam in the side of the head (by accident, of course) in the process. With one leg on the floor of the car, and the other crossed, Sam sat sideways on the backseat, and I circled my legs around him, and took his cock in my hand. As I stroked him, the tunnel opened on one side, letting in the daylight in flashes that acted as a strobe – making my motions look as though they were in an old-time movie.

Sam was ready, and I managed to lift myself, and put him in me. Sam and I hugged, and rocked back-and-forth, with added jerky movements caused by the rough train ride. We held each other and kissed achingly, the vibrations of the train running through our connected bodies. I closed my eyes, and let the vibrations – and my fantasies – turn me on.

Sam and I continued rocking, and I thrust my pelvis against him, my thoughts finally breaking through my consciousness, and I orgasmed – just as we exited a tunnel. Sam wasn't far behind, and we held each other tightly afterward, savoring our combined warmth, and love for each other. Sam climbed back into the driver's seat, and I slipped on my underwear and jeans.

We didn't quite make it: The train came to a stop and engines revved, then a long line of cars drove off the train and onto the highway that descended into the valley. I had gotten my pants back on, but was maneuvering myself back into the front seat, as we drove off the train.

Less than an hour after we had boarded the car train, we were driving south again, down a switchback road into a long valley, finally arriving at the small town of Tasch, where we left our car, grabbed our rolling cases and backpacks, and boarded a shuttle train for the quick ride up the mountain to the car-free village of Zermatt.

CHAPTER 15: WHAT'S ZERMATTER?

The train chugged up the mountain – only a three mile route, but very steep, passing through covered bridges and tunnels through the mountain. We got off the train, and Sam pointed to a cute, golf-cart like vehicle with our hotel's name. We hopped aboard, and were driven through narrow, winding streets up the hill.

Sam pointed, and I saw it: The Matterhorn. It was like something from a fantasy ... something from Disneyland. I blinked, and it was still there, towering above us, wisps of clouds on either side of the peak, in the otherwise spectacularly clear air.

Six months ago, I could never have imagined that I would be visiting the Matterhorn. Nor would I have believed that I would have had such a shift in perspective about relationships and sex.

Sam was not a billionaire, but he had given me something incredibly valuable: A renewal of my belief in myself, and finding some of my true sexual turn-ons – such as being with women as well as men, and taking a dominant role. Being with Sam had forced me to look inward, to decide who I truly was ... and who I was going to be.

There was a brisk breeze, and I snuggled close to Sam, as the electric vehicle climbed further up the hill; the hotels and houses had thinned out, and we turned on a lane that rose to our hotel. It was like a small chalet, with a backdrop of trees and mountains.

We were shown to our top-floor room, and walked directly out onto the balcony. The Matterhorn – *the* Matterhorn – loomed far above us. It was a perfect view: The sloping, rolling ground covered with green grass, dark green conifers dotting the landscape, a handful of other chalets, cottages, or farm buildings, a few cows, and above it all, the most-recognized peak in the world – triangular, it's summit seemingly 'bent', and mostly covered in snow. The wisps of clouds were now thickening, and crowding around the peak of the Matterhorn.

Sam and I walked down the hill, nearly the length of the town, to the center, where we window-shopped expensive watches and artwork. We walked into several shops and saw dozens of types of music boxes, and even more varieties of cuckoo clocks. We visited one of the ski shops, and rented equipment for tomorrow; it would be waiting for us at the cable car.

It was a very cute town, obviously catering mostly to tourists, but it was very much how I had envisioned Europe. The Matterhorn museum was interesting, but we decided to pass on the mountaineers' cemetery. Even though there were a lot of tourists, the village felt empty to Sam and I, after our Oktoberfest experience.

We dined by candlelight at a typical Swiss restaurant that served *raclette* – a special cheese that is heated and scraped onto your plate (this particular restaurant still holding with the tradition), along with small white potatoes, hearty bread, gherkins, and a pickled onion. Sam also ordered the special dried ham appetizer, that covered an entire platter; the slices were paper thin – nearly transparent; I'd never eaten anything like it. Sam poured more of the Pinot Gris wine, and we toasted to a great trip so far, and to good skiing tomorrow.

It was a long walk back up the hill to the hotel, and wasn't too dark to make out the outline of the Matterhorn. We gathered things we would need for skiing tomorrow, filling our packs with gloves, caps, extra sweater, and a pair of cheap goggles that we had bought at the ski shop.

Sam insisted that I try on my new silk long underwear – of course, asking me to put them on without wearing my bra or underwear. He did the same, and we had a fun romp on the bed. For a few minutes, it turned into a wrestling match, Sam first pinning me down, and putting my silk-covered breasts in his mouth – until I complained that I didn't want to wear wet clothes skiing tomorrow. That distracted him enough for me to turn him over, and climb on top of him, pinning him to the bed.

But when I reached down and held his erection, our wrestling match ended, and I quickly pulled off my long john bottoms, and mounted Sam, his dick sticking through the opening in *his* long john bottoms. I leaned forward, pinning him by his shoulders, as I had my way with him, riding his cock to satisfy myself, while also sating Sam's sexual appetite, at least for a while.

We undressed and laid out our clothes for tomorrow, then turned off the lights and opened the curtain; we could feel the mountain's presence. We snuggled with each other until we fell asleep.

Waking to the towering Matterhorn framed in our window was a real treat. We watched the first rays of the sun light up the summit in an orange-pink pastel shade, the clouds having disappeared, and the sky above us an incredibly deep blue.

We dressed, and ate at the breakfast buffet in the hotel's small restaurant. Then, we walked the relatively short distance to the cable car, picked up our skis, boots, and poles, and positioned ourselves at the downhill end of the car.

As the car ascended, and the town fell below us, Sam said, "If we just had a couple of extra days ... there are some great hiking trails around here below the snow level, and an incredible cog railway to the summit of another mountain with a great view of the Matterhorn. There are beautiful mountain lakes, and waterfalls."

We watched, as the town became a tiny dot on the magnificent landscape. Sam continued, "And, with still another couple of days and we could have seen Chamonix – in the valley below Mont Blanc – and gone up another incredible cable car ... and maybe even had an exciting ski experience."

I laughed, "Yeah, I've heard about those 'exciting' experiences – where you ski off the edge of a cliff, or fall into a crevasse."

Sam nodded, "Actually, if we skied there, it would probably be with a guide. And you don't have to worry about much here – it's a popular year-round ski resort." Sam pointed down the hill, and we could barely make out the town. "Later in the season, when there's more snow, you can ski all the way back down to the village. I've never done that, but if you like this area, maybe we could come back, sometime?"

I just nodded. It still seemed like a fantasy that I was even here. We switched to another cable car, and continued the ride up the mountain. Finally at the top, we found lockers, put on our ski boots, and exited to the snow. It had evidently snowed last night, only an inch or two, but enough to make the skiing soft. We had a great morning of schussing down the slopes, and I was glad that I'd had some practice a couple of days ago. Sam was a very good skier; actually, we were pretty well matched – my youth balancing his skill.

It was nearly noon, and my stomach was growling; I eyed the mountain-top lodge, and began to pole in that direction. Sam stopped me and said, "I'm getting hungry." I nodded; maybe he could read my mind? He smiled, and said, "I really feel like some good pasta for lunch." Then, he snapped his fingers, as he gave me a devilish smile, and asked, "Why don't we have lunch in Italy?"

I wasn't sure I was hearing Sam correctly, "Italy? Aren't we in Switzerland?" Then, I added, "And aren't there big mountains between Switzerland and Italy?"

Sam nodded, "Yeah, like this one." He pointed to a signpost, pointing in many directions, and we skied over to it. "It's actually a very easy ski – mainly a long winding road, with just a few exciting slopes, and we'll be in Cervinia, Italy in only ten minutes. There are quite a few restaurants there – and they're probably better than the restaurant at the ski lift."

I shook my head. Ten minutes? From Switzerland to Italy? And we appeared to be in an isolated – and, if not for the people, desolate – spot near the Matterhorn. I followed Sam, and we skied continuously down the mountain, taking closer to 20 minutes to reach the Italian town. We had a delightful lunch, foregoing the wine, as we still had some skiing to do.

We skied until late afternoon, taking the cable car down again, dropping off the equipment, and returning to our chalet. We took a hot shower together, bathing each other caressingly, then dressed and walked down to the town for dinner. We ate at a tiny restaurant, and drank a reserve chianti that Sam had wanted to try.

This restaurant was very romantic, very small, decorated nicely, and had flickering candles ... that, upon further inspection, I realized were electrical – a small switch on the bottom turning the device on and off. It did look realistic, and the restaurant had an air of the old-fashioned Europe I had envisioned.

It was quite chilly as Sam and I walked together up the hill, passing ancient storage huts typical of this region. When we got back to the room, we undressed and slipped into bed. It really felt good, after a hard day of skiing. When the covers were over us, Sam said, quietly, "Kelly, I'd like to make love to you ... but I don't think I have the energy for anything fancy.

I laughed, and said, "Do you want to be on top, or bottom?"

Sam said, without hesitation, "On top, if you don't mind." Sam made love to me slowly; we were both slowed by the day's exercise, and the bottle of wine. He stopped and asked, "Kelly, could you please tell me about your sex club experience? A quick synopsis may be all I need, to come."

As Sam slowly, and repeatedly, filled me with his manhood, I told him the basic story: I had spanked the guy, and masturbated in front of him. Zöe had come in, and given me a 'lesson', and I jerked off the guy, who seemed to be satisfied with the experience. Of course, I told the story a little more sexily, than that.

Sam tensed, and then came, driving into me frantically, until finally relaxing, and putting his full weight on me. It felt good ... comforting. I reached around and held his butt, then pretended to give him a shot on each side, using my fingernail to simulate the needle.

I thought Sam was nearly asleep, but he got up on his elbows, gave me an evil smile, and said, "Can we do that again?"

I was amazed at Sam's fortitude, as I knew how tired he had to be, after the skiing we'd done on the 'little' Matterhorn. If he wanted to try, I would let him.

He kissed me, as he rubbed along my flame-shaped patch of hair, until he was hard again. I had really expected him to fall asleep during his efforts ... but I knew that Sam was always an over-the-top kind of guy. Now, he was ready, and putting himself into me, filling me again with desire, passion, love.

It took much longer this time – for both of us. And we were totally spent, afterward. The curtains were open, the moon illuminating the Matterhorn. Last night, the clouds had kept the mountain dark, but now, it was as majestic as in the daytime.

We slept well, the presence of the mountain felt in all of our muscles, joints, and bones. The Matterhorn! I drifted off as the tune from 'It's a Small World' rattled through my head.

CHAPTER 16: PARIS LIGHTS

We ate breakfast at the hotel's buffet and were off early again. As we descended from Zermatt in the shuttle train, it was hard to believe that we would be having dinner in Paris. Paris! I knew that Linda would be a bit jealous, as she had dreamed of visiting Paris someday. And, someday, her prince may come ... but my prince *had* come. In many different ways.

We retrieved the car in Tasch, and drove through mountain passes and beautiful valleys, arriving a couple of hours later at Montreaux, on Lac Leman, the huge lake on the other end of which was Geneva. It was a bit early for lunch, so we continued to Lausanne, and ate at an upscale bistro overlooking the lake.

"This is a big medical development area – I have quite a few contacts here. Maybe we could come back in the summer, take a boat on the lake, and do some hiking?" I nodded. There were a lot of places to visit, and many to come back to.

Sam continued, "We're going to also miss seeing Geneva, since we'll be arriving at the airport, which is before we would get to the city. It's probably the most 'cosmopolitan' city on the continent, one of the top three most expensive places in the world to live, along with London and Paris ... and also Zurich; and Lausanne, where we had lunch."

We returned the car and checked in for our mid-afternoon flight, and Sam led me to one of the executive lounges. I was excited to be going to Paris and London, but was a bit sad that we were leaving Switzerland, so soon.

The hour flight was uneventful, until we circled over Paris, and I saw the Eiffel Tower; then, it became real. The half-hour taxi ride was also interesting, as we crossed through the city to our left bank hotel. The room was classic, with tall ceilings, wainscoting, and a narrow balcony with wrought iron railing that overlooked the 'Luxembourg Garden'.

Sam asked, "Are you ready to do some walking, today?" I nodded. It was nearly four in the afternoon, but we had been in a car or plane all day, and the weather was nice; I was ready to see some of the sights of Paris.

We walked past the Sorbonne, and across the bridge to the *Île de la Cité*, circling around the massive Notre-Dame Cathedral, from the twin belfries in front, to the flying buttresses in the back. Sam explained, "It was built about 800 years ago, with more glass and thinner walls than ever before ... so they needed those external supports."

We entered the cathedral, and I was stunned at the beauty, the scale, the height of the arched ceiling; it was truly impressive. We walked down the nave, and Sam pointed out the beautiful stained glass windows, the 'rose window', and the organ pipes. The vaulted ceiling above the altar had a field of stars on a bright blue sky. With the gold, the marble columns, and the incredible stained glass, it was the most beautiful church I'd ever seen.

We took the tour, saw the crypt, and even climbed to the top of one of the towers, where we were rewarded with a fabulous view of the city, and the Eiffel Tower in the distance.

I couldn't stop raving to Sam about Notre-Dame, as we walked a few blocks farther up the island, and entered *Sainte-Chapelle*. I was floored: This small chapel was even more impressive, with its high walls of stained glass. It was beautiful, and I hugged Sam, as my eyes began to tear.

I'm not religious, but the awesome beauty of this place became an emotional experience for me. I sat in one of the pews, and stared upward: We were surrounded by intricate stained glass walls; not windows, but *walls* of the deep-hued glass, in reds, and blues and purples, in vertical stripes, each having hundreds of small scenes.

Walking back outside, we headed to the far west end of the island, where we took another selfie, the Seine River and Eiffel Tower in the background. Sam led me across the *Pont Neuf*, and we continued walking west, along the Seine. A couple of bridges further, and we hung a right, entering *Place du Carousel*, with the huge glass pyramid surrounded by the Louvre Museum.

Sam said, "We'll see the Louvre tomorrow. Let's walk through the gardens." We passed through formal gardens, and Sam explained, "These are the *Tuileries*, originally the gardens of Catherine de Medicis' palace, built around 400 years ago, which became a public park after the French revolution." We watched, as several young boys sailed radio-controlled boats in the huge octagonal pond.

As we approached the *Fer à cheval*, a horseshoe-shaped plaza, Sam pointed to our right. "That is the *Jeu de Paume*, France's national gallery of contemporary art – now, mostly modern photography exhibits. It used to house the most incredible collection of impressionist art – which is now in the *Musée d'Orsay*, which we'll see tomorrow."

Sam checked on his phone, and smiled, "The Jeu de Paume is open late; why don't we take a look?"

The museum featured modern photographers and videographers, including a wide range of realistic to abstract works. As we strolled through room after room of art, Sam chuckled, "By this time tomorrow, you'll understand why it would take two or three weeks to see Paris properly."

We walked out onto the gigantic *Place de la Concorde*, which appeared to actually *have* a Concorde airplane, on the other side. Sam said, "That other one looks like a Mirage stealth fighter! I thought they would only have something like this displayed on Bastille Day, which is July fourteenth, and celebrates the beginning of the French revolution, when the Bastille – a fortress used as a political jail – was stormed."

I posed near one of the fountains, and Sam took a picture of me, with the Eiffel Tower in the background. As we walked toward the river, we looked down a beautiful stretch of the wide, tree-lined *Champs-Élysées* boulevard, tree-lined, and – in the distance – the *Arc de Triomphe*. In the center of the plaza was a huge Egyptian obelisk.

Sam chuckled, "This was originally at the entrance to the pyramids of Luxor, one of a pair given to France by Egypt. They managed to get this one here, but couldn't transport the other one, so finally gave it back to Egypt."

Sam was a fount of information – more than I needed. I was enjoying the 'feel' of the city, with its bustling traffic, but still lots of trees, their leaves now mostly oranges and reds, and the sky blue. We walked to the river, where we continued west, passing many tour boats. On our right, across the road was a huge building that Sam said was an exhibition hall and science museum.

Sam pointed, "We'll take one of those boats – called *'bateaux mouches'*. They're more like barges, but have a nice open deck on top … which will be great, as the weather is so beautiful." I looked up, and the Eiffel literally towered above me. My eyes were teary again; it was still surreal to believe that I was actually here. I pulled Sam over to me, and kissed him.

"What was that for?" he asked, unnecessarily.

"Thank you for taking me on this trip, Sam. It's been wonderful." I kissed him again, and we held hands, as we walked down onto the dock, and bought tickets for the next boat tour. There were plenty of tourists, but when we boarded, and went to the top deck, we had plenty of room to ourselves; most others looking like lovers, also, snuggling together in the crisp breeze, as the boat left the dock.

We headed up the river, and I couldn't take my eyes off the Eiffel Tower; it was huge, from our vantage on the water. We turned around a small island, heading back downstream, and saw the 'Statue of Liberty', a ¼-scale model of the one given to the U.S. by France. A bit further, and we were directly under the Eiffel Tower. "Can we go up there today, Sam?"

Sam nodded, "Sure, since we're in the area; it will be nice around sunset. I just don't know how long the lines will be …"

"Can't we book it on the Internet?" That only seemed logical. Sam hit his forehead with his hand and, within five minutes, had booked it using his phone.

Our boat tour continued down the river, going under arched bridges with just enough clearance. Sam and I snuggled together, as Paris passed by. We took a few more 'selfies', as the boat cruised past Notre-Dame, then necked like a couple of teenagers. That's how I felt, also:

Somehow 'rejuvenated', enervated but relaxed; with the man I loved.

Sam asked, "Would you like to 'play around', a little?" He gave me the evil eye.

I looked around: There were only a handful of other couples up here, all involved in themselves. I looked at Sam, and shrugged. He patted his lap, and I sat, my back to his chest, my legs straddling his, and his arms around me, holding my breasts. As I started to rock, giving Sam another lap dance, He said, "It will be too easy for me to come, and too messy, if I do. How about if I take care of you? Don't even think about me being behind you; I'll just put my hand down your pants, like this ..."

What was he talking about, 'don't think about him'? I glanced around, and subtly undid my belt, and unzipped my pants, pulling my sweater down over Sam's hand. We both rocked, and my eyes involuntarily closed, as Sam 'hit the spot'. Then, I opened them, and looked forward, as Sam had suggested – taking in the incredible view of Paris from the river, and thinking how 'sweet' Sam was, to take care of me.

And, how uptight he still was, being worried about the 'mess'. I realized that I would be on a mission, to 'reform' Sam. He was doing pretty well, so far, but had a long way to go. That was OK; I would be patient with him.

Suddenly, my PC muscles clenched repeatedly, and I was again in the 'real' (or surreal?) world, on the cusp of an incredible orgasm. The thought of glancing around crossed my mind, but I forced myself to close my eyes, and feel the experience.

A brief cry came, unbidden, from my throat, before I could regain control, thrusting my pelvis into Sam's groin, and forward, only being restrained by Sam's left hand holding my breast, and his right hand deep in my folds. I didn't care whether others watched.

But when I had calmed, and opened my eyes, I realized that the boat was gliding through the water very close to the wall, on the top of which was a line of people, looking down at us. Probably tourists. Well, I hope we gave them a good show. It had been good for me!

After the boat ride, we walked across a bridge and were about to head down a main boulevard towards the park in front of the Eiffel Tower. Sam suddenly pulled me left, and we read a sign – it was the 'Sewer Museum' of Paris. Sam said, "This could really be interesting. I wonder whether they also have tours of the Parisian sewers?" I was about to tell him how romantic 'Parisian sewers' sounded, when he said, sadly, "Oh. They're closed today."

We walked past hotels and apartments, restaurants and pastry shops, and finally through a park, then turned to look down the long grass stretch, with tree-lined dirt paths on either side, leading to the Eiffel Tower. It was the typical tourist postcard view, but it was still impressive. We took a few more 'selfies', and Sam handed his phone to a passerby to take a few snaps of us. Then, we walked to the huge iron structure.

There was a line, but we went through the pre-ticketed gate, and a few minutes later we were going up in the elevator, as the tour guide gave us all the facts. The tower had been built in 1889 to celebrate the 100th anniversary of the French revolution, but was actually used for some of the first radio transmissions, and the first public radio broadcasts.

We stepped out onto a deck, and walked around – the view incredible in every direction. Sam pointed out many of the sights, including the *Montmartre* hill, where he said we would be, watching the sunset, 24 hours from now. We took the elevator to the top level, and walked out onto a windy, metallic deck. I looked over the edge, and signaled to Sam, but he stayed back from the rail, and I remembered that he was afraid of heights.

We took more pictures, and took our time, as the sun set, the sky becoming orange, then pink – wisps of clouds refracting the light in a kaleidoscope of colors.

Several tours had come up and gone down, but we were enjoying our time up here – I even looked through a couple of the telescopes mounted on the railing. It was getting darker, and I could see a star in the sky. Sam and I leaned into each other, our motions slow and deliberate, putting our arms around each other, smiling, looking into each other's eyes, and finally putting our lips together, in an electrified kiss ...

Sam and I *both* jumped, when we heard a loud 'clunk' and thousands of watts of light illuminated our kiss. It really *had* been electric! It was ten minutes of eight, and I suggested we head down, but Sam insisted we stay up here for a while longer. He had made dinner reservations at nine, which was early for a Friday night in Paris.

I was getting bored, now, but Sam looked at his watch and smiled. His timing wasn't perfect, but a minute later, we were illuminated again – this time with 20,000 twinkling lights, above and below us. It felt like we were in a Disney film, having been sprinkled with the twinkles of Pixie dust.

Sam kissed me again, passionately, lovingly, then took my hand firmly, and said, "*Now*, we can go down." He had obviously known the schedule when the lights would go on.

The restaurant was not far from our hotel, and we had walked everywhere today, but our feet were tired, and we were running late, so we took a taxi, the short ride taking nearly half an hour; still, we walked in within five minutes of our reservation time. The bistro was on a corner, with a dark green awning, and the word '*Papillon*' – butterfly – in yellow script.

The place was crowded and intimate, and most people were dressed better than us, although there were also quite a few younger couples who were dressed casually. It was dark, and nobody seemed to be worried about our attire. I looked at the menu, and didn't recognize much, everything being in French. Sam translated a few items, but I told him to make a choice for both of us.

He did well: The dinner, and the wine, was incredible. We started with a terrine of rabbit with crusty bread, and were then served a seafood tower (enough for dinner by itself), and then we shared two main courses – the duck in lingonberry sauce, and the veal with a juniper cream sauce.

We were floating – from the wine, and from the long day – by the time we finished our main courses. But Sam wanted to try the Grand Marnier soufflé ... so we ordered espressos, and Sam – as usual – went overboard by also ordering a well-aged brandy.

When it came, he rolled the snifter in his hands, explaining that the additional warmth would increase the vapors, enhancing the drink. He took a deep whiff, and handed the snifter to me: I took a tentative breath, the vapor burning, and I couldn't stop coughing. After a swallow of water, I drank some of the thick orange liquid, and agreed that it was amazing. I gave the glass back to Sam, and our soufflé was served.

The waiter cut into the center of it – which I thought was a bit rude, after it had risen perfectly to a beautiful peak; then, he poured in the Grand Marnier sauce, leaving a dish of it at the table.

I wasn't really a 'food person'; at least, I hadn't been, before I met Sam. But one bite, and I was in heaven again. The meal had been amazing, and the dessert was totally awesome – light but rich, the orange flavor of the Grand Marnier permeating the dish. I licked my spoon and glanced up: Sam was smiling.

He was looking at me – in a nice way. He stared into my eyes, and I saw myself in his; he reached over and put his warm, comforting hand on top of mine. Love in a tiny bistro; on the left bank. In Paris. France. Europe.

We walked the short distance back to our hotel hand-in-hand, and I thought of the old movie, '*Singin' in the Rain*', where Gene Kelly did his famous song-and-dance routine. Somehow, I felt 'happy again'. I was happy with my life, I was happy with Sam and, as I felt the first drops of a drizzle, I was happy we'd had beautiful weather nearly the entire trip; so far.

Saturday was a whirlwind of touring. Fortunately, the rain had ended by morning, leaving a clear atmosphere, and small cumulus clouds floating lazily over the city. I had to take Kelly to the major sights, and we started at the Louvre at nine in the morning, covering it shamefully quickly. Of course, we saw the Mona Lisa, Winged Victory, and Aphrodite - among many other famous pieces – but my favorite was the Egyptian art.

Then, we crossed a bridge, and walked along the river to the incredible Musée d'Orsay – which houses impressionist and post-impressionist art. We took our time, and toured the art chronologically, from Delacroix and Courbet, through the heart of impressionism: Manet, Monet, Degas, Cézanne, Renoir, Gauguin, and even two dozen van Gogh paintings that we hadn't seen in

Amsterdam. We saw some expressionist art, including Edvard Munch, modern pieces from Klimt and Mondrian, and even the famous 'Whistler's Mother', by the eponymous American artist.

We walked across the river and were going to use the Metro, Paris' efficient subway system, but we decided to continue walking, up the *Champs-Elysée* – the famous upscale shopping and entertainment boulevard. From Cartier to the Disney Store, restaurants, clubs, and nice hotels, we – and a crowd of other people – window shopped, and enjoyed a beautiful day on the boulevard.

Kelly commented, "I'm glad we're walking; look at the traffic!"

I laughed, "Yes, this boulevard, and lots of others, are continually gridlocked – I would only take a taxi here if I weren't in a rush getting anywhere. But it's Saturday, so there's only *light* traffic today!" The traffic was one of the worst things about Paris, in my opinion. But between the Metro and a pair of strong legs, there was usually no need to suffer in the congestion.

After making a few stops at jewelry stores, art galleries, a lingerie store, and pastry shop, we finally arrived at the Place l'Étoile, in the center of which is the '*Arc de Triomphe*', the famous arch built to commemorate Napoleon's victories. Kelly asked, "How are we going to get across all these lanes of traffic?" There were at least four or five lanes circling the monument, with cars turning onto and off of the circle from a dozen streets – like the spokes of a wheel.

I led Kelly to the stairs down to a tunnel that took us under the huge plaza to the monument, where we toured the exhibits, saw the Tomb of the Unknown Soldier, and climbed the stairs to the top. It was a magnificent, clear day, small clouds floating by, framed by deep blue sky.

Looking back towards the Louvre, we saw the length of the *Champs-Elysée*, twin rows of trees on each side, now multihued, in greens, yellows, oranges, and reds.

Walking around the top of the monument, we looked out over a dozen different streets, and I pointed out the *Palais de Congres*, a modern conference center where I had attended many pharmaceutical industry meetings.

We took the Metro to the *Palais*, and walked a few blocks to a good Algerian restaurant that served the best *couscous* dishes I'd ever eaten. As we were seated, at a nice window table with a flower box just outside, my phone beeped.

Now that I was retired, I didn't get many messages. I glanced at the text, and put my phone back in its holster. We looked at the menu and ordered a multi-course Algerian meal. We were ready to relax for a while, before continuing our tour.

"Kelly, I need to discuss something important with you," I began. Kelly put her Diet Coke down, and her hands in her lap, giving me her full attention. "You know that I did a lot of research, and considered meeting a Dominatrix, in London." Kelly nodded, now all ears.

I continued, "Well, it turns out that there are *hundreds* of Dommes, many specializing in certain things. For example, the rage now seems to be the 'financial dominatrix', who commands you to spend money on them, until you feel it financially."

Kelly picked up a piece of Middle Eastern bread, and said, "That's ridiculous! Who would let them do that?" Then, she smiled, and added, "I could do that, easily!"

I shook my head, "Don't get any ideas! I guess there are a lot of men, and probably women, who have more money than they know what to do with. I wouldn't know."

Kelly ate her bread, and I took a piece, realizing that I had to steer the conversation back to the main point, the decision we would need to make. "So I found several Dommes who seemed to be appropriate for giving us a half-day session, to show us a few things, train us."

Kelly just nodded, so I continued, "And I contacted three of them. One is booked, another is on holiday someplace in the Balkans, and the third responded positively. Since we're on such a tight schedule, I tentatively reserved a date – next Tuesday. But there's a 48-hour cancelation, and she just texted me, saying that she would be happy to meet with us Tuesday morning, and is keeping her afternoon schedule free, if we decide we want to 'go farther'."

Kelly asked, "What does 'go farther' mean? And what would she want us to do?" Kelly looked a little nervous, so I navigated the browser on my phone to the Domme's website, where there were 'testimonials' from other clients. I enlarged the column, and handed the phone to Kelly. As she read, her eyes went big, and she glanced up at me. Then, she continued reading, and finally handed my phone back to me.

"It looks like she is a really *serious* Domme. Are you sure that this is what you want to do? Want us to do?" Kelly looked down to her lap, and was quiet for a few moments. Thankfully, I was able to keep my own mouth shut, while she pondered the thought of having a 'session' with a dominatrix.

"Sam," she continued, "I would like to do this with you. We've talked before about me getting some training from a professional, to explore my dominant side." She looked at me obliquely, and said, quietly, "But I'm not sure that you will be happy with the experience." That was strange; I cocked my head, and let Kelly explain.

She said, "From what I am reading, it looks like this Domme has a very similar approach to yours ... by making people submit to things they don't like. Surprising them. I don't think it's just going to be a quick over-the-knee spanking."

I had to consider this; Kelly had a point, and I wasn't sure whether this would be a turn on or turn off – perhaps ruining the fantasy that I had now successfully implemented with Kelly and her friends. On the other hand, I really should be trained, also; although my medical experience gave me a leg up (get that vision out of my head!), my spanking experience was mainly vicarious – from the Internet, and experimental – from the 'play' I had done with Liz and Kelly.

My bottom hurt, as I thought about how painful this training session could be. But Kelly and I had both gotten used to hard punishment – at least, as 'used' to it as could be. But I was also turned on by the idea of seeing the Domme; especially, with Kelly: To see her reactions, and to test my own.

"Kelly, if you want to do it, I think it would be interesting – for both of us. I *am* a little scared, now that I'm thinking about it actually happening. And I'm also a little scared of what it might do to our own 'play', and fantasies." I realized that my face was contorted, and I was looking down, not at Kelly.

I looked up and smiled, trying to act carefree, "Well, I guess there's only one way to find out!" Kelly nodded, her face impassive, as I responded to the text message, and our couscous was set on the table.

After lunch, we walked a short distance to the *Bois de Boulogne*, a large park on the western side of Paris. There were a lot of people on the walks, but after we passed the kiddie park, the crowd thinned out. It was beautiful in every season. We passed formal gardens, a winding stream with a small waterfall, and finally a huge grass area.

There were lots of people lying on the grass but – unlike Munich – nobody was nude; a few women had taken off their blouses, and wore their bras, but the cool weather kept most people in jeans and long-sleeved tops. We walked along a huge lake, with dozens of boats being rowed – filled with either lovers or families. "Are you ready for some more sightseeing?"

Kelly nodded enthusiastically, then asked, "Isn't that what we've been doing?"

We walked out of the park, and Kelly pointed – we now had a view of the Eiffel Tower from the opposite side. We ducked into a small museum featuring the paintings of Claude Monet, which was an amazing, unexpected gem. Then, we took the Metro to the Army Museum, where we saw Napoleon's tomb, and toured an interesting museum connecting war and art.

Another 'must' on our tour was the Rodin museum, which seemed to have grown dramatically, since I last visited. Kelly was enjoying the art, and we held hands, as we gazed at some of Rodin's racier pieces. I pointed at the 'Kneeling Fauness', who appeared to be kneeling, with her hands behind her head, as in our 'standing position' – very subservient. Then, Kelly pointed to 'Naked Balzac', and said, "And that guy's dick has turned to stone." 'The Thinker' and 'The Kiss' seemed to be among the least interesting of Rodin's pieces.

We decided to return to the hotel, taking the Metro, and walking through the Luxembourg Gardens, which our room overlooked. I checked with reception, and was amazed to hear that our hotel had a sauna – a 'mixed' one, both genders together, as we had experienced in The Netherlands and Germany. I turned to Kelly, "How about it? Maybe a quick sauna before we dress for the evening?" Kelly nodded, mumbling something about preferring a slow sauna.

After undressing, putting our things in lockers, and showering, we entered the small sauna. Surprisingly, there were two cute women already inside. They smiled at us, then frowned, as I carried the still-folded towel; I excused myself in French, and let the towel fall in front of me. The women continued talking quietly. It was apparent that mixed saunas here required men's and women's pubic areas to be covered in the sauna, although breasts and butts were obviously acceptable.

Interestingly, when the women exited, we could see them showering, through the smoked glass sauna door. But they had been 'proper' in the sauna. It was funny, the variations of acceptability – where people 'drew the line'. The women disappeared, leaving Kelly and I alone in the sauna. It was similar in size to the one in my house, perhaps a bit larger.

I told Kelly, "I would like to take you to Montmartre, this evening – it's the 'original' artist area of Paris – where Dali, Picasso, and van Gogh, among many others, painted. At the top of the hill is the *Sacré Coeur* cathedral; we'll try to be there at sunset. There are hundreds of restaurants, and dozens of clubs and cabarets in that area."

I turned, and sat cross-legged on the bench next to Kelly. "I hadn't planned on taking you to the *Moulin Rouge*, or *Crazy Horse*. They have Las Vegas style productions, with topless or nude dancers; some only have dinner shows, and we would need to make a reservation – so that might be a possibility for tomorrow, if you're interested."

Kelly shook her head, "Why?" I looked at her questioningly, and she said, "We've seen plenty of nude people, without going to a fancy show. And I like shows, and music and dancing, but it doesn't have to be a big production."

Then, I offered, "And, I know there are quite a few 'sex clubs' here – some specializing in spanking scenes."

Kelly kept shaking her head, "Why, again? I think our visit to the Domme will be enough spanking for the rest of the trip." I smiled and nodded, and again my bottom hurt, just thinking about what might happen in a couple of days.

I agreed, "So let's play it by ear, walk around the area, and see what happens." Kelly nodded, and lay back on the sauna bench, resting her feet in my lap. I gave her a foot massage ... until we were finally overheated, and had to get out and cool off in the shower. We did two more cycles, still the only ones in the sauna, and we were well relaxed for whatever the evening held.

We took the Metro to the *Anvers* stop, and walked up to a street lined with cheap-looking sex shops and kebab shops; then we turned down a narrow lane, made some more turns, and up some steps to a small plaza leading to a sloping grass lawn, with steps on either side, rising to the *Sacré Coeur*, a huge white basilica at the top of the hill, its three domes looking like they had been compressed and lengthened, reaching to the sky.

Kelly asked, "Are we going to climb these steps? Or take that train-thingy?"

Shaking my head, I led Kelly back down to the street. "Neither; we're going up the more interesting way." We walked up one cobblestoned street, and then up a steep street to another level, where we walked back down the next street, continuing as if we were on a switchback trail.

There were lots of tourists, diminishing the romance of this area, and restaurants were already filled – hours before any Parisian would consider dining. We passed artists, making pastel drawings of the tourists, and plenty of shops filled with tourist 'junk' – from key chains and miniature Eiffel Towers to postcards; and, somewhat surprisingly, people were actually *buying* the junk. There was no accounting for taste.

These tourists probably hadn't walked through the park or taken a sauna today. But, at least they were on their own, and not part of a bus tour. We continued walking up the hill – only a few hundred feet above the city, but made more interesting by the circuitous route we were following.

Finally, we walked up the steps to the esplanade in front of the cathedral. The view – as expected – was incredible: Over the rooftops of Paris, we saw a few tall buildings and domes of other churches in the distance, but towering above all, clearly dominating the vista, was the Eiffel Tower. "Here's one more view, to add to your collection," I told Kelly.

Of course, we had to take more selfies. The sun was low, and I had planned for us to watch the sunset, after a tour of the cathedral. There was a line, and I hoped my timing would still work out, and fortunately, it did. After the short tour, we walked back out to the esplanade, the clouds now a deep orange, and the lights of the city just coming on.

We sat on the grass, Kelly – now in her jacket – huddling with me, as we watched the sky dim. Suddenly, in the far distance, the Eiffel Tower was illuminated in golden light. We had been at the top, enjoying our electrified kiss, 24 hours before. We kissed again, and it seemed no less electric.

We walked down the hill and ate at a brasserie that wasn't overly touristic; both the food and the atmosphere were terrific, and I was sure that Kelly enjoyed the experience. Further down, we passed by a cabaret; it wasn't one of the famous ones, but looked interesting. "What do you think, Kelly? Would you like to see a show tonight?"

Kelly and I were both feeling relaxed, and this particular cabaret was more low-key than the others, and reasonably priced, so we entered, and were shown to a nice booth that had a great view of the stage. The drinks were overpriced, and I paid about double the restaurant price for a nice bottle of wine.

The show, however, was well worth it: Every act surpassed the next, in terms of talent and sexiness. In fact, the show seemed more like a sexy version of Cirque de Soleil than that of a Paris nightclub. All of the women were beautiful and, more importantly, natural.

The initial act was a sexy strip-tease, where a tuxedoed gentleman undressed several women, each wearing different sexy underclothes – including garters and stockings. Then, there was a series of incredible pole dances, the women completely nude, and doing moves that would challenge any circus acrobat. Another act was an 'oil wrestling' contest between several young beauties, in which their bodies were twisted into impossible-looking positions.

Kelly's eyes were wide, and I have to admit that I was turned on by watching this show. Kelly saw me adjust myself, and put her hand down my pants, stroking, as we watched the next act, which involved six girls and three large boas – real snakes, not the fashion accessories.

The show continued, becoming more and more outrageous, as the night turned into morning. There were several sex acts, and several acts with sex … including a half dozen nude women dancing onto the stage, and into a knee chest position facing the audience, while half a dozen men danced onto the stage, and entered them from behind, the positions morphing acrobatically, the men never coming out of the women. By the time we left the cabaret, both Kelly and I were ready for a little sex of our own.

Sunday morning, we got up amazingly early (before eight!), and visited a nearby *patisserie*, where we enjoyed a couple of pastries, and some very dark coffee. Then, we took the RER train, from near our hotel, changing once, out to the palace at *Versailles*.

It was another beautiful day, with the puffy clouds still overhead, but not threatening to rain on us. As we walked across the *Place d'Armes*, and through the courtyard of the palace, Kelly exclaimed, "A whole block of houses where my parents live could fit inside the courtyard!"

I chuckled, "Just wait until you see the gardens." We took a guided tour of the palace – the royal chambers, hall of mirrors, and the rest, and then we walked out into the gardens. There were plenty of tourists, but also a lot of French families, with children, having a picnic, or rowing a small boat in the 'grand canal'.

We walked past statues, fountains, and manicured lawns, and between hundreds of trees lined up in intricate patterns. We saw the many *bosquet*, formal gardens, each in a unique style. We visited Marie Antoinette's estate and the gardens of the *Trianon*.

It was still beautiful, but seemed a lot more commercial these days, with many restaurants, snack bars, and other concessions, such as pony rides ... and even free WiFi. After we had finished the formal tours, we walked far out into the gardens, where the crowd thinned, and we could look back at the palace.

It was quite a sight; and so was Kelly, her face radiant, auburn hair flying in the wind, and contrasting with the green of the hedges around us, and blue sky above. We held each other, and I ran my fingers through her hair, down to her waist, and below.

I held her bottom with both hands, as Kelly's arms encircled my neck, pulling me to her. We kissed, and then pulled back, looked into each other's eyes, and said, "I love you," spontaneously, together, synchronized ... in stereo. We laughed comfortably, and walked hand-in-hand on a random path through the gardens, making our way back to the chateau.

We ate in the town, and took the train back to Paris after dark. As we bumped along the track, the train went underground, and I did some research on my phone. Handing it to Kelly, I said, "There's still time to get dressed up - I mean down – and visit one of the sex clubs." I saw her scrolling through the never-ending list, with her finger.

She handed the phone back to me, and said, "I *am* impressed by how many clubs there are ... and all the things they cater to ... but I'm not sure I'm up for something like that tonight. Aren't we flying to London early tomorrow morning?"

I nodded sheepishly, as I knew we would have to be up early ... but I was still thinking about the club that was featuring 'lingerie' night tonight. And there were several BDSM clubs, where we could just view the action.

Kelly held my arm and said, "Don't pout, Sam; we can have our own private 'sex club' tonight.

And that's exactly what we did.

CHAPTER 17: DOMINATING LONDON

Sam and I took the RER train to Paris' Orly airport, and flew in a small jet to City Airport, London. Most of the other passengers were businessmen in suits and ties, flying in to London on a Monday morning for meetings, or to work the week. I had a great view, as we flew over the winding Thames, passing the O2 Arena, and landing on a small island reclaimed from the old docklands.

A short tram ride brought us to the Tower station, where it connected with London's subway system, the 'tube'. Ever-efficient Sam suggested that we put our bags in a locker, and see our first sight: The Tower of London.

Before we had bought our tour tickets, Sam had explained that this castle and fortress was built nearly a thousand years ago, and was the royal residence for hundreds of years, before being used as a prison and execution site for a few hundred more years. Anne Boleyn – 'Anne of 1,000 days' – was executed here.

We saw the famous *Beefeater* guards, in their uniforms, and took a full tour of the site, even seeing a chopping block still stained with blood from centuries ago. We learned that many ghosts inhabit the Tower, including that of Anne Boleyn, who has been allegedly seen carrying her decapitated head under her arm.

On a more uplifting note, we visited the incredible crown jewels of England – including dozens of incredibly bejeweled crowns, scepters, orbs, and swords.

Sam wanted to try something new, so we retrieved our bags, and took a taxi to the 'Shard' – an 87-story skyscraper that had been built since he'd been here. We checked our bags and took the elevator to the observation deck: The view was breathtaking. The tower, at 1,000 feet, was the tallest building in Europe.

We walked out onto the open-air deck 800 feet above the city. It was spectacular, and I insisted that we get our picture together, with London in the background; Sam stayed back from the rail, and couldn't look down through the grated floor of the observation deck. When we were back inside, he said, casually, "I think it's almost time for a pub stop. Let's get checked in to our hotel. Back on the ground."

The next thing we did was underground: We took a ride on the tube – more than 30 minutes – to our boutique hotel in the Knightsbridge area, near Hyde Park. Our room had just become available, so we got settled then headed back out for a whirlwind day in London. Sam asked, "Do you feel like walking, a little?"

We walked into Hyde Park, far enough to see the 'Serpentine' – a large lake. Then, we walked through a park behind Buckingham Palace, and down 'The Mall' to Trafalgar Square. There were red, double-decker busses circling the huge plaza, and crowds of people around the fountains and the tall 'Nelson's Column' that dominates the space.

Sam led me through a maze of streets with bars, restaurants and shops, to 'Picadilly Circus' and Regent Street. Sam explained, "This is one of the main shopping streets of London, with all the big brands – from Burbury to the Apple Store." Sam laughed – an evil laugh, it seemed, then admitted, "Actually, we're only two tube stops from our hotel. I just wanted you to get an idea of this area by foot."

I shook my head, as Sam led me down to the tube, and we rode another couple of stops, then walked through another maze of streets, Sam finally pointing, "This is one of my favorite pubs in London." Sam chuckled, as he held the door open for me, saying, "Of course, there are around 7,000 pubs in London. And I haven't tried them all, yet."

We had a pint and the daily 'pie' – steak and kidney; it was good, if you didn't think about the organs in it. We drank pints of warm beer from rounded mugs, and toasted to our 'day with a Domme' tomorrow. I wasn't as eager about it as Sam, but was still curious, and wanted to learn more about expressing my dominant side.

Sam spent most of the lunch whining about what we *wouldn't* be seeing on this trip. "We'll be seeing a little of the British Museum next, which is almost across the street. And, maybe we can see Madame Tussaud's wax museum. I'd love to visit the Tate Gallery, one of the great modern art museums. And I'm going to feel guilty not bringing you to the Maritime Museum in Greenwich – where world time and longitude starts."

He sighed, "But there are dozens of other museums, and hundreds of sights to see. You really need a couple of weeks here, just to get started. And now, we're using half our time here seeing a Domme."

"I didn't expect to see all of London on this trip, Sam. But if you'd rather tour some more, instead of seeing the Domme, I'll understand." Sam shook his head, unwilling to go that far.

We walked to the British Museum, an imposing place even before stepping inside. Sam wanted to walk through the ancient artifacts – from Egypt, Assyria, Greece, and Rome. We wandered, seeing random rooms – such as one having an amazing collection of watches and clocks. It was obviously too much. "I think we could spend a week just touring this museum." Sam nodded, and bent over, stretching his back. I was glad I wore good walking shoes.

As we walked out of the museum, Sam asked, "Kelly, I know you were planning on getting back late Thursday, so that you could see your advisor on Friday. But if we could just extend our trip a day or two, you'd be able to see much more of London. We could still get back on Saturday, and recuperate on Sunday. What do you think?"

I didn't really have to go to school on Friday – there were no classes, but I had planned to meet with my advisor. Now that I was more convinced that my new 'invention' was feasible, I realized that I would need at least a day to prepare, before I presented it to him.

Sam checked with the airlines, asking them on which day they could confirm our first class upgrades. It seemed optimistic, but he was able to get us on a flight from Heathrow on Thursday morning, first class all the way home. At least, we would have one more day in London, and time for our bottoms to recover before we had to sit ten hours on a plane.

As I thought of sitting, and watched another red bus go by, I asked Sam, "Maybe we could take one of those tour busses, rather than rush around to all the museums?"

"We can take a bus tour, if you like. Let's just see a couple of other things, first." We toured Madame Tussaud's, which Sam said was touristy, but I had never been to a 'wax museum', and I was into the personalities much more than Sam. They were incredibly lifelike, almost haunting.

We walked behind the museum a couple of blocks, into another park. It was a beautiful setting, and we stopped on a small bridge over a stream.

Sam put his arm around my waist, as we watched a flock of birds take flight. "London is a huge metropolis, but it has some nice parks." Sam pointed, "If you want to go to the zoo, it's just a short 'walk in the park'. But, I had something else in mind; another of London's modern icons." We walked down the steps to the tube, and rode a train that bumped along through the smelly tunnels, finally exiting on the other side of the river, in a neighborhood of big, modern buildings.

Sam took my hand, and led me a short way to the 'London Eye' – the giant Ferris Wheel on the Thames. We rose in one of the huge glassed-in cages, and got another perspective on London. Directly across the river was Westminster Abbey, the houses of Parliament, and Big Ben. Sam wanted to see the aquarium, so we spent an hour watching sharks and rays, and seeing other exhibits.

Our walking tour continued as we crossed the Westminster Bridge, taking another selfie – of course – with Big Ben in the background. I could show these pictures to my friends, but never be able to explain the 'feeling' of being in these famous cities. And I knew that I hadn't learned enough history to really understand the significance of all the buildings I was seeing; we passed by 10 Downing Street, one of the few addresses I *did* know.

Finally, we were back in Trafalgar Square, and boarded a tour bus, sitting on the open upper deck. I snuggled with Sam, as the tour guide explained the sights and the history surrounding them. The weather was clear, but cool, and we took advantage of shared body warmth. I chuckled as I thought about 'body heat', and how 'hot' of a guy Sam was. I snuggled closer, and Sam leaned his head against mine.

Our bus tour ended around sunset, and we walked past bars and restaurants, swank shops, and theaters. Sam suggested we get tickets for a play on Wednesday afternoon, which again triggered a thought about how our bottoms would be feeling, after our Domme experience.

As we passed a movie theater, Sam laughed, and said, "Look! They're playing the Roman Polanski remake of 'Venus in Fur'. I've been wanting to see that movie with you." We walked to the ticket booth, and saw that the movie was starting in a few minutes. So, on the spur of the moment, we went into the theater. At least my feet would be able to rest for a while!

The movie was fascinating, the story based on the original *Venus in Furs* by Masoch-Sacher, of 'masochism' infamy. In the film, a director is casting a stage play of the story, and an actress appears who seems to know the role intimately. In the story, the man wants to be dominated – in theory, but finds out that the reality isn't as much of a turn on. In the movie, the actress becomes the dominant one, as the director becomes obsessed with her, or perhaps with the character in his play.

This was a deep and moving portrayal of S&M and D/s (dominance and submission), which Sam and I would discuss at length. But it hit me that the story paralleled ours – the man wanting something from his fantasy, but real life presenting something different than what he had expected; and the woman realizing that she was truly the dominant one, forcing the man into submission beyond his will. But, in the movie, it wasn't clear that the woman was even real; perhaps she had been a figment of the director's fertile imagination?

Sam wanted to take me to an Indian restaurant for dinner, but I was still stuffed from lunch, and suggested that Indian might not be the ideal thing to eat before our Domme experience. Sam agreed, and we ate at an up-scale tapas bar, where we shared several smaller dishes, washed down by a Rioja wine from Spain. Again, we toasted to our upcoming experience, which we now both realized could potentially be life-changing; in one way, or another.

We returned to the hotel, and Sam had to ask the reception to remind us of which room we were in – as the keys were all-white electronic cards. We'd dropped off our bags, but had hardly spent any time in the room.

Undressing quickly, we crawled into bed together. I think we were both nervous about the experience tomorrow – not really knowing what would happen. Sam reassured me, "I'm sure you'll do fine tomorrow." As we made love, I thought about it, and wondered how well *Sam* would do, in the presence of a professional dominatrix.

Tuesday morning, we went to Starbucks for coffee and a scone. Kelly and I hadn't talked much, this morning, as we were both a little nervous about the day ahead. Just wanting to make idle conversation, I asked Kelly, "So what do you think our Domme will look like? I'm picturing a chubby, older woman, with black hair ... wearing a shiny black PVC rubber suit."

"Sam! You're full of stereotypes. She could be my age." Kelly munched her scone, and added, "From what I could see from her website, it looks like this is going to be pretty serious – not play-acting. I don't think it's going to matter what she looks like, or what she is wearing." That could be true. But I couldn't get the stereotypical image out of my head.

I had packed a few 'supplies' in my backpack, in case the Domme wanted us to do a demonstration ... but I really wasn't sure exactly what we would be doing. Through e-mails, I had explained that Kelly and I wanted to experience an introductory session, get a little 'formal' training – safety tips, etc., and learn how to use new implements.

In my original letter to her, I took great pains (!) to explain that I was turned on by submission – including my own – and that Kelly and I had tried spankings and some types of medical fetish. And, that each of us was a 'switch', although my main role had been as 'top', and Kelly's as 'bottom'.

We took the tube, and then two short over-ground trains to an area called Kew Gardens, where there is a botanical garden, and an upscale residential neighborhood. It was supposed to be a '10-minute' walk from the station, but took us nearly twenty minutes. Altogether, it had taken more than an hour to get here.

The town was cute, and the residential streets were quiet, the only signs of life being a few mothers perambulating their small children. The houses, in long rows, had designs in white on a background of red or brown brick – not dissimilar to the designs on the buildings we had seen in Rothenburg. There were many bay windows, but none had flower boxes, as they would have in Germany.

I glanced at Kelly, as we walked up the steps and rang the bell; my stomach suddenly felt hollow, and my knees were weak. Kelly smiled thinly, and held my arm.

The door opened, and we were ushered in to the house, and then into a study – more like a formal library in dark wood, with heavy furniture. The woman ushering us was older, heavyset, with short black hair, and she wore all black. She asked if we would like something to drink, and Kelly answered, "Some water, please?"

When the woman left, I turned to Kelly and smiled, "See! What did I tell you?"

At that moment, a younger woman entered the library – perhaps in her late thirties – wearing a black silk blouse, with a deep V-cut in front, and a stylish gray and black skirt, that came down to a few inches above her knees. She wore a simple gold necklace with some kind of pendant, and an expensive-looking gold watch on her wrist.

She was good-looking, in a mature way, perhaps ten pounds overweight, but her buxom body being well proportioned. She had sandy hair that fell straight to her shoulders, and a muted cinnamon-colored lipstick that complimented her brown eyes.

We introduced ourselves. She asked to be called 'Mistress Elena', and she sat down on the other side of the large desk, and smiled at us. Then, she leaned forward, her hands clasped on the desk, and asked, "So why are you here, Sam? And Kelly? What are your expectations, and what would you like to accomplish?"

I looked at Kelly, and back at Mistress Elena, and responded, "Well, we're both turned on by submission, and we've tried a lot of different things – like spanking, medical fetish, and needle play. For our spankings, we've used our hands, paddles, straps, the tawse, hairbrush, spoon, switch, and cane. We've only tried serious spankings a few times. And as far as medical stuff, we've done examinations, rectal insertions, enemas, and intramuscular saline injections. We've tried a few other things also, such as electrical stimulation and hot wax."

Mistress asked, "Have you visited a dominatrix, before? What kind of training have you received?" She was starting to look concerned.

"I've never met a dominatrix before today, but I've done a lot of reading and Internet research." Mistress rolled her eyes, but I persisted, "I realize that the responsibility of the 'top' is to ensure that the 'bottom' has an intense experience, but not beyond the limits set, and nothing that would be damaging. I'm retired from the medical field, so I know how to use aseptic technique, and we always use fresh, sterile supplies. And Kelly has a safeword that she can use to stop a scene."

Mistress was nodding, "That's all fine ... those are all important things to remember. But there is much more to being a top or a Dom – especially developing the sensitivity to know how your bottom is feeling at each moment."

Mistress lifted a cup of coffee, and sipped some, looking at us over the upturned coffee cup. Kelly took a sip of her water, and I could see that she was nervous, also. Mistress put down her cup of coffee, and continued, "And you're into trying new experiences? Seeing how people react and respond to the 'challenges' you give them?"

I was nodding, "Yes. It's a turn on for me to see how someone will react, and even more of a turn on if they will submit to something, even if it might involve some pain or embarrassment."

Kelly and I received icy stares from Mistress. "I want to make it clear what will happen here, today." I think Kelly and I both swallowed at the same time; the room was silent, as we awaited Mistress' explanation. "This is my home and my dungeon. While you are here, you are my guests, and will do exactly as I command."

Mistress was nodding, and finally pushed her chair back and stood. "Come with me," she commanded. Kelly and I followed her like two puppies not yet weaned from their mother. We went down some stairs, into a large room that was modern, but well-equipped as a 'dungeon'.

There were racks of punishment implements, spanking benches, stocks, a Saint Andrew's cross, a torture chair of some type, and – in one corner – a swing with chains and leather harnesses. I saw a kind of cage, a rolling exam table, and suspension apparatus on the ceiling. Now *this* was a dungeon! Although I didn't know what many of the fixtures and pieces of furniture were for, it was an impressive set up.

Mistress pointed to the privacy screen – a metal structure with white cloth, as in a clinic – and said, "OK. I want you two in your underwear," she glanced at Kelly, "and bra, and at attention, when I return." Under her breath she said, "I'm going to get into some work clothes." Then, she turned, and walked back up the stairs.

As we undressed, I said, "And, *now* is when she appears in the black latex suit, with her breasts ..." Kelly just shook her head. I wasn't sure why she was so worried – we had done most of these things before, and would learn better techniques. And, I'd paid for the session ... and told Mistress what we wanted.

Kelly had worn a simple, cream-colored bra and bikini underwear, and I was in my 'racy' European underwear ... now thinking that the larger and thicker 'tidy whities' might have been a better choice. We took the standing position near one of the spanking benches, glancing once at each other before staring ahead ... to our fate.

Kelly had given me another grim smile, and my stomach felt hollow again.

Mistress didn't return for another ten minutes or more – and I wondered briefly whether this was a sort of financial scam – the dominatrix making the client wait, as part of the scene, while she relaxes. Then, I realized that Kelly and I were quiet, staring ahead, ready; we hadn't discussed it, but somehow knew – instinctively – that we were already in the 'scene', whatever that would be. We were being tested.

I thought about moving my hands to my hips, but decided that would be a too-aggressive posture; I kept my hands clasped behind my head, as did Kelly.

Mistress returned, and I heard Kelly chuckle: Mistress wore a pair of black jeans, and a black tank top; the only nods to her role as Domme were the pointed black boots she wore, and the riding crop in her hand.

Kelly and I stared ahead, and waited. Mistress pulled a straight-backed chair from the wall, and pointed to a small table on which were a dozen or more spanking implements, and said, "OK, Sam. Why don't you give me a little demonstration, as a top?"

I nodded confidently, and smiled; I knew this wasn't going to be that bad! I sat on the spanking chair, looked at Kelly, and pointed to my lap. Kelly nodded, and stood to my right side, and I pulled her panties down to mid-thigh; then, Kelly got over my left thigh, my right leg out straight. Kelly's toes were on the floor, and her hair obscured any view of her head. I said, quietly but firmly, "This will be a 50 spank warm-up." I put my hand on Kelly's bare bottom.

The mass of hair moved slightly, and I heard Kelly say, "I'm ready for my spanking, Sir."

I smiled, proud that I had taught her so well. I spanked Kelly's bottom, alternating sides, with fairly hard strokes. Kelly held her position well, and made only a few grunts during her warm-up. I then had her stand, as I got up, and asked her to take the 'over-the-front-of-the-chair' position, which she did, immediately. I selected a small strap from the table, and told Kelly, "Here's a level-5 with the strap." I proceeded to give her 18 hard strokes of the strap. Then, I picked up a round, wooden paddle.

Mistress interrupted, and said, "I've seen enough."

I put the paddle down, and told Kelly that she could stand; she took the standing position, facing forward, as I explained, "I measure spankings in 'levels' – with each implement requiring a different number of strokes to reach, for example, a level-10. It takes 200 spanks with my hand, or 36 strokes of the strap, or 24 of the paddle, or 6 of the cane, to equal a level-10 spanking." A solid spanking might be a level-30 or level-40, and a really hard spanking might be a level-100." I smiled at Mistress.

She shook her head, and looked at Kelly, "You can relax, now." Kelly stood more casually, her panties still down around her thighs. Then, Mistress asked Kelly, "Is he always like this?"

Kelly stifled a quick laugh, and nodded, "Yes, Mistress. He's a scientist, very mathematical, so he has it all worked out."

I jumped in to explain further, "I like seeing what someone will choose, when I offer her the choice of implements for a spanking – for example, a level-30."

Mistress was still shaking her head, as she looked at me. "That's interesting, Sam. But I don't think about numbers when I'm giving a spanking – it's only necessary to see how red the bottom's bottom is getting … and listen to the breathing, watch the reactions. The top must be sensitive to the bottom's needs, not just go by a script, counting the strokes." I nodded.

Mistress picked up a small, leather paddle from the table, and sat on the chair. She smiled at Kelly, who walked up to Mistress, again assuming the standing position. Mistress smiled at Kelly, and said, "And, you must give the bottom a much longer warm-up before she is ready for heavier implements." She pointed, and Kelly clumsily got over Mistress' lap. Mistress put her leg over Kelly's legs, rubbed Kelly's bottom for a few moments, and then added, "Like this …"

The room was immediately filled with the staccato sound of the leather implement smacking hard against Kelly's buttocks. There had been no warning, no announcement of the number of strokes., and no let-up once it had begun. Kelly was already squirming, after the first couple of dozen strokes. I lost count, but Kelly began whimpering, as the strokes rained down on her already-pink butt.

Mistress took her work seriously, continuing to apply hard, and loud-sounding, slaps of the leather to Kelly's bottom, only momentarily looking up, to smile at me and, apparently, to look at the clock. The spanking continued, as Kelly tried to maintain her position, her legs crossing and uncrossing at the ankles, her hair bobbing, and her hips rocking.

It felt like time had slowed: The spanking was continuing at full force, while the hands of the clock seemed to stand still. The sounds of the paddle impacting Kelly's rear filled the room, as Mistress focused on her work; if anything, the strokes were now even harder and faster than before.

Kelly sobbed quietly, and it was clear that it took a concentrated effort for Kelly to stay in position over Mistress' lap. My knees grew weak, as I watched the small leather paddle make its rounds, covering Kelly's bottom, hips, and upper thighs completely. Kelly's ass was now a uniform, deep red, and my own bottom hurt, a psychological 'phantom' pain, as I empathized with Kelly.

When the clock showed that ten minutes had elapsed, the room suddenly quieted, as Mistress rubbed Kelly's raw, red rear. She smiled sweetly, and asked, "Would you please hand me the hairbrush, now?"

I was shocked: Kelly was already in pain, from what Mistress considered a 'warm-up', and now she was going to feel a much more serious implement. I handed the hairbrush to Mistress, and I hoped she hadn't noticed that my hand was shaking, slightly. Kelly's sobbing had subsided, but she was taking gasping breaths, as she relaxed her body over Mistress' leg.

Mistress said, "I'm not going to give Kelly a full hairbrushing, only a few sample strokes." She looked up at me, "I'd like her to feel – and you to watch – a few strokes, just to 'calibrate' you," she chuckled, using the scientific term, "what a spanking should be." She rubbed Kelly's bottom, and laid the back of the hairbrush on her right buttock.

Again without warning, Mistress began spanking Kelly, the hairbrush impacting Kelly's butt with a dull 'Splat!' on each stroke. This time, it was only one minute, but Kelly must have received at least 50 strokes. She was crying, now, her body shaking, but she still held her position; she had not once tried to bring her hand back to shield her bottom.

I was again proud of Kelly. But I also felt bad for her: She was taking a very hard hairbrushing just so Mistress could demonstrate her technique to me. Kelly was a stoic woman; she was not afraid of pain. I realized that *I* was the one who was 'afraid of pain' – and that's why it turned me on to see someone else voluntarily submit to some pain.

But, as I had explained to Kelly during our second lunch, I'm not turned on by seeing someone in real pain, just seeing their submission to the *expectation* of receiving pain.

I watched, as the hairbrush fell on Kelly's sore bottom; again, and again. Mistress didn't seem 'playful' about it – she was entirely serious, the strokes coming at a fast and uniform pace; no playing around. This *was* a good demonstration of how much Kelly could take ... and would voluntarily take. But I realized that my body was jumping with every stroke that Kelly received.

Finally, there was silence ... except for the persistent ringing in my ears; a ringing that came in pulses, as if the hairbrush were still smacking down on Kelly. Mistress commanded, "Stand up, Kelly!" Kelly slid off Mistress' lap, and stood as quickly as she could, taking the standing position, her legs spread, her back straight, hands on head, and eyes forward.

There was a moment of silence, as I watched in awe, then Kelly said, "Thank you for my spanking, Mistress." Her eyes were still forward, face serious, voice quavering.

Mistress stood, and walked around Kelly, picking up her crop. She looked like a military commander, inspecting her troops. She stood close in front of Kelly – their faces not half a foot apart – then smiled, "Kelly, I'm impressed by how well you took that spanking, You showed very good stamina and control over your body."

She glanced at me, and I gave her a quick smile back, before she looked back at Kelly and continued, "I'd like to see how you do, as the top. Would that bother you?"

Kelly, hands still on her head, smiled and said, "Oh no, Mistress! I get more turned on by being the top than the bottom. Fortunately, Sam lets me spank him sometimes." Mistress was nodding, and I saw Kelly's hips move, as she slightly repositioned herself.

"That's what I suspected. I would like you to demonstrate for me; Sam's going to need a warm-up." Then, she laughed, "And maybe we can let him give us a numerical rating to see how well your spanks reach my standards?" Kelly laughed.

But I wasn't laughing: I thought that I would be the one taught, perhaps with a few demonstration strokes; but Kelly had just taken a very hard spanking, and now it was clear that I should have heeded Kelly's warnings about our experience today. I suddenly thought maybe it *was* a good thing I had changed our flights, so we didn't have to sit on sore bottoms for ten hours.

My thoughts were interrupted, when Kelly asked, "Same implements, same intensity?"

Mistress nodded, "Yes. But we'll do the warm-up paddle only half the time – five minutes." Well, at least that was something! Then, I was deflated to hear, "Then, I'll demonstrate the flogger, and let you finish warming up Sam's butt with it. That's a good implement for starting easy, and working up to more serious." I was in a daze, as Kelly sat on the chair, and signaled me with a crooked finger.

I walked to Kelly's right side, and got into the standing position. Kelly lowered my underwear, having to lift it over my semi-erect penis. I glanced down, and could see a silvery thread of stickiness connecting the tip of my penis with the edge of my underwear, until Kelly suddenly yanked them down, and they were around my knees.

"No, no – that won't do, at all," Mistress said, as she walked across the room, and returned with a small device. Handing it to Kelly, she instructed, "This cock shield will be held in place by the ball rings. There's no need to let him drip on you ... and keep getting turned on."

As Kelly slipped the shield over me, and fiddled with my sensitive parts, Mistress looked at me severely, and said, "Sam, you asked for some training and a demonstration, and you told me you wanted to try some new things; and, that you were turned on by your own submission." I nodded, blankly.

She continued, "This session is for your benefit, later; it is not going to turn into a sexual experience while you're here." Then, she smiled at Kelly, "Although, if Kelly wants to satisfy you, before you go back out into the world, I will probably let you guys use the bed over there," she pointed to a corner of the room opposite the corner with the swings and chains, "but only if you complete the session satisfactorily. Doing as I say. Without question. Immediately."

I nodded, and said, "Yes, Mistress, I understand."

"Then get over Kelly's lap, and let her demonstrate her technique to me. Now!" I hurried to position myself correctly over Kelly's lap, the strange device on my genitals hindering my efforts. I put my feet slightly apart, toes touching the floor, and felt Kelly's hand on my bottom ... for a moment. Then, my bottom stung, as if a swarm of bees had attacked me, the small leather paddle coming down very fast; and hard.

I tried to relax, but it was difficult: My bottom was already on fire, and Kelly had just started ... and this was only the 'warm-up'. I focused on the floor, an intricate parquet pattern, as Kelly covered my thighs and upper legs; at least, until my eyes filled with tears, uncontrollably, blurring any vision I might have had.

Mistress said something, and Kelly stopped spanking me. My bottom must have been radiating heat. And, Mistress needn't have worried about me getting turned on, as I was now entirely flaccid, resting in that clear plastic container somewhere underneath me.

"Sam! Get up now, and bend over the chair, like Kelly did. Get those underwear off." I got off Kelly, and she stood up, as I slipped off the underwear, and got into position, holding the base of the chair.

Now it was Kelly, "Get down on your forearms, Sam." I tried to comply, but the seat of the chair was too low, forcing me to bend my knees.

I felt the many strands of the flogger come down on my hips, alternating left and right, brushing them, caressing them. Then, the strands began to sting. The strokes continued at the same pace, but harder now, my hips burning. I got my wish – for the flogging of my hips to stop. But, it was replaced by the flogging of my already-sore bottom; from top down, left and right, and then from underneath.

"Ow!" I cried, as a few of the strands hit my balls. The flogging stopped, and I mentally relaxed, even as I stayed physically in position. That hadn't been too bad. But my hips now hurt as much as my butt.

I heard Mistress say, "Five minutes." And then the flogging started anew – moving in an 'X' pattern, upper left to lower right, and upper right to lower left. The center of the 'X' slowly moved down, until my well-flogged bottom was in searing pain. And it continued. I shut my eyes, and concentrated on maintaining my position – which was getting difficult, as my leg muscles were tired, in this half-bent position. Finally, I had to change position.

The flogging stopped, and I looked back: Kelly was holding the flogger, a frown on her face, while Mistress stood there, tapping her palm with the crop. "Over here!" Mistress directed, as she walked to a spanking horse. She glanced at me, and adjusted the height of the horse, then pointed. I had seen these on the Internet, but had never actually been on one.

Mistress put padded cuffs on my ankles, as Kelly did the same on my wrists, and I was shackled to the horse, my body in a 'U' shape, legs and arms held in position. I felt a searing pain on my left buttock ... and then another one on my right side. Mistress said, "You'll get to feel the crop more, if you don't behave!"

Then, I heard Kelly and Mistress whispering, and I was sure I heard 'we'll start the five minutes over'. Then, louder, Mistress said, "He's ready for some hard strokes, now. It will make it easier when you use the hairbrush on him." My discomfort faded, and I relaxed into position, as best I could.

Then, the flogging started – again – and I couldn't help but whimper. I don't know how long Kelly flogged me, but it suddenly stopped, and there were two more searing flashes of pain from Mistress' riding crop. She said, sternly, "Sam! Stop that sniveling. Kelly's just warming you up."

Then, I heard Kelly say, "He's such a baby!" A moment later, the flogging started again. By the time it ended, I was crying – and didn't care. My bottom felt raw, already. And, now, I was supposed to get a hairbrushing? I wondered whether my money had been well spent. Presumably, Kelly was getting trained ... but I wasn't sure I would survive the ordeal.

Kelly asked, "May I rub him?" There was some shuffling, and Kelly rubbed my bottom, which dulled the pain a little. The cuffs were released from the spanking horse, and Kelly whispered, "OK, Sam. Get over my knee." As she sat, and I began to get down over her, Kelly added, "And try to behave yourself. Be strong."

It was hard – literally – to get over Kelly's thigh with that protector thing on me, which forced me to move higher up on her, my feet now leaving the floor. Kelly put her leg over mine, as Mistress had done with her. Then, I felt the hairbrush sliding over my sore skin; Kelly was 'rubbing' me lightly with the hairbrush. I glanced at Mistress, upside-down in my field of view, and saw her smile and nod.

Then, I felt a searing pain – this time huge, compared to the crop – and then more, covering each side of my bottom with what must have been raised welts. I was crying almost instantly. Kelly smacked me on the upper thighs, and then pulled my buttocks up to allow access to the crease between my butt and my legs – the gluteal fold, or 'sulcus'.

I was getting frantic, and near using my safeword. But I was crying so hard that I was heaving, and probably couldn't have used the safeword if I had tried. The hairbrushing suddenly stopped, and Kelly rubbed my bottom carefully. "I think he's had enough. At least, of the hairbrush." Kelly, the monster; the monster I had created.

There was a difference between the carefully applied pain of the spankings I'd given Kelly, and today's experience. But maybe it was only a matter of degree. For all I knew, Kelly had 'felt' the same amount of pain that first time, as I was 'feeling' now.

We didn't really know how another person felt, and there was no way to communicate it. How hard was hard? I guess you had to go by the reaction of the person. But people also responded differently, showed their feelings differently. I felt sore, tired and confused.

Mistress pointed, and said, "Please drink some water from that cooler. It looks like you're tired from standing in that position for so long." Ha! I was probably *more* tired from the spanking I'd just endured. Mistress continued, "So I'm going to let you lie down for a while. We'll move on to something different."

That sounded good to me. I took a small paper cup of water from the cooler, and drank it in one gulp. Then, I went over to the other side of the room, where Mistress and Kelly were standing next to a rolling exam table. Mistress pointed to the table, and I climbed onto it, and lay on my back. Suddenly, Mistress and Kelly were putting straps around my chest, my legs, and my arms, and I was immobilized on the table. "Just a precaution," Mistress explained.

I said, "I'm surprised that you don't have me lie on a towel or something to keep the table clean."

As she tightened the strap over my legs, she laughed, "We disinfect everything after every guest leaves. Mildred does a very good job." I guessed Mildred was the chubby one with black hair – who I had initially thought might be the Domme.

I then realized that my bladder was getting full. "May I please pee, before we do whatever we're going to do on this table?"

Mistress shook her head, "No, Sam." I was confused; maybe Mistress hadn't heard correctly? My sore bottom was pressed to the table, and I knew that I'd have to go, before long. Mistress removed my balls from the rings, and pulled the cock shield off of me.

She explained to Kelly, "You have to think ahead!" She laughed, as something was slipped over my penis. Then, I heard a rolling table being moved into position, some ripping of sterile packages, and some whispering. Then, there was a hand firmly holding my penis.

"It's handy to be able to catheterize your bottom, if it's going to be a long scene. Either that, or give him something to pee into. It's fun to watch a guy trying to pee into a Coke bottle." Then, some chuckling, "But you can't find a Coke bottle very easily any more." She rubbed the tip of my penis with a cold alcohol swab, startling me.

I said, "Coming from the medical field, I don't think it's a good idea to access sterile parts of the body – like the bladder, or do an IV; it's just too dangerous, and can lead to infection, or worse."

Mistress disappeared for a moment, and returned holding something in her hand – an orange ball, with straps. She looked at Kelly, "Sometimes, you don't want to hear from your bottom." Before I could object, she put the ball into my mouth, and tied the straps around the back of my head. I whimpered, but it was no use: There would be no communication, and I would have to take whatever Mistress gave me.

Mistress then explained to Kelly, "Always use a gag that holds his mouth open; if he vomits, at least it won't get aspirated into his lungs. And be careful not to damage his teeth." I tuned out, not wanting to hear the rest.

"Sam is correct that it can be dangerous, so it's important that you follow the proper procedure." I heard the sterile package being torn, and Mistress explaining how to insert the catheter. I felt a pressure as Mistress explained to Kelly, "Just a few cc of saline will inflate the balloon, and the catheter is now retained inside Sam's bladder."

A few moments later, she said, "So the urine bag is connected, and now we'll open the valve." I felt the pressure in my bladder lessen, as the urine flowed. This had been a new experience: I had never been catheterized before. I began to relax, and Mistress stood over me, "That feels better, doesn't it, Sam?"

I 'ahhh'd' through the ball gag a few times, and Mistress shook her head, "I guess you can't answer me. I'll take that ball gag out for a few minutes, so you can answer a few questions." She unstrapped the ball gag, and asked me again, "Does your bladder feel better, now?"

"Yes, Mistress," I replied.

Mistress asked, "So you've done some needle play, and saline injections?" I nodded. "Where did you inject the saline?" she asked.

"In the butt – like a normal intramuscular shot. We've injected as much as 6cc in one shot, and we've given – and received – two shots simultaneously," I explained.

"And where have you inserted needles, in the needle play?" Mistress was grilling me like a trial lawyer.

"I've made a corset down Kelly's back, and a spiral design on her butt and hips. And, I've inserted needles radially around her nipples." Actually, now that I thought about it, I'd inserted a lot of needles into Kelly.

Mistress asked, "And, you've taught Kelly how to insert needles and give shots safely?" I nodded, and Mistress followed-up her question with another, "So how much needle play has Kelly done on you?" Uh. I thought about it, and realized that while I'd let Kelly stick a few needles through pinches of skin on my thigh, I'd never had more than a couple of needles inserted at any one time.

Mistress said, "We'll just try a couple of simple things. To give you a bit more experience. Some needles through the skin on your penis, and some saline injected into your balls."

It was a good thing the ball gag was out of my mouth, as I was gagging already, "What!?? I know needles there will really hurt ... and it might bleed." I'd never even heard of saline injections into the testicles.

"Yes, it might. But, Sam, you have to face your fears. You know that." I didn't have a choice, being bound to the table.

Then, she told Kelly, "Go ahead and stroke him a little; it will be easier if he's hard." Kelly stroked me and, despite my increasing fear, my manhood grew – at least the part of my 'manhood' now being stroked down below. Mistress positioned the cock ring, and explained, "This will keep him hard, even if he isn't turned on by what we're doing."

Mistress laughed, and reminded Kelly, again, "You have to plan ahead. That's why I threaded the catheter through the cock ring before I inserted it into him." She then manipulated the device, my balls fitting into the fixture, the ring now against the base of my penis.

Mistress laid my penis on my stomach, and manipulated the skin. I closed my eyes, but could hear her preparing the needles. Suddenly, I felt a cold shock – alcohol being liberally swabbed on the underside of my erection.

Mistress leaned over me, and twisted my nipples roughly. "Since you're sensitive to the possibility of infection, I can swab you with Betadine, if you like; but then, half your penis will be orange." I kept my eyes closed and shook my head.

A moment later, Mistress commanded, "Look, Sam!" I opened my eyes, and saw a huge needle – not that long, but fat, probably 18-gauge. Mistress stepped alongside my middle, and I closed my eyes again. I felt Mistress pinch my frenum, lifting it, and she abruptly skewered me with the needle. It took a moment, but I couldn't help but scream. Mistress told Kelly to put the ball gag back on me, and I was again held incommunicado.

"If you would like to watch, I can put a pillow under your head," Mistress offered. I shook my head, keeping my eyes closed. Over the next few minutes, several more needles were inserted through my sensitive tissue. I tried to control myself, but couldn't help yelping a few times. I felt Mistress tamping me with gauze, and knew that I must be bleeding.

I whimpered. This was significantly more edgy than the things that Kelly and I did together.

Then, Kelly inserted several needles; thankfully, they felt smaller than the ones Mistress had used. Kelly positioned them between each of the needles that Mistress had inserted. I opened my eyes briefly, and saw Kelly using my phone to snap a picture of my skewered cock.

Then, Mistress entered my view, and showed me a very large syringe and needle: It had to be at least 20cc – twice as large as the syringes we used. At least the needle seemed to be smaller, perhaps 22-gauge. I closed my eyes again.

I felt the skin of my testicles being manipulated, and then swabbed with alcohol. The needle stung going in, and Mistress held it in place, as she spoke to me. "We're going to do a 'scrotal infusion' – a small injection of saline into each of your ball-sacs. Usually, it's done by slow infusion through a thin needle, using a bag of sterile saline. Often, people infuse hundreds of cc of saline into each testicle – they become the size of grapefruit."

I whimpered again, and Mistress put her free hand on my left hip, and stroked me soothingly, "Don't worry, Sam. This is just a sample experience – we'll only be injecting 50cc on each side." I couldn't stop myself from whimpering again; and I didn't care. Maybe Kelly was right, and I *was* a baby?

Mistress injected the saline slowly, over a couple of minutes, creating a strange sensation in a location where I usually didn't feel anything (and didn't *like* to feel anything). She and Kelly talked, and I heard 'only a bit larger than normal', 'you can do the other side', and 'hold the skin well away'.

Kelly swabbed me on the other side, and I felt the needle pierce the skin; then the saline flowed into me, my balls now feeling about the size of plums, although they apparently didn't look much larger than usual.

Kelly and Mistress stood over me, on opposite sides of the rolling exam table. Kelly smiled at me, while Mistress roughly twisted my nipples again. She turned to Kelly, and asked, "Shall I demonstrate the procedure for doing a nipple piercing? We could use the relatively-small 14-gauge needle, and I have some sterile, gold jewelry that you could select." I whimpered louder, this time, and Kelly patted my chest.

"No, that's OK. You can demonstrate on me, if you want to show Sam how to do it."

Mistress responded, "That's very gallant of you, dear. But I think Sam is still a little short of endorphins. So, maybe I'll just insert a couple of smaller needles through his nipples – maybe 20-gauge or 18-gauge." I closed my eyes tightly; this was becoming a nightmare. It was not the experience I had envisioned, with the Domme instructing me on the best way to cane Kelly. I opened my bleary eyes, and looked at Mistress entreatingly.

She shrugged, "OK, Sam. Since you like choices so much, I'll give you one: Either I insert a needle through each nipple, and then Kelly and I will leave you for a while ... or we can take out the needles in your dick, you can get on the spanking bench, and Kelly can put some needles in your butt – and a butt plug, just as you like." She smiled at Kelly, "And *then*, Kelly and I will go and have some tea."

I didn't like either of the choices, but the needles were hurting, and I really didn't mind a few needles in the butt – we'd done plenty of that. I tried to answer Mistress, but the ball gag prevented any actual words from coming out of my mouth. Mistress nodded, and took off the ball gag, and I said, "I'll take the needles in the butt."

Mistress pulled each of the needles out of my frenum, and it was painful as they slid through two layers of skin. There was more patting with gauze, and then Mistress taped a gauze pad to the underside of my penis. I was unstrapped, and Kelly helped me off the table, and over to the spanking bench, holding the tubing from the catheter, as Mistress brought the urine bag.

I got onto the spanking bench, my knees on padded ledges, and my chest on a diagonally-raised, padded bench. My forearms went down onto another set of padded ledges, and Mistress fastened the cuffs that were still around my ankles and wrists. Mistress went to a counter, and put a number of supplies on a small, metal, rolling table, and positioned it next to the spanking bench.

"Here are some supplies – a nice big butt plug, box of 100 needles, alcohol swabs, and gauze pads. After you insert the plug, please make sure your hands are washed. I've also provided some exam gloves, if you'd like to use them."

Mistress leaned over me, and whispered, "They're only 22-gauge needles. Nice and thin. I'll let Kelly take care of this," Then she whirled around, and walked out of the room, laughing, "50 on each side ... while I make some tea."

I nearly screamed, "Fifty! There's not even room on my small butt for that many needles!" Kelly laughed, and opened an alcohol swab, then swabbed my entire bottom. As the alcohol dried, she prepared the butt plug, and showed it to me: It was fatter than most we had used, and all I could say to Kelly was, "Take it slowly, please." It took several minutes to get the butt plug in, and then Kelly washed her hands.

Standing next to me, Kelly said, "Well, let's get this done. I'm ready for some tea." Very funny. I remained quiet, as Kelly began sticking me with needles. They were done randomly, all over my bottom, sometimes two or three on a side, then moving to the other side. I was feeling faint. I wondered whether Mistress was prepared to deal with anaphylactic shock, if one of her clients had a reaction to so many needles.

Kelly said, "I think we're about halfway." My entire bottom hurt, and Kelly was now sticking needles between the other needles. I closed my eyes, and tried to think of something nice: A tropical island. Then, I saw Kelly and I there, on the beach, splashing warm water on each other. Now Kelly's friends had joined us: Julie, Linda, and Kathy, frolicking around and laughing. We were all nude; I hadn't noticed that at first.

I bellowed suddenly, as Kelly inserted a needle that must have hit a nerve; she pulled it out, and I let out a continuous 'Oooowww'. "Don't whine, Sam. We're almost done." Yeah, *you're* almost done, and get to have tea, while I'm strapped down here with a hundred needles in my butt. I thought about an island experience, again; playing with Kelly and her friends.

Finally, Kelly announced, "OK, Sam. That's 100. Take it easy for a while." Then, she walked out. 'Take it easy' – that was an easy thing for *her* to say! I groaned, and dropped my head, wondering how I had gotten myself into this.

Mistress Elena and I sat at a formal dining table, covered by an embroidered, lace tablecloth, and sipped our tea. It was very good, slightly sweetened by Sam's 'suffering' downstairs. Sometimes he acted like a little boy, not a grown man; I had thought he would have been much more brave for our Domme, even if he was whining inside.

My bottom still hurt, and Mistress had provided a pillow on which I could sit without squirming too much. I'm sure Sam's bottom also hurt – especially now that it was a double-puffed pincushion.

Mistress put her tea down, and commented, "When Sam contacted me, he mentioned that each of you was a 'switch', but that he was the 'dominant in the family'. I can see, now, that you have the attitude and aptitude to be the dominant one ... unless you would like to leave him thinking he's in control, and submit to his discipline."

I had to think about that a moment. "Mistress, I'm willing to submit to Sam, if he wants, sometimes. In fact, he and I have submitted to each other whenever we were asked. But Sam doesn't want to hurt me, and his spankings are just play, compared to yours."

Mistress smiled, her teacup pausing briefly on its way to her mouth, "And you've only received a warm-up and a brief hairbrushing. Just wait until I've caned you." She sipped her tea, eyes looking at me over the rim of the cup.

I nodded, "Yes. I know there's much more. And I'd like to explore that. But I think Sam will need to be the bottom; and I don't know how far he will go, in his submissiveness to me. He still fantasizes that he is the dominant one, the open one, the teacher."

Mistress put her cup down, "Sam's a nice man, and I'm sure he will learn to be the bottom. You, dear, have a knack for domination." She studied me, taking her time, as I sat in my bra and underwear in her formal dining room. "Actually, I would like the opportunity to train you; as a dominatrix." She smiled, "I think we would have some fun together."

On the one hand, I was shocked to be receiving such an offer – and I hadn't really done anything so far to merit it; on the other hand, I had secretly hoped that I would have the opportunity to be trained as a Domme. I stammered, "That's quite an honor, Mistress."

Mistress stood and walked to me, putting her hands on my shoulders, "Kelly, you must understand that being trained to be a dominant also means that you will need to be trained to be a submissive." She chuckled, "Your bottom will probably be pretty sore for the month that you're here."

I shook my head, "A month! I can't do that, since I'm in school, and doing my research. I'm not worried about a sore bottom – and I would *like* to be trained as a sub, so that Sam will be better topping me – but I could never afford to take a month course with you." I had peeked at the credit card receipt, as Sam signed it, and today's experience had cost a cool $1,000 – way over the budget of a student.

Mistress squeezed my shoulders, "Dear, it would be my pleasure to give you a substantial discount. And there *are* some scholarships available, for a talented woman like you."

"Scholarships?" What was this, BDSM University? Just the idea of a scholarship for me to become a Domme sounded ridiculous.

Mistress nodded, and explained, "Yes. I have a few wealthy benefactors ... who take advantage of my services, and the services of the few women I train. They will provide the funds, and you would live here, as you will get 24 hour-a-day instruction. The only thing they ask in return is to have a graduation session with you."

I knew there would be a catch. I shook my head, and started to object, when Mistress calmed me, "There would be no sex. That's not relevant to your training. Most of these men like to be tied up – in very creative and fancy ways – and then be spanked or humiliated in some way. I have an agreement with them: They will get a session with you – up to 24 hours, but they have agreed to respect you, and do exactly as you say; you will be the one in control."

Then she cackled, "We're getting ahead of ourselves, dear. Why don't you think about it? Maybe, we can schedule some time in the summer, when you can take a month from your research."

I nodded, my mind now filled with new possibilities, as Mistress took my arm, and I stood up. "Shall we go downstairs and see how Sam is doing?" I just nodded again, and walked with Mistress down to the dungeon. Sam was still over the spanking horse; where else *could* he be? He moaned, as he heard us enter the room. I knew Sam would be happy that we were back to remove the hundred needles.

Mistress picked up a couple of items from the counter, and showed one to Sam, "I'm sure you've seen these? A Trachtenberg wheel – with tiny teeth that I can roll over your skin to give you lots of needle-like sensations."

Sam nodded, "Yes, Mistress. I have one; we've played with it once."

Mistress was suddenly animated, "Oh, they're *lots* of fun! Have you seen *this* kind?" She showed Sam another wheel, this one with half a dozen wheels of teeth that could be rolled over the skin. Sam shook his head, and Mistress appeared delighted. "Great – I can introduce you to something else new!" Sam groaned again, as Mistress set the multi-toothed wheel on Sam's upper back, and then suddenly rolled it down to his hips.

"Ow! Ow! Ow! Ow! Ow! Ow! Ow!" Sam was screaming. Mistress put the wheel back on Sam's upper back, on the other side, and rolled it down again. "Ow! Ow! Ow! Ow! Ow! Ow! Ow!" Sam yelled, softer now, like the echo of the prior screams. Then, Mistress put the roller on Sam's left thigh, just below his butt; suddenly, she rolled it down the back of Sam's leg, and Sam yelled again. By the time Mistress had finished Sam's right leg, Sam was sobbing.

Mistress turned to me, and said, "See, you don't need needles; it's easy to make someone cry with a little tool like this." I nodded, and Mistress told Sam, "This was just a preview, to demonstrate a few new things that you might not have considered. Now, if this had been a serious session ... I would have injected at least 500cc in each of your balls, and then rolled over them with this wheel. There would be a fountain of tiny jets of saline, each time I squeezed your ball-sac."

Mistress was laughing, but purposely making it sound evil. And Sam was responding. He had been good to not ask about removing the needles. Mistress asked me, "Do you think he's had enough needles for one morning?" I nodded, and we pulled them out, Mistress on one side, and me on the other. We dropped the needles into a Sharps container, as Sam moaned and groaned.

Then, Mistress poured some rubbing alcohol onto two large gauze pads, and handed one to me. We wiped down Sam's back, and legs, then turned the pads over, and wiped down his butt. There were dozens of tiny pinpricks visible, some of them showing a small drop of blood. We cleaned Sam, and removed the butt plug – which had been the least of his worries.

Then, Mistress and I walked to a rack on the wall, where she showed me her cane collection. "Most of these are rattan, which is a type of palm; a few are bamboo. The thicker canes usually bruise more, and the thinner canes are more whippy and sting more." Mistress selected one of the medium-sized canes, and we walked back to Sam. "Sam, I'm sure you know that you shouldn't cane someone too high up – or you could damage the tailbone."

Sam nodded, and Mistress added, "So being elevated on a spanking bench like this is a good approach." She leveled the cane, and slid it across Sam's bottom.

Sam reacted instantly, "You're going to *cane* me, now? With my bottom still having a thousand holes in it?" He was exaggerating, but very serious. Mistress pointed to the rolling table, and I retrieved the ball gag and put it into Sam's mouth. I wasn't sure what would happen, next, and watched – fascinated – as Mistress slid the cane back and forth across Sam's rear, and he alternately moaned and whimpered.

She turned to me, and asked, "Is Sam romantic?" I nodded. Then she asked, "Is he gallant?" I shrugged and nodded. Sam really was a polite person, and – without being chauvinistic – *was* a gallant gentleman.

Mistress smiled, and said, "OK. Kelly, please help me." She put down the cane, and we dragged another spanking bench alongside the one Sam occupied. She pointed, and I nodded, removing my underwear, and getting into position. Mistress fastened the straps around my wrists and ankles, as I glanced over to Sam; he was watching, but there was no smile on his face.

Mistress said, "OK, you guys. We're going to finish up the morning with a demonstration of the cane. I'm going to give six strokes ... and you guys can decide who gets them. Then, Kelly will give Sam another three strokes – unless I want her to change her technique, in which case it might be more ..." Sam groaned again.

"We'll do one more thing, while Sam is in this position, and then Sam will take his turn giving Kelly three strokes of the cane." Mistress looked back and forth at us, and said, severely, "And you *will* give a hard caning. Or else, your own bottom will receive a reminder of how it should feel, and then you'll be given a chance to give your partner another stroke."

I knew our bottoms were going to hurt, by the time the Domme was finished. "Who wants to take the first stroke?" Mistress asked.

I swallowed hard, and said, "I'll start with two strokes, Mistress." Mistress stepped behind me, and I felt the cane cutting across the middle of my bum. Then it left me, but only for a moment; the cane crashed down on my butt with a 'Thwack!' and, after a very brief moment, I felt as if I had been sliced by a sword. A loud 'Ugggh' emanated from my mouth.

I felt Mistress rubbing the searing line of heat, and then the cane was against my butt again. 'WHAP!' the cane sliced through me again. I screamed, and tears came to my eyes. It was a good thing that I had been strapped down, as I never would have been able to hold my position, otherwise.

"Who wants to take the next ones?" Sam groaned, and said, "I guess I'll take two, also." I turned my head and watched, as Mistress gave Sam a couple of hard strokes. Just the 'whoosh' of the cane through the air was frightening, and the 'CRACK!' was truly intimidating, and not only for the person being caned.

Sam squealed after each of the strokes, and started crying again. Mistress had said we were almost done; at least Sam could have *pretended* to be strong, and take his caning with dignity.

Now, Mistress paced behind both of us. "I've got two more strokes left in this arm. Who's going to take them?" Sam and I were both quiet. Sam was sniffling, and shaking his head. I was prepared to take the last two strokes, if necessary. I sighed, and turned my head back to face Mistress, about to request the two strokes … when Sam – still sniffling – said, weakly, "I'll take the last two strokes." He let his head drop, and sniffled a few more times.

I couldn't believe it! Sam had actually offered to take both of the last strokes, even though his bottom was still hurting from the needles. Sam really *was* gallant; at least, he was trying.

Mistress placed the cane across Sam's bottom, and quickly administered a very hard stroke, Sam screaming again. Mistress paced back and forth again, giving Sam time to settle down. As she put the cane on Sam's bottom again, I sputtered, "Mistress. I'll take the last stroke."

I hadn't planned to offer that, and wasn't sure why it had come out. But I was willing to share the pain with Sam, and he had been very nice, offering to take both of the last strokes. Mistress shrugged, and moved over to me. I looked straight ahead, trying to will my mind into a blank, Zen state, as the cane slid across my already-sore bum. The stroke was a zinger, slicing into my bottom, and I cried out. As tears fell from my eyes, I turned slightly, and said, "Thank you, Mistress."

Mistress unstrapped me, and we walked back to the rack of canes, where she hung up the cane and selected the smallest cane, handing it to me. I turned to Mistress, and pleaded, quietly, "Do we have to?"

My question surprised Mistress, and she paused a moment, before replying, "I'll be satisfied to see you each give the other one stroke ... but it had better be a good one!" I swallowed hard and nodded.

Positioning myself behind Sam, and to his left, I put the cane across his bottom. Mistress gave us several tips, to avoid causing damage to tissue, or unnecessary 'hot spots'. I pulled the cane back and, just before swinging it, whispered, "Sorry, Sam."

The cane flew, and I flicked my wrist at the end of the stroke, as my father had taught me, with several sports – for example, golf and softball. The cane landed on Sam's poor bum with a 'CRAAACKKK!'. Sam yelped and panted heavily. Mistress smiled and nodded.

I put down the cane, and Mistress pulled another rolling metal table in front of the spanking bench, where Sam could see it. She used an electronic lighter to ignite a Bunsen burner, and adjusted the flame. Then, she picked up a long metal rod, with a disc at the end, and tilted it, so we could see the raised pattern on the disc: There was a small circle, appearing to be rope, divided into three segments, the whole thing crossed by what looked to be a riding crop, and another spiked implement.

"To show your commitment to each other, and willingness to submit, you will each be branded with this BDSM symbol." As Sam predictably reacted, I looked at Mistress with concern, and she put a finger over her lips. I smiled: Sam was such an easy tease!

Sam squealed, beside himself, and Mistress quickly put the ball gag back into Sam's mouth and tied the straps behind his head. He was still making a racket, but at least we didn't have to listen to his rant.

Mistress clamped the branding iron so that the disc was in the flame of the Bunsen burner; before our eyes, it turned red, then orange, and then yellow. Mistress opened a drawer and took out a couple of items. One of them was a blindfold, with which she covered Sam's eyes, saying, "It's much easier this way, Sam. You won't see it coming, and it will be over before you know it."

She showed me the other item, a small piece of fur, and put it on a small block of wood on the metal table in front of Sam. Then, she stepped quietly to the other side of the room, and opened a small refrigerator, taking something out of the freezer compartment. When she came back, she picked up the now white-hot branding iron, passing it under Sam's nose before handing it to me. She signaled what to do, and I nodded.

I picked up the wood block with the fur around it, skin-side up, and held the branding iron next to it, near Sam's waist. Then, Mistress positioned the frozen duplicate over Sam's left hip. She mouthed 'three, two, one' and – simultaneously – she brought the frozen iron into contact with Sam's hip, and held it there several seconds, while I pushed the real – and really hot – branding iron into the fur skin, which sizzled loudly, and smoked. I moved the fur under Sam's nose, so that he would get a whiff of the putrid smell of burning flesh.

Even with the ball gag in his mouth, Sam shrieked – sounding like the high-pitched, blood-curdling scream in some horror movies. It was a mean joke, perhaps, but not cruel: Sam had arranged to meet with the Domme, and had asked her for some new experiences. This certainly appeared to be one, as Sam was now breathing heavily, unsure of what had just happened.

I took off Sam's blindfold, and kissed him on the cheek. His forehead was beaded with sweat, and he was still shaking. Mistress removed the cock ring and the urinary catheter, and I unstrapped him from the spanking bench. Then, I brought him a small paper cup of water.

Sam stood before us, nude but without the hint of an erection; he was shaking his head and, just to be sure, turned his head, and pulled his bottom so that he could see the 'brand'. Of course, there was nothing showing, except slightly whiter skin from the cold.

Sam looked at me, and I shrugged, and commented, "If you remember our lunch together, all those months ago, you told me that pain wasn't really necessary, just submission, to get you turned on. Thank you for submitting to the cane, and for letting us 'brand' you."

Sam was still shaking his head, "But I didn't have a choice! I was strapped down to this thing." He pointed to the spanking bench.

Mistress explained, "Sam, it's all a matter of degree. You could have put up more of a fight. And, it's the same with the spankings and needles: We didn't really do anything new, today; you had done it all ... but at a lesser intensity. Hopefully, I've given you a taste of what you can expect, being punished by a professional Domme."

Then, she smiled and said gaily, "And you're welcome to come back for a 'real' session sometime; I promise to tan your hide thoroughly!" We all laughed, despite our sore bottoms.

Then, Mistress frowned, and said, "Oh! We almost forgot ... to give Sam *his* chance at trying the cane." She handed Sam the cane, and he examined it closely.

Sam turned to me, and said, "Kelly, I'm willing to forego this 'lesson', if your bottom is too sore. I don't want to see you hurt any more." I hugged Sam, and took my position on the spanking bench.

"It's only one stroke. How bad can it be?" Sam didn't have to answer that, as I knew exactly how bad it would be. But it was the thin cane, and I had used it on Sam ... so I was willing to play fair and let him take his turn. I turned and faced forward, and realized that I was not strapped down.

I heard Mistress remind Sam of the consequences, if his stroke was not up to 'standards'. Sam positioned himself behind me, and spent some time moving the cane across my bum. I hoped he would just do it, already.

I didn't have to wait long, as I heard the 'whoosh' and the 'Crack!' against my own bottom. It hurt like hell, but I was determined to behave, and bit my lip, rather than scream. I tasted blood, as I turned to Sam and said,

"Thank you, Sir." Sam helped me up, and hugged me tightly. I still wore the bra that I'd worn all day.

Mistress handed me a tube of lotion, and said, "You guys can use the bed, if you like. Then, please use this lotion on each other, and get dressed. I'll meet you up in my office."

I looked at Sam and asked, "Are you interested in making love now?" After what Sam had gone through, I was happy to satisfy his needs ... but I wasn't very turned on at the moment; certainly not as much as I would be later, thinking about this experience ... and a possible future month of training.

Sam smiled, and said, "Would it be OK, if we made love when we get back to the hotel?" I laughed, and opened the lotion, while Sam bent over one of the tables. We soothed each other's bums, and got dressed, without saying another word to each other.

We knocked on Mistress' office, and she called us in. As we sat in front of her desk, she shuffled some papers, and said, "Sam, I hope you feel that your experience was worthwhile. I would be pleased to have a more 'normal' session with you, anytime. But today I wanted to let you see how much more there is to BDSM than what you've been exposed to previously."

Sam nodded, "My bottom is telling me that I got my money's worth." We all chuckled, quietly. "And you have opened my eyes to many things ... that I'll have to ponder later." Then, Sam looked at me, while addressing Mistress, "And I'm very impressed at Kelly's performance today."

Mistress nodded vigorously, "Yes. I am, also. I have offered her a month-long formal training experience. There will be a few other students, who will 'practice' on each other. It will be a challenge, but very rewarding, when Kelly is certified as a dominatrix."

Sam looked at me with narrowed eyes, and I said, "We'll discuss it later." Sam nodded, and we rose to say our goodbyes. It had been an interesting experience, albeit a little painful. But it had also been enlightening; especially, when Sam offered to take the cane on his very sore bottom, rather than force me to endure another stroke. We had learned more about BDSM, and more about each other, today.

We spent much of the afternoon in our hotel room, and made love three times. Sam bought tickets for tomorrow's activities, and made reservations at one of the upscale restaurants in 'The Shard' for dinner tonight.

We dressed nicely – as nice as the clothes we had brought on the trip would allow – and had a very enjoyable dinner. It was a multi-course affair, with wine pairings, and we had an incredible window seat, looking out over the heart of London, glimmering with a multitude of lights.

Holding his wine glass high, Sam toasted, "With only one day left, I hope you have enjoyed your first visit to Europe. We didn't see much of it," Sam smiled seductively at me, "but we did see some interesting things … and had some interesting experiences." We sipped the luscious deep purple Bordeaux.

Sam's toast was an understatement: We had experienced a lot in the past three weeks; a lot that had brought us even closer together. I looked forward to more travel with Sam, and wondered where our next trip might take us.

I also looked forward to *being* with Sam more, and decided that I wanted to move in with him, provided his offer still stood.

CHAPTER 18: FLIGHTS OF FANCY

We had a very busy morning on Wednesday – our last day in Europe – touring Westminster Abbey and Parliament. We even managed to see the 'changing of the guards' at Buckingham Palace. Then, Sam got his last chance to visit a Pub – at least, on this trip. I hoped we would be able to return soon; perhaps for a formal training in domination and submission.

In the afternoon, we attended a matinee performance of a long-running play in the West End theater district: *Cats*. Neither Sam nor I had ever seen it, but we both recognized several of the songs. It was a great performance, and our bottoms survived sitting for a couple of hours on hard wooden seats, even though we were both still sore.

We went back to the hotel, meowing at each other, and began packing for our flights tomorrow. As Sam pulled out each sex toy we had bought on the trip, he looked at me, and raised his eyebrows. I just raised my eyebrows at him, in return.

Finally, when he had everything laid out, and ready to repack, I said, "OK, Sam. We can do anything you want ... but only one thing. And it can't involve spanking or needles." He laughed, and I had to join him. Our bottoms were still sore.

Sam answered, "I think we should masturbate together."

I raised my eyebrows, this time for real, and asked, "Really?"

He nodded, and finished his sentence, "while you try out your new strap-on, on me." Now my brows went up and I smiled. We undressed and, as I put on the strap-on, Sam put one of the used hand towels on the corner of the bed. Then, he positioned himself with his legs straddling the corner of the bed, and his head on a pillow. I lubed the dildo of the strap-on, which caused it to bob, hinging on the phallus inside me, and causing the forked-tongue-like top portion to diddle my clit.

Stepping behind Sam, I asked him, "Should I lubricate you with my finger, or one of the vibrators?"

Sam chuckled, and said, "Don't bother with it. I think I'm still dilated from that huge butt plug you left in me for an hour yesterday."

I chided him, mockingly, "It wasn't an hour!" We laughed, and I added, "It couldn't have been more than 45 minutes." I rubbed the tip of the strap-on's dildo against Sam, and used my hand to gently angle it, and advance it into him. Then, I began moving my hips, slowly, as I watched the dildo disappear inside Sam, and emerge from him again. Each time, the other end of the dildo stimulated my clit.

I didn't even have to reach down to do myself; I used my hands to lightly rub Sam's bottom. It was still a dark shade of red – like mine – and I could still make out a few of the tiny pinpricks from the needles.

Sam rubbed himself on the hand towel, our motions sometimes together, sometimes opposite, as we each attended to our own needs – but both of us being stimulated by what connected us, the dildo. And, our shared experiences. And fantasies.

That evening, we dressed up again, and ate at a famous, old, restaurant that specialized in English roast beef and Yorkshire pudding. Actually, the beef was Scottish, the wine Australian, and the dessert classic French – Crème Brulée. I once again vowed to go on a diet when I got home.

Near the end of the dinner, I looked at Sam, and tears came to my eyes. "What's wrong?" Sam asked, very concernedly.

"I love you, Sam." That was all that need be said. But when Sam looked enquiringly at me, I added, "And, I'm sad to be going home. It seems like we've been traveling a long time ... but I could keep this up forever, traveling with you; seeing new things, and having new experiences together."

Sam nodded, "It's been a nice trip." He smiled, devilishly, "And we seem to have gotten along pretty well. No major arguments. No major disasters."

I sipped the last of the wine, and agreed, "Yes, you behaved very well; although I was close to leaving you the night of the Oktoberfest. You were really out of it. But, I guess I can grant you that, every once in a while."

Sam smiled, "I didn't cause a scene. There were a lot of other people sleeping on the lawn, also."

I laughed, "Yes, but I wasn't so sure about letting you go down to the sauna ... until we saw all the other guys passed out on the chaises, too."

Sam said, resentfully, "I never passed out." He smiled again, "But I might have closed my eyes for a while. They were really tired." He couldn't help but laugh. I shook my head. Sam had taken good care of me on this trip – even though he'd made me drive from Munich to Zurich, since he'd been hung over. I chuckled. Sam was pretty well-hung, also.

We took the tube back to our hotel, and Sam made love to me, taking the 'top' position. As he entered me, I asked, "Do you need to keep your hot spanked buns in the air?"

Sam laughed, and said, "You've got 'hot buns', too, lady."

As we made love, I thought briefly about 'hot crossed buns' – my train of thought running from the delicious cinnamon buns in the airports, to the English nursery rhyme:

> Hot cross buns!
> Hot cross buns!
> one a penny, two a penny,
> Hot cross buns!
> If you have no daughters,
> Give them to your sons
> one a penny,
> two a penny,
> Hot Cross Buns!

That seemed to be the story of my life, at least how I felt about it. My father had spent his time with his sons, not his adopted daughter. And my mother had wanted a 'doll', not a daughter who had her own thoughts and ideas. Tears came to my eyes again. Why was I even thinking about this?

I held Sam, as we made love. He put his lips on mine, and we kissed, slowly, as our hips thrust faster, finally reaching near-simultaneous orgasms.

Thursday morning, Sam and I were up early, and at Heathrow two hours before our flight was scheduled to depart. We waited in the airline's first class lounge, and I knew to skip the breakfast buffet. When our flight was announced, we walked to the gate, and were among the first to board.

This time, we turned left into the first class section. I had imagined our seats being together, but they were across the starboard aisle from each other, Sam letting me take the window seat, while he took the center seat. There was a short barrier dividing Sam's seat from the one next to him, on the other aisle, which was occupied by a gentleman in suit and tie.

We were served drinks as other passengers boarded, both Sam and I electing the French Champagne – which we examined with fresh eyes, trained by a few wineries on the Mosel River. We reached across the aisle and clinked our glasses.

I took time to explore my seat, which had a shelf next to the window, a fancy entertainment system, and it even swiveled. I smiled at Sam, as the plane taxied to the runway. Looking out the window, I watched Heathrow recede behind us, as we rose through broken clouds. We flew over green fields separated by long lines of trees. It got hazy outside, and I closed the window most of the way, and reclined my seat.

A male flight attendant provided a menu and wine list, and returned a while later to take our orders. I decided to 'do it all'. First was the caviar and blinis, along with sour cream, chopped egg, minced onion, capers, and fresh dill. Sam insisted that I try the chilled Russian vodka, and I was floating by the time the salad course arrived.

We took our time, happy to spend some of the flight hours enjoying the meal. The salad was served from a huge wooden bowl, and came with a crab claw, and smoked duck breast. I tried one of the German white wines, and was surprised that I could recognize the taste, and remember the classifications.

Sam was watching a movie as he ate – and there were plenty of movies to watch – but I was more interested in enjoying the food, getting slightly tipsy, and occasionally lifting the window a bit to peek out. When my salad plate had been taken away, I was rewarded with a spectacular view of Iceland; Reykjavik sure looked small, from up here. I saw a volcano smoking and, when I had lowered my shade, was amazed to realize that none of the other passengers had bothered to look out the window and catch that magnificent view.

I felt lucky: Lucky that I had emerged from my 'wild' days relatively unscathed – not even any tattoos. Lucky that I had found a subject that interested me enough to go on for advanced degrees. Lucky that I had met Sam, a most wonderful person ... and that we had fallen in love. And lucky that I'd had the experiences that Sam had introduced me to – that we'd *shared* – over the past six months.

I briefly considered how I could explain this trip to my friends; especially Linda, who was expecting a full report on our romantic visit to Paris. Some of it had been truly romantic – like our electric kiss on the top of the Eiffel Tower. It was always romantic, when I was with Sam.

Although, now that I thought about it, our experience with the Domme had not been that 'romantic'. Until Sam had shown that he was willing to make a sacrifice for me. I was really feeling the wine, now.

Our main courses came – I had ordered the rack of lamb, but I wasn't that hungry. After I'd had a taste of the sauce, I ate more of the lamb than I had expected, and all of the vegetables. Now, Sam wanted me to try still another wine ... or another still wine ... I wasn't sure which. I took one swallow and nodded to him, smiling.

The lights were dim, and Sam leaned halfway across the aisle to kiss me. I yawned, and said, "Sam, after all that wine, I hope you don't think we're going to have another mile-high club experience."

Sam shook his head, "No, Kelly." Then he reconsidered, "Unless you'd like to, of course." He smiled, "I'm always happy to oblige a lady." I playfully slapped him on the cheek, and then took a pinch of it, as a grandmother would with an infant.

Sam whined, "Ow!"

I added, "You couldn't get it up, if you had to, after all that alcohol." As I said that, perfectly timed, the flight attendant brought the brandy that Sam had ordered to go with dessert.

Sam sat back in his seat, looked down into his lap, and shrugged. Then, he put his headphones back on, and took a sip of brandy from the snifter.

The flight attendant came, and I decided to go with the cheese and fruit plate, rather than the sundae. The cute guy leaned over me, glanced around, and said – conspiratorially – "Don't worry. I'll put your name on a sundae for later in the flight, if you're hungry." I chuckled, realizing that I'd probably sleep through the rest of the flight.

And, I wasn't far from wrong: I tasted one of the cheeses – a smelly French variety, along with a couple of slices of apple. Then, I put the plate on the side shelf, put the tray away, and adjusted my seat into a bed. The pillow was huge, and the blanket soft, as I covered myself. Sam whispered to me, "Put your seatbelt over the blanket, so they won't have to wake you." I did as Sam suggested, and was asleep a minute later.

I woke up once during the flight to use the lav, and stumbled down the aisle, even though there was only a little turbulence. As I sat on the toilet, I realized that I should be getting my period soon ... hopefully, not *this* soon. It was OK, and I would be home in a few hours. At *Sam's* home. I was spinning.

As I made my way back to my seat, Sam looked up and smiled at me; he was still watching a movie. I got back into my 'seat bed' and fastened the seat belt over me.

I woke again somewhere over Canada, according to the route map on the seatback LCD, although I didn't recognize the names of any of the towns. The cute flight attendant came over and offered to bring the sundae, any way I liked it. Hot fudge and cold ice cream sounded good, so I let him indulge me. Now, my jeans were feeling tight; it could be water retention ...

The next flight was also in first class, and they served a dinner, which we skipped, as it was totally unnecessary for those of us coming off an international flight. This time, Sam and I sat together in the bulkhead, and were able to talk.

"Sam, we haven't really discussed our experience with the dominatrix." It was a simple statement. Sam and I were both relatively detoxified, now, and I knew that Sam was bothered by something.

He looked at me a moment, and said, "I'm not sure it was such a good idea." Maybe he was upset that I had been invited to be trained ... and he hadn't?

Sam expanded on the thought, "I might have been happier, left with my fantasies, not quite as 'educated' as we were a couple of days ago. Of course, I knew there was much more 'to it', and that I had never really been trained. But I felt like she was putting me down. And, I was the 'bottom' for most of our session."

I looked at him, "And you didn't like it?"

Sam was getting flustered, "Well, it certainly was painful."

I shook my head, "Sam, didn't you expect that? We *knew* that she would be using her techniques on our bottoms – because that's what you told her you were interested in ... as well as needles, and doing something 'new'. Well, you got to try several new things."

Sam grumbled, "They were tried on *me*."

I tried to get Sam to see the situation logically. "Sam, what did you expect? Did you see some of the photos on the walls of that dungeon?" I knew he had, as I'd seen him staring, with his mouth open, at one of them.

"Did you want Mistress to hang us by huge hooks through our skin?" I shivered, remembering the grotesque image. "Or, would you have preferred if Mistress had gone through with piercing your nipples? Or, maybe you wanted us both to be *really* caned – two dozen strokes of the medium school cane?"

I sighed, hoping that Sam would 'get it'. "Mistress Elena did exactly what you requested of her: She surprised you with some new things, most of which are your 'old' things at a slightly higher intensity."

Then, I chuckled, "We really will have to try infusing half a liter of saline into your balls."

I knew that would get to Sam, and it did. He turned from me, and put on his headphones. And, a minute later, he took them off, and put them down roughly on the armrest of his seat. "Do you want to tell me what you guys discussed over tea and crumpets? And about your invitation to be 'trained'?"

Inwardly, I smiled. "Sam, first of all, we didn't have crumpets. If we'd had them, I would have brought you one; of course!"

Sam grumbled, "You didn't offer me any tea."

My mind's eye saw Mistress unfastening the straps holding Sam's wrists, and me handing him a cup of tea – him lifting the cup with his little finger outstretched, while at his other end, there were a hundred needles in his bare bottom. I continued, "Secondly, we discussed how badly you behaved," Sam reacted, as I knew he would, "and how I had a natural talent for domination."

Sam looked down and nodded, saying quietly, "I knew that."

I held Sam's hand. "And Mistress Elena has offered to train me ... as a Domme." I could see Sam's eyes cloud over, and knew he would ask about the money, so I quickly added, "She said that she would discount the price, and that I could get a scholarship."

He bellowed, "Ha! Get a scholarship? For 'the school for dommes'?" Sam fell back into his seat, shaking his head.

I explained what Mistress had said, that I would need to 'perform' for one of her wealthy clients, but that there would be nothing sexual. Sam bellowed again, and I could see a few people around us look up from their books or tablets.

"Sam, wasn't that *your* approach, when we met? Make me promise to do something submissive with you, your promise in return being that there would be no sex? At least, no 'sex', as you defined it."

Sam was shaking his head again, "No! Not at all. I didn't offer to pay to have you trained, so that I could have an 'experience' with you."

"You paid plenty, to 'play' with me. Again, as Elena said, 'it's only a matter of degree'."

Sam gave me a strange look, "Now, it's 'Elena'?"

I chuckled, and looked out the window at the view. Then, I turned back, "Sam, if you don't want me to be trained, I don't have to do it."

Sam shook his head, "It's not that I don't want you to be trained; I think it would be great – you would make a fine Domme."

Then Sam looked away and back, pained, "Kelly, frankly, I'm worried about the same thing you were, when I made that Italian dinner for you (and served you in nothing but an apron) – that I won't be able to satisfy you, especially, if you become a professional dominatrix. And, I'm not sure how often I would want to take a spanking like we had two days ago." He reached down and rubbed his bottom.

I laughed, "Sam, we're never going to be able to divine whether we'll satisfy each other in the future. And, I don't plan on becoming a 'professional' ... I think I'll be able to make enough money in the biotech field."

Still laughing, I reasoned, "And if I *were* professional, I'd have lots of clients to 'satisfy' me, and you wouldn't need to, that way." I thought about what Sam had said about his relationship with Sarah. "As you've told me, you can't always expect one person to satisfy *all* your needs."

Sam whined, "But I *want* to satisfy all your needs, Kelly." Then, he was quiet, thinking. Turning to me, he put his hand on my arm, and said, "I'm tired, Kelly. Let's think about all the ramifications of this, when we're rested."

I nodded, and patted Sam's hand. Then, I stroked the back of his hand, and his arm, like stroking a kitten; such soft fur. I purred, and batted my eyelashes at him.

CHAPTER 19: HOME, SWEET, …

It was great to get back home. Not that I hadn't enjoyed the trip, and traveling with Kelly … but there really was something to the old phrase, I thought, as I opened the kitchen door to the backyard. Home, sweet backyard. Kelly came downstairs, having unpacked her rolling case and backpack.

"Are you going to let your parents know you're back?"

Kelly gave me a strange look, and said, "Yes, Sam. I'll go home and see them – at least, my mother – Saturday morning. My advisor's hours are tomorrow afternoon. I'm going to have to prepare a presentation to him on my proposed project … and invention."

I nodded absently, checking the house, and turning on lights. The yard looked pretty good, considering it was fall, and leaves had been falling for the past couple of weeks. The gardeners had obviously been here, but had not kept up with the trees.

We got settled in, each catching up on some of our routines, and finally sat on the playroom sofa together. I handed Kelly a Diet Coke, and toasted her with mine, "Here's to 'Home, Sweet Backyard!' – my first thought, as I opened the back door."

I looked at Kelly, "You know, if I were a billionaire, we would have a lot of choices – we could live almost anywhere in the world. I could get used to living in downtown London, or Manhattan, if I had that kind of money. But, as you know, Kelly, I'm comfortable, but not wealthy. So, considering the prices everywhere else, I'm pretty happy to come back to this house; and backyard.

Kelly smiled, and raised her glass, "I agree, Sam. It's not just comparative – you have a very nice house, and an especially beautiful backyard. I'd come back here, from my international travels, anytime." She chuckled, and then put her glass down, and took my hands in hers. Was she going to propose? I suddenly felt tired, and wasn't sure what was going to happen.

"Sam, you know that I love you."

I nodded, and said, "I love you, too, Kelly."

Kelly put a finger on my lips, and continued, "And, I want to be with you. More than 'sometimes'. And I'm now happy with my dissertation project; of course, I'll have to see what my advisor says, tomorrow. But I think I have a direction, so it's just hard work from here – nothing magical." That sounded logical, but I still could not fathom where Kelly was going with this.

Then, she deduced, "So, I would like to move in with you. If you don't mind." I was a little stunned; I shouldn't have been, but I was tired, and perhaps already jet-lagged.

Before I could respond, Kelly offered, "I would be happy to sleep in one of the guest bedrooms ... and just 'visit' you when you request ... if that's what you would prefer. But I'm sure that I can manage my project from here. And, I'd like to let my parents know ... Saturday morning ... that I'm going to be living with you.

I was surprised: Kelly had not – to my knowledge – been concerned with her parents, and now she was going to let them know about 'us' ... whatever 'us' meant. I knew what it meant to me, and was pretty sure I knew what it meant to Kelly. This would be a big decision, and bigger milestone. I suddenly felt pressured, and knew that I wasn't at my 'optimum' performance level. It may have been the alcohol on the flights, or that I hadn't slept in more than 24 hours.

"Kelly, I would be very happy, if you decide to move in with me. You may have your own bedroom, if you like. And, if you want to share a bed with me, I can convert one of the bedrooms to an office for you."

I took a deep breath, "But could you please hold-off telling your parents, until we've slept on it, and discussed it once more ... when there's less than 0.2% alcohol in our blood?"

Kelly laughed, put her arms over my shoulders, and said, "Sure, Sam. Let's discuss it tomorrow. I can see my parents over the weekend. But I don't want to hide you any longer: We don't have to have any stated future plans ... but could we please just be a 'couple'?"

My mind was fogged, and I nodded, vacantly, and stood. I chugged the last of my Diet Coke and put the glass down on the bar.

Then, I led Kelly upstairs, to the master bedroom. *Our* bedroom.

###

Thank you for reading Book 5 of the Experiences series. If you enjoyed it, please take a moment to leave a review at your favorite retailer. And, if you liked this story, you'll LOVE the continuation in Book 6: Friends' Experience!

- Simone Freier

Discover other titles by Simone Freier

Experiences Series Book 1: Origins of a Fetish

Experiences Series Book 2: First Experience

Experiences Series Book 3: Weekend Experience

Experiences Series Book 4: Birthday Experience

Experiences Series Book 5: European Experience

Experiences Series Book 6: Friends' Experience

Experiences Series Book 7: Island Experience

Experiences Series Book 8: Domme Experience

Connect with the Author

Follow me on Twitter: http://twitter.com/SimoneFreier

Friend me on Facebook: http://facebook.com/SimoneFreierAuthor

Subscribe to my blog: http://SimoneFreier.com

Favorite me at Smashwords: http://smashwords.com/SimoneFreier